Withdra~~~ ~~~~~~
Dor~~~~~~~~~

CONSO~~~

James Wilson has written plays, TV documentaries (including the award-winning *Savagery and the American Indian* for the BBC) and a critically-acclaimed history of Native Americans, *The Earth Shall Weep*. His three previous novels were *The Dark Clue*, *The Bastard Boy* and, most recently, *The Woman in the Picture*, described by Kate Saunders in *The Times* as 'a multi-layered, deeply absorbing and entertaining novel'.

CONSOLATION

A Novel of Mystery

JAMES WILSON

First published in 2008
by Faber and Faber Ltd
Bloomsbury House
74–77 Great Russell Street
London WC1B 3DA
This paperback edition published in 2009

Typeset by Faber and Faber Limited in Minion
Printed in the UK by CPI Bookmarque, Croydon

A CIP record for this book
is available from the British Library

ISBN 978–0–571–23806–4

2 4 6 8 10 9 7 5 3 1

For my family

I

It happened, as near as I can fix it, at twenty-seven minutes past six. When the church clock struck the quarter, I was still indisputably my old self. By the time it chimed the half-hour, I had already begun my queer journey to what I am now. Though I couldn't have told you what it was, and hadn't the faintest intimation where it would lead me, I knew – as certainly as if it had been a physical hand, reaching out and closing about my wrist – that something strange had taken hold of me, and would not lightly let me go.

I had been walking, at that point, for three days. The first evening I had put up at a small pub in a riverside hamlet, but the snugness of the bar, and the sweet-natured banter between the landlord and his pretty young wife, and the trusting way their small boy asked me to admire his toy engine, all tormented me as a hot bath does cold flesh. By the time I went to bed, I was in such mental anguish that I could hardly sleep. So the next night I decided to stay in the woods. I lit a fire in the crater made by a fallen tree, ate a supper of bread and cheese, then wrapped myself in my coat and lay down in the shelter of the overhanging root. I slept no better, as it turned out, than I had at the pub. But at least my mind, when morning came, was as numb as my limbs.

The following day I trudged on, taking the most out-of-the-way paths I could find, and keeping myself going by scooping handfuls of water from every little stream I passed, and grubbing among the leaves for a few old cob-nuts that the squirrels had missed. When dusk began to fall, I looked around for another place to camp, and in a few minutes had discovered the perfect spot: a shallow, leaf-strewn hollow, almost completely enclosed by a straggly wild rhododendron. As I set down my rucksack and started gathering sticks for the camp-fire, some small, critical part of my consciousness observed that I was behaving oddly, and that I should go in search of a hot meal and a change of clothes before hunger and solitude unhinged my mind. But I was already so faint and light-headed – the pulse thrubbing in my ears; my arms and legs turning to string – that it was easy enough to ignore it. Hunger, I knew now from experience, wasn't so terrible: once you were past a certain point, in fact, it was actually rather soothing. And, in any case, I was in no state to go anywhere, or see anyone, tonight. Only let me sleep, I thought, and I'd be better in the morning.

I rummaged through the fallen leaves, but couldn't find any dry enough to serve as tinder; so I reached into my pocket, and drew out the note my wife had thrust into my hand as I was leaving. I crushed it into a ball, and set a match to it – illuminating, for a second or two, a few random words on the crumpled surface: *Black bear sez good by, and be shor to change yor soks.* I should, I knew, have felt a pang of compunction; but the only emotion I was aware of, as I watched the flames, was a strange, unworldly kind of serenity, as if my soul were finally parting company with my body.

The next second there was a rustling in the bush behind me. I turned, and saw a trembling spaniel looking at me, one paw in the air. For a second or two we eyed each other curiously. Then its soft pouchy mouth began to move, and I heard it say:

'Well, you're a rum 'un, and no mistake.'

Dogs can't talk, shouted the critic from his box. But that didn't stop me bridling, and snapping back:

'What a damned uncivil greeting.'

I was still speaking when the branches parted again and a well-dressed woman appeared. The instant she saw me, she made a barrier with her hand, to prevent someone behind her from coming any further. Then she stood staring at me for a few moments, before whistling for the dog, and backing away nervously, her arm still outstretched, and her startled gaze never leaving my face – as if she feared that, if she allowed her attention to lapse for a moment, I might commit some frightful outrage. All I could see of her companion was a felt hat garnished with a feather; but as they stumbled noisily through the undergrowth together, I heard sobs – whether of fear or laughter I couldn't tell – and a rapid fire of half-whispered female conversation, from which I was able to make out only the word 'lunatic'.

The critic was right: if I wasn't careful, I could find I had drifted irrevocably beyond the edge of the known world. There was nothing for it: I needed an infusion of the real, before it was too late. I quickly stamped out the fire, and took up my bag again.

But where to go? I had only the vaguest notion of where I was, and it was so long since I'd last looked at the map that consulting it now would be useless. The two women must have come from somewhere, but there was no telling how far it was, or in which direction. And even if I managed to find the place, I doubted, after the incident with the dog, whether I could expect a very cordial reception.

I peered about me, searching for a sign of human life. Blankets of mist were starting to hang between the trees, reducing the view on every side to a few smudged-out pencil strokes, and when I held my breath all I could hear was the slow pop and prickle of dripping moisture. But I knew that I was close to the top of a hill, and that, if I could only find a path down, it was bound, sooner or later, to lead me to a road or a track.

The women had continued on along the ridge, so – to avoid the risk of another embarrassing encounter – I set off back the way I had come. And, sure enough, after a quarter of a mile or so, I spotted a small gap in the bushes to my right, and a dark line zig-zagging away through the undergrowth below it.

3

It was a treacherous descent, the mud spiked with flints and riddled with slippery, half-hidden roots, and more than once I lost my balance. But after no more than ten minutes I was rewarded with the unmistakable smell of wood-smoke, and then – a few hundred yards further on – the faint glow of a lighted window.

It came, I saw, as I drew nearer, from a square cottage tucked into a fold in the steep hillside. Beyond it stood a tall, overgrown structure that looked as if it might once have been the gateway to a much bigger house, though the drive – if that's what it was – had now disappeared under a wild tangle of scrub.

I hesitated. And then it occurred to me that even if the two women did live here (and their clothes and their manner suggested something rather grander), they would not have been able to get back before me. So I pushed open the garden gate, walked up the flagged path, and knocked at the door. Almost at once, I heard the shuffle of feet on tiles, and then the click of the latch.

The rank sawdust-and-bile smell should have warned me. But it took me so much by surprise that for a moment I couldn't identify what it reminded me of. And by the time I had the answer – Mr. Angwin's butcher's shop – I was looking into the milky eyes and blood-matted faces of five dead rabbits stretched side by side on a table.

I dropped my gaze and turned abruptly away, to keep myself from retching. A fair-haired child was staring at me round the edge of the door. She was perhaps eight or nine, and dressed in a patched and darned Alice-in-Wonderland smock. It was a second before I noticed the red spatters on the front of it.

A black iris closed around my vision, and I only managed to stay on my feet by clutching at the door-jamb, and resting my forehead against the angle of the wood. From what sounded like the end of a long tunnel, a deep male voice said:

'Hullo! You look all-in.'

4

I felt a hand taking my elbow. I opened my eyes again, and found a thin, dark-bearded man examining me. He was so close that I could smell the oil of his hair, and the oaty fust of his tweed waistcoat.

'Come on,' he said, gently trying to draw me inside. 'Let's sit you down.'

If I got any closer to those rabbits, I knew for a certainty that nothing in the world would stop me from being sick. So I pulled free of his grasp, and clung on to the door-post.

'Thank you,' I said. 'But I'm perfectly all right. I was just wondering if you could tell me where I might find a bed for the night?'

He frowned, trying to square the way I spoke with my appearance. Then he jerked his thumb over his shoulder and said:

'If you go up there, to the big house, they'll give you something to eat. And maybe let you sleep in one of the stables. Tell them Davey Riddick –'

'No, I'm quite willing to pay,' I said. 'If you could just point me in the direction of the nearest village . . .'

He studied me for a second – calculating, I suspect, my chances of getting there on my own. Then he said:

'I'll be going that way myself in a couple of ticks, so if you just hang on a moment, I'll show you.'

I had little appetite for company or conversation, but I couldn't very well refuse. I propped myself against the wall and waited while he retreated into the nauseating fug of the cottage and exchanged a few words with another man. As he came out again, shrugging on his coat, I heard the little girl calling:

'Goodbye!'

I could not bring myself to look at her again, so I waved blindly into the gloom, and then turned hurriedly towards my companion.

'This is very kind of you,' I said. 'Is it far?'

'A fair step,' he said, striding off ahead of me. 'But most of it's through the park. So easy enough on the feet.' I found him as hard to place as he had found me. He didn't sound like a Sussex man, and wasn't dressed like either a gentleman or an estate-worker: to see and hear him you might have imagined he was a board-school teacher. But I had met him in what appeared to be a game-keeper's cottage, and he had a countryman's easy alertness to his surroundings.

'This used to be the main entrance, I believe,' he said, as we approached the overgrown gateway. 'But a few years ago they cut a new drive, so now you can get to the big house directly from the village, rather than having to take the long way round through the woods. Which is lucky for you, because it'll save you a mile or two.'

The arch was clogged by a jungle of brush and ivy, which had shrunk the opening to a ragged wound no more than eighteen inches across.

'Good thing we're a couple of bean-poles,' said my guide, as he squeezed through sideways. I took a deep breath and followed him, my clothes snagging on twigs and thorns, and a bristly stem grazing my face – so that when I emerged again on the far side, I felt as if I had been re-born in another world.

And indeed the atmosphere *was*, all of a sudden, strikingly different. A breeze had started to blow up from the valley below; the moon was edging above the horizon; and through the thinning mist I could see the puckered scar of the old drive winding ahead of us across a lake of silvery grass dotted with little islands of trees.

'Invigorating, eh?' said the man. 'No refuge, in a landscape like this. You have to take what the elements fling at you. But at least you know you're alive.' He took a few paces forward, then stopped abruptly, and lifted his nose like a pointer. 'Smell that?'

I shut my eyes and snuffed the air. Mingled with the down-land sweetness I could just make out a faint spice of salt.

'Christ,' he said. 'Don't you wish you could run away to sea sometimes?'

'Yes. Everyone does, don't they?'

'I mean the real thing. Hawsers, and capstans, and engine-rooms, and the stink of coal. Pitting your muscles and marrow against the might of nature.' He hesitated, then turned towards me with a short bark of laughter. 'What do you say? Shall we do it? I'm game, if you are.'

It sounded off-hand enough; but I could feel on my cheek the power of his gaze boring through the darkness.

'I'm not sure my muscles and marrow are up to it,' I said.

He laughed again. 'Nor mine, I expect, worse luck.' He looked at me for a moment more, then wheeled round and began walking again – so abruptly, that I was left standing for a second or two, like a runner who has missed the starting pistol. By the time I had finally forced my enfeebled legs into motion, he was so far ahead of me that – try as I might – I could not close the gap between us. From time to time he would glance surreptitiously over his shoulder, and, if I had fallen too far behind, ease his pace a little. But he always increased it again before I had a chance to catch him up.

And then, finally, he stopped on a knobby prominence, and stood peering out over the long swoop of the hillside below us. It was a minute or so before I had climbed high enough to see what he was looking at: a large, square country house lying comfortably at the bottom of the valley, protected by a little copse and a horse-shoe of outbuildings. I expected him to move on again as I drew near; but instead he fumbled in his pocket, pulled out a packet of Players, and offered it to me companionably.

'Thank you.'

I found my matches and managed to strike one, but my hand trembled so much when I held it out to him that he had to take my wrist to steady it. He quickly puffed his cigarette into life. Then, still grasping my arm with one hand, and shielding the flame with the other, he leaned forward to study my face in the light of the match.

'Heavens,' he said. 'You *are* in a state, aren't you? What was it? The sight of those rabbits?'

I said nothing. He continued to stare intently at me, until the match started to burn my fingers. He blew it out, and flicked it on to the ground.

'Well,' he said. 'You look like a man who's seen a bit of life, and got dirt under your nails. I can't imagine it comes as much of a shock to you to realize that a rabbit's a flesh-and-blood animal, and not a character in a picture-book.'

'I was feeling a bit faint, that's all. Haven't slept or eaten much recently.'

He drew smoke into his lungs, then slowly let it out again. 'When'd you last have a meal?'

'Two nights ago.'

He nodded again. 'And where was that?'

'Oh, just some little wayside inn. In a village somewhere.'

'What, round here?'

'I don't think so. Though to be honest, I'm not sure. I don't *really* know where I am *now*.'

'About ten miles from Portsmouth. Is that where you're going?'

'I'm not going anywhere in particular.'

'Ah.' I suddenly noticed he was still holding my wrist, and found myself wondering if – having established just how lost and helpless I was – he meant to attack and rob me. But after a moment, he merely nodded again, and said:

'So where'd you start out from, then?'

'Brighton.'

'You're a Brightonian?'

I shook my head. 'I took the train there.'

He waited for me to explain myself – to tell him where I *did* live, and who I was, and why I was there – but I couldn't do it. It wasn't just weariness that prevented me, but the fear of being thought ridiculous, too. I couldn't expect much sympathy for my predicament from a man who liked engine-rooms and the stink of coal.

'Well,' he said at last. 'You're a rum 'un, and no mistake.'

I couldn't help laughing. He squinted curiously at me.

'You put me in a bit of a quandary,' he said. 'My way' – jerking his head back, towards the house – 'lies down there. Yours is straight ahead. So by rights, this is where we should part company. Only I'm not sure I ought to leave you.'

'Oh, I'll be all right, thank you.'

He scratched his chin irritatedly. 'That wasn't what I meant.'

Exhaustion doesn't only weaken you: it makes you stupid, too. It should have been perfectly obvious that my dirty clothes and unshaven face and distraught manner were bound to arouse suspicion, but the idea hadn't even occurred to me before. Now, trying to make light of it, I said:

'Ah, I see, you think from my appearance I must be some poor desperate fellow who's murdered his wife or something, and is fleeing the retribution of the law. Well, I can promise you I'm not.'

His fingers tightened on my wrist, and he peered into my eyes, as if – despite the darkness – he thought he might be able to see there whether or not I was lying. Then, after a couple of seconds, he let me go again, and pulled away.

'No,' he said, 'I don't believe you are. A pity. I should like to meet a murderer.' He turned towards the house, and raised a hand. 'Well, whatever you are, and wherever you're going, good luck to you. Don't waste your time on the Three Crowns. You'll find the Railway comfortable enough, though. At the far end of the village.'

'Thank you,' I called after him; and watched until he had dwindled to no more than a faint sinuous shadow slipping across the grass below me.

It was only now, as I resumed my journey alone, that it struck me how quickly the weather was changing. The breeze had grown to a gusty wind, blowing away the last rags of mist and flinging angry spatters of rain into my face. To protect myself, I pulled up the collar of my coat and walked with hunched shoulders and half-closed eyes. When I came to the new drive, I knew it more by the crunch of fresh gravel beneath my boots than by anything I could see.

There was a squat, newly built lodge at the entrance. I tiptoed past it, for fear of being challenged by the gate-keeper, and then out through the open gate on to the road. A hundred yards or so ahead of me a straggle of cottages marked the beginning of the village. Beyond them, I could just make out the black witch's hat of a church spire. As I turned towards it, the clock in the tower below it struck the hour.

The rain was falling continuously now, and with almost every step I took it seemed to become fiercer and more insistent. By the time I had passed the cottages it was an unremitting onslaught, jabbing my eyes and stinging my cheeks and working its way relentlessly through the seams of my coat and boots. If I kept going, I knew I should be drenched to the skin long before I could reach the haven of the Railway Inn.

Looking around for somewhere to shelter, I spotted the dark bulk of the church porch. The lych-gate was still some way ahead; but it was easy enough to scramble over the low wall, and take a short-cut through the jungle of headstones. The porch was unlit, so I had to grope my way on to the stone bench running along the side. As I did so, my hand brushed against something that felt like a cut flower. I picked it up, and gave an *oof* of pain as a thorn embedded itself in my fingertip.

I held it to my nose. Yes: it was an unseasonal rose. For an instant, as I smelled it, time dissolved, and I glimpsed soft summer shadows on a golden lawn, and caught the distant squeals of a playing child, and had the odd sense that any second I should see her jump out from her hiding-place, and run laughing towards me. So desperate was I to hold on to the vision that I leaned back against a wall-beam and shut my eyes, to stop it from bleeding away into the darkness.

The next moment, from no more than five feet away, I heard a soft intake of breath.

I sat up so abruptly that the rough wood grazed my neck. A woman's voice said:

'The vicar's in the church, you know.'

I peered into the depths of the porch, but my eyes still weren't sufficiently accustomed to the gloom to see anything. The woman, however, could evidently see *me*: her tone had been assertive – as if she feared I might attack her, and was letting me know that she could summon help if I tried.

'Well,' I said, 'I'm glad to hear it. On balance, that's pretty much where you'd want a vicar to be, isn't it?'

There was a short silence, followed by a snuffling sound that might have been a stifled giggle. Then she asked:

'Do you know him?'

'No, I'm afraid not. I've never set foot in this place before in my life. But I don't doubt he's a splendid fellow.'

'I hope so.'

'For any particular reason? Or just from a very creditable concern for the well-being of the church in general?'

She did not reply. Though I still couldn't see her, I sensed her tortoising further back into the blackness. I flourished the rose, and said:

'Is this your flower?'

'Yes. I must have dropped it.' Her intonation was flat, squashed to a monotone by some heavy weight. 'Did you hurt yourself with it?'

'Oh, just gave my finger a little jab, that's all.'

'I'm sorry, it was careless of me. May I have it, please?'

I held it towards her. A hand appeared to take it. For the first time, I glimpsed the murky silhouette of a high-collared coat, and a pale blob of a face. Then they diffused into the gloom again.

'Thank you,' she said.

'A lovely scent.'

She said nothing. But I could hear her delicately sniffing it – and then the start of a sob, which she quickly strangled.

There was, of course, only one remotely likely reason why a solitary woman would bring a hot-house flower to a country churchyard on a damp February evening – and good manners plainly demanded that I should avoid alluding to it. So I was startled to hear myself suddenly saying – as if someone who had never *learned* good manners had taken control of my vocal cords:

'Your parents, is it?'

'No.' She paused, and I wondered if I had offended her. But the instant she went on again, I knew I hadn't. The load had lifted from her voice: she sounded surprised, certainly, at the frankness of my question; but relieved, too, that it allowed her to be equally frank herself.

'The truth is, I haven't a clue where my parents are buried. Or if they're buried anywhere at all. They may both still be alive, for all I know.'

'Do you mean to say that you've . . . completely lost touch with them?'

'I never knew them.'

'Heavens,' I said. 'But surely there must be some way you could find out? Somebody you could ask?'

I could hear the stirring of her clothes, and feel a whiffle of cold air as she shrugged. 'They've shown no interest in me. Why should I be interested in them?'

First talking dogs, murmured the critic from his box. *Now soul-baring strangers.*

'Hm,' I said. 'Well, of course, I don't know the circumstances . . . But if for no other reason, I'd have thought – well, just out of simple curiosity.'

'I was curious for a long time. You can't imagine the stories I told myself. I'd been stolen by gypsies, and my grieving parents

12

were even then scouring the country, looking for me. Or my mother was a grand duchess in the Balkans, who hadn't wanted to part with me, but had been forced to by her wicked uncle, so he could seize the throne for himself.'

She paused.

'But would a grand duchy *have* a throne?' I said, blurting out the first thing that came into my head, merely to keep her talking. 'And if it did, could a daughter inherit it?'

She gave a broken-glass little laugh. 'That's the advantage of stories, isn't it? They don't have to bear any relation to reality at all.'

An odd gargling sound erupted in my throat, which I tried – and failed – to turn into a cough. I was saved only by a sudden bluster of wind outside, which set the trees cracking and creaking, and hurled a ferocious scattershot of rain on to the paving stones, turning them into a spitting lake.

'Goodness,' I said. 'The old gods are in a taking about something tonight.'

She drew in a long unsteady breath, that sounded like a series of hiccoughs.

'Here,' I said. 'Would you like my coat? It isn't awfully dry, I'm afraid, or awfully clean, but it'll help to keep the cold out.'

'Oh, that's very kind of you, but really . . .' But her jaw was quivering so much that she sounded as if she were biting the words rather than saying them.

'Come on.' I removed it, and held it out to her. After a moment she relented, and edged closer – her face still hidden, and her back turned towards me. As I draped the coat round her shoulders, the *substantiality* of her body, even through so many layers, took me by surprise. Not that it was large: it felt, on the contrary, delicately-framed and slender. But there seemed to be a kind of super-solidity about it – as if it were made not of flesh, but of gold.

'Thank you,' she said. And then, as she retreated again, huddling the coat around her, I heard a fastidious sniff.

'Yes,' I said, 'I'm sorry. I've barely taken it off for three days.

And last night I was sleeping under the stars, so it had to do duty as my blanket, too.'

'Why?'

'Ah, well, now, there's a question.' I sighed, and cleared my throat. 'Home, you might say, lost its power to hold me. The hearth was reduced to cold ashes. And nothing I could do would warm them up again.'

She hesitated a moment. 'Because of your wife, is it?'

For a fraction of a second I was dumbfounded by her directness. Then I remembered the way *I* had spoken to *her*.

'My wife, yes, I suppose that's part of it,' I said.

'Oh, dear, has she – ?'

'Oh, no, not that, she's still very much alive. Or was, at any rate, the last time I heard. But we're – we're not awfully close any more. Actually, that *any more*'s a bit redundant. We've *never* been awfully close, that's the truth of it. We just muddled along, a bit like England and Germany, eyeing each other suspiciously across the North Sea of the dining-room table.'

She laughed again – more gently, this time. 'So why did you get married?'

'Well . . . It seemed the thing. People do, don't they?'

'Yes.' There was a kind of unsurprised acceptance in the way she said it that made me think her case might not be very different.

'Not that I blame her. It's at least as much my fault as hers. A perfect stranger would have seen at a glance that we were destined to make each other unhappy. We just didn't see it ourselves, for some reason – until the first morning of our honeymoon, when I suggested a cliff-top walk, and she favoured an expedition to the shops, followed by a saunter along the sea-front, and tea in front of the bandstand. And we've gone on in much the same vein ever since. Which is why I'm here, and she's staying with her brother in Hove.'

'Oh, dear.' She laughed – but with so much ruefulness, that it was almost a confession.

'Well,' I said. 'This *is* a queer business, isn't it? Two people meet by chance in a church porch. Neither of them really knows what the other looks like – let alone what he – or she – is called. And yet in no time at all they're talking like old friends. *More* than old friends. Well, in my case, anyway. My closest pal's a chap called Cyril Jessop, and I couldn't have this kind of conversation with him. Or with anyone else, for that matter.'

I paused. After a second she said:

'*Moi non plus.*'

'So should we introduce ourselves, do you think?'

The idea appeared to surprise her.

'Yes, I suppose we should, shouldn't we?'

'My name's Corley Roper.'

I was braced for the inevitable: 'Not *the* Corley Roper, surely?' But she merely replied:

'I'm Mary Wilson.'

'How do you do?'

Our hands briefly touched, before withdrawing into their own worlds. For a few seconds, neither of us spoke. Then, falteringly, she began:

'And why . . . how . . .?'

'Did England and Germany finally fall out?'

'Yes.'

'Ah, well.' I hesitated. But having already revealed more to her than I had to any other living person, there seemed little point in now clinging – as it were – to my last few undergarments. So I showed myself in all my nakedness:

'We lost our child.'

She said nothing. But at that instant I knew, from the sudden flutter of her breathing, that she had lost hers, too, and that that was why she was here.

'You'd have thought it might perhaps have brought us closer together again,' I said. 'But it had the opposite effect.'

'Why, does she hold you responsible in some way?'

15

'For . . . Elspeth's dying? No, I don't think so. But she – my wife's – interested in spiritualism, you see. And I think it's pure humbug, I'm afraid. I did, finally, reluctantly agree to go to one séance with her, after . . . You know . . . But I simply couldn't bear it. The dark, and the suffocating warmth, and all that cheap flummery. The thought that my daughter, whom I'd held on my knee, should be reduced to trying to communicate with us like *that* . . . It was worse than simply accepting that she'd gone, and there was an end of it.'

The woman whimpered.

'Oh, I'm sorry,' I said. 'I didn't mean to . . .' I hesitated. Then, so softly that it came out as a whisper, I asked:

'Was yours a boy or a girl?'

'A boy.'

'How old?'

'Nothing at all. He was still-born. Strangled by his own . . . his own . . .'

I reached into the darkness and found her hand again.

'What a dreadful thing. I'm sorry.'

'You can't bury a still-born baby,' she said. 'Not in consecrated ground. Because he hasn't been baptized. So they just took the body away, and . . .' She swallowed hard to suppress a sob. 'I don't know what they did with it. But I managed to save a lock of his hair. And I wanted to put it over there, under the yew tree. Only there seemed to be a constant stream of people. Families leaving flowers on graves. A grave-digger digging a new one. So I sat here all afternoon, reading my book, hoping no one would notice me, and looking out every few minutes, to see if the coast was clear.'

'Heavens! You must be frozen!'

'Yes,' she said, in a flat, dismissive voice that suggested physical discomfort was her usual condition, and she was surprised I should even bother to mention it. 'And then, just when everyone had finally gone and I at last got my trowel out, the vicar turned up.'

'Ah, and what, he objected, did he?'

'I didn't give him a chance to. I slipped everything back into my bag, and tried to look as if I'd just wandered in to admire the architecture.' She gave a little huff of derision. 'And it must have been a pretty convincing performance, I think, because I was rewarded with a twenty-minute lecture on ogees and trefoil windows. And then, of course, no sooner had he finally gone inside than the heavens opened, and I had to take refuge in here again to avoid being drowned. As it is, my hat's ruined.'

There was something unnerving in the way her tone had shifted from grief to sarcasm, without her apparently being aware of it – as if she found it hard to differentiate between the loss of her child and the arrival of the vicar and the onset of the rain, and saw them all merely as ploys of a vindictive life that was determined to spite her at every turn.

'Do you not think', I said, as gently as I could, 'that it might have been better simply to tell him the truth? My guess is you'd have probably found him quite sympathetic. I mean, this isn't the middle ages, is it – ?'

'No!' she said, so forcefully that it cannoned off the stone walls. The noise seemed to startle her as much as it had me. She gave a gasp of surprise. Then, almost sheepishly, as if she feared she might have offended the spirits of the dead lying all around us, she said: 'The thing is, you see, it isn't as if I've any right to be here. It isn't even my parish.'

'Oh, really? Then why did you choose it?'

'Well . . . When I was a girl, I was at school in Southsea. And one of the mistresses had a cottage here, and sometimes I'd spend some of the holidays with her. So –'

She stopped abruptly. The clock in the church tower was striking the quarter. When it had finished, she said:

'You didn't by any chance happen to see a motor-car on your way here, did you?'

'No. Why?'

'Oh, it's only that there should be one coming for me soon.'

She stirred, as if she were preparing to venture out to look for it. 'Well,' I said, 'we'll hear it, won't we?'

'Yes, I suppose so.'

'We *will*,' I said. And then, without giving her time to reply: 'So, anyway, you were happy?'

'Hm? Oh, here, you mean. Yes, yes – the happiest I've ever been anywhere in my life.' She pondered for a moment. 'The *only* place I've *really* been happy.'

'Well, that's easy enough to understand, at any rate. The downs are the best of England, pretty near.'

'Yes, *I* think so.' She paused for a moment, and I heard an odd grating noise, as if she were slowly scratching the stone with her fingernail. 'All the time I was abroad, whenever I tried to picture home, *this* is what used to come into my head. You know: the grass, and the wild flowers, and the sheep . . .'

'I *do* know,' I said. 'And the glorious loneliness. And the feeling that any moment you might stumble on a fairy ring, or a sleeping giant –'

'Yes. And the rabbits. That was what *I* liked best. There was a big warren about half a mile above the house. I'd go there almost every day, and sit and watch them scuttling in and out of their burrows. They were frightened at first, but if you kept still they'd soon get used to your being there. I even persuaded myself I could recognize some of them, and gave them names, and pretended they were my friends.'

A blade seemed to slip between my lower ribs. I hunched forward, but managed to keep myself from crying out.

'There was one – or I *thought* it was just one, anyway – Alexander, I called him – who seemed to be the old grandfather of the family. And I was convinced he could remember me from one year to the next, and was glad to see me. Stupid, of course. It was probably a different animal every time.'

'Not stupid,' I said, between gritted teeth. 'Perfectly understandable.'

18

'No.' Then she registered the change in my voice, and paused for a second or two, trying to interpret it. 'What's the matter? Have I upset you?'

'Please,' I said. 'You must forgive me. It just so happens that I'm rather in flight from friendly rabbits at the moment.'

'Oh, oh, I'm sorry.' But it was too hasty, and said with a kind of sulky resignation that directed the feeling to her predicament rather than to mine – as if it was just her luck to pick the one subject that would offend me, and she really should have known better than to open her mouth at all.

'No, no,' I said, 'you couldn't possibly have realized. The truth is, I'm afraid, that I've just spent far too much time with them. Whenever *my* life's proved too troublesome, I've simply taken refuge in *theirs*. Only now it's failed me. The sanctuary has been violated.'

I heard the soft whisper of my coat as she started to shift position, and assumed she must be edging nervously away. But then, just as I was about to try to explain myself, her face swam out of the darkness towards me. It was small and pale and heart-shaped, with a long nose and straight black eyebrows that looked as if they'd been pencilled on in charcoal. It was not exactly beautiful; but for some reason – perhaps just that, having entertained so many possibilities about her appearance, it was a shock to find them all suddenly reduced to a single concrete reality – the sight of it seemed to knock the wind from me like a blow to the stomach.

'Your child, do you mean?' she said.

'Yes,' I stammered.

'What, you used to make up stories for – ?'

'Yes. Well, I don't know about *make up*. I never felt I was *inventing* anything, exactly. It was more like drawing aside a curtain in my own head, and leading her through into the world of Alcuin Hare, and Mr. Largo Frog, and their friends the Coneys.'

Her brow creased in puzzlement.

19

'Coney?' I said. 'A fine old English word. Pretty much banished from polite society these days, though you still sometimes find country people using it. It's wirier than *rabbit*. And not so babyish as *bunny*. Anyway, that's where we went, whenever she was ill or upset. And it always worked. Because, of course, it was a magical place, where nothing could be amiss for long.'

My voice was starting to thicken. She tactfully dropped her dark eyes.

'So . . . When the doctor told me she was dying . . . I sent him out of the room, and sat by her bed, and – though he'd said she couldn't possibly hear me – I began to . . .' I paused, trying to get my ragged breathing under control. 'I really don't know why, I must be a savage, I suppose, but I honestly believed that – if I could only nerve myself to it – I'd be able to bring her back again. It would be like trying to rescue someone from a burning house. Just one supreme act of enchantment. Do it with enough faith, enough conviction, and it would have the power – even at that late stage – to overcome the ravages of scarlet fever.'

She twitched, as if something had stung her. Then she reached out her hand, and laid it over mine.

At that moment, outside, we heard the bathetic goose-honk of a motor-horn.

'Oh!' She whipped back her hand and started to her feet, like a child caught doing something shameful. Then she turned abruptly, and began frantically patting the seat where she had been sitting.

'What's lost?'

She didn't answer. I found my matches, lit one, and held it above her, cupping my palm over the flame to make a tiny lantern.

'Ah!' She lunged forward, and snatched something up. Then she stood looking past me at the rain, nibbling her lips and lacing her fingers so tightly that I couldn't see what they were clutching.

'Is there anything I can do to help?'

She was so absorbed in her own thoughts that she seemed momentarily to have forgotten I was there. She stared at me, frowning with the effort to assimilate what I'd said.

The horn sounded again.

'Who is that?'

'My . . . my . . . school-mistress friend.' She was grimacing, and the tension in her throat had squeezed her voice to a girlish falsetto. She was either in great fear or great distress all of a sudden, that was obvious – but what the cause was, I was at a loss to understand. Behind me, I heard the lych-gate squeak, and the leisurely clack of a woman's footsteps starting along the path.

Mary Wilson stiffened, then hunched forward slightly, pressing whatever was in her hands against her belly. And in that small, unconsciously protective gesture I suddenly glimpsed what it was that was anguishing her.

'Ah,' I said, 'I see. Even *she* doesn't know what you came here for, is that it?'

She blinked at me aghast, as if I'd performed some startling act of mind-reading.

'No,' she stammered. 'I didn't tell her. I didn't tell anyone, except –'

'Would you like me to take that, and bury it for you?'

She hesitated a second. Then – after peering round me, to make sure her friend was still not close enough to see what we were doing – she impetuously thrust a small wooden box into my hands. By the time I had managed to fumble it into my pocket, she had already edged past me, and was standing shivering in the entrance, clutching her sodden hat like a rag. Something in the narrowness of her shoulders, and the forlorn slant of her bare head as she bowed it against the rain, made me think of a frightened child steeling herself for her first day at school.

'Under the yew tree?' I said.

21

She nodded. 'Here.' She slipped off my coat, and held it out to me. 'Thank you.'

Her teeth were chattering. I said:

'Please – keep it if you want –'

She did not even reply, but simply dropped it over my knees, and hurried out into the night.

I wanted to call after her; but that, I realized, would only embarrass her further, by forcing her to explain my presence to her friend. So I shrank back into the gloom, and waited until I heard the chug of the motor-car rise to an imperious roar, and then start to dwindle away into the distance.

I pressed my ear against the church door. All I could hear were some indistinct scuffling noises, which – to judge by their dullness and faintness – seemed to be coming from the vestry. I couldn't guess what the vicar was doing – but, whatever it was, it certainly didn't sound as if he was about to leave.

I crept down the path, glanced round quickly to make sure I was still unobserved, and then darted for the cover of the yew. In no more than five seconds I was crouched beneath the matted canopy of the branches – quaking with cold, and my shoulder stabbed and scraped by small sharp twigs, but miraculously shielded from the deluge pummelling the ground all around me.

I took out the box. The darkness under the tree was so impenetrable that I was unable to see even the merest outline of its shape, but when I ran my fingers over the surface I could feel a regular pattern of something cooler and harder than wood, which told me it was inlaid with ivory or mother-of-pearl. Indian, I imagined: perhaps a treasure from her own childhood, which had fuelled her fantasies about the exoticism of her background. It was impossible not to think of the artistry that had gone into making it, and feel a pang at the wastefulness – it seemed almost like a tiny murder – of burying it where no one would ever be able to appreciate its beauty again. But it was its very preciousness, of course, that – in Mary Wilson's eyes – fitted it for its purpose.

I could not resist easing it open, and slipping my finger inside. Yes, there it was, lying under a square of card: a curl of silky strands, tied together with a piece of thread.

I closed the box again, and started scooping out the soil between two roots. It was dry and crumbly, and in only a couple of minutes I'd made what I judged to be a big enough hole. I laid the box inside, and began pressing earth on top of it.

What happened next was so utterly unlike anything else I have ever experienced that no image can more than dimly suggest it. The closest I can come to it is to say that it was like finding a wild bird has somehow got into your sitting-room, and is whirring its wings against the window. There was the same shock at encountering something familiar in the wrong place; the same fear that a creature so small and fragile might inadvertently hurt itself, or break its neck. But the room, in this instance, was my own skull; and the bird nothing I could put a name or even a shape to. And it was beating so hard in my temple that I feared I should faint.

I stumbled out into the open again. My mind was in chaos: thoughts and memories harried into a wild swirl, like papers threshed by a gust of wind. The only idea I could hold on to from one moment to the next was that I must be ill, and needed help.

I stared about me. Nothing – not the church, or the graveyard, or the glow of lights from the village, or even my own dirty hands – seemed familiar. Some instinct, though, drove me towards the lych-gate. As I went, I was startled by a sudden sound, which frightened me into a run.

I know now – but didn't then – that it was the church clock striking the half-hour.

II

I have no recollection of finding the Railway Inn, or of how the landlord received me; and my only memory of my first night there is of a strange delirium, in which Mary Wilson's fractured reflection appeared, dazzlingly bright, in a broken looking-glass. At the same time, I was engaged in an endless struggle with the sheet, which seemed in some way to be a part of me, clinging to my over-sensitive flesh like the half-sloughed skin of a grass-snake. In my confusion, the two things seemed somehow connected: if I could just arrange the sheet properly, the image of Mary Wilson would be whole again, and I should be at peace. But, try as I might, I was never able to manage it.

In the morning, I was drenched with sweat, and conscious of a painful throbbing in my finger where the rose had pricked it. I tried to get up, but my legs folded under me, and I collapsed on the floor. The noise brought the landlady running upstairs to knock on my door and ask if I was all right. Hearing nothing from inside but a feeble moan, she immediately called the doctor – who helped me back into bed, swabbed my swollen finger with carbolic, and told me I must stay where I was until the fever had abated.

Though I never again sank into the madness of that first night, the hallucinations of Mary Wilson's splintered face continued to trouble me. Over the next day or two they would suddenly, without warning, dart up in front of my eyes like brilliantly coloured tropical fish, so vivid that they seemed more real than the faded rose wallpaper and cracked ceiling on which they superimposed themselves – giving me, for an instant, the odd impression that there were really two of me, each of us using the same apparatus to look at something different. Gradually, as my finger began to heal and my temperature returned to normal, these spectres started to retreat – until finally they were no more than a kind of ever-present potential: a luminous quality around the edge of my vision, like the rim of light you see on the horizon just before sunrise.

By the third day, thanks to the care of the landlady, Mrs. Grant, I was strong enough to get up for an hour or so; and – knowing that my wife must be starting to grow anxious about me – I thought I should take the opportunity to cable home. My kindly nurse protested, saying I would only set myself back again if I went out, and offering to go in my place. But I was too embarrassed to let her see what I had written; so I hobbled down to the post office, and shamefacedly slid my message across the counter:

Tell Bear have narsty case of sniffles. Will tellygrarf when comin home.

The post-master scanned it a couple of times, then looked up and said:

'Are you sure that's the right spelling, sir?'

'Quite sure, thank you.' And, before he had time to question me further, I hurriedly paid him, and left.

On the way back, I decided, on an impulse, to stop at the church. I told myself that I was simply being practical – that the effort of walking had tired me more than I had expected, and it would be prudent to take a rest before making a final assault on the hill up to the pub – but as I went through the lych-gate, I knew from the sudden tingling of my skin that something else entirely had driven me there. It was only when I found myself stumbling not towards the church itself but across the graveyard to the yew tree that I realized what it was.

I knelt down, and lifted the nearest branch. Yes, there was no doubt about it: the earth was freshly turned. Mary Wilson had not been – as I had begun to suspect she might be, though I had scarcely acknowledged it – simply a feverish chimaera produced by an infected finger. I *had* actually met her. I *had* buried her box.

I experienced a tremendous gush of relief – mingled, incongruously, with the sense that I had just assumed some momentous burden. Slowly, I clambered to my feet, and limped to the porch. I had just gone inside, and was about to lower myself on to the seat, when I noticed a red-covered book standing on the window-sill. From the way it was displayed – upright, and half-open – it looked as if someone had found it on the floor, and put it in as prominent a place as possible, so that whoever had left it there would immediately see it when he (or she) came to retrieve it.

I took it down and opened it: *She*, by Rider Haggard. On the fly-leaf was written: *Mary Stone. Southsea. May 1898.*

Mary. Southsea. Surely it must be hers. Everything was right except the surname – and that could be explained by the date. She would have been only a girl in 1898. *Stone* must have been her maiden name.

Pressing the book to me, I hobbled back to the Railway Inn, and passed out on my bed.

The landlady was right: by venturing out so soon, I *had* set myself back again; and as a result it was almost another week before the doctor finally pronounced me fit enough to go home. On the eve of my departure, I made myself as spruce as I could, trimming my moustache, and slapping some colour back into my pasty cheeks, and putting on a clean shirt; then I slipped *She* into the poacher's pocket of my coat, and went down to the bar. Mrs. Grant smiled at my changed appearance, as you might at a child showing off his new school uniform.

'Gracious, sir, I'd have hardly known you. You going calling on Sir Humphrey Darby?'

I smiled back. 'I don't know where I'm going. I have to return something to somebody, but I'm not sure how to find her. All she told me was that she was staying with a friend who has a motor-car.'

'What, here in the village, you mean?'

I nodded.

'Oh, that'll be Miss Shaw, up at the Motte, I expect. She has the only motor-car round here that *I* know of.'

'How far is it?'

'About a mile past the church. On the Buriton road.'

'Thank you,' I said. As I turned towards the door she called after me:

'But I can do that for you, Mr. Roper, and gladly. You didn't ought to be going out on an evening like this. Remember what happened the last time.'

'That's very kind of you, Mrs. Grant,' I said. 'But a short foray will do me good. Brace up my muscles for tomorrow.'

I was, indeed, dreadfully weak still, and had to keep stopping to catch my breath; and it was almost dark by the time I finally found the Motte. It was some distance from its nearest neighbour, and hidden by tall untidy hedges. I opened the gate, and started up the gravelled drive. Ahead of me I could see a neat whitewashed house, with a stable block to one side, and a line of tattling fir trees to the other. The only feeble light came from a delicately veined fanlight above the front door, but I could just make out the other windows – large, and arranged with classical regularity – glinting in their recesses like dirty pewter. There was something eerily desolate about the place, as if it had been hastily abandoned after some disaster. But if an accident had really befallen Miss Shaw, then surely Mrs. Grant would have mentioned it?

I rested my head against the door-jamb for a moment, then tugged on the bell-pull. There was no response. I tried again, using both hands this time. After a few seconds, I heard foot-steps, and then the heavy clunk of a bolt, and the squeak of unoiled hinges. The door cracked open eighteen inches, and stopped abruptly as it hit a chain. A lamp appeared, and then – a foot below it, and jaundiced by its glow – a round, unsmiling woman's face.

'Yes?'

'Good evening. Is Mrs. Wilson in?'

She craned forward, frowning, her eyes screwed half-shut with the effort of trying to see me.

'There's no Mrs. Wilson here.'

'Oh, I'm sorry. I thought she was staying with Miss Shaw.'

'She was. But she went home last week.' She began to close the door. I drew out the book and thrust it into the shrinking rectangle of light.

'She left this at the church,' I said. 'I was hoping to return it to her. Would your mistress be able to let me have her address, do you think?'

Her face softened, as if merely by mentioning the word *church* I had demonstrated my trustworthiness.

'No, sir, I'm sorry. The mistress is away herself.'

'Do you know when she'll be back?'

'Not this side of Christmas, I'm afraid. She's gone to India. To visit her brother in Simla.'

'Ah. And you wouldn't . . . you wouldn't, I suppose, have any idea where her address book might – ?'

She shook her head. 'She'll have taken it with her, sir.'

'Well, that does seem rather conclusive.'

The obvious thing, of course, would have been to give her the book in any case, and ask her to keep it until her mistress got home, or until Mary Wilson wrote enquiring after it. But that would have robbed me of the opportunity of returning it in person – which for some reason I was peculiarly reluctant to lose. So, before the housekeeper could offer to take it, I said:

'I'm sorry to have troubled you, then. Good night.'

And without waiting for a reply, I turned and set off briskly down the drive. I had gone no more than ten paces, however, when she called after me:

'I can tell you one thing, though. Where her ticket was for. Mrs. Wilson, I mean.'

I stopped. 'I beg your pardon?'

'She left it behind in her room, see, and the housemaid found it and gave it to me, and we ran after her, and just managed to catch her in time. And I noticed the name on it. And it stuck in my mind, because it seemed a funny thing to call a railway station. It sounded more like a farm or something. Somewhere you'd expect someone to live.'

I took a step back towards her. 'What was it?'

'Langley Mill,' she said. 'Langley Mill.'

Early the next morning, still carrying the book, I at last set off for home. Thinking that it might possibly be on my way, I asked the station master, before I got on the train, if he could tell me where Langley Mill was. He frowned as if I were mad, and grumbled:

'Oh, it's miles away, sir. In Derbyshire. Heart of the mining country.'

Being forced to travel like an invalid, wrapped in a borrowed rug, and entirely dependent on the goodwill of porters and cab-drivers to get me from one stage of my journey to the next, I made frustratingly slow progress, and didn't finally arrive until the last silver threads of daylight were fading from the sky. The house was dark, except for a dim yellow glow from the drawing-room; and the only other sign of life I could see, as the gardener's boy helped me down from the trap, was a great black swirl of rooks gathering in the skeletal branches of the trees at the end of the garden. It was a desolate enough homecoming – but at least, I thought, it meant that I should find my wife alone, and would not have to contend with anyone but her and the servants.

I was wrong: I realized it the instant I switched on the light in the lobby, and saw a greatcoat that didn't belong to me swagging out from the jumble of jackets and mackintoshes hanging on the hooks. Beneath it was a pair of muddy boots – not neatly stowed against the wall, but splayed with proprietorial carelessness in the middle of the floor. There was only one man I knew who would behave like that in my house: my brother-in-law.

I started towards the drawing-room, but stopped abruptly again when I reached the door. There were muffled animal sounds coming from inside, like the grunts and squeals of a pig sty. I pressed my ear against the wood. My wife (there was no mistaking the whooping-cough bray of her sobs) was crying angrily, while her brother tried to smother the flames by murmuring, over and over:

'Come along now, Violet Roper. Brave kid. Brave kid.'

I crept away, meaning to wait out the storm in my study. But when I got there, I found a book lying open on the table, and a couple of Hubert's pipes next to it, and the stale air thick and scratchy with his smoke. I should have known – when he was in the house, nowhere was safe from his presence: it permeated every crack and corner like an invisible gas. In my weakened state, I could not compete with it: it made me feel an intruder even in my own sanctuary.

I turned, and impulsively hurried into the kitchen. Mrs. Chieveley stood with her back to me at the stove, peering beneath the half-lifted lid of a steaming saucepan. Her husband was sitting at the table, one hand on his teacup, reading the newspaper. The hubble of the boiling water must have disguised my footsteps, because neither of them seemed to have heard me.

I cleared my throat. Chieveley looked up sharply, then jumped to his feet.

'Oh, I'm sorry, sir, we didn't know you were back.'

'That's all right, Chieveley. How are you?'

'We're very well, sir, thank you.'

'Good, good, good.'

'But what about *you*, sir?' said his wife, turning towards me.

'Ah, well, you know . . .'

'We were so sorry . . . to hear from the mistress . . . you'd been so poorly . . .' There were tears in her eyes, and she was frantically kneading her apron with her red hands – as if that was the only way she could keep herself from lunging forward to kiss me.

'Thank you. You're very kind.'

'But you really are better now?'

'Just about back in the land of the living. But still weak as a kitten, I'm afraid.'

She made an odd noise with her tongue. 'Then you really shouldn't be walking about, should you, sir? Why don't you go into the drawing-room, and I'll bring you some tea?'

'My wife's in there, with Colonel Ashburn. They seemed to be having a bit of a confabulation about something, so I didn't like to disturb them.'

I avoided Chieveley's eye, for fear of the pity I knew I should see in it.

'The study, then,' said Mrs. Chieveley.

I felt myself starting to sway. 'Look, would you mind if I just sat here for a minute or two?'

'Of course not, sir.' Her husband pulled out a chair at the head of the table, and helped me into it. She hesitated a moment, then nodded at the big earthenware teapot. 'If you don't mind *our* tea, sir,' she said tentatively, '*that's* just freshly made.'

'I'd love a cup, Mrs. Chieveley. Thank you.'

We sat in companionable silence for half a minute or so, smiling at the novelty of the situation. Then, from somewhere in the depths of the house, I heard a door close.

'Who's here?' I said. 'Apart from the Colonel?'

'Only Mrs. Ashburn, sir,' said Chieveley. 'They didn't like the idea of the mistress being on her own in . . . you know, under the circumstances. So when they brought her home they decided to stay on for a few days. Just until you got back.'

'Hm,' I said. 'Well, that seems a bit odd, doesn't it? The simplest thing, you'd have thought, would have been for *her* just to stay a few more days with *them*.'

Mrs. Chieveley blinked with surprise. And indeed, I was quite shocked myself: this was the first time, in ten years of married life, that I had ever said anything in front of her or her husband that might have been construed as a criticism of my wife, or as an unseemly attempt to enlist their support against her. Perhaps, I thought, my encounter with Mary Wilson had eroded my sense of propriety. I felt myself flushing, and hastily took a sip of tea.

'Ah,' I said, waggling my cup histrionically. 'Very welcome, Mrs. Chieveley.'

She looked away in embarrassment. But her husband, with his usual aplomb, rose effortlessly to the occasion:

'I rather think, sir,' he said, 'that Mrs. Roper was anxious to see her friends again.'

'What, the spiritualists, you mean?'

I tried to sound off-hand, but could not keep the exasperation from my voice. Chieveley, though, was the perfect diplomat: he avoided my gaze, and gave not so much as a twitch of amusement or disapproval to suggest that he shared my opinion.

'Yes, sir,' he said. 'There's a new gentleman, in particular, comes here every afternoon. A Mr. Dolgelly.'

'Dolgelly, eh?'

'Yes, sir.'

'Ah.'

Chieveley is one of the astutest judges of character I have ever met, but – curious as I was – I naturally couldn't come straight out and ask him his opinion of a visitor to the house. So I contented myself with nodding encouragingly. After a couple of seconds my patience was rewarded:

'He's a very decided gentleman, sir. At all events, that's my impression.'

'Oh, dear. Not rude, I hope?'

'Not *rude*, sir, no. Just exceedingly *definite*. The furniture has to be just so. There mustn't be any noise. So Mrs. Chieveley and I have to stay in here with the door closed during the sittings, so as not to disturb them.'

'Hm, well that's a bit of an inconvenience, isn't it?'

'Oh, please don't think I'm complaining, sir.'

'And anyway,' put in his wife hurriedly, 'what *really* matters is the change there's been in the mistress. I couldn't hardly believe it. I don't know what he says to her, but whatever it is, it's done her the world of good. She's always more cheerful when he leaves, isn't – ?'

She stopped suddenly, as she turned towards her husband and caught his warning glare. Her throat worked painfully, and her face started to redden. Neither she nor Chieveley, I noticed, was looking at me. I studied my teacup and said:

'Well, that's something at least, I suppose.'

The words seemed to be sucked into the void, like pebbles in a quicksand. There was a lull, in which we all tried in vain to think of some way to re-start the conversation. We were saved, finally, by the sharp clip of a man's boots approaching us along the passage. Chieveley got up and moved quickly to the door. The footsteps stopped. I heard my brother-in-law's voice saying:

'Ah, Chieveley.'

'Good evening, sir.'

'Your mistress isn't feeling very well, I'm afraid. She's gone upstairs to lie down. So dinner at eight rather than seven-thirty, please.'

'Very good, sir.'

'Right. Thank you. Oh, and, er –'

'Yes, sir?'

'Would you make up the bed in the cabin? And light the stove? Mrs. Roper thinks her husband would be more comfortable out there than in the –'

Chieveley silenced him with a tiny jut of the chin; then – as an angler reels in a trout – took a couple of backward steps to draw him further into the room. Hubert appeared in the doorway. He was holding three or four stuffed toys, which he thrust at Chieveley, as if he couldn't wait to be rid of them.

'And put these in there, too, could you?' he said. Then he caught sight of me, and started.

'Ah, you're back,' he said, his face softening into an apologetic smile. 'Didn't know. I'm sorry.'

I nodded. 'Mrs. Chieveley's very kindly restoring me with a cup of tea.'

'So I see. Splendid. Splendid.' He hesitated a second. 'Look, old chap, why don't you come through? We need to have a bit of a pow-wow. And no time like the present.'

I was in no mood for a pow-wow with anyone, but there was clearly no way of avoiding it. So I thanked the Chieveleys, and followed him back into the study.

'Now, Corley Roper, you make yourself nice and cosy here,' he said, graciously ceding me my own chair as if he were the host, and I some peevish guest. He arranged a blanket round my knees, then scooped up one of his briars from the table, knocked it out in the fireplace, and perched himself on the corner of the desk.

'Well,' he said, starting to fill the pipe from his pouch, 'I don't mind telling you, you gave us all quite a scare. Why didn't you at least let us know where you were, for heaven's sake?'

'I didn't want to be a nuisance.'

'It never occurred to you, I suppose, that you might have been a bit less of a nuisance if we'd had some means of reaching you, just to find out how you were getting along?'

I shrugged. 'I was very well looked after.'

'Well, I'm glad to hear it. But you know what Violet's like. How highly strung she is. She was awfully upset about the whole thing.' He rattled his pocket for matches, and slowly lit his pipe. 'Sounds a bit far-fetched, I know,' he said finally, letting the words out gently on a billow of smoke, as if to soften their impact, 'but she somehow got it into her head that you weren't really ill at all, but had met some other woman, and run off with her.'

'*What*?' But I couldn't keep a treacherous blush from spreading up my face. Hubert, mercifully, was still too busy fussing with his pipe to notice it.

'I know,' he said. 'But there it is. So it was a bit of a shock to her when she had your wire saying you were coming back.'

'And that's why she doesn't want me in the house?'

He raised his eyebrows, and nodded gravely.

'I see.' But I didn't. I knew, in fact, that it couldn't be the truth – or, at least, not the *whole* truth. Violet had her passions and idiosyncrasies, but jealousy was not among them.

'Is Mr. Dolgelly involved in this, by any chance?' I said, as casually as I could.

Hubert coloured. 'What do you know about Dolgelly?'

'Just what Chieveley told me,' I said, feeling the heat spreading up my throat. 'That he seems to have a great influence over her.'

'Well, there's no denying that. I can't say I care for the fellow myself. But it's obvious he's been a great comfort to V.'

I shook my head despairingly.

'I know,' said my brother-in-law, rolling his eyes. 'I absolutely agree with you, of course: it's pure mumbo-jumbo, all that eye-wash about auras and spirit guides and manifestations from the other side. But when it comes to the gentler sex, ours not to reason why, what?'

'And banishing me to the cabin was this . . . this *table-tapper's* idea, was it?'

He grimaced, and spread his hands in a gesture of baffled impotence.

'You know me, Corley: I'm a simple chap. I've never understood women, and I never will. But the best policy, I've always found, when some strange little beastie has taken up residence in their crania, is just to go along with them.'

For a moment I was speechless. This was a man whose own wife was the most timid, mouse-like creature I had ever met; and in the twelve years I had known them, I could not remember one occasion on which he had consulted her opinion on anything – let alone *gone along with it*. It was hard to believe he was now suggesting I should indulge his sister by tacitly conniving at her adultery with a spiritualist – and yet I couldn't immediately think of any other construction to put on what he had said.

'Perhaps I'm being obtuse,' I said, when I had found my voice again. 'But I'm not entirely sure what beastie you're talking about?'

'Well, I told you, old chap. She thinks –'

'But surely – I mean, the fact that I'm here – doesn't that prove pretty categorically that I *haven't* run off with another woman? In which case . . .?'

He sighed. 'That would seem to be the logic of the thing, I know. But unfortunately, logic isn't what we're dealing with here.' His voice was steady enough, but his face had darkened. 'You've been through it too, of course you have: we all know that. But a woman's bound to feel the loss of a child more keenly than a man, isn't she? That's just nature. Damned unfair, I know, when she takes it into her head to lash out, and you happen to be in the way, but . . .' He shrugged. 'In a couple of months, you'll see, everything will have calmed down a bit, and she'll be more amenable to reason. But till then, I'm afraid, there's nothing much for it but to ride out the storm.' He tinkered with his pipe. When he spoke again, his voice had dropped to a murmur: 'To be honest, old chap, in your shoes, I'd see it as a blessing in disguise. I mean, I know all you really want is a quiet life – and, frankly, you'll have a much better chance of it out there than you would here. It's your own little lair. No one's going to barge in and bother you there. You'll be able to do exactly as you please, without fear of let or hindrance.' He laughed. 'Sounds like heaven to me.'

I suddenly felt too tired to resist.

III

And that is how I came to find myself living in my own work-room, at the end of my own garden. Chieveley attended to me like a steward on a ship, bringing me my meals, and cleaning and tidying round me as I lay on the bunk. The doctor looked in a couple of times, and pronounced me *on the mend*. My wife slipped a note under my door saying: *Black Bear sez you wer very norty to giv us orl such a fright, and you ar to <u>stay</u> <u>there</u>, and not cum in the howse*. Otherwise, I had no communication with anybody.

I had been away almost two weeks longer than I had meant to be, and knew I must start to reassert control over my own life. But the most I could manage during the first few days, as I slowly recuperated from my journey home and the welcome I had received, was to set about answering the condolence letters that had come in my absence. Most consisted entirely of stock etiquette-book phrases, and required nothing more emotionally demanding in reply: indeed, there was something quite soothing about the mechanical process of answering them, which gave me the spurious sense that I was helping to return the world to some kind of order. The only one that breached my defences was a messy note from my old friend Cyril Jessop, written in pencil on sheets torn from an exercise book, and offering me a restorative holiday *wandering the by-ways, as we did in days of yore* in his gypsy caravan. This provoked such a sharp jab of loss that I crumpled it up and hurled it on to the fire, before hastily opening another *Please accept our deepest sympathy* to regain my equilibrium.

But as I sealed the final envelope, I realized that my last excuse had gone, and I could no longer avoid confronting the larger questions that were pressing in on me.

The first and most immediate, naturally, was: what should I do about the strained relations with my wife? I had still heard nothing more from her, and had no notion how much longer she meant to leave me living in exile in the cabin. There were moments, indeed – particularly at dusk, when the garden looked especially desolate, magnifying the sense that I had been marooned on a desert island – when I even began to wonder whether she saw it as a permanent arrangement. I briefly considered writing a note, asking her – but quickly rejected the idea on the grounds that it would only weaken my position, by implicitly conceding her the power to decide my fate. I could, of course, bring the thing to a head by giving her notice that I intended to move back into the house on such-and-such a date, and then just turning up; but that risked precipitating a crisis that might drag on for weeks, absorbing all my small stock of energy and stopping me from doing anything else.

So in the end – though I knew I was being feeble – I decided simply to leave things as they were until I had dealt with the second urgent problem: my career. Sitting on my desk was the story I had been working on when Elspeth had fallen ill. Although my publisher had grudgingly accepted that the finished manuscript would now be delayed, he still expected me to deliver it eventually – and I was by no means certain, any longer, that I could. During my conversation with Mary Wilson, some vague nauseous unease about my work had crystallized into positive disgust – and, having once made it conscious and put it into words, I could not seem to banish it again.

Which brought me to the third question: Mary Wilson herself. In some shadowy way I could not quite define, my encounter with her seemed to have wrought a fundamental change in me. For one thing, though the delirium had gone, a hint of it remained in the strange aura of light which continued to hover around the edge of my vision. The effect was rather like hearing the murmur of a garden party you cannot see: it gave you the unsettling sense that life – *real* life – was happening somewhere else, just beyond some unreachable horizon.

And sometimes, still, I found, without warning, the image of her face erupting before my eyes. Often, these apparitions seemed to set off a sudden, overwhelming yearning to see her again, which left me weak and trembling, and pricked with guilt at feeling so much more intensely about someone I barely knew than I appeared to about my own poor beloved girl. And once or twice they were accompanied by an odd sensation in my temple – something between a tic and a headache, that would last for anything up to a minute, before abruptly stopping again. I thought of mentioning it to the doctor, but in the end decided it was too difficult to describe, and too trivial, to warrant troubling him with it. The problem of my obsession with Mary Wilson, I decided, like that of my marriage, would have to wait until I had finished my new book.

But when I took up the pages and tried to read them, they seemed as impenetrable as if they had been written in an alien language – and on the rare occasions when a meaning did some-how push its way through, I found it so repellent that I felt physically sick. I forced myself, nonetheless, by an enormous act of will, to sit down at my desk every morning and try to continue the story. It was useless: the words were so many individual atoms, that refused to connect themselves into even the simplest organic structure, and I invariably ended either by drifting off into thoughts of Mary Wilson, or else by simply slumping in my chair, and gazing dully at the bare trees stirring in the wind, and the robins and blackbirds scouring the sodden garden for worms.

What finally shook me from this lassitude wasn't, in the end, a conscious act on my part, but an irruption from the outside world. One afternoon, at the start of my second week there, I noticed my wife coming down the path towards me. It was the first time I had set eyes on her since my return; and – rather than wait passively for her, like a tame rabbit in its hutch – I pulled on my coat, and hurried out to meet her. As soon as she saw me, she hastily produced her battered toy bear from her pocket and flourished it at me.

'Bear says you're to stay inside!' she called. 'You'll catch cold!'

'Good to get a breath of air!' I hunched my shoulders against the spitting drizzle, and charged unsteadily towards her like an ailing bull. She responded by starting to walk faster herself; and we met, finally, red-faced and breathless, under the big spreading cedar in the middle of the lawn.

'Bear thinks you're very bad, don't you, Bear?' she said, nodding its head in reply. 'He's a good mind, now, not to give you your letter.'

'What letter?'

'Shall we, Bear? Oh, all right, then.' She slipped a letter from her sleeve and handed it to me. 'Here. This came for you this morning.'

My first thought was: why is she giving this to me in person, rather than letting Chieveley bring it with my other post? The envelope was dimpled with raindrops, which had left the ink badly smeared; but enough was left for me to see that the handwriting was large and expansive, the 'o's and 'a's formed with big looping curves, and the 'p's and 'y's with luxuriant curly tails. No man, I was certain, would write like that – but how would a strange woman have come by my address, since the occasional letters I received from enthusiastic readers were always sent via my publisher?

She craned forward, watching me. 'Bear says aren't you going to open it?'

'I will in a minute.'

'Why not now?'

And suddenly I thought I understood: she suspected – perhaps even hoped – that it had been sent by my supposed *inamorata*.

Which set, as it were, a parallel hare wildly running in my own head: what if it was from Mary Wilson? The writing did not immediately remind me of the *Mary Stone, Southsea* on the flyleaf of *She*, but it was too smudged for me to be sure – and, in any case, that inscription had been written more than ten years ago, when she was still little more than a child.

I peered up through the dense spines of the tree. 'It's raining.'

'We're dry here.'

'But then it'll get wet on my way back.'

She lunged forward, as if to snatch it from me again. But at that moment, the garden door to the house opened, and a man came out on to the terrace. He was perhaps forty, with black hair and the waxy complexion of an undertaker, and wore a sober dark suit that would have looked more appropriate in the city than in a country garden. He did not speak; but cleared his throat so noisily that Violet stopped abruptly, and spun round to look at him. I could not see her face, of course; but there was a kind of trembling anticipation in the way she held herself that made me think of a sheep-dog awaiting orders.

'Is that Mr. Dolgelly?' I said.

She did not reply. Still saying nothing, the man slowly lifted his hands, and pressed the palms and fingertips together to form a crude circle. I couldn't imagine what this sign meant, but it must have had some significance for Violet, for without so much as another glance in my direction, she lowered her head submissively, and started towards the house again.

I stood and watched until they were inside, then turned and began making my way back to the cabin, carefully tucking the letter under my coat to protect it from the rain. Despite my curiosity, I was in no great hurry to open it. Reason told me it could not really be from Mary Wilson – and yet, until I knew for certain, there was always a dim hope that reason might be wrong. The thing was not, after all, impossible: perhaps she had seen my name in a bookshop – recognized it – employed a detective to track me down . . .

I shut the door, riddled the coals in the stove, and sank into my chair. Then, slowly, I slit open the envelope.

Inside was a single sheet. I forced myself not to cheat by going to the end and looking at the signature. Instead I read:

As from: Fleming's Hotel, Half Moon Street, London W.

February 26, 1910

Dear Mr. Roper,

Let me begin by saying just what a warm admirer I am of your work. As a little girl, my favorite playmates were the children in 'The Mists of Time'; and then, years later (when I was older than I care to admit), I discovered Alcuin Hare and his friends, and <u>they</u>, in their turn, became my boon companions. And all the while, my dearest hope was one day to meet the creator of these wonderful characters, and to see for myself the woods and streams where their adventures took place. For a young woman growing up in Albany, New York, this was not – as I am sure you can imagine – an easy ambition to fulfil!

And yet here – thanks to a large dose of good old Yankee grit and resourcefulness – I am! For weeks I besieged Bailey's Magazine, asking them to commission a series of articles on modern European authors; and when it finally penetrated their poor heads that I had no intention of going away until they said 'yes', they relented. And top of my list, needless to say, was Mr. Corley Roper.

Mr. Charles Derrington of Derrington and Mayes was good enough to give me your address, so I do hope you will forgive my taking the liberty of writing to you direct . . .

I stopped reading, screwed the thing into a ball, and wrenched open the door of the stove. Only as I was about to drop it on to the flames did it strike me how unreasonable I was being.

Sheepishly, I smoothed the pages out again, and slid them into my desk drawer.

But the damage was done. Feelings do not lie, and the violence of my reaction had brutally demonstrated, beyond any doubt, the truth of what mine had been telling me for days, and I had been steadfastly trying to keep from myself: I simply could not write any more.

And it had shown me something else, too: just how deeply Mary Wilson had penetrated my soul. The faintest possibility that the letter had been from her had been enough to lift me, in an instant, from torpor to giddy exhilaration; and the discovery that it wasn't had as quickly plummeted me into despair. Just *why* she had had this effect on me I was at a loss to understand: the most obvious explanation, of course, was that I somehow imagined I had fallen in love with her, but – try as I might – I could not quite make that idea fit the case. The nearest I could come to it was to say that I felt as if I were imprisoned in a small smoky room, and knew that if I could only get to her I should be able to fill my lungs with fresh air – oxygenating, perhaps for the first time in my life, not merely those few muscles required to get me through my day-to-day existence, but every corner of my being. In any event, it was pointless, now, to pretend that she was simply one problem among many: she had unsettled my very foundations, and nothing else could be put right until – one way or another – I had made them strong again.

From that moment on, I could not keep her from my thoughts. During the day, thinking it might bring me closer to her, by offering me an insight into her character, I would sit reading her copy of *She* – until the story of a man in thrall to a mysterious woman disturbed me so much that I had to set it down again. At night, I would lie hot and twitching in my bunk, trying to devise some means of finding her, and wondering how, if I succeeded, I could conceivably explain myself to her. When I did manage to sleep, she haunted my dreams – usually as I remembered her, but sometimes, unaccountably, in the guise of an enormous giant, who held me helpless in her hands.

I started taking longer and longer walks – ostensibly to wear myself out, but also in the half-acknowledged hope that destiny would somehow lead me to her again. One evening, after a long ramble over the hills, I found myself sitting in the porch of our village church, muttering into the darkness – as if I imagined that some kind of sympathetic magic must have brought her there, too, and at any moment I should hear her answering. I heard nothing, of course, except the sound of my own voice, and the whistle of the wind. But the eccentricity of my behaviour had seriously alarmed me. Before I was half-way home I had persuaded myself that I was in danger of losing my mind, and must seek help and advice without delay.

To whom, though, could I turn? Not Violet, obviously; nor the doctor, who would be bound to attribute my condition to some digestive disorder, and prescribe a strict regimen of liver pills and water. Flicking mentally through my address book, I found only one name that might be of some use: Cyril Jessop. And even the thought of confiding my predicament to *him* filled me with a certain heaviness. As I trudged the last few hundred yards through the village, I could not help imploring Fate, even at this late hour, to spare me the necessity, by *hey-prestoing* Mary Wilson out of thin air, and setting her down before me.

The instant I turned in to the drive, I thought Fate must have heard my plea. There, in front of the house, was a motor-car. Aside from my wretched publisher (and it was inconceivable that he would call on me unannounced) I knew of only one person who owned a car: Mary Wilson's friend, Miss Shaw. So great is the power of wishful thinking that, by the time I had reached the front door, I was three-quarters convinced that this gleaming blue monster must be hers, and that Mary Wilson had borrowed it, in order to come and see me.

I took off my coat and hat, and – like a victorious soldier

planting his flag to mark the retaking of some lost possession – hung them next to Violet's in the lobby.

'There's a lady to see you, sir,' said Chieveley, emerging from the shadows as I went into the hall. 'I showed her into the drawing-room.'

'Anyone we know?'

'No one *I* know, sir. I should remember if I'd seen her before.'

Ah, I thought. *Better and better*. 'Thank you, Chieveley. Could we manage some tea, do you think?'

'Yes, sir.'

She was standing in front of the fireplace, looking at the portrait of my father-in-law above the mantelshelf. I hesitated for a moment in the doorway, struggling to reconcile the trimness of the figure and the modishness of the high-waisted cowrie-pink dress with the woman I remembered. I turned her round in my head and tried to fit the long nose and the straight eyebrows and delicate forehead beneath the brim of her flamboyant hat. Difficult, but just possible, surely . . .

But at that moment she heard me and twirled round herself, and I knew it was a lost cause. She was, if anything, younger than Mary Wilson, with the unlined skin and fresh-from-the-chrysalis lustre of a girl who has still not yet quite completed the transition into womanhood. And her face, though equally pale, was broader and more rounded, with a dusting of freckles, and a tiny mole like half an apple pip on the upper lip.

'Good afternoon,' she said. There was something unusual about her voice, but I couldn't immediately identify it.

'Good afternoon.'

For a few seconds, we stood staring at each other. Her large, unnervingly direct grey eyes seemed to be looking for something they couldn't find. Her mouth was a tight pink bud, ready to blossom into a smile as soon as I recognized her.

But I didn't recognize her. I knew, in fact – as certainly as Chieveley had done – that I had never seen her before in my life.

'I'm sorry . . .' I said.

She started to blush. 'You weren't expecting me?'

'No, I don't think . . .'

'I'm Alice Dangerfield.'

'Ah.' I was so overcome with disappointment and confusion that I couldn't think of anything more to say. I did just manage a half-hearted grin, but I knew it was useless. A child would have been able to see that her name meant as little to me as her face had.

Her blush deepened. 'Oh, my Lord. I did write you. And at home you can always count on the mail, so I guess I just kind of assumed . . .' She grimaced. 'Oh, dear, this is so embarrassing.'

Write you. Home. Mail.

'Ah,' I stammered. 'You're a . . . you're the young American lady?'

She nodded.

I ran my hands over my cheeks, trying to draw the heat from them into my fingertips. 'In that case,' I said, 'I'm afraid I have a dreadful confession to make. Please – won't you sit down?'

She settled herself on one end of the sofa. To avoid having to look her in the eye, I perched on the other, and addressed myself to the window.

'I did get your letter,' I said. 'But I didn't *know* it was from you, because – well, this sounds awful, I know, but I didn't read it to the end. I hadn't been very well, you see, and I put it in a drawer, meaning to deal with it later, when I was better. I really can't tell you how dreadful I feel –'

'No, please, there's no need for you to apologize. It was *my* fault, I'm sure, for blithely saying *I'll be calling on you on such-and-such a day, unless I hear from you that that isn't convenient.* I dare say that's seen as a very forward and improper way to behave on this side of the ocean.'

'Not at all –'

She laughed. It was not an unpleasant sound, but it had an uncomfortably penetrating quality, like a stab of sunshine finding its way through the blinds into a cobwebby room.

'Now you're just being polite,' she said. 'My aunt came to Europe in the eighties, and she told me you do things differently here, so I can't say I wasn't warned.' She laughed again. 'Will you forgive me?'

'Really, there's nothing to forgive.'

'No, but there is. Please, Mr. Roper, don't keep me at bay with good manners. If I've been rude, I'm truly sorry. And I should truly like to be forgiven.'

For a moment I was quite nonplussed. There was an odd mixture of contrition and assurance in her tone – as if she really *did* feel in need of my forgiveness, and yet was so used to getting what she wanted that she imagined all she had to do to be certain of receiving it was merely to draw my attention to the fact, just as one would give a shopping-list to a grocer. And yet, for all my irritation, I couldn't help recognizing that I was more to blame for the awkwardness of the situation than she was.

I didn't want to do it, but there was no alternative.

'Really,' I said, 'you've nothing to reproach yourself for. It was inexcusably negligent of me. All I can plead in extenuation is my . . . personal circumstances. My daughter, you see . . . You know, Elspeth?'

She nodded: she had read my dedication to *The Little Mouse*.

'Well, she died. Last month. Of scarlet fever.'

Miss Dangerfield let out a strangled whimper. I turned towards her. Her face was as white and frozen as if she had toothache. For a moment she couldn't speak. Then she whimpered again.

'Oh, how terrible!' she said.

'Yes, I'm sorry. Not quite what you were expecting, I know.'

She gave a quick shake of the head that said: *don't worry about me*. 'But why didn't Mr. Derrington tell me?'

'Oh, I think that's easily enough explained. He's been pressing me for my next book, and I've been putting him off. Since . . . since Elspeth . . . I find I simply can't write. In fact, to be perfectly

47

honest with you, I've more or less come to the conclusion that it's a permanent condition, and I shall never be able to do an animal story again. But Derrington doesn't know that yet. And he probably thought: *perhaps a charming young American woman will succeed where I failed. But I'd better not let her know about the loss he's suffered, or she'll be too delicate to go.*'

She flushed. 'Oh, I hope that's not true!'

'I'll bet you it is.'

'No' – colouring even more – 'I mean about your never doing an animal story again.'

'I'm afraid that is, too.'

'But –'

But before she could say anything more, Chieveley came in with the tea things, and began laying them out on the table. I could tell from the way she watched – bright-eyed, her fingers in a constant fidget – that she was frustrated at being interrupted, and impatient for him to be gone again. But she smiled graciously enough, and managed to hold her tongue until he'd closed the door behind him. Then she hunched forward quickly and asked:

'Would you like me to pour?'

'Thank you, yes, if you wouldn't mind.'

She laughed. 'I am an expert pourer, Mr. Roper. I've been playing mother since I was ten. That's what comes from being the eldest of four girls and two boys.' She leaned over to hand me my cup, bringing her face to within a foot of mine. 'All of whom have grown up enchanted by the adventures of the Coneys and Alcuin Hare and Mr. Largo Frog. You have no idea how desolate they would be to learn that the spell has finally been broken. And I can vouch for it that there are tens of thousands of American readers who would feel the same.'

'Well, I'm sorry to hear it, Miss Dangerfield. But everything must come to an end.'

'Yes, but *such* an end. It's too sad!'

I felt a surge of heat in my neck. 'It was not of my choosing.'

She blushed. 'No, of course not. But . . .' She paused, and studied me with a curious abstracted gaze, like a sapper looking for a weak point in the enemy's defences. To forestall her I said:

'Rotten luck for *you*, of course, to find it's been a wasted journey, but there it is. You'll fare much better elsewhere, I'm sure. What other authors are you going to see?'

'I beg your pardon?'

'Didn't you mention, in your letter, that you were hoping to talk to some – ?'

'Oh, yes, yes.' And in the lacklustre voice of a schoolboy declining Latin nouns, she recited a list of names – of which the only one I recognized was H. G. Wells. Then, without giving me time to reply, she returned to the attack:

'So, anyway, am I really to tell your American admirers that you have nothing to say to them?'

'You may tell them I am sensible of the great honour they have done me.'

She gave another dismissive little shake of the head. 'All they will want to know is when they may expect another book.'

'Miss Dangerfield, I have tried to explain . . .'

'Yes, I know, but . . . Oh, dear . . .' She sighed, and dropped her gaze, and started worrying at a stray tendril of hair that had come loose above her temple. I began to relax, thinking I'd finally succeeded in putting her off. But then she abruptly looked up at me again and said:

'But – this may sound awfully impertinent, I know – but I truly think . . . if you just thought about it . . . you'd see . . . it all comes from a misunderstanding. You feel . . . at least, I'm guessing you do . . . that the stories are somehow to blame for what happened to your daughter. You figure that if they'd been any good, they'd have been able to save her.'

Tears tortured my eyes.

'But that's to have a wrong idea of what you do,' she went on.

'You're a magician – but not of the Merlin kind. What you do can't prevent suffering – it can only make it more bearable. And it does. Wonderfully. As I can testify . . .' She paused. Then, very gently, she said: 'The question you must ask yourself is whether Elspeth's life would have been *better* without Alcuin Hare and his friends, or worse. And I think you know the answer. I certainly do.'

I was crying – I could not help it – and my throat seemed to have turned to concrete. I got up, and starting edging towards the french window. Behind me, she said:

'You do not betray your daughter by giving other children the same delight you gave her. In fact, what could be a lovelier memorial to her?'

I was boiling with some emotion so intense I could not tell whether it was anger or grief or self-loathing, or a mixture of all three. But I knew I could not hold it in for more than a few seconds – so I quickened my pace, hoping to have gained the safety of the garden before it exploded. As I did so, I glimpsed a blurred figure scurrying guiltily out of sight behind the box hedge at the edge of the terrace. I could not see the face, but something in the angle of the neck and shoulder told me it was Dolgelly.

The Vesuvius inside me finally erupted. I lunged at the french window and hurled it open, wrenching the handle so violently that it snapped off in my hand.

'What the devil do you think you're doing?' I yelled.

There was no response. I ran towards the hedge. He immediately broke cover, and – despite his undertakerish suit and town shoes – sprinted across the lawn with astonishing agility. It was obvious I had no chance of overtaking him; so I spared myself the indignity of pursuit, and bellowed after him:

'Do you know whose house this is?'

He stopped just short of the cabin and faced me. He said nothing, but slowly held up his hands, and formed the same strange ovoid sign with the thumbs and forefingers that I had seen him make before.

'I've no idea what that means,' I yelled. 'But if I catch you trespassing on my property again, I'll report you to the police!' And, without waiting to see his reaction, I turned and went back into the house.

Miss Dangerfield had finished her tea and was standing expectantly at the end of the sofa, like a passenger waiting for a train.

'I'm sorry –' I began.

'No, no,' she said, backing away. 'I'm the one who should apologize. This is obviously an awfully difficult time for you. I can see it was wrong of me to impose myself on you –'

I shook my head. 'Oh, that was nothing. Just some disreputable fellow who keeps hanging around the house. Please. Sit down again.'

'No. Thank you. I really must be going.'

She had already half opened the door into the hall, so I had no choice but to say, 'All right,' and ring the bell for Chieveley. As we were shaking hands, I said:

'You do understand, don't you, that I am not being deliberately perverse? I should like to do as you ask, if I could. But it is simply not possible.'

'I understand,' she said, with a smile. 'But don't expect me to give up on it.'

I stood by the front door, waving my handkerchief as her motor-car chugged and fumed its way down the drive. To my amazement, I saw she was driving it herself.

The next morning, after a night in which I barely slept, and a breakfast I could barely touch, I hurried to the post office and sent a wire to Cyril Jessop:

Does holiday offer still hold? If so, yes please. C.R.

Less than two hours later, Chieveley brought me the reply:

Splendid. Make haste. C.J.

51

IV

Having effectively banished me from her life, my wife could not
reasonably expect me to consult her about mine; so rather than
trying to see her before I left – which would have given her the
opportunity to argue with me – I merely scribbled a brief note to
explain what I was doing. For a few seconds, I struggled with the
urge to soften it by starting *I am orf for my hols wiv Sirril Jesup* –
but then, reflecting that even that would seem to assume a
degree of intimacy (or, at least, a kind of habitual complicity)
that no longer existed, I contented myself with merely writing: *I
am going away, and do not know when I shall be back.*

It is a complicated journey from Oxfordshire to southern
Dorset; but the connections were so miraculously arranged that
I never had to wait more than five minutes for a train, and it was
still only late afternoon when I finally found myself approaching
Jessop's cottage in the hills above Lyme Regis. He called it his
redoubt – the one place on earth he could return to, after weeks
of wandering in his caravan, and be certain of finding a refuge
from *the noise and inanity of the modern world*. And indeed, as
my trap lurched towards it through the gathering dusk, and I
saw the thick circling wall of hedges and the keep-like slab of the
barn silhouetted against a fading March sky, it did strike me, for
the first time, that it resembled nothing so much as a small fort.

Independence was Jessop's watchword; so, refusing the driver's
offer of help, I shouldered my own bags, and staggered through
the gate. The house itself – a low huddle of whitewashed cob
under a beetling bonnet of thatch, set twenty yards back from
the road – was unlit, and for a few moments I wondered if after
all I had arrived too late, and Jessop had left without me. But

then I noticed a square of paper fixed to the front door, and hurried up the path towards it. There was still just enough light for me to make out what was written on it – a single word, scrawled in soft pencil: *Vannery*.

I set down my bags, and walked round the house and across the muddy yard to the barn. The door was half-open, and the blackness inside tinctured by a yellow haze. I leaned against the jamb, and peered in. The interior – as always, when Jessop was at home – was dominated by the half-visible bulk of the caravan, which loomed and glinted like a decrepit dragon startled in its cave. A hurricane lamp stood on the platform beneath the fretwork canopy, sending faint hieroglyphic shadows on to the barn-walls. Below it, on the steps, sat Jessop, with a screw clamped between his lips, a screw-driver and a pair of seamstress's scissors poking from his carpenter's apron, and a large wooden hoop balanced on his knees. Something about his appearance – slight, and bent, and oddly creased – made me think of a newly opened nut still that bore the marks of the shell that had shaped it.

'Don't strain your eyes,' I said.

The screw dropped. 'Ah, Roper,' he muttered, without looking up. 'Forgive me. This thing's being the very devil.'

'Can I help?'

He shook his head; but when I retrieved the screw and held it out to him, he said: 'Yes, you're right, I suppose: three hands are better than two.'

'We can make it four hands, if you like.'

He shook his head again. 'I shan't be needing more than one of yours, thank you. Just hold this for a moment, would you?' He handed me a heavy ring, then waggled his thumb to show where it fitted on the hoop. 'There,' he said, as he screwed it home, 'that should keep old Tankard from breaking free and leaving us stranded in Farley Puddock or Dimbles Bottom. Why don't you sit down?' He got up, laid the hoop aside, and started gingerly probing the space beneath the caravan with his foot. 'Sybil, bless her, has gone into town to get provisions for us, so you'll be cosier here with me than in the house. Ah, here we are.' He stooped down, and pulled out a little portable oil heater. 'A bit new-fangled for my taste,' he said, setting a match to it. 'And'll never be a substitute for the real thing, of course. But takes the chill off well enough if you have to be inside.'

I found an empty crate and kicked it towards the fire. 'Is she coming with us?'

'Hm, what, Sybil? Oh, no. No.' He settled himself back on the steps, took up a tangle of straps and started teasing them apart. 'Thought it best not to, this time. I mean, there are things you can't ask a woman to put up with, aren't there? And she doesn't want to spoil our fun.'

I turned the crate over to make a stool and sat down. 'That seems a bit hard on her.'

'Oh, she'll be happy enough to have a holiday from me. You forget what an exasperating fellow I am. In a couple of weeks you'll be ready for a holiday from me yourself.'

I laughed. 'Even so . . . The spring's her favourite time, I know . . .'

He shrugged, then edged round to catch the light, and began minutely examining the stitching on a buckle. I could see his lips moving; but the noise that came out – a low hum, like the inconsequential muttering of a doctor at a patient's bedside – was so faint that it was a couple of seconds before I could decipher what he was saying:

'She really was dreadfully sorry, you know . . . As I was, of course. About your . . .' He shook his head. 'A fairy child, Elspeth. Not of this world. Makes you wonder whether Life really knows its business, doesn't it, when it snatches the best from us, and leaves so much dross behind? Financiers, and factory-owners, and politicians . . .'

I tried to speak, but my tongue had swollen in my mouth.

Jessop plucked a loose tuft of thread from the strap and fumbled in his apron pocket for a needle and cotton. 'How's Violet coping?'

That was easier. I swallowed, and said: 'Oh, all right, I think.'

'Still seeing her spiritualist friends?'

'I'm afraid so.'

He nodded and glanced up at me. There was a kind of melancholy gentleness in his eyes that said: *it isn't something I'd do myself, but don't be too hard on her: we must all take comfort where we can find it, mustn't we?* I shivered suddenly, like a man on a winter's night who doesn't realize how cold he has been until he comes in and feels the first warmth of the fire.

'But the truth is,' I heard myself blurting out, 'I really don't know. She seems to have fallen under the spell of a chap called Dolgelly – a *medium*, I suppose that's how he'd describe himself – and he doesn't want her to let me into the house, for some reason. So ever since I got back I've been living in the cabin.'

Jessop was licking the end of the cotton. He removed it for long enough to *tch* his tongue sympathetically.

'Oh, it's really not as bad as you might think,' I said. 'In some ways I actually prefer it. There's certainly no denying it's a lot more restful.'

'Lonely, though,' he murmured.

'No lonelier than being in the van on your own, I'd have thought.'

'I'm not in the van on my own very often. And when I am, I'm on the move. Surprising the people you meet on the road. A postman here. A sheep-drover there. So at least you have the *illusion* of company.'

The illusion of company. I'd meant to wait a day or two before mentioning Mary Wilson, until Jessop and I had had time to re-establish our old easiness with each other. But however long we spent together, I knew I should never have a better *entrée*. For a few moments I sat watching him. He looked the very soul of patient understanding, hunched over his sewing like a kindly grandmother. And surely, I thought, if he did not judge Violet, then he will not judge me?

'I have had the illusion of company, too,' I said.

'Really?'

I nodded. 'Or something like it.'

And then, before I could check myself, I was telling him. For the first few sentences I stuttered and stumbled; but soon the phrases were jostling each other in their impatience to get out. When I had finished, still staring at his work, Jessop said:

'Oh, my poor old friend.'

'Do you think I'm mad?'

He shook his head. 'No, of course not. I think it's all too understandable. You were hungry. You were tired. You were soaked to the skin. You craved the kind of warmth and comfort that only a woman can give you. And you knew . . .' He paused, and cleared his throat noisily. When he went on again, he was mumbling so softly I could barely hear him. 'You knew you weren't very likely to find it at home. So when you chanced upon an attractive young stranger in peculiar circumstances, it was only to be expected that your feelings would be more than usually roused . . .'

'But the feelings aren't quite of that kind, Jessop.'

'No?'

'No. That's what's so unaccountable.'

He appeared to be completely absorbed in re-threading his needle, but I knew from a slight stiffening of his shoulders that he was waiting for me to tell him what kind of feelings they *were*, in that case.

'I mean, that, obviously, was the first thing I thought of,' I said. 'But I'm not giddy and dry-lipped whenever I think of her. I don't feel I'm about to drift off like an untethered balloon. I feel . . . Well, all I can say is that the few minutes I spent in her company seem like the most *real* experience I've ever had. As if what is *truest* in me is somehow bound up with her.'

'Hm.' He pinched his lower lip and drew it out, like the end of a thick rubber band. 'And all *I* can say is that love's a strange animal. Sneaks up pretending to be something else entirely, and then, when it's too late, rips the mask off and shows itself for what it is.'

'If that were the case here, I can't help thinking my eye would have fallen on someone a good deal softer and sweeter than Mary Wilson. My landlady at the pub, say . . .'

He shrugged. 'Well, there's no means of knowing, is there, except by seeing her again? Since you're married and she's married, that can only make the thing more painful for you, if I'm right. But it's plain as a pikestaff you won't rest easy until you've settled the matter, one way or the other.'

'You think I should look for her?'

He nodded.

'I don't even know where she lives.'

'You know she lives in Derbyshire. At a place called Langley Mill. Or somewhere close, at any rate.' He was silent for a moment. Then he glanced up at me and said: 'I'd been planning to venture into Devon. But I'm happy to go north instead. Only if we're going to' – jerking his chin towards the caravan – 'we should be on our way. Even with Tankard at his best, it'll take us a fortnight to get there, if we're lucky.'

I was so moved and surprised I could only stammer:

'Oh, no, you mustn't . . . I mean, I couldn't . . .'

'Yes, you could. It'll be easier for you if we go together. Won't look as if you've had to make a special journey. You'll have a pretext for being there – so if you do manage to find her, you can simply give her the book, and say we just happened to be passing.'

'But what about you?'

'Oh, there'll be something for me to do, don't you worry. There always is. You show me ten Derbyshire miners, and I'll show you – I guarantee it – at least one bonnie fiddler, and a fine dancer or two, and a crafty-eyed fellow who's a catalogue of old country songs, and'll sing you half a dozen of them for a sup of ale. The trick is just to know how to burrow beneath the grime.' He stood up. 'Come on. Help me to get my recording-machine stowed.'

Imagine that one day when you are out walking, you come upon an enclosed garden, with a small green-painted door in the wall. You turn the handle and step inside – and immediately find you have somehow managed to slip back twenty years or more. You haven't forgotten the present: you know it still exists beyond the walls, and you can even glimpse it sometimes through the open doorway. You know, too, that at some point soon you will have to return to it – and that, when you do, it will be exactly as it was when you left it. But – for as long as you are able to remain there – you miraculously seem to know again the long-lost sensations of youth, in all their innocent, skin-tingling intensity.

So it was with the next ten days, as Jessop and I plodded northward in the van. Spring had not yet quite arrived, but you could sense it waiting eagerly in the wings – catch the sharp, urgent smell of sap, and see the stark outlines of the trees starting to soften under a fuzz of fresh green. And sometimes, when the wind eased and the cool air started to warm a little, you could hear the first tentative stammering of birdsong in the woods.

Every morning, we rose with the sun, and – our feet drenched with dew – padded across the meadow where we had spent the night to wash ourselves in a brook. Afterwards, sprawling luxuriously on an old tarpaulin, we would breakfast on home-made sausages from the local farm, or a couple of perch we had caught ourselves the previous evening. When we had finished – an almost religious ritual, this, that Jessop insisted on with quiet devotion – we would light our pipes and lie back for a few minutes, gazing up at the heavens and absorbing the peace that seemed to enter us at every pore. Then, as one of us cleaned and stowed the dishes, the other would fetch Tankard from his overnight lodging, and blinker him, and harness him into the shafts, ready for the day's adventure.

We did not talk much as we went – not as a result of any awkwardness between us, but rather because we were so sated by the shared experience of jolting and rattling along the road, with the countryside unrolling magically before us and the breeze cutting at our cheeks, that any commentary would have been superfluous. Sometimes we would stop for lunch at a wayside inn, but more often we merely pulled up on the verge for an hour or so, and feasted on bread and cheese and beer bought in a nearby village, while Tankard cropped contentedly at the young grass. Then we would pack up and trundle on again, until fading light and a deepening chill told us it was time to look around for a resting-place. Having found a suitable field, and delivered Tankard over to the hospitality of the farmer, we would take ourselves for an hour or two to the closest ale-house – where Jessop would invariably cajole some wizened old fellow into singing a couple of songs, which he gleefully scribbled down in his notebook – before returning to our portable little kingdom, and building a fire, and cooking a simple dinner beneath the stars. And so to bed, to sleep until a new morning – and then get up, and pull on just enough clothes to be decent, and tramp shivering across yet another meadow, to wash in yet another stream . . .

This idyll lasted almost unbroken from the day we left Dorset to the moment of our arrival in Derbyshire. Only once, in all that time, did the world beyond the garden-wall break in, and rudely drag me back into the sad complexity of my real life. It happened, as these things so often do, at the very instant I should least have expected it, when – so glorious was the weather, and so arcadian the landscape of woods and valleys and tree-dotted pastures in which we found ourselves – I could almost have deceived myself into thinking we had moved beyond the power of the present to recall us. In order to take advantage of an especially lovely camping place overlooking a burbling, willow-fringed river, we decided to stop rather earlier than usual, and I had volunteered to lead Tankard to his quarters, while Jessop got the van ready for the night. On my way, I saw three children playing on the river-bank below me. One of them, a slender boy in a norfolk jacket, looked up and waved at me. I waved back, and called:

'Good hunting!'

The farmer's wife was a friendly enough soul, but rather over-particular, and would not let me leave until she had given me a choice of stables for Tankard, and written down every last detail of his dietary requirements. As a result, it was three-quarters of an hour before I was finally able to get away and hurry back to the caravan. I'd expected to find it all shut up, and Jessop sitting waiting for me, his pipe in his mouth and a book open on his knee; so it was something of a surprise to discover the door still open, and a young girl wrapped in a blanket huddled on the steps in his place. As I drew closer, I could see she was shivering, and wincing with cold or pain.

'Hullo!' I cried out, while I was still fifty yards off. 'What happened to you?'

She was too caught up in her own anguish to respond, but the next second Jessop appeared on the platform above her, with a roll of bandage in one hand, a water-jug in the other, and a towel draped over his arm.

'There's been an accident,' he said, as inconsequentially as if he were muttering a platitude about the weather. 'Nothing too serious. But a bit of first aid's called for, I think.' He edged past her, then knelt down and carefully folded back the blanket from her left leg. A graze ran from the knee to the shin. It looked uncomfortable but fairly superficial – except at the bottom, where fresh blood was pulsing from an inch-long gash. He took

60

a sponge from the jug and dabbed at the wound. The child –
who could not have been more than six or seven – whimpered,
and involuntarily jerked her leg away. He grabbed the ankle, pinioned it, and went on working, gently but with quiet persistence.
The girl cried out, and began to struggle.

'I know,' he murmured. 'Hurts like anything, doesn't it? But
this is the worst bit. Start counting now, and by the time you've
got to a hundred, it won't be so bad. That's a promise.'

The girl tried, but couldn't keep it up, and dissolved in a wel-
ter of moans and shrieks.

'What happened?' I asked.

Jessop shook his head. 'The victim has so far been unable to
tell us,' he said, drying the leg with the towel. 'And I've
despatched the only witnesses to fetch wood for a fire.'

I looked around. For a second or two I could not see anyone
else. Then, at the far end of the field, at the edge of a small copse,
I noticed the boy who had waved to me earlier. Next to him was
a smaller companion, also wearing a norfolk jacket. They were
both darting about like actors in a comic moving picture,
frantically snatching up twigs and broken branches from the
ground and piling them into their crooked arms. After a few
moments, they evidently decided they could carry no more, and
started running back towards us. Jessop cocked an eye at them,
then squinted up at me and said:

'Get us a good blaze going, would you? Our poor wounded
heroine's chilled to the marrow.'

I fetched newspaper from the van, then went and intercepted
the two young fellows, and showed them where to drop the
wood. As I squatted down to build it into a fire, they stood
watching me, pale-faced and breathless, like a couple of errant
schoolboys waiting in the headmaster's study to hear what their
punishment will be. Finally, unable to bear the silence any
longer, the taller one said:

'You must think awfully badly of us, sir.' He was about twelve, with delicate features and large apprehensive grey eyes. His upper lip trembled visibly, though he was doing his best to control it.

I shook my head. 'I'm not in a position to think anything of you at the moment. Just slip into the van, will you, and bring out the tarpaulin and a few cushions, so we can make the patient as comfortable as possible?'

He hesitated, until the younger one tugged his sleeve and said: 'Come on, Ced! Sharp about it!'

In less than a minute they were back, staggering under what looked like half the contents of the caravan, and between us we managed to fashion a kind of rough *chaise longue* next to the fire. Then Jessop, having finished bandaging the girl's wound, gently carried her over and laid her down. Her face was was still white and contorted, but she had stopped crying, and when I wedged a pillow under her head she unclenched her stiff little body and settled back with a grateful sigh.

'How is she, sir?' asked the older boy.

Jessop shrugged. 'I've cleaned her up. And the bleeding's stopped. But she'll need to see the doctor. You live here, I take it?'

'Yes. I'm Cedric Adair.' He paused for a second, caught between childhood and manhood, and then held his hand out, first to Jessop and then to me. 'This is my sister Daisy. And my brother Charles. And our father *is* the doctor.'

'Well, that's handy, at any rate,' said Jessop.

'He's going to be frightfully cross, I'm afraid. And, of course, I *know* we should have been more careful. But honestly . . . It was an accident. Daisy was the princess, you see, captured by pirates. And we were rescuing her from the island they'd taken her to. Only she slipped –'

The girl interrupted him with a dreadful wail. It was the sound not of pain, this time, nor of protest, but of dismay at the sudden realization – for the first time, probably, in her young life – of her own shocking vulnerability.

'That's because she didn't *want* to be the princess,' said the younger boy, casting her a nervous glance. His voice was oddly slack and neutral, as if he couldn't make up his mind where his loyalties lay. 'And she didn't want to be rescued. She wanted to be left alone to talk to Mr. Largo Frog.'

The skin on the back of my neck tightened. The older boy caught my eye and pulled a humorous face, making common cause with me against his sister's silliness. I looked away, blushing.

'Ah,' said Jessop, smiling. '*There's* a coincidence.'

I twitched my head, but it was too late: he had already turned back to the girl.

'Well,' he said, taking her hand in his. 'If you really want to meet Mr. Largo Frog, then you're in the most tremendous luck. Because it just so happens that my friend here is the one person who can introduce you to him. Can you guess my friend's name?'

The girl shifted her head and stared at me for a couple of seconds. Then she looked up at Jessop again, and I saw her lips move.

'That's right,' he said. 'Mr. Corley Roper.'

A glow spread up her throat and over her whey-coloured cheeks.

'Is it true?' she asked.

'Yes,' I said.

She shivered and clenched her fists. Pin-pricks of light appeared in her eyes. 'Will you tell me a story?'

'About Mr. Largo Frog?'

She nodded. 'And Alcuin Hare. And the Little Mouse.'

My mouth was dry. I had a momentary vision of being able to vanish in a puff of smoke, like a pantomime genie.

'Please?'

'Well, to tell the truth, I'm a bit out of practice . . .'

I could feel Jessop searching my face, trying to fathom my

reluctance. He must have misinterpreted the reason for it, because after a moment he turned to the two boys and said:

'I expect you two chaps think you're a bit old for this sort of thing, don't you? So why don't you cut along home, and bring someone back with you who can help get your sister up to the house?'

'We'd as soon stay, if you don't mind,' said the younger boy hastily. 'And then we can help her ourselves, can't we?'

Jessop cleared his throat, then threw the question to me to decide. 'Well . . .?'

Eight eyes looked at me expectantly. I knew, of course, that it would be unpardonable to disappoint the little girl. But I also knew that the springs of my invention were quite dried up, and that nothing I could do would make them flow again. The only choice open to me was to tell her the half-written tale I had been working on at the time of Elspeth's death – and the thought of *that* made me feel faint with disgust.

The girl started to sob. I took a deep breath, then settled myself cross-legged on the ground beside her.

'Well, Daisy,' I began. 'The story I'm about to tell you is one I had from Mr. Largo Frog's own rather big lips, when I chanced upon him the other day. And it's all about – who do you think?'

'The Little Mouse?'

'Our friend the Little Mouse, that's right. And of course Alcuin Hare, and the Coney family, and Mr. Largo Frog himself.'

The girl nodded happily, and shut her eyes.

'It all started one morning not so long ago, when the Little Mouse got up, and stretched, and yawned as usual, and then pulled open her curtains –'

'The red-check ones?' murmured the girl.

'That's right. The ones her mother made from the table napkin.'

'And did they still tickle her paws?'

'They did. But you must stop asking questions and let me get on with the story, or else we'll never be finished.'

'All right. I promise.'

She was as good as her word. And – astonished at my own fluency, and the treacherous ease with which felicitous details and embellishments suggested themselves to me – I related the story of the spring-clean at Badger's Bakery, and Mr. Largo Frog's accident with the hot-cross buns.

When I had finished, there was a long silence, as if the children – and even Jessop – found it difficult to come back from the Little Mouse's world into our own. Then the older boy said:

'That was absolutely first-rate, sir. Thank you.'

And the younger one jumped up, wheeling his cap through the air, and shouted:

'Three cheers for Mr. Roper!'

The little girl joined in the cheering, and then rolled over and impetuously kissed me.

'I'm better now,' she said, getting up like Lazarus from her makeshift sick-bed. 'I think I'll go home.'

We shook hands all round, and then they set off towards the gate – the girl in the lead, limping so slightly that a casual observer wouldn't have noticed she was doing it at all, and her brothers hovering a few paces behind, shaking their heads incredulously, and marvelling at their luck.

'Well done,' said Jessop softly. 'That was splendid. Quite took me back.'

'And me,' I said. I did not add: *And I would rather it hadn't* – but he must have seen the thought in my face, because after a couple of seconds, instead of pursuing the subject, he got up and went into the van to make tea.

I built up the fire, watching the light drain from the sky, and bats flickering in the thickening dusk.

And, then, for the first time in more than a month, I sat down and wept for my dead child.

V

My encounter with Daisy Adair left me feeling oddly depleted, as if telling the story had used up some vital element that the normal processes of eating and sleeping could not replace. I spent much of the next two days inside the caravan, stretched out on my bunk; and when we came to a hill, and I had to lighten the load by getting out and walking, I found myself creeping along like an old man, broken-winded and hollow-legged. At the same time, the strange sensation in my head became noticeably more troublesome – erupting without warning just as I was falling asleep or waking up, and continuing, on at least one occasion, for almost half an hour. I told myself that I had merely suffered a minor relapse – caused, no doubt, by sitting so long outside, and catching a slight chill. But this explanation didn't altogether satisfy me, since I didn't seem to have a fever; and I began to wonder whether perhaps something more serious might be amiss.

Jessop, of course, couldn't fail to notice the change in me, and I often caught him glancing curiously at me out of the corner of his eye. Only once, though, did he come out directly and ask me if I was feeling all right – and, when I assured him I was, he let the matter drop.

In the long hours of solitude, when I could muster the energy for it, and was not being distracted by the agitation in my temple, I considered the increasingly urgent question of what I should say to Mary Wilson, if and when we actually found her. And here, at least, my brush with the three children seemed to suggest an answer. We would establish ourselves in Langley Mill – which I still conceived of as a little island of rusticity, somehow miraculously preserved in the middle of a black sea of pits and mining towns, with cosy stables for Tankard, and a tranquil meadow for us – and let it be known that we had come in search of folk songs, and would be staying for an indefinite period to record them. And then, when (as was bound to happen, sooner or later, in so small a place) I happened to see Mary Wilson in the street one day, going to the post office, or taking her dog for a walk, I could merely attribute our meeting – just as Jessop had attributed the marvel of my being Corley Roper, and able to effect an introduction to Mr. Largo Frog – to the power of coincidence.

Why, how extraordinary! I heard myself exclaiming. *It's Mrs. Wilson, isn't it?*

She would certainly be startled, but she could not very well be angry.

But, when my strength recovered, and I began to spend more time outside, sitting next to Jessop on the driver's seat, my faith in this idea started to wane. As we rattled our way north through Warwickshire, the brilliant green of the countryside started to dim to a slate grey, as if someone were gradually turning down the lamp illuminating it; and by the time we finally crossed into Derbyshire, there seemed nothing left that could properly be called countryside at all, but only a smoking desert sketched in charcoal, with black chimneys lording it over the horizon, and miserable little farms and clusters of soot-blackened houses huddling in the hollows. Jessop and I tried to keep each other's spirits up by saying *this cannot go on for ever*, and *there are very pretty parts of Derbyshire, I believe*; but every mile that carried us closer to Langley Mill seemed to make it less likely that it could possibly match my idealized conception of it.

Even our worst fears, however, fell short of the reality. Cresting a ridge one drizzle-soaked Friday afternoon, we passed a skewed name-board welcoming us to A GLEY MILL, and the next moment found ourselves looking down on one of the ugliest sights I have ever seen. If Langley Mill had once been a village of even the most wretched sort, there was certainly no evidence of it now. At its heart was a sprawl of roads and canals and railway tracks, which converged like the tentacles of an injured octopus, and tangled themselves together in the centre in an untidy knot. Crowded next to them, along pretty well their entire length, were wharves and warehouses, engine houses and engine sheds, offices and factories – the most prominent of which was proudly crowned with an illuminated sign: *Langley Mill Gaslight and Coke Company*. In the remaining space, as if they had been squeezed in as an afterthought, were mean little terraces, their gloom relieved only by a scattering of public houses and – here and there – a brightly lit corner-shop.

Jessop stopped the caravan and stared, tight-jawed and frowning with dismay.

'Heavens,' I said. 'I didn't know such places existed.'

He shrugged. 'It's the logic of the modern world. How else are our industrialists to get their wealth, but by setting other poor souls to disembowel the earth, and then selling the lights and liver to the rest of us?'

I pressed a handkerchief to my nose, to keep the raw coal-fumes from stinging it. 'But what on earth would a lady be doing there? Or someone who *seemed* like a lady, at any rate?'

He laughed. 'Probably a missionary, wouldn't you say? They look as if they're in need of one. Or perhaps one of the cannibal chiefs has decided to lay out some of his ill-gotten gains on acquiring a well-bred wife.'

Tiredness and disappointment had made me irritable; and for a moment I felt so affronted by his tone that it was all I could do to keep myself from snapping: *How* dare *you talk about her like that?* But then I reflected that I actually knew nothing about Mary Wilson's personal circumstances at all, and that – though I might object to his language – his hypothesis was at least as plausible as any other. Certainly she had given me the impression that she was not happy in her marriage – and wouldn't that be precisely what you would expect, if it had been made for the calculating reason he suggested? So after biting my lip for a couple of seconds, I freed it again, and contented myself with merely asking:

'Do you want to leave me here, and go on on your own?'

He shook his head. 'It's not quite what we expected, I know. But I still think you'll have a better chance of finding her if we stick together.'

'That's awfully decent of you,' I said, touched. 'But are you sure you can bear it?'

He nodded. 'The pressing question, though, is: where can we stay?'

We did pass a couple of poor little farms close to the outskirts of the town, but at one, though the door was open, we got no reply; and at the other a toothless old man shook his fist from an upstairs window, calling:

'Be off with you, before I set the dogs on you: I'll have no gypsies on *my* land!'

I was beginning to think we might have to turn back, and spend the night by the side of the road, with no shelter for poor Tankard, and nothing for him to eat except the dirty grass on the verge, when I felt Jessop stiffen at my side, and heard him mutter:

'Let's try there.'

'Where?'

He pointed down the road, where, a couple of hundred yards ahead of us, an empty dray was turning in at a large gateway. I screwed up my eyes to read what was written on the side, and just had time to make out *Divot's Dairy* before it disappeared from view.

'What good will that do us?' I asked. 'There won't be anywhere for us to camp there.'

'No, but at least the entrance will be wide enough for us to get through, and they may have a stable to spare for poor Tankard, and a yard where we can leave the van, while we go off and avail ourselves of Langley Mill's doubtless princely hospitality.' He gave me an odd sidelong look, his mouth twisted into a sly grimace. 'Don't you think clean sheets and a hot bath might put you in a fitter state to go looking for Mary Wilson tomorrow? Don't want *her* to think we're gypsies, do we?'

It was such a novel suggestion that it took me a moment to grasp it. Then I said:

'Yes, that does sound very appealing.'

We found the owner – a plump, egg-faced man stuffed into a brown work-coat that was too small for him – sitting in his frowsty office, puzzling over a ledger. He was not unfriendly, but so slow-witted that Jessop had to explain what we wanted three times over. Once he had understood it, however, and agreed a price with us, he seemed quite taken with the idea, and insisted on coming out himself to show us where we might put the van, and which stall we could use for Tankard. The gate, he said, would be locked at seven o'clock, but opened again at four a.m. – *which* (tapping his nose, and grinning complacently at his own roguishness) *I trust is early enough to suit, gentlemen, and means you won't be kept waiting in the morning.*

We packed a couple of bags apiece, and then – having canvassed Mr. Divot's advice on the best place to stay – set out to find the Midland Hotel. It turned out to be a squat, square building, as charmless and functional as a waterworks; but the manager was welcoming enough, and the rooms clean and comfortable. I was worried that the proximity of the station might disturb Jessop; but when I asked him he merely shook his head and said:

'You can't avoid having a machine for a neighbour in a place like this; and a railway engine's no worse than any other.'

It was too late, we thought, to do anything productive that evening: Mary Wilson, wherever she lived, would almost certainly be at home now, and very unlikely to stir out again before morning – and even if she did, and by some outlandish accident we saw her, I was far too dishevelled and travel-weary to speak to her. So after taking it in turns to luxuriate in the promised bath, and eating a passable meal in the hotel dining-room, we fixed when we should meet in the morning, and then closeted ourselves – for the first time in more than two weeks – in our own bedrooms.

After so long on the road, I was quite unprepared for the stuffiness of the room and the *hiss-clank-thud* of the trains. As a result, tired as I was, I lay awake for more than an hour, trying to devise some strategy for the next day. In the end, I only managed to inveigle myself to sleep with the anodyne assurance a nurse gives to a distraught child: *there, there, don't you fret: everything'll come right in the morning, just you wait and see.*

After breakfast, having agreed to extend our stay at least one day more, Jessop and I decided to go our separate ways, and then meet again in the evening to pool what we had learned. He donned his red kerchief, a Tyrolean felt hat and an old jacket plucked from the hotchpotch of clothes he called his 'travelling wardrobe', and set off in search of miners' clubs and the workingmen's institute. I, for my part – conscious that, however unlikely it was, I must still be prepared for the possibility of happening upon Mary Wilson in the street – settled for a more sober getup: my battered but still respectable tweed suit, spruced up by the addition of a stiff collar and a tie. Then, tugging on my overcoat, I ventured out into Langley Mill.

In the light of day, it seemed less desolate and menacing than it had the previous night. The morning was not bright, exactly, but the strengthening sun, filtered through a dense, ever-present shroud of smoke, produced a shadowless silver sheen so brilliant that it hurt your eyes to look at it. Daytime, it was obvious, was what the place was made for, and the moment when it came into its own. Everywhere you looked there was an exhilarating bustle

71

of horses and wagons and hand-carts, interspersed here and there by a snorting steam- or motor-lorry, and with a constant thread of people braiding its way through the centre and around the edges. A few of the men stumbled along like worn-out work-horses, and one or two of the children were pinched and wide-eyed with hunger, but most of the people looked cheerful enough, and at least adequately clothed and fed. The same variety was visible in the buildings, with squalid little alleys crammed with hovels giving way to streets of modest bay-windowed villas, and even the occasional larger house – square, and comfortably settled in a pleasant garden behind a laurel or a monkey-puzzle tree – where, with some effort of the imagination, I could almost visualize Mary Wilson living.

And then, after I had been pacing back and forth for a couple of hours, I thought I spotted her. I was hovering in front of the post office at the time, debating whether I should go inside and enquire after her there; and, having more or less concluded that it was almost certainly pointless, given how little information I had, and might even appear suspicious, I had begun to turn away. As I did so, I half-saw something out of the corner of my eye that immediately drew me back again: a young woman in a pearl-grey dress and a feathered hat emerging from the entrance. By the time I had swivelled round and brought her into focus she was already hurrying away from me on the oppo-site side of the street; and I managed to catch no more than a glimpse of a pale cheek and a strand of black hair before the ineluctable logic of geometry reduced her to a back-view.

Don't forget Alice Dangerfield, I cautioned myself. But – though of course I had never seen Mary Wilson absolutely clearly – in my mind I had frequently taken out and burnished the few images of her I *did* retain, and *this* woman's gait and fig-ure seemed to match them far better than Miss Dangerfield's had done. While it had obviously been a foolish fantasy, more-over, to imagine that Mary Wilson might really have just turned up unannounced to visit me at home, I had solid grounds for linking her with Langley Mill, and supposing I might find her here.

I set off in pursuit, increasing my pace when I had to breast a sudden surge of people, and easing it again as soon as they were past, so as to avoid the risk of coming up too close behind her and making her look round. After a couple of hundred yards or so she suddenly turned right. I hurried to the corner, and was just in time to see her disappearing through a doorway in the middle of a parade of modest little shops and public houses. There was something surreptitious in the quick, darting way she moved; and when I came up to the place I realized why: above the entrance, in discreet gold lettering on a black board, was painted: *J. Hawker. Pawnbroker.*

I pressed myself to the wall, then gingerly craned my neck until I was able to peer inside. Beyond the usual display of clocks and cheap jewellery and boxes of cutlery in the window, I could just see a dimly lit room no bigger than a small parlour. At the back, behind a cluttered counter, stood a bald man in a black suit, watching attentively as the woman drew something from a bag. I could not tell what it was; but I saw him examine it through an eye-glass, before sorrowfully shaking his head. The woman started to gesticulate angrily, shifting her weight from one foot to the other like a thwarted child. I held my breath, willing her to move enough to give me a clear view of her. But before she could, the man suddenly responded by pocketing his eye-glass and looking up – forcing me to shrink back against the wall to avoid being seen.

I was conscious there were footsteps approaching me along the street; but so absorbed was I in watching the entrance to the pawnbroker's, and wondering who might emerge from it, that I paid them no attention until they were almost upon me. Then, all at once, I heard them stop, and a voice saying:

'Why, if it isn't my fugitive!'

I spun round, and found myself looking at a thin, heavily bearded man with the sharp eyes of a consumptive. I had seen him before, I knew, and not too long ago – but *where*? Not at home, I was sure of it. Perhaps he was someone we had met on our way here – and yet when I tried to connect him in my mind with Jessop, and our experiences together over the last two weeks, he seemed to spring away like a repelled magnet, as if he didn't belong there.

'Don't you remember?' he said, smiling at my perplexity. 'We were going to run away to sea, as I recall, the pair of us.'

'Of *course!*' I said, suddenly seeing again a glimpse of moonlit downland, and feeling the first cold spits of rain on my cheeks. 'Sussex. A month or so ago. You showed me the way to the village.'

He laughed. 'I failed, then, in my civic duty. Should have taken you to the police, and I let you go instead. But you shan't escape so easily this time. I'm not letting you out of my sight until you've given me a full account of yourself. And if I'm not entirely satisfied, why then' – stretching out a hand, and turning an invisible key with it – 'it's off to the cells with you.'

I knew he must be joking; and yet there was a kind of wild-eyed intensity in his expression that left a tiny pocket of unease in the pit of my stomach. What made it infinitely worse was the thought that at any second Mary Wilson might appear, and I might find myself having to explain what I was doing here to both of them simultaneously.

'It's really nothing particularly sensational, I'm afraid,' I said, with what, even to me, sounded like an uncertain laugh. I started to move away, hoping to draw him into step beside me; but he reached out and grabbed my arm:

'Hold on, there, not so fast. I think I'm beginning to see.' He nodded towards the pawnbroker's window. 'Not content with murdering your wife, you've decided to take up burglary, is that it?'

I couldn't run: it would be tantamount to admitting that I really *was* a criminal. I tried to invent some convincing subterfuge, but my brain seemed paralysed. Finally, in desperation, I blurted:

'Please – there's a woman in there. She'll be coming out directly, and I don't want her to see me when she does.'

'Ah, so that's the way the land lies. But you still want to be able to see *her*, is that it?'

'Yes.'

'What, and follow her?'

'Only if she's the person I'm looking for.'

He nodded. Then – in a sudden rush, as if the idea had only just struck him – he said:

'Not a detective yourself, by any chance, are you?'

'No.'

'Well, this is all damned mysterious. But I'll give you the benefit of the doubt – for the moment.' He pointed to the end of the street. 'We'll wait down there. If it turns out it *is* your woman, we'll follow her together. If it isn't, you'll come and have a drink with me, and tell me the whole story. Agreed?'

I could hear the tick of the seconds beating away in my ears. Reluctantly I nodded.

He nudged my elbow. 'Come on, then.'

We set off down the street, but had gone no more than ten yards when we heard the *ting* of the pawnbroker's door behind us. Stopping in unison, we peered back cautiously – just in time to see the woman stepping out into the road, clutching her bag. She hesitated a moment; then, seeming to sense our presence, she glanced in our direction – giving me, for the first time, a look at her face.

Damn, I thought. And, in the same instant: *Thank heaven*.

I could see how I had been deceived: she was much the same age as Mary Wilson, and had the same luminously pale complexion. But her chin was rounder, her features heavier – and her eyebrows, far from being thick and charcoal-black, were so light as to be almost invisible.

'Well?' asked the bearded man.

'No. The person I'm looking for is rather more delicate –'

'I dare say she would be.'

'And darker-haired.'

The woman – wondering, I suppose, why two strange men should take such an obvious interest in her, and no doubt reaching the inevitable conclusion – scowled fiercely, and scurried away in the opposite direction. My companion watched her for a few seconds, then stepped back into the middle of the road, scanning the buildings on either side.

'Right,' he said. 'We have a choice, it seems. The Black Lion or the Dewdrop.'

We chose the Dewdrop, largely because it seemed to be the emptier of the two. It was small, but bright and pleasant, with a cheerful smell of beer and smoke and furniture polish. We settled ourselves at a table in the corner, and my companion went to the bar to order our drinks – glancing back at me every few seconds, as if he still thought I might try to make a bolt for it. When he returned, carrying a brandy for me and a bottle of stout for himself, he said:

'I'm Davey Riddick, by the way.'

'How do you do?'

He put the glasses down carefully, took my hand, and waited for me to tell him *my* name. When I didn't, he said:

'And you?'

I was in a quandary. I still found it hard to imagine who or what he was, but his manner did not suggest a man of much natural reticence. At the very least, he was likely to be an incorrigible gossip – and, given the nakedness of his curiosity, was it not possible he might even turn out to be a journalist? The idea of my story being reduced, at best, to an amusing anecdote, and at worst to a newspaper article full of knowing hints about my sanity and proclivities, made me feel sick with dread.

'Roper,' I said finally.

'*Roper*? Your parents didn't think to christen you?'

'They did. But my Christian name's rather an embarrassment to me, I'm afraid.'

He nodded impatiently, as if he expected me to give it to him anyway.

'Augustus,' I said. That much, at least, was true enough. I was not obliged to add that, as a result, I used my second name instead.

'*Augustus Roper*,' he said, sitting down. 'That has a good rough sound to it. Like sticking your fingers on a sack of spuds, and feeling the hard round knobbles inside.' He saw my expression, and laughed. 'Not the way *you* think of it, I dare say. But I'm a hungry man, Mr. Roper. Hungry for the queer awkward cross-grain of real life. And when I get a bit of it, even just a name, I can't help relishing it.'

'But surely', I said, snatching gratefully at the opportunity to shift the conversation away from me at last, 'it's here all around you?'

'I know. But six months I was starved of it. And that leaves a man feeling pretty famished, I can tell you.' He coughed, holding the back of his hand to his mouth with a surprising womanish delicacy. 'Angry, too. I mean, how many years has any of us got? Thirty? Forty? And then to find you've wasted half of one of them with people whose veins are full of rosewater.'

I laughed, despite myself. 'Why didn't you just leave them, if they were as irksome as that?'

'I should have done. But they'd invited me to stay with them while I was finishing a book, and I was desperate to get it done. The house was meant to be a sort of artists' community, you see: my host – a *belletrist*, as he was pleased to call himself; and his tubercular sister; and two lady novelists. We were *all* supposed to be painting, or writing novels. It was only after I'd been there a while that I realized *their* novels were draining the life out of *mine*. All that minute analysis of what they felt about the colour

77

of the wallpaper . . .' He shook his head. 'I was dying of anaemia. So I started roaming the countryside, looking for blood. In fact' – unfolding a finger and pointing it at me as he remembered – 'that's what I was doing the night we met.'

'Well, you found it then, as I recall.'

He frowned for a moment, then nodded and smiled. 'Oh, yes. The rabbits. But more to the point, I found you. You kept me going for at least a week. I spent hours afterwards wondering who you were, and what you were running from. So now's your chance to satisfy me.'

It was inescapable; so, after fortifying myself with a sip of brandy, I told him – though in the simplest and most conventional terms, and leaving out any reference to my profession, or my imagined conversation with the dog, or my strange experience when I was burying the box. Riddick watched me closely, saying nothing – even at moments, such as when I was describing Elspeth's death, that seemed to demand at least a minimal expression of sympathy. When I had finished, he nodded and said:

'And what about this dark-haired beauty of yours?'

'I'm not sure I should call her a beauty –'

'This *woman*, then. Who brought you to Langley Mill?'

'Ah, well that's more difficult to explain.'

He gave a low growling laugh that dislodged something in his throat and made him cough again. 'It always is, isn't it?' he said, dabbing the corner of his mouth with a handkerchief. 'When the case concerns a man and a woman. Though I really don't see why it should be. I mean, we're all caught up in it, aren't we? It's just the old dance of life and death, that's been going on since the beginning of time, and'll still be going on at the end.'

I started to blush.

'Well,' I said, 'I don't know about that. But I'll tell you a funny thing. It's only just occurred to me: if it hadn't been for you, I'd probably never have met her.'

'*Really?*'

I nodded. 'Because you directed me to the village. And that's where I found her. Sheltering in the church porch.'

'And what's her name?'

'Mary Wilson.'

'Is it, now?'

A frightening, exhilarating idea suddenly hit me.

'You don't know her, do you?'

He let out a soft, almost noiseless whistle, and shook his head. 'No.'

The collision between disappointment and relief squeezed the air out of me. 'Ah, well,' I wheezed. 'It would have been astonishing if you had, I suppose.'

He took a deep gulp of beer, emptying his glass. 'But I think I know where you might find her. St. Lawrence's church, up in Heanor. Tomorrow morning. Stand outside after Sunday School, and see if you can spot her there.'

My first thought was that this must be a piece of *braggadocio*: I had simply not told him enough about Mary Wilson for him to be able to make a reasoned guess about where I might find her. But then it struck me that – having seen the woman I had been following – he already had a rough guide to Mary Wilson's appearance, and there could not be very many other people of a similar age and colouring and figure in a place the size of Langley Mill.

'Why Sunday School?' I asked.

'There's a Mrs. Wilson just started there, who teaches my niece. I've seen her a couple of times in the street, and she looks like enough your lass.'

'But you've never spoken to her?'

He laughed. 'I shouldn't trust myself. I think it's a crime. Cramming children's heads with all that bread-and-butter pudding. But I'll wager you five bob that she's the one.'

I longed to question him further, and find out what else he

could tell me about her. But I knew that if I did he would almost certainly demand more confidences from me in return; and I feared I had said far too much about Mary Wilson already, and risked compromising her reputation. So I merely thanked him; and then – as if as an afterthought – added:

'By the way, I wouldn't want you to get the wrong impression. There is really nothing improper about my relations with Mrs. Wilson, or my intentions towards her. And *her* behaviour towards *me* has been absolutely beyond reproach.'

He laughed again. 'What makes you think I'm the man to reproach her? Or reproach you, either, if it comes to that?'

VI

When Jessop and I met for dinner that night, I felt strangely constrained with him – mentioning my encounter with Davey Riddick only in passing, as an amusing curiosity, and saying nothing at all about the Sunday School teacher, or my plans to go in search of her the next day. At the time, I justified this simply as prudence: what, after all, was the point in raising his hopes, when the chances were that I was following a false lead? But now, looking back, I think I can identify another, barely conscious motive: the sense a hunter has, when he thinks he may have caught a distant glimpse of his quarry, and fears that if he draws too much attention to it he may frighten it away.

Thankfully, Jessop compensated for my reserve by being more than usually ebullient himself.

'Here,' he said, slapping his notebook on the table and riffling the pages with his thumb. 'Two new songs. And tomorrow I'm invited to Sunday dinner with a mill-worker, whose mother is eighty-two, and a living encyclopaedia – or so he tells me – of the old ballads. Do you want to come with me?'

'No, thanks.'

He looked at me curiously for a second or two, but did not seem particularly dashed or surprised – and, to my relief, did not bother to ask me what I was intending to do instead.

In the morning, I hovered in my room until Jessop had gone. Then, after quickly dressing as churchily as I could, and slipping the copy of *She* into my pocket, I snatched a hurried breakfast, and set off on my quest.

Heanor, it turned out, was not part of Langley Mill, but a separate little town, standing a mile or so away on a low rise above the valley. I climbed towards it up a winding road that seemed unable to decide whether it was urban or rural, but stuttered uncertainly from one to the other, with rows of neatly kept cottage gardens suddenly giving way to a sprawling carriage-works or the sweet steamy stink of a knacker's yard. Only at the very top did it finally abandon the countryside, emerging through a tight bottle-neck of buildings into a small market square lined on every side with sooty-faced shops and houses and inns. There was no difficulty, at any rate, in finding the church: it stood in one corner, on the highest point of the hill, its thickset, crenellated tower louring over the landscape like the keep of a mediaeval castle.

I had heard the faint sound of the bells starting to ring out soon after I had left the hotel, and by the time I arrived the service was clearly well under way: I could see lights inside, and just make out the muffled drone of a hymn wafting through the stained glass. Behind the nave was a functional modern hall, where presumably – although I could see no sign of it, except for a half-open door – the Sunday School was being held. I did not want to make myself conspicuous either by barging into the service half-way through or by loitering outside, so I decided to make a tour of the square – keeping one eye more or less permanently fixed on the church.

It was one of those days when spring suddenly seems to lose its nerve and take a step backwards. A vicious wind blew up from the north, harrying black-edged clouds across the sky and flinging tiny spatters of snowflakes into my face. Uncomfortable though it was, I couldn't help feeling grateful for it, because it gave me a pretext for tugging down my cap and turning up my collar without appearing strange – so allowing me the comforting sense that I was, if not quite invisible, at least so thoroughly disguised that even a close friend would not know me. Some flinty little part of my mind told me this was a delusion, but I chose to ignore it, knowing that without a belief in my own invulnerability – and hence my own power to control events – I would simply turn tail and flee in panic.

It took me a couple of turns round the deserted market-place to discover that the best shelter from the weather came from a dingy hotel called the King of Prussia. I stationed myself in front of it, rubbing my hands and peering into the distance, doing my best to look like a man who was waiting for a companion to arrive before going inside. I had been there for more than ten minutes, and was beginning to think it was time to assume another character and go somewhere else, when I suddenly became aware of the clatter of footsteps and a surge of children's voices coming from the direction of the church.

I started towards the sound, travelling in a wide arc, so that I ended up not directly by the churchyard gate but across the road from it. A seemingly endless procession of children was marching from the hall to the church. I looked around for their teacher, and finally spotted a young woman sauntering beside them at a slower pace, as if she were waiting for the end of the line to pass her so she could bring up the rear.

I squinted at her, trying – as I had with Alice Dangerfield, and the woman in the pawnbroker's – to superimpose her figure on my memory of Mary Wilson's. It did not seem to fit: it was too willowy. But I was still too far away to be absolutely sure, so – pulling my cap even lower, and hunching my shoulders – I began to sidle closer, and reached the the churchyard wall just as she passed in front of me.

No, there was no question about it: she was at least three inches taller than Mary Wilson, and I could see a curl of golden hair poking out from beneath her hat.

I suddenly noticed that two small girls were pointing at me and whispering. I started to back away again, trying to move out of reach of their curiosity, but something at the edge of my vision stopped me: a point of intense stillness in the middle of all that jostling motion.

I turned towards it. Another woman had emerged from the hall and was standing in the doorway, staring at me across the stream of children flowing between us.

It was her. I knew it instantaneously, not through the usual process of mental comparison that tells you you've seen someone before, but as a kind of self-evident truth about the nature of the world, like the colour of grass, or the regular passage of night into day. And it was absolutely clear that she recognized me, too. Her mouth was half-agape, and she clung to the door-jamb with both hands, as if the shock of seeing me had robbed her legs of the power to support her.

I raised my cap in greeting. She was still too dazed to smile, but managed to give me an abbreviated nod in reply. As the stream of children thinned to a trickle, we started to edge towards each other – and then found ourselves having to wait while the last stragglers dawdled their way between us. She stood watching, her lips pursed and her fists tight with impatience, as they meandered, infuriatingly slowly, towards the church. Only when they had finally disappeared inside did she turn back, and totter the last few steps to meet me at the wall.

I held out my hand. She did not take it, but merely went on looking at me – her chin tilted slightly forward, her brow creased. Then, suddenly, she began to sway. I caught her elbow, and lowered her gently until she was sitting on the wall. She was very pale, apart from a vivid rash of pink on her throat. I sat down next to her, so that we faced each other like a couple in a love-seat.

'I'm sorry,' I said. 'I didn't mean to startle you.'

She did not seem to hear me, but tentatively reached out and touched my wrist.

'You must wonder at seeing me here, I know,' I said. 'But –'

'I have been very stupid.'

'No, it's perfectly understandable –'

She shook her head. After a moment, her voice flat with resignation, she said:

'The box, is that it?'

'I beg your pardon?'

'The box I gave you. Something's happened to it?'

'I buried it, as you asked me to.'

'But then the vicar found it, and dug it up again?'

'Not as far as I know. I think it's pretty safe where it is.'

'Then why are you – ?' she began, then spread her hands in a despairing gesture that said: *no, don't answer.*

I started to take the book from my pocket, but it seemed such a puny thing to put into the scales against so much unhappiness that I dropped it back again.

'You must forgive me,' I said. 'If I'd known how upset it would make you, I would never have dreamed of coming.'

I began to walk away. I'd gone no more than a dozen steps or so when I heard her start after me. I stopped and turned to face her.

'You don't realize,' she said, hurrying up to me. She was trembling, and her fists were balled like an angry child's – as if by apologizing I had taken some unfair advantage of her, and forced her into making a response against her will.

'No,' I said. 'I can see that. But you really don't have to explain if you don't want to.'

'Yes, I do.' She glanced towards the church. 'Only I should be in there. They'll be wondering where I've got to.'

'Please go, then. The last thing I want is to be a burden to you.'

She considered for a moment, then shook her head. 'No, it'll only cause more raised eyebrows if I go in now. The sermon's the same in any case, inside or out: *For whosoever hath, to him shall be given; but whosoever hath not, from him shall be taken away even that he hath.*'

'What have I taken from you?'

She looked round nervously. 'We're not safe here. People might see us.'

'Does that matter?'

85

She nodded again.

'Let's go for a walk, then.'

She hesitated. 'I'm meant to be having lunch with the rector and his wife. My husband's away, you see, so they're doing their Christian duty and taking me in.'

'Oh, I'm sure it's more than duty . . .'

She turned towards me. Her eyes had a kind of bottomless darkness that reminded me of looking into a tin of treacle.

'Are you? Why?'

I had no answer. She nodded curtly, then glanced at the church clock.

'I'll need to be at the rectory by half-past one,' she said.

'That gives us almost two hours. Is there a park here?'

'Someone would be bound to notice us there.' She thought for a moment, then stood up abruptly. 'Let's go to Langley Mill. We'll say you're an old friend of the family, who turned up unexpectedly to see my husband, but then discovered he wasn't here. So I'm walking you back to the station.'

'Do you honestly think we need to make up a story like that? Surely no one'll think there's anything wrong in a man and a woman talking publicly to one another in broad daylight?'

She shook her head. 'People are terrible gossips.'

She was trembling with fear.

'All right,' I said, relenting. 'What's your husband's name?'

'Christopher. Chris.' She looked up at the church spire, as if we might see him peering down at us from the battlements. 'He's the curate here.'

'And how do I know him?'

'You were at school together?' She squinted at me, assessing my age. 'No, that won't do. Theological college, then.'

'I don't think I'd make a very convincing clergyman.'

'No.' She continued to stare at me, biting her lip. 'Ah, *I* know what it is: you met him in Tenerife.'

'*Tenerife*?'

'He was the English chaplain there. A couple of years ago. And you could have been on your way to India. Or South America, perhaps.'

'India's safer, I think. Let's say I was going to visit my sister. Who's a school-mistress in Simla.'

Her eyes narrowed slightly. She nodded and said:

'Come on, then.'

We started walking, retracing my journey down the hill. Neither of us spoke again until we were clear of the town. Then I said:

'Why were you so taken aback to see me?'

She glanced behind her, to make sure there was no one following us.

'You will laugh at me,' she muttered, turning back. 'You will think I'm the stupidest woman you ever met.'

'No, I shan't.'

'How can you say that? You don't even know what I'm going to say!'

Again, it was unanswerable. She seemed to relax slightly, as if she had scored a small victory over me, and it had made her more confident.

'I thought you were an angel,' she said.

I mastered the impulse to laugh. 'An *angel*?'

She nodded. 'An angel in disguise. Sent to take care of my child. To lead him to a better place. So you can imagine – when you turned up again like that – in broad daylight –'

'Ah.'

'There, doesn't that seem ridiculous to you?'

I shook my head. 'Or, at any rate, it's no more ridiculous than what *I* thought about *you*.'

'What was that?'

'You . . . You seemed, somehow, the *realest* thing that had ever happened to me.'

She nodded again, then bit her lip, frowning abstractedly.

'Isn't that odd?' she said finally. 'When I felt *you* were the

87

unrealest thing that had ever happened to *me*! Well, not *un*real, exactly. Real in a different way. In the way a *story* is real.'

'What, you mean I was a . . . a happy ending? For your child?'

'Yes, I suppose that was it.' A savage little gust of wind hit her, buffeting her sideways and whipping loose a strand of black hair which she distractedly tucked back behind her ear. After a few seconds, she looked up at me and said:

'And for me, too, in a way, I think. Because he was the best of me. The truest part of me.'

For a moment I was too embarrassed to speak. Then I managed to stammer out:

'Well, I'm sorry. I can see it must have been a dreadful disappointment to find I'm just flesh and blood after all. But it was awfully dark in that church porch, of course, so it was a natural enough mistake to make.'

Even before I'd finished speaking, I was cursing myself. She had the grace to try to smile, but it was clearly a struggle, and the result – a tremulous, thin-lipped crater in her pale face – was heart-breakingly sad. She shivered, and pulled her cloak tighter about her shoulders, retreating into her own misery. In an effort to draw her out again, I said:

'Do you often see angels?'

Her neck stiffened, and a tiny circle of colour appeared on her cheek. I held my breath. Finally she said:

'Not *see*, no.'

She sounded surprised, but not angry. I let the air out of my lungs as noiselessly as I could. After a moment she went on:

'But I used to *believe* in them, when I was a child. Or *half*-believe. In one, at any rate. *My* angel.'

'What, a *guardian* angel, you mean?'

She started, and her blush deepened.

'Yes, that must have been it, mustn't it? I hadn't thought of that. But then I haven't ever spoken to anyone about this before. So I never had to find a word for it.'

'Did you hear him? Did he talk to you?'

She considered, then shook her head. 'I just always felt that he was there. No, *always* isn't right. What I mean is, there were always *times* when I felt he was there.'

I nodded.

'It must have begun, I think, with my French nurse,' she said, teasing the words out slowly, as if she were explaining as much to herself as to me. 'When I was two or three, it started to dawn on me that all the other children we met in the park had mamas and papas. So I asked her where mine were. And she said: "*Tes parents terrestres sont partis. Mais tu as le bon Dieu comme père.*"'

She glanced towards me suddenly, roused from her self-absorption by the thought that I might not have understood.

'"Your earthly parents have left. But you have God for a father."'

She nodded. '"And he will send an angel to protect you."'

'And was he a French angel?'

She gave a quick surprised smile. 'I'm not sure. Do angels have nationalities?'

I shrugged. 'Perhaps you should ask your husband. He'd know, I presume, if anyone does.'

From her reaction, you would have thought I had suggested something indecent. She shuddered, and then immediately hurried on:

'But the answer is yes, probably: he *was* a French angel. Because *everyone* was French in those days. Apart from my governess – and she was the least angelic person you can imagine.'

'*Everyone*?' I said. 'Why? Where were you living?'

'In Paris.'

'So are *you* French, then?'

She shook her head. 'But France is where I was born. And where my mother chose to abandon me.'

Her voice had dropped almost to an inflectionless stage-whisper. I inched my head sideways until I could see her. She was swallowing repeatedly, as if trying to shift something in her throat.

'Why did she abandon you?' I said.

She turned towards me. The skin had tightened around her eyes, giving her face the flat look of a mask.

'Why do you suppose?'

'I don't know. I could guess, of course, but –'

'Guess, then.'

I shook my head, refusing the responsibility of saying it.

'Because I am a bastard.'

I tried not to blush, but could not help myself. 'That's scarcely your fault.'

'No, of course it isn't!' she snapped. 'Any more than it's the fault of all those thousands of poor little mites who clutter up the workhouses. But that doesn't save *them* from being . . . *thrown away*, does it?'

'No,' I said, as gently as I could. 'But the difference is: most of the poor little mites in the workhouses are there simply because their mothers can't afford to keep them. Which can hardly have been the case with your parents, can it, if they were able to provide a nurse, and a governess – ?'

'Oh, an entire household! Everything I could possibly need! A housekeeper. A piano. Music lessons. *Sur le pont d'Avignon.* Just as long as I didn't trouble them by . . . by . . .' Her voice faltered, and she shook her head, to express some depth of disgust she couldn't trust speech to convey.

'Did she never come to visit you?' I said.

'Mm?'

'Your mother. In Paris?'

'No.'

'And you have not met her since?'

She shook her head again.

'Have you tried?'

'What?'

'To meet her?'

'I told you before,' she said unsteadily. 'I have no idea where she lives.'

'I had no idea where *you* lived, and I managed to find you. Surely someone at your old school would know? Or would at least be able to point you in the – ?'

'Why should I want to find her?'

'To bring about a reconciliation.'

'It is not up to *me* to be reconciled to *her*. She –'

She stopped suddenly, unable to go on – not because she was weeping, but because her whole body was trembling so uncontrollably that she could not form the words. She looked so helpless and bereft that, without thinking, I put a hand on her arm. She started to lean towards me, shoulders hunched, like a small child seeking comfort – and then abruptly pulled away again, crying furiously:

'What are you doing? What are you doing?' She hurriedly smoothed her dress and straightened her hat.

'I'm sorry. I –'

'Someone will see!' she said. And then, with a kind of perverse triumph, nodding at the road ahead: 'Look!'

Coming towards us were a dozen or so people on bicycles. Most of them stared directly in front of them as they puffed and wobbled up the hill, too occupied with the business of merely turning the wheels to pay any attention to anything else. When they were almost upon us, however, a boy of fifteen or sixteen looked up and called:

'Morning!'

'Good morning,' I replied.

Mary Wilson said nothing, but kept glancing back at them as they passed. Finally, when they were out of earshot, she whispered:

'What do you think?'

'Mm?'

'Those people. Did they notice us?'

'Yes, of course they did. Or at least the young chap did . . .'

'Will he say anything, do you imagine?'

'To whom? About what?'

'About us!'

'Look,' I said. 'I do understand that you're concerned for your reputation. But I really don't believe you are putting it at risk by being seen walking down the road with me on a Sunday morning. If you act as if you have nothing to be ashamed of, people will just naturally assume that to be the case, and won't give it another thought. Look: my hotel's just over there. Why don't we go in and have some coffee?'

She followed the direction of my outstretched finger. 'The Midland, you mean?'

I nodded.

'But I'm known in there.'

'That is exactly my point.'

We sat in the over-heated lounge, and drank tepid coffee from scuffed silver-plate jugs that looked as if they had been retired from a railway dining-car. It was the first time I had seen Mary Wilson in a social setting, and I was struck by the change in her behaviour. She made a heroic effort to appear easy – muttering sly little jokes about some of our fellow-guests, and asking me polite questions about myself, and whether my life at home had improved since our last meeting. But the instant I began to reply, her gaze flickered away, and she started glancing round surreptitiously to see if anyone was watching us. It was perfectly obvious that, try as she might, she could not free herself from the quicksand of her own anxiety; and after a few minutes, as she turned back towards me for the tenth time, and suddenly caught the look of pained concern in my face, she gave up, and acknowledged as much herself:

'I'm sorry, I'm not being awfully good company, I know.' She forced her lips into an unwilling smile, which promptly sprang out of shape as soon as she started speaking again. 'But this really is very dangerous for me. My husband . . . My husband and I are not . . . not what we should be. But still: a wife is all I am. If my marriage is ruined, I have nowhere to go. No family to take me back. Even the child I thought might grow up to care for me is . . . is . . .'

I nodded, and touched her hand. 'What about your guardian?'

She shook her head. 'He was kind to me when I was at school. But he would not help me now.'

'You cannot be sure –'

'I can. I *am* sure.'

There was a kind of saw-blade sharpness to her voice that warned me not to press her further on the subject. I said:

'Well, there's always the school itself, isn't there? You did say you were happy there. And –'

'What, Sussex Place? I *was* happy there, but it's closed now. And the Misses Robinson are old, and very frail. Besides, a school-mistress is always a school-mistress, isn't she? She can never really be a *friend*. That's a different thing altogether.'

'What about Miss Shaw – ?'

She started as if I had slapped her.

'What do you know of Miss Shaw?'

'What you told me. That you used to spend holidays with her, and still go to see her sometimes, even now. She is obviously a true friend – someone you could really count on, if it came to –'

'How do you know her name?'

'I beg your pardon?'

'I didn't mention that she was called Miss Shaw, did I? Only that she was an old school-mistress of mine, and had a motor-car.'

I was so unprepared for this sudden attack that for a moment I did not know how to respond. Then, very cautiously, I said:

'Yes, and that was enough to identify her. It's thanks to her that I am here at all.'

93

'But she has gone to India!'

I laughed. 'All right, then. Thanks to her housekeeper –'

'Her *housekeeper*? I barely know the woman. What did she say about me?'

'Nothing. She just told me she remembered seeing your railway ticket. And it said "Langley Mill" on it. So we knew where to start, at least.'

'*We*?'

I was at a loss. I frowned and shook my head.

'You said "*we* knew where to start". Who else was looking for me?'

'Oh, I see. My friend, Cyril Jessop.'

'Why? He's never met me, has he? I've never so much as heard of him.'

Even frowning was beyond me now. I merely stared blankly at her, like a boxer slumped against the ropes. I thought seeing the state she had reduced me to might jolt her into apologizing for her rudeness, but she seemed more pleased than ashamed, and could not, indeed, repress a tiny smile – as if, again, witnessing the full extent of her own power had dulled her fear, and momentarily made her feel safer.

'Well?' she prompted me, when I didn't answer.

'Cyril Jessop's my oldest pal,' I said. 'And the best fellow alive. So when he saw my predicament, he immediately offered to help me find you.'

'What predicament?'

I pulled out the copy of *She*, and laid it on the table. 'I found this in the church, and wanted to return it to you.'

I braced myself for another onslaught: *you're lying; I don't believe you; no one would have taken so much trouble just to deliver a book.* But to my astonishment, the shrewishness left her face, and she gave a shiver of delight.

'Oh,' she said quietly. 'Thank you!' She turned to the first page and read a few lines, before looking up at me again and saying:

'No one's *ever* been so kind to me. It must've taken you *days*.'

'Longer, actually. But we've only ourselves to blame. We decided to come by caravan.'

Her brow puckered, as if she suspected I were pulling her leg.

'Honestly,' I said. 'That's how we did it. Two weeks on the road, living like gypsies.'

'Where is it, then?'

'What?'

'You said you were putting up here. So where's the caravan?'

'Oh, oh, I see. There was nowhere we could stay in it in Langley Mill. So it's at Divot's Dairy.'

'Truly?'

I nodded. She gazed at me – but with a kind of steady, unblinking abstraction that suggested she was really seeing something in her own imagination. Then – tentatively, as if she expected me to say no – she asked:

'Could I look at it, do you think?'

I glanced at my watch. 'Well, there should just be time, I suppose. But we'll have to hurry, if you're not to be late for your lunch.'

I paid, and we set off through the town. The streets were far less crowded than they had been the day before, and we reached the dairy in no more than ten minutes. It being Sunday, the gates were locked; but by craning our necks we could look into the yard where the van was standing, and see one of the wheels, and the gracefully curving yellow shafts, and the brightly painted canopy above the driver's seat, and a dab of the red panelling behind it.

'It's true!' said Mary Wilson. She grasped two of the upright bars of the gate and pressed her face between them, like a prisoner peering longingly at the outside world. 'How beautiful!'

'It is a lovely thing,' I said. 'Though not altogether practical, I have to say. There are times when you find yourself wishing devoutly for a bath and a proper bed.'

'But still, you are free, aren't you?' She gazed at it for a few seconds more, then turned away abruptly – and for the first time, to my immense surprise, I saw tears in her eyes. 'I don't like seeing it penned up like that,' she said. 'It makes me sad. Like looking at a zebra in a zoo.'

'Don't worry,' I said. 'It'll soon be at liberty again. We'll be back on the road in a day or two.'

'I wish I could go with you.'

I felt a vertiginous rush – whether of desire, or dread, or simple astonishment, I was too dazed to know.

'Are you not feeling well?' said Mary Wilson.

I shook my head. 'Just a little tired, that's all. But you really ought to be on your way, or you won't be at the rectory in time.'

She sighed, her breath wavering with a kind of infinite resignation – as if, having tantalized her, yet again, with some tempting prospect, life had once more vindictively snatched it from her grasp.

'No,' she said. 'I suppose you're right.'

We barely spoke on the way back – though this time it was not awkwardness that silenced us, but rather the knowledge of our impending separation, which, as it approached, seemed to drive us both further and further into our own trains of thought. I had no idea what she was thinking – although from time to time, when she imagined I wasn't aware of it, I would catch her looking in my direction, as if she was still trying to reach some firm conclusion about me. And I, meanwhile, was snatching curious glances at her, and wondering whether Jessop was right after all, and the truth was that I was in love with her? Certainly, the sight of her pale heart-shaped face provoked, every time, a violent spasm of emotion in me. But, powerful though it was, it still did not quite *feel* like love – or, at least, not the conventional, romantic love he meant. It was more elemental: a sense that I was touching the very marrow of life, and that everything else must seem, in comparison to it, insipid and unimportant.

'Would you like me to walk you back to Heanor?' I asked, as we drew near to the hotel.

She hesitated a second, then shook her head sadly.

'No,' she said. 'We must say goodbye at the station, as we agreed.'

When the moment came, neither of us seemed quite to know what to do. In the end, unable to think of anything more appropriate, we merely shook hands again, as limply and formally as a couple of strangers. Only when she had already started to leave did she suddenly look back and say:

'It isn't fair to say I have no friends. You are my friend.' She held up her book, like a priest displaying the word of God. 'Perhaps you *are* an angel after all.'

I shook my head, grimacing with embarrassment.

'An angel who doesn't know it,' she said.

Then she turned back, and went on up the hill.

I stood watching her, promising myself that I would wait until she was out of sight, and then – since by this point my mind was lagging so far behind events that I no longer knew what I thought or felt about them – take a long solitary walk, to give it time to catch up. She had not gone more than ten paces, however, before there was a sudden explosion in my temple, so violent that it felt as if my skull would crack open. For perhaps five seconds, I didn't know where I was – or, rather, I seemed to be in three places at once: in front of Langley Mill station; crouched under the yew tree in the churchyard; and somewhere I couldn't identify, though it was dazzlingly bright, and smelt faintly of starch. Then – though the tumult continued unabated – the tree and the light shrank back to the very edges of my vision. Clutching my head, I blundered into the hotel, ignoring the startled glances of the handful of guests in the lounge, and started towards the stairs.

'Are you not feeling well, sir?' asked the pleasant woman at the desk.

'Migraine,' I muttered.

'Have you tried aspirin?' She proudly produced a small bottle from her drawer and shook a couple of white discs on to my hand. 'Take these with a glass of water. See if they help.'

Once inside my room, I locked the door, closed the curtains and swallowed the tablets. Then I lay down on the bed and shut my eyes. Whether it was thanks to the aspirin or not I couldn't tell, but almost immediately the movement in my head started to grow less frantic, until, after a few minutes, it was no more than an insistent steady pulse. Safe in the calm of my own little sanctuary, I suddenly began to feel limp and drowsy. I needed to think, but I couldn't hold on to the disconnected flashes in my mind for long enough to fashion them into a train of thought. Soon, a sense of gentle dissolution was spreading through my body, and I felt an invisible current starting to carry me away.

When I woke, the room was almost dark. I groped for the light switch and looked at my watch. Nearly seven o'clock: I had slept through the entire afternoon. I didn't feel ill, exactly, but I was strangely tired, as if some succubus had battened on me and was draining me of energy. I lay down again, and shut my eyes. Immediately, I was aware that something had changed: not only could I *feel* the movement now, but I could *see* it, too – a vague shadowy mass stirring at the edge of the light-prickled night sky behind my eyelids.

I panicked, clenching my fists and thrashing my head from side to side in a frantic attempt to dislodge it. For a moment I thought I had succeeded; but when I stopped long enough for my jangled vision to clear again, I realized it was still there – stronger and more obtrusive, if anything, than it had been before.

'What are you?' I said, startling myself with the loudness of my own voice.

I thought I caught something in reply – a muffled cry or whimper – but it might just have been the hum in my ears, or a dog barking half a mile away in Langley Mill.

'What are you?' I said again.

The next moment, as clearly as if she had been sitting in the room with me, I heard Mary Wilson saying:

The best of me. The truest part of me.

I opened my eyes. There was nothing there.

'Roper! Roper!'

I jumped violently, ricking my neck. Jessop was rapping the door.

'What is it?'

'I don't want to intrude, but it's dinner-time.'

The small of my back was a puddle of sweat. But at least – as if it, too, had been frightened by the noise – the thing in my head was suddenly still.

'All right,' I called, levering myself from the bed. 'Give me five minutes, and I'll be with you.'

I felt so unsettled – so precariously balanced on the edge of some unfathomable river that might sweep me away to destruction – that I made up my mind, in the short time it took me to wash and change my shirt, to say nothing to Jessop about my strange experience. But this resolution crumbled within seconds of my reaching the dining-room. I had not even finished sitting down before he looked up sharply and said:

'Who were you talking to?'

'I beg your pardon?'

'You were talking to someone in your room. I heard you.'

Normally, he approached any delicate subject so obliquely that you barely knew you were being interrogated at all. Now he sounded like an irate headmaster.

Flustered, I burbled:

'I wasn't with a woman, if that's what you were thinking.'

'Who, then? Or what? You're looking very pale, I must say.'

The waitress came to collect our order. I waved her away.

'Have you ever heard of anyone reacting strangely to aspirin?' I asked.

'Strangely how?'

'Having hallucinations?'

He shook his head. 'So it was a hallucination, was it?' he said softly.

'I . . . Look, I'm sorry, I'm not very well,' I said, getting up. 'I need to see a doctor.'

'Oh, you poor chap. We'll ask nice Mrs. whatever-her-name-is at the desk. She's bound to be able to recommend some more or less decent local fellow.'

'My *own* doctor. I'll have to go home tomorrow, I'm afraid.'

'Oh, but –'

'Don't worry,' I said, 'I'll take the train.'

And bolted for my room.

VII

I came closer to true mania that night, I think, than I have ever been in my life. The poles had vanished from my world, leaving me compassless. I just managed to get myself into bed – but then lay there, rigid with fear, waiting for the movements in my head to start again, pushing me irrevocably into madness. They never did – but the depth of my dread left me powerless to protect myself against the terrors crowding around me. When a strange billowing shape suddenly appeared at the window, I tried appealing to common sense – and immediately found I had hardly more reason, now, for believing it to be merely the curtain, stirred by a gust of wind, than I did for thinking it was a vengeful spirit. On the few occasions I managed to doze off, I would come to again with a jolt a few minutes later, wondering why the recollection that I had succeeded in finding Mary Wilson again seemed to fill me not with joy, but with an overwhelming dread. And then, with the force of a tidal wave, the answer would burst in upon me.

It was not until the first light of dawn began to dissolve the darkness that I was at last able to get my imagination under some kind of control. I got up, and quickly packed. I could not face Jessop again, so I left him a note, apologizing for my abrupt departure, and thanking him for all his kindness to me. Then, after wiring Chieveley to say I should be back that evening, I took the first train from Langley Mill to Derby, where I was able to pick up the London express. Five hours later, I was pulling into Henley.

I had originally intended to go back and settle myself in the cabin before doing anything else; but, as I came out of the station, and saw the all-too-familiar jumble of buildings that told me I was no more than half an hour from home, it suddenly hit me that in my present condition I would be quite incapable of sustaining a conversation with Violet, or even the Chieveleys. So I found a cab, and asked the driver to take me direct to Dr. Lewis's house instead.

Lewis's housekeeper answered the bell, and told me that he had already left on his evening visits. But just as she was shutting the door, I saw Lewis himself striding into the hall behind her, clutching his bag. He reached for his coat, then caught sight of me and dropped it back on the hook.

'Hullo, Roper!' he said. He smiled, and nodded at my suitcase. 'You look as if you've come to stay.'

I just managed to laugh.

'Something the matter?'

'I was wondering if you might be able to spare me ten minutes?'

He peered at me, then glanced at his watch. 'All right. Come in.'

'Thank you.'

He lifted his arm, weighing the bag. 'Shall I be needing my instruments of torture?'

'No.'

'Let's go into my study, then.'

I followed him into a dark, chilly room smelling of stale cigar smoke. It was smaller than I would have expected, and more untidy, with papers strewn across the desk, and piles of journals on the floor, and books stuffed at odd angles into the shelves. Lewis pokered the dying fire into life, and lit an oil lamp on the mantelshelf.

'Useful stuff, electricity,' he said. 'Wouldn't be without it. But I still think this is cosier.' He waved at the two armchairs flanking the fireplace, and then at the desk. 'Friendly, or formal?'

'Friendly.'

He nodded, and we sat facing each other across the hearth. He tugged at his trousers, then leaned back with a comfortable sigh and smiled.

'So, what can I do for you?'

I cleared my throat. 'This is all a bit awkward, I'm afraid. I should have mentioned it weeks ago, only . . . Well, it was pure hubris, that's the long and the short of it. I thought I could manage on my own, and it turns out I couldn't.'

He nodded sympathetically. 'Well, you're telling me now, at any rate.'

'I really don't know what you're going to think of me.'

He raised his eyebrows. 'I shouldn't worry. You hear some pretty queer things when you're a doctor.'

'I doubt whether you've ever heard anything as queer as this.'

He nodded again and opened his hand, inviting me to go on.

'All right,' I said. And, taking a deep breath, I told him the entire history of my meeting with Mary Wilson, and what had happened since. I knew that if I watched him too closely it would only inhibit me, so I studiously avoided his gaze as I spoke – until, that is, the very end, when I was so hungry to see his reaction that I could not keep myself from glancing surreptitiously at his face. I expected to see horror there, or at least perplexity; but the mask of polite professional interest had barely changed.

'Is that it?' he said.

'Yes.'

'Hm.' He pressed his fingertips together and stared at them meditatively for a few seconds, a secular monk at prayer. 'Well, the best thing I can do for you, I think, is to refer you to a specialist in nervous diseases.'

'You think that's what it is, then? A –'

'I'm certain of it – though I can't give you a more precise diagnosis myself. The human mind's a complex and sensitive mechanism, and I'm no expert in it. All I can say with any confidence is that *yours* has taken a nasty knock, poor old fellow, and been thrown a bit out of kilter. And the sooner we can take steps to put things right again, the better. So . . .' He consulted his watch again. 'There's one chap in particular I have in mind, a Dr. Enticknap. He's up in town, of course, as you'd expect. So doubtless gets a lot of fashionable ladies suffering from the vapours. But don't let that put you off. He's got a first-rate reputation. You won't find a sounder man anywhere.' He got up, moved nimbly to the door, and held it open for me. 'And now, I'm afraid, I really must be on my way. Ailing infants to see, and worried mamas. But I'll write to Enticknap tonight, I promise, and let you know how we get on.'

'Thank you,' I said. But I could hear the disappointment in my own voice. And Lewis must have noticed it, too, because as I walked past him he added:

'No, tell you what, even better: why don't I telephone him in the morning, and see if we can get things moving at once?'

It took me almost an hour to get home, because my suitcase was so heavy that I had to keep setting it down to rest my arms. But at least the physical effort stopped me from dwelling too much on the implications of what Lewis had told me.

I was still hoping to slip in unobserved and make my way straight to the cabin – and only then, when I had staked my claim, as it were, by depositing my luggage, to go in search of the Chieveleys. So, rather than walking up the drive, I took a detour across the lawn, darting – as well as I could, under the burden I was carrying – from the sanctuary of one bush to the next. I had almost reached the side of the house, where I knew I should be safe, when the front door suddenly opened, and a man appeared. Though I could not see his face, I recognized him immediately from the silhouette he made against the light of the hall.

I froze, but it was too late: he stiffened; turned towards me for a moment; then spun round, and started to go inside again.

He was the last person I wanted to talk to; but he had caught me skulking through my own garden like a criminal, and if I failed to acknowledge him, he must take it as tacit proof that, indeed, I felt I had no right to be there.

'Mr. Dolgelly!' I called.

He said nothing, but stopped, and looked back at me. I dropped my case and began towards him. He made no move to come and meet me, but merely stood there, one hand on the door – as if he had not quite decided how to respond, and wanted to leave open the possibility of slamming it in my face at the last moment.

'A word, if you please,' I said, as I approached, though I still had no idea what I was going to say, or what tone I should adopt.

'A word about what?' he said. His voice was deeper than I had expected, and marked by a faint Welsh accent.

And then, all at once – as if someone else had slipped the thought into my mind – I heard myself saying:

'I want to consult you about something. You are a spiritualist, are you not?'

He shrugged. 'That is what people call us.'

'What would you call yourself?'

'A bridge. Between this world and the other side.'

I was almost upon him now, and could see the scowl on his face, and the nervous way he jigged his weight from one foot to the other.

'Well, then,' I said. 'What I want to know is this. A still-born child. A little boy. Would it be possible for him to cross the bridge?'

'Of course. We all do, when our time comes.'

'But what I mean is: could he then come *back* again? And haunt someone? Possess someone, even?'

He looked startled – though whether at the question, or simply at the fact that I was asking it, I couldn't tell. Then, to my surprise, he smiled, and said:

'No. A still-born child would be insufficiently *developed* to have an individual spirit. It would be nothing more, at that point, in fact, than raw undifferentiated energy. All that would happen is that it would be reabsorbed in the One, and then reappear in a new form altogether.'

'You are certain of that?'

'Yes.'

'All right. Thank you,' I said, with a perfunctory nod. 'Good night, then.'

I could feel his gaze on me as I made my way back to the suitcase. He was desperately curious to know why I had raised the matter, but he could not bring himself to ask me. Only when I was past the corner of the house, and he could no longer see me, did I finally hear the front door closing again.

I felt a sudden flurry in my head – and, the next moment, a tiny voice seemed to whisper above my ear:

'And yet, here I am!'

I stopped and leaned against the wall, to keep myself from falling. My neck and back prickled with sweat. This time, no question about it, I wasn't dreaming.

I stood there, my head resting on my arm, waiting for the initial shock to fade and be replaced with an overwhelming sense of horror. But it wasn't: in fact, to my astonishment, I found myself suffused with a kind of giddy lightness that felt very like exhilaration.

Baffled though I was, I decided not to risk provoking another catastrophe by examining the roots of my feelings too closely. It was, after all, the recognition of my own failure to understand them that had brought me to this crisis, and driven me to seek medical advice. I had agreed to put myself in the hands of a specialist: now there was nothing to be done but wait for his opinion.

At nine the next morning, while I was still finishing my breakfast, my wife came to see me. The only warning I had was a quick faltering of the light as something passed the window. A few seconds later, there was a knock, and I heard her calling:

'Are you decent?'

I got up and opened the door. She was shivering, despite her grey winter coat, and her eyes were puffy and rimmed with pink, as if she hadn't slept.

'Hullo, Violet,' I said.

I was expecting an outburst, but instead she strained her face into a smile and started fumbling inside her sleeve.

'A certain someone wanted me to bring him to see you,' she said.

I knew what was coming, and tried frantically to think of some way to avert it; but after ten years of marriage the conversational tram-lines were worn so deep it was impossible to escape them without causing a catastrophe.

'Here.' She drew out the black bear, and held him towards me. He was more battered than ever: one ear had come adrift, and the left eye had disappeared altogether, leaving nothing but a little pig's-tail of cotton.

'He wants to know if you're *orl right*. Don't you?' she said, then bobbed his head in agreement.

'I'm well enough, thank you.'

'Only you were gone a *dredful long time*, he thinks. And a little bird told him that when you got back last night *you wented to the doctor*.'

She must have heard it from Lewis himself. For an uneasy moment I wondered how much more he might have said. Then I steadied myself again: it would have been quite out of character for him to betray a professional confidence, even to my wife – and if by any chance he *had* done it, she would not be behaving like this.

'Well, that's perfectly true,' I said. 'But nothing to worry about.'

She waited for me to go on. When I didn't, she said:

'You can't expect Bear to be satisfied with *that*.' She put her lips against the good ear and bellowed, '*Can* he?' before turning back to me and mouthing: 'You know what an old fuss he is.'

'Yes,' I said. 'But really, I'm all right.'

'Well, we'll see about that, won't we? What's that?' She held the bear to her own ear. 'He says: *it's jolly cold out 'ere. Why don't 'e ask us in?*'

'All right,' I said.

She heard the reluctance in my voice, but misinterpreted the reason for it.

'Oh, don't worry,' she said, as she bustled through the door. 'We're used to a bit of muddle, aren't we? Kissy?'

She waggled the bear against my face. I kissed it.

'That makes him feel better, doesn't it?'

She hovered for a moment, uncertain where she should go. I waved her to my place by the stove. She inspected it apprehensively, as if she imagined I might have hidden a knife among the cushions. Then she sat down gingerly and looked round, searching for something she evidently couldn't find. Finally she asked:

'Where are all Bear's pals?'

'The other toys? I put them away weeks ago.'

'Well, that's not very friendly, is it, Bear?' She paused, then gave a shrill little laugh. 'Do you know what he says? He says: *That's coz the only pal you ever fink about now is that Cyril Jessop.*'

'Why would he say that?'

She started to blush. 'Because you've just spent two weeks with the man, I suppose.'

I wheeled out the desk-chair and sat down to face her.

'How do you know that?'

She grimaced, trying to cover her mistake. 'You'll have to ask Bear.' And then, when I didn't reply: 'Sybil dropped me a line.' She laughed uneasily. 'Suggesting that since the husbands had gone away on holiday together, the wives really ought to do something similar.'

'But you weren't tempted?'

'Good heavens, no!' she said, as if the very thought of a woman having the same freedom as a man were absurd. But then, realizing how false it must sound, sitting in the hut to which she had banished me, she went on brightly:

'Anyway, you had a jolly time?'

'Yes, thank you.'

She nodded. 'I always thought that life would suit you. Camp-fires, and countryside, and fresh air. And absolutely no need to dress for dinner, or make polite small talk.'

'Well, yes,' I said, thinking perhaps she meant to try to use it as a pretext for excluding me from the house permanently. 'But it has its inconveniences.'

'Really? I'd have imagined it would have been perfect heaven for you.'

'You make it sound as if you wish I hadn't come back.'

'Oh, no, of course I don't wish that! I'm just thinking of you, my dear, that's all.' She tried to laugh, but it sputtered out, like a motor-car engine that refuses to spring into life. 'You *oughted to have married a gypsy woman*. That's what Bear says. He thinks she'd have made you much happier than I ever managed to do.'

She had never talked to me like this before – and for her to concede so much now, even in the character of Black Bear, could only mean she wanted something tremendous in return. I still had no idea what it might be, but I knew it would be unwise to seem to accept the logic of her argument too readily, in case it carried me somewhere I didn't want to go.

'Hm,' I murmured. 'I don't know about that.'

'Well, the other toys would agree, wouldn't they, Bear? *Yes*, he says, *they would*. Why don't you get them out and ask them?'

It was no good: catastrophe or no, I had lost the power of ventriloquism, and nothing would revive it. As gently as I could, I said:

'Look, do you think, just for once, we might try to communicate with each other directly? Rather than putting words into the mouths of imaginary animals, and expecting them to do our business for us?'

She gasped and stiffened as if I had hit her. I readied myself for a storm of tears and recriminations. But in the end she only gulped and said quietly:

'All right.' She put the bear down, picked him up, put him down again, and began nervously smoothing her dress with her fingertips. 'The fact is, my dear, I've been doing a lot of thinking since you went away. This obviously isn't a very satisfactory arrangement for you. And I'm well aware, believe me, that it's partly my fault. I haven't been as . . . well, as *understanding* as I might have been. So now I want to try to put things on a better footing.'

'Ah.'

'Wouldn't you like that, too?'

'Difficult to say, when I don't know what sort of footing you have in mind.'

'Well, I mean . . .' She caught my eye, and gave me a quick appeasing smile. 'You can't go on living here, can you?'

'It's not ideal.'

'Not *ideal*! You can't work – at least, not properly. You can't use the telephone. You can't entertain –'

'You're suggesting I should come back into the house?'

'Well, that would be one possibility, wouldn't it?' she said. 'But I'm not sure it would be a good idea. After all, we did live in the same house for ten years, didn't we? And I don't think anyone' – attempting a smile – 'would probably count it as having been a howling success.'

'No,' I said, still wary of giving anything away, until I knew for certain where this was leading. 'I don't suppose they would. But then that's nothing particularly unusual, is it? I mean, an awful lot of couples are in pretty much the same boat, and most of *them* seem to get by well enough.'

She raised her eyebrows, and the ends of her mouth puckered

like the corners of a purse. It was a look I had often seen before, expressing – at the same time – surprise that I should be prepared to settle for something less than perfect, and an absolute refusal to accept it herself.

'And the other possibility?' I said.

'Well . . . Well, it's rather obvious, isn't it? That we should each of us have our own establishment.'

She was right: it *was* obvious. But it was still a shock to hear her saying it so matter-of-factly. The coldness of it took my breath away, like the first slap of the sea when you're tiptoeing in for a swim. I could not keep myself from shivering.

'You're probably thinking about the expense,' she said. 'But provided we're careful, we really ought to be able to afford it, oughtn't we, thanks to Alcuin Hare and Mr. Largo Frog?'

'Where would you . . . What would you . . .?'

'I would stay here,' she said softly. And then, seeing my face: 'Oh, no, darling, don't!' She leaned forward and began gently stroking my temple with her forefinger. 'Honestly, just think about it. It'd be a clean slate. You could go anywhere you chose. The downs – you always said you wished we'd settled there. Or the seaside –'

'I –'

'Or what about Dorset? Then you'd have the Jessops for neighbours. That'd be nice, wouldn't it?'

'But this is where . . . this is where . . .' I was fighting to keep my voice under control, and was surprised how quiet it sounded. 'Where . . . You know . . . Where Elspeth –'

She coloured abruptly, then started frantically fluttering her hand, like a woman whose bag has just been snatched by a thief.

'I know you have suffered, too –' I began.

She shook her head. 'You should not have made me say this,' she murmured, so softly I could barely hear her. 'But there's no avoiding it now. What I have gone through and what you have are different things altogether. You are sad, of course you are: any man would be. But I . . . If *I* had to leave here, it would kill me.'

This, I knew from experience, was a contest I could not win: unhappiness was her province, and she would always manage to trump my anguish with her own, leaving me feeling an insensible clod. My only hope was to shift my ground.

'Well,' I said, 'I will think about it. But I'm afraid I can't give you a firm decision at the moment.'

She sniffed. 'Why ever not? I mean, surely –'

'There'd be no point to it. I still haven't seen the specialist.'

'Ah. I hadn't realized it was that . . .' She left the word *serious* hanging unspoken between us, in hope I would pluck it from the air myself and tell her what was wrong with me.

'I'd rather not discuss it,' I said.

Her eyes narrowed, then widened again as she wrestled with herself, wondering whether she could still assert a wife's privilege to know, or whether, in suggesting a separation, she had forfeited her last claim to it. After a few seconds she nodded, admitting defeat.

'All right,' she said. 'And when are you going?'

'I don't know yet.'

She retrieved the bear and got up.

'Well, be sure to tell me when you do.' She moved to the door, then stopped and looked back with her hand on the handle. 'It *is* a good idea, Corley. Honestly, I know when you've thought it over you'll agree it really would be the best thing for us all.'

'For us *all*? What, for Mr. Dolgelly as well, you mean?'

'No, no, I'm just talking about the family.'

'But you and I *are* the family now, aren't we? And you said *for us all*, which suggests more than two.'

She flushed. 'I'm sorry. A slip of the tongue. I'm an old silly, aren't I, Bear?'

I was numb after she had gone – not just mentally, but physically, as well: my feet felt like blocks of ice, and my hands seemed to have turned into lumps of rubber, too clammy and ungainly even to lever myself out of my chair. So I was still slumped there when, an hour or so later, Chieveley appeared with an envelope.

'This came for you from the doctor, sir,' he said.

I waited until he had left, then fumbled it open and drew out a note smelling faintly of chloroform.

Dear Roper (it read),

This morning, as promised, I spoke to Dr. Enticknap on the telephone. I told him something of your case, and – in view of the extremity of the symptoms – he has agreed to see you tomorrow at 3.00 pm at 12, Fairfield Gardens, St. John's Wood. I trust this will suit.

Yours very sincerely,
Arthur Lewis

VIII

At five to three the following afternoon a cab delivered me to Fairfield Gardens. Two passing women looked curiously at me as I paid the driver, and – fearful that they would guess my business – I hovered on the pavement until they had gone. Then I climbed the steps to number 12, and rang the bell.

It was only then that a disturbing thought struck me: what if Dr. Enticknap decided that I *was* insane? Or – even worse – if Lewis had already come to that conclusion himself, and referred me, not to a conventional doctor, but to the director of an asylum, who after the most cursory examination would order me to be put away? Perhaps, even now, a couple of burly fellows were lurking in the shadows of the hall with a straitjacket, waiting to pounce . . .

I had turned, and was already hurrying back down into the street, when I heard the door opening behind me, and a woman's voice saying curiously:

'Mr. Roper?'

I tensed myself, preparing to break into a run. But then I reflected that the two burly fellows, if they existed, would have no difficulty in overtaking me. And if I was trying to prove my mental stability, it would not help my cause to be caught ringing the door-bell and scampering off like a naughty child. So, bending down, I quietly dropped one of my gloves at my feet, and then made a great show of retrieving it.

'Ah, here you are, you wicked chap,' I said. 'No more larks for you.' I shook a reproachful finger at it, before ostentatiously stuffing it into my pocket.

The woman giggled. I turned back towards her, and immediately felt better. Instead of the brawny-armed nurse I had expected, I saw a slender, pink-faced girl in a parlour-maid's uniform. Her eyes were bright, and she was nibbling on a thumb-knuckle to keep herself from laughing. It was hard to imagine her being an accomplice to kidnapping.

'Would you please come this way, sir?' she said – and then immediately began to giggle again, and had to ram the thumb back into her mouth as she turned to lead me inside.

The last remnants of my fear of violence evaporated the instant I stepped through the door. This plainly was not a house adapted to desperate struggles with lunatics: the brightly lit hall was furnished with spindly legged Regency chairs and a huge old looking-glass that looked as if it would crack if you breathed on it; and the waiting-room the girl showed me into was nothing more than the doctor's dining-room, still smelling of lunch, and fitted for its temporary purpose simply by the addition of a few magazines on the table. I had time enough only to open a copy of *Punch*, and puzzle over what made a cartoon of a washer-woman and a fish-knife funny, before the girl reappeared and said:

'Dr. Enticknap will see you now, sir.'

The first thing that struck me, as she opened the consulting-room door, was how dark it was. Thin winter-afternoon daylight seeped through the blinds at the window, but it was too feeble to penetrate more than a few feet, so all you could see at the extremities of the room was a dim fog where the heavy brown carpet met the dingy walls. The only other illumination came from a small electric table-lamp, which inscribed a sharp circle of light on the blue leather surface of the desk, leaving everything beyond it vague and indistinct.

'Mr. Roper, sir,' said the girl.

'Thank you, Esther.' A grey-suited figure erupted in the gloom, stretching a hand towards me. 'How do you do, Mr. Roper?'

He was younger and less imposing than I had imagined: a slight, wiry man with steel-rimmed *pince-nez* and a neatly trimmed black beard flecked with iron filings of grey.

'Won't you please sit down?' he said. As soon as I had done so, he stepped nimbly round the desk, placed his hands under my chin, and began to examine me as a vet might a horse, moving my head this way and that so as to be able to see into my ears, eyes and nose. The sensation was surprisingly pleasant: his fingers were soft and warm, and smelt of Pears soap, and worked with a kind of calm authority that was oddly reassuring.

'Would you be so good as to do this?' he said, when he had finished – pulling back his lips so I could see his teeth. I imitated him as best I could, and he peered into my mouth for a few seconds. Then he nodded, went back to his place opposite me, and leafed through a small pile of papers.

'So,' he said finally, looking up. 'Mary Wilson. And her stillborn son.'

'Yes.' I don't know what I'd expected – a few bland introductory civilities, probably – but indubitably not this. I swallowed painfully, uncertain how to respond. I was still far from sure how he regarded me, and had counted on having at least a minute or two to size him up.

'Well,' I began, nodding towards his notes, 'I don't know how much you already know –'

'Assume I know nothing.' The arrangement of the lamp allowed him to see me more clearly than I could see him, but I could feel the uncomfortable force of his eyes looking into mine.

I hesitated a moment. And then, reflecting that there was really no point my being here at all, if I did not intend to be honest, I took my courage in both hands, and told him more or less what I had told Lewis two days before – only faltering, as I had then, when I reached the disturbing episode in the hotel room in Langley Mill. For a second, my tongue seemed to knot in my mouth, and I found myself mutely searching Enticknap's shad-

owed face for some sign of unease or incredulity. But he immediately reassured me with an encouraging nod, as if he heard
stories of spirit possession every day, and regarded them as
entirely normal. And when I had finished, to my great surprise,
he did not even mention my hallucinations, but instead – after
jotting a quick note – settled back in his chair and said:

'And can you offer any explanation for the intensity of your
feelings towards this woman?'

'No, not really,' I mumbled. 'Unless . . .'

He raised his eyebrows, inviting me to say unless *what*. But my
courage deserted me, and I shook my head instead.

He nodded. 'Well, let's begin by trying to identify exactly what
those feelings are, shall we? What does the name *Mary Wilson*
mean to you?'

'It . . . Well . . .'

He snapped his fingers. 'Quick! Quick! Don't think about it!
First thing that comes to mind!'

'Real. Solid. Strong. True.'

He waited for me to continue. When he saw I had nothing
more to add, he said:

'*True*. That's interesting. Can you elaborate?'

'It's as if . . . as if when I'm with her, I have found my true
vocation.'

I paused, trying to grasp hold of the fugitive images darting
through my mind.

'When I met her,' I went on finally, 'it suddenly seemed that
every other relationship I had known had been limited to only
two dimensions. Even with intimates, I mean to say, I had always
found I had had to censor myself, to a greater or lesser degree, in
order to prevent them from seeing some . . . some part of me I
thought they would not . . . understand. And they, doubtless,
were doing the same thing with me. But Mary Wilson and I
appeared to experience each other in three dimensions. That, at
any rate, is what it felt like.'

117

'Even during your second encounter with her?'

I pondered a moment, then nodded and said:

'Well, needless to say, the circumstances were rather different. But yes, I think so. It wasn't an easy conversation, of course. But there was none of the usual pretence. We were both quite . . . naked, I suppose you could say.'

'Hm.' He picked up his pen and flourished it back and forth, as if he were conducting a miniature orchestra. 'Tell me, Mr. Roper, how would you describe the state' – clearing his throat – 'of your marital relations?'

'I should say they are almost non-existent.'

'And for how long has this been the case?'

'My wife has never been ardent. We have always had separate rooms. But she would generally tolerate my going to her once or twice a month – except after our daughter was born, of course – until about a year ago. It's only since then that her bed has been entirely barred to me.'

Enticknap did not reply, but leaned closer, still holding my gaze – and giving me, all of a sudden, the unnerving sense that a stranger had scaled the walls of my house, and was shining an electric torch through the bedroom window. I started to blush, and looked away. Immediately he said:

'Onanism?'

'I beg your pardon?'

'Have you ever resorted to onanism?'

I heard myself gulp. Staring at the desk, I said: 'If I have . . . it was only very occasionally. Never a matter of habit.'

'And when you were younger?'

'I . . . Look, do you really think it is pertinent to my case?'

'It's hard to say *what's* pertinent at this juncture. But, as I'm sure you're aware, there is a view – maintained by no less an authority than Professor Maudsley, among others – that repeated self-abuse can lead to mental degeneration, and even, ultimately, lunacy.'

'If that were the case, it seems to me a great many of my school-fellows would be mad.'

He had the grace to smile.

'Was either of your parents susceptible to mental infirmity?'

'No. Not unless you count drunkenness.'

'They were inebriates?'

'Only my father. And even he, not all the time. But brandy did inflame his imagination. When he'd been drinking he would hit my poor mother and me, if we said we couldn't see the big black dog on the stairs, or the *kaffirs* surrounding the house.'

Enticknap nodded, and scribbled something.

'And what of *your* imagination, Mr. Roper?' he asked, looking up. 'I understand from Dr. Lewis that you are an author of children's stories. About talking frogs, and dress-making rabbits, and so on?'

'Yes.'

'Well, it strikes me that if you spent enough time in the company of talking frogs, and then, while in a state of nervous excitement, encountered a *real* frog, you might well start to suppose that *he* could talk, too. Was it not, indeed, something of exactly that kind that took place when you thought you heard the spaniel speaking to you in the woods?'

I didn't like the drift of his argument, but I couldn't deny its logic.

'Yes,' I said reluctantly. 'Perhaps.'

'Well, and might not the same mechanism have been at work when you met Mary Wilson?'

'What, you think I *imagined* her talking?'

'No, no, I don't say that. My point is that it's quite natural for a *woman* to talk. And, from what you've told me, I don't think a dispassionate observer would feel there was anything very remarkable in what she said – on either occasion. So your imagination was obliged to endow her with another miraculous attribute. An extra dimension.'

'I confess I hadn't thought of it in that light,' I said – feeling like the apostle Peter denying Jesus.

He smiled. 'Neither should I have done, five years ago. The only choices before me then would have been to prescribe you a strict regime of liver pills and cold baths and vigorous exercise – or else, if I thought the case warranted it, to have you admitted to an asylum. But the world of psychology is changing. Giving us new ways of understanding what is really happening in the patient's mind.'

'But surely, I am either mad or not mad?'

He nodded. 'That would certainly have been the prevailing view when I first began to practise. A madman was not like the rest of us: you could identify him immediately, by the asymmetry of his features, or the malformation of his ears, or a spasmodic movement of the eyes or mouth. But now the distinction does not seem quite so clear. We're being forced, in fact, to reconsider some of our most fundamental assumptions about it. You might perhaps liken our situation to that of astronomers at the time of Copernicus.'

He stood up, and drew aside a blue velvet curtain hanging behind the desk. I expected it to reveal another window, but to begin with all I could make out was a shadowy, rectangular recess like the mouth of a cave. Then he switched on an electric light, and I saw a shallow alcove, with an examination table in the middle of the floor, and shelves and pictures lining the walls. In pride of place in the centre was a life-size, coloured anatomical drawing, showing the complex tracery of the human nervous system. Nodding towards it, he said:

'That is a map, as it were, of our Ptolemaic universe. It sees mental phenomena as no more, really, than the expression of our various organs working on our nerves. When those organs are grossly diseased or degenerated, usually as a consequence of some inherited weakness, the result is madness. So – since you exhibit none of the associated physical symptoms – I would conclude that you are not mad, but merely suffering from some temporary neurasthenic disorder that can be corrected by enforced rest, and a change of diet. It is all very simple. The only difficulty is that it does not seem to have been very effective – or not, at any rate, in more than a small number of cases. So our new Copernicans are abandoning that model' – pointing to the drawing, and then switching off the light again, so that it was lost in darkness – 'and replacing it with another.' He closed the curtain, then sat down facing me again. 'Our organs have been deposed from the centre of the solar system. And what has taken their place is individual experience. In particular, *childhood* experience. And that, of course, does not require any inherited propensity. It is common to all of us. What happens in a disturbed mind is no more than an exaggerated form of what happens in *every* mind.'

This seemed the most outlandish idea I had ever heard – and yet at the same time, so dazzlingly obvious that I could not imagine why I had not hit upon it myself.

'Is that what you believe?' I asked finally.

'I've yet to see conclusive proof of it. But I have used it successfully in the treatment of several patients, which inclines me to hope it's only a matter of time before our Galileo appears. Some of my more enthusiastic colleagues, indeed, are convinced that he is here already.'

'And you think this . . . new approach . . . would be effective in my case?'

'Well, naturally, I cannot say for sure. But in my opinion it's certainly worth trying.'

I had no idea, of course, what the *new approach* might entail, but I could not help imagining phials of bitter-tasting potions, and tangles of electric wires. But, not wishing to appear a coward, I swallowed my curiosity, and asked:

'And what is your diagnosis?'

'Oh, there's no question *there*: obsession.'

'You mean I am obsessed with Mary Wilson?'

His eyes widened. 'Well, yes,' he murmured, as if it were so obvious as not to require saying.

'And what about the . . . the hallucinations?'

'I have no doubt what they are in principle. But –'

'Not the spirit of the child?'

One corner of his mouth puckered. 'No.'

'Well, that's a relief.' And it was, in a way, because it restored me to a world I could understand. But at the same time, to my surprise, I felt a sharp jab of disappointment.

'It was natural enough, no doubt,' said Enticknap, 'for a man of your . . . unusual gifts, having just lost *his* child, to imagine that he had been possessed by another.'

'Why should I not imagine I had been possessed by my own?'

'You were too much on your guard against that. It would have meant, in effect, accepting your wife's spiritualism, and that you were not able to do. So the idea had to find some other way of getting past your defences.'

'I still don't see why it should have taken that particular form.'

'Neither do I, at the moment. I have a few tentative ideas, of course – but it's far too early to know whether or not any of them is right.'

'How can you find out?'

He smiled. 'There is a school of thought that favours hypnosis. Have you ever been hypnotized, Mr. Roper?'

I shook my head. 'But I suspect I wouldn't prove a very suitable subject. And I can't see what the point would be, in any case.'

'Well, the theory is that there's a part of your mind that's completely unknown to your normal waking self. Difficult to conceive, I know. Perhaps the easiest way to think of it is architecturally. Imagine, say, your house has a whole other wing that you didn't realize was there, and which can't be reached by the usual doors and passages, but only through an underground tunnel concealed behind a wall in the cellar. Hypnosis allows you access to it, by taking you *down* into the cellar, as it were, and unblocking the closed-off entrance.'

'That,' I said – a sudden surge of rage lifting my voice almost to a shout – 'is the most absurd thing I ever heard in my life!' I was shocked by my own vehemence, and had to pause for a moment to bring myself back under control. 'And,' I went on, more calmly, 'even if it were true, I fail to see how it could possibly help.'

'I think you've just suggested at least a part of the answer yourself.'

I jerked my head irritably. 'How?'

He smiled again. 'Why did what I said make you so angry?'

'I told you. I thought it absurd.' But the feeling had unaccountably begun to evaporate, and the words seemed to deflate as I said them.

'Absurdity makes us laugh. You were incensed.'

I started to try to rebut it, and then realized I couldn't. I felt hurt and puzzled, like a child reproached for breaching some rule of etiquette he had not even been aware of. It would have been too much of a concession to say *Yes, you're right*, so I merely gave him a nod instead.

'Do you know *why* you were incensed?'

I shook my head.

'Well, we get angry when we feel threatened by something, don't we? In hope that if we yell and beat our chests enough, we'll manage to intimidate whatever it is into retreating.'

It was half a statement, half a question – and there was a kind of cajoling sweet-reasonableness about it that made me feel more like a disgruntled child than ever. But, again, I couldn't refute it.

'Yes,' I said. 'I suppose so.'

'So the notion of the sealed-off wing seems *threatening* to you. That isn't altogether surprising. According to the theory, you see, it's sealed off for a reason. Which, put simply, is this: that it would be too difficult and uncomfortable for you to acknowledge its existence.'

'I really can't see why it should be –'

'Because it's where you've banished the memory of your most painful experiences. And those aspects of yourself you find most disreputable and unacceptable.'

This notion was so startling that I had to grapple with it for several seconds before I even knew what I thought of it. The effect was rather like holding a portrait of yourself next to a looking-glass, and finding that while the artist's vision – a turbulent swirl of blacks and reds – is quite unrecognizable, it still somehow manages to deprive the familiar mirror-image of some of its substance, making it appear thin and shadowless. I felt unnerved and strangely violated, as if he had suddenly leaned across and put his hand on my knee.

'I know,' he said gently. 'It *is* a disturbing idea, when you first meet it. It seems to run counter to everything we've been taught about the world, and about ourselves. But it has the power, I promise you, to make you well again. Not at once, but over time. Bit by bit, you will come to see that Mary Wilson is just an ordinary flesh-and-blood woman. And that her "child" is no more than a mental aberration – some rejected part of yourself, cowering in a corner, which – as you bring it more and more into your conscious mind – will simply dissolve away into nothing, and never trouble you again.'

I was struck by that tottery sensation you get when you're standing at the sea's edge and a retreating wave sucks the sand from under your feet. I blinked, and tried to swallow, but my throat was dry.

'Don't worry,' said Enticknap, smiling. 'I shan't be using hypnosis. There is a way into the tunnel without it.'

'Which is?'

'Sit back in your chair. Close your eyes. Take a deep breath.

That's it. Now, without thinking about it, say the first words that come into your head.'

For a moment, *nothing* came into my head. And then, in the darkness, I saw *it* again. It was more clearly defined this time, so that I could just make out what seemed to be tentacles or limbs, moving with the balletic grace of a sea creature. As I watched, it rolled towards me, and I glimpsed what appeared to be a face. I gazed into the eyes: huge, and strangely passive, like craters on the moon, as if it had no inkling that its fate hung in the balance. And somewhere – in my hand, or in my own chest – I thought I felt the flutter of its pulse.

I was startled, of course – and yet, at the same time, flooded with unbearable tenderness at the odd, alien beauty of the thing, and the sense of its utter dependence on me.

'Anything,' said Enticknap. 'Just whatever suggests itself.'

Could I do this? Could I pluck it out, and still its heartbeat, and reduce Mary Wilson in my own mind to the unhappy, closed-in woman the rest of the world must see? Or should I accept the destiny that had somehow linked me to them, and try to find some way to restore them to life?

'Whatever it is,' said Enticknap, 'I promise you, I shan't be shocked.'

'I must be going!'

I shouted it so loudly that he started, and then twitched back in his seat as I jumped up, as if he feared I was about to attack him. To my surprise and relief, he didn't try to stop me, but simply nodded, and rang the bell for the maid to show me out.

But, as I left, I noticed he was scribbling something on my notes.

IX

You will conclude, I am sure, that I really *was* mad – and, indeed, I half thought so myself. But, odd as it may seem, the idea did not particularly trouble me. In fact, as I retrieved my coat from the parlour-maid and hurried back into the street, I felt strangely liberated. I had made a decision: after weeks of vacillation and uncertainty, I finally had a star to navigate by. And even if it was no more than an illusion, as Enticknap believed, I still had a strong enough grasp on reality to know that I should be harming no one but myself by following it. Deranged I might be, but I was not dangerous.

I spent the entire journey back trying to come to terms with my new situation. The implications were dizzying, and I could not assimilate them all at once; but one thing, at any rate, was immediately clear: it was impossible for me now simply to return to my old life, and carry on as before. Whatever else I had done, I had plainly accepted a responsibility, and must begin to find a way of fulfilling it. By the time I got home, though I still had no long-term plan, I had at least clarified my thoughts enough to know what my next step should be. So when my wife saw me crossing the lawn, and came out to intercept me, I was more or less prepared for her.

'Hallo, my dear.'

'Hallo.'

'I've a message from Bear. He's been silly with worry about you. He –'

I clicked my tongue. It was enough. She stopped, and in the light from the drawing-room window I saw her grimace.

'Sorry,' she said. 'How did you get on?'

'Oh, well, you know . . .'

'I don't, as it happens. You didn't even tell me who you were going to see.'

'Just a specialist.'

'And what did he say?'

I shrugged. 'I wasn't entirely satisfied by his approach. So I've decided to take myself in hand, and prescribe my own treatment.'

'Oh, but darling, is that wise?' She reached out impulsively and touched my arm. 'I mean, surely, he'll know best, won't he?'

I shrugged again. 'In any event, you should be pleased. Because it means I shall be going away. Indefinitely.'

I waited for her to respond, but she said nothing.

'Isn't that what you wanted me to do?'

'I think it's very cruel of you to say that,' she said. 'You make it sound as if I'm a hard-hearted woman who's just trying to get rid of you, and doesn't care what happens to you afterwards. And that just isn't true. I *do* care, very much. I only suggested . . . what I did . . . because I want us *both* to be happy. And I think we would be, if we were leading our own separate lives.'

The back of my neck started to burn, but I knew it would be pointless to waste energy remonstrating with her.

'Well,' I said. 'Let's see, shall we?'

'But where will you go?'

'The seaside, to begin with.'

She did not reply. I started to pull away. She reached out and grabbed my wrist.

'Well, all right, then,' she said. She leaned forward, and for a moment her cheek brushed against mine. 'Good night, darling.'

'Good night.'

She nodded me on my way, then turned and went back into the house.

It took me three whole days to pack, to settle matters with the bank, and to arrange for my post to be forwarded to my lawyer in London; and most of a fourth to make the zig-zag railway journey to Southsea. I had never been there before, and had no idea where I was going to stay; but the cab-driver who picked me up at the station said he knew just the place, and drove me to an unpretentious little private hotel on the sea-front.

'How many nights?' asked the woman at the desk, eyeing my mountain of luggage.

'That depends,' I said. 'But at least two.'

I had dinner in the dining-room, watching the last faint glow of the sunset melt into the Solent, and clusters of light starting to speckle the black bulk of the Isle of Wight in the distance. Afterwards, I asked the waiter for directions to Sussex Place, and sauntered out to look for it – not in the expectation of making much progress in my quest, since it was obviously far too late to go knocking on doors, but merely out of curiosity, and to save time by finding out where I had to go in the morning.

It turned out to be no more than half a mile from the hotel: a dark little cul-de-sac, crammed into an odd corner next to the grounds of a large grammar school. The street-lamps were lit, but the houses were set so far back that all you could make out clearly was a lintel here and a window there looming out of the darkness. I walked up and down a couple of times, searching for some clue that would tell me where the Misses Robinson's school had been; but the gloom was simply too impenetrable, and after a few minutes I gave up.

I had just reached the corner when I heard a rapid rattling sound approaching from the main road. Imagining I might be about to collide with a child on roller-skates, I stopped abruptly, and the next second saw a girl in a house-maid's uniform push a bath-chair into Sussex Place. As she caught sight of me, she gave a gasp of surprise and jolted to a halt. I was conscious of something being catapulted towards me from the seat, and – instinctively leaning forward to catch it – found myself holding an old woman swathed in a blanket. She was pitifully light, and trembling with cold or fear.

'Ooh, I'm sorry,' squeaked the girl. 'Are you all right, m'm?'

'Yes, yes, no harm done,' muttered the woman, as I helped her back into the chair. 'Thanks to this gentleman.' She peered up at me, as if she were trying to decide whether she should offer me a tip. Finally, she smiled and said: 'Very improper, being in a man's arms before we've even been introduced. My mother would be scandalized.' She held out her hand. 'I'm Agnes Winterton. How do you do, Mr. – ?'

'Roper.'

We shook hands. 'Well, I'm indebted to you, Mr. Roper,' she said. 'You showed great presence of mind.'

I bowed, and tucked the blanket around her, then stood aside to let them go on. Only when they were already past me did it suddenly occur to me that – unless she had moved here very recently – Agnes Winterton would almost certainly know the answer to my question.

'Excuse me,' I called. 'But could you by any chance tell me which of these houses was the Misses Robinson's school?'

She made an odd barking noise, and jerked her head on to her right shoulder. The girl immediately stopped the chair and wheeled it round.

'Number five,' said the old woman. 'Why do you ask?'

'I want to talk to them about a former pupil of theirs.'

'Do you, now?' She was obviously curious to know more, and slightly suspicious. But when I didn't reply – guessing, perhaps, that I was a lawyer, and bound to be professionally discreet – she decided to give me the benefit of the doubt.

'They aren't there now, you know,' she said. 'They left years ago.'

'I realize that. But I thought the people who *are* there now might be able to give me their new address.'

'You don't need to trouble them. *I* can give it to you. Or at least, I can give you an address for *Marion* Robinson. She's the only one who's still in Southsea. She lives a stone's throw from here, in Western Parade. We play whist together every week. I was with her just yesterday.'

'Really?'

She nodded. 'In fact, I'll do better than that. I'll write her a note, telling her to expect you. And then you can be certain she won't just plead age and ill-health, but will actually see you.'

'That would be ripping,' I said. 'Thank you.'

'What was the name again?'

'Roper. Corley Roper.'

Anxious though I was to meet Miss Robinson, I could not reasonably call on her before the afternoon, so the next day, rather than fretting in my room all morning and then lunching at the hotel, I decided to walk out to the Roman castle at Portchester, and find a waterside pub where I could eat more simply. As I was coming back, a ray of sunshine suddenly broke through the clouds, scattering brilliant fish-scales of light across the surface of the sea. I stopped to admire the effect; and all at once felt a familiar stirring in my temple.

'Yes, old fellow,' I murmured. 'It's lovely, isn't it?'

The boom of the wind and the crashing of the waves made it impossible to be sure, but I was almost certain that I heard an answer: one word, split childishly into two:

Love-ly

I wasn't frightened, this time: I was elated. Not for myself, but for the child. Even if Enticknap was right, and he was there only in my imagination, I could still give him existence of a kind, by letting him use my eyes and ears and touch to experience the world that would have been his.

'And just think,' I said. 'It's what your mother would have looked at every day, when she was a schoolgirl.'

Mo-ther.

'And now we're going to help her, if we can.'

At four o'clock, having returned briefly to the hotel to change my clothes, I presented myself at 10, Western Parade. A maid answered the bell and peered timidly out, as if she half expected to find a criminal on the doorstep. Before she could say anything, a voice from upstairs called:

'If that's Mr. Roper, Fanny, show him up! Otherwise, I'm not at home.'

The girl coloured, and smiled apologetically. 'She doesn't hear very well, sir,' she said in a half-whisper, tapping her ear. 'Probably thought I hadn't opened the door yet.'

'It doesn't matter,' I said. 'Luckily I *am* Mr. Roper.'

The hall was dark, lit only by a stained glass fanlight that left little shimmers of red and blue on the tiled floor. She led me up to the first floor, and stopped at a door in the middle of the landing. It was already ajar, but she knocked on it anyway, and waited meekly until she heard the reply:

'Come in!'

She gave me a conspiratorial glance, then ushered me inside.

'Mr. Roper, miss.'

My first impression was that I was entering a hot-house. The atmosphere was warm and clammy, and spiced with a heavy smell of earth and leaf-mould and sap. There were plants everywhere: ranged along the mantelshelf; crowded on to table-tops; bursting like giant fireworks out of huge tubs arranged either side of the fireplace and around the walls. The effect of so much foliage was to give the air itself a greenish tinge that seemed to seep into every other colour – so that even the furniture and the pictures on the walls appeared to be covered with a thin dusting of mildew.

'How do you do, Mr. Roper?'

It took me a second to find her: sitting in the furthest of a pair of Queen Anne chairs in the window, half hidden by the tendrils of what looked like a small tree. She was wearing a sombre purple dress, and a lace cap that would have seemed old-fashioned when Mary Wilson was a child. Her hands – shrivelled, and dappled with liver-spots – were carefully folded on her lap; but I noticed that she could not keep them from shaking slightly.

'Agnes Winterton tells me that you saved her life,' she said, as I began towards her.

I laughed. 'She's exaggerating, I'm afraid. Saved her from a nasty bruise would be nearer the truth.'

'There's often not a great deal of difference, when you get to our age. Anyway, whatever you did, I'm grateful to you. Agnes is a dear friend.' She nodded to the empty chair. 'Won't you sit down?'

'Thank you.'

She glanced towards the door and smiled. Her face, I saw, as the light caught it, was older than her voice: the skin dry and seamed, and the eyes so sunken they appeared to be glittering through slits in a sheet of crumpled paper. It struck me with a jar that she must be almost eighty.

'Would you bring us some tea please, Fanny?'

'Yes, miss.'

'That would be splendid.' She waited until the maid had gone, then turned back to me and said:

'Now, please. I'm on tenter-hooks. Agnes said you wanted to see me about one of our old girls. Not bad news, I hope?'

'No.'

'Well, that's a relief, at any rate.'

She widened her eyes and nodded, encouraging me to explain why I *was* there. I said:

'I'm aware that what I have to say to you may seem rather out of the ordinary. Well, no, it *will* seem out of the ordinary. And for reasons that will become apparent, I'm afraid I have to ask you to ... to promise never to mention it to anyone else.'

She drew a deep breath, then let it out slowly. 'Well, I'm sorry, Mr. Roper, but I don't feel I can do that.'

'I give you my word, it's nothing criminal. Or –'

'That may well be. But the law is one thing, and one's conscience is quite another.'

'I don't think your conscience will be troubled.'

'Forgive me, but that's not really something you're qualified to say, is it? We scarcely know each other. I hadn't even heard of you before this morning.' She caught the severity of her own tone, and softened it with a smile. 'I have to say that you've given me no reason to doubt you. But you must see that stopping Agnes Winterton being hurled out of her bath-chair, though very commendable, is not really a sufficient testimonial to your character, when what, in effect, you are asking me to do is deliver into your hands my freedom to judge what is right and what is wrong.'

'Mm,' I said, 'well, I take your point. But the trouble is, it puts me in a very ticklish position. I'm not thinking of myself. My aim in coming here is to help someone who has already suffered a great deal – and I know that if she were ever to hear of it, it would only cause her more pain. And that, of course, is the last thing I want to do. So we're at something of an *impasse*, aren't we?'

'Yes, I'm afraid it seems we are, doesn't it?' But she said it carelessly, as if it were simply an automatic response, and from her abstracted gaze I had the impression she was still considering the problem. Finally she said:

'Very well: this is what I *will* promise. I shall do as you ask just so long as I see no *moral* objection to it.'

They were, I knew, the best terms I should get – and the very fact that she had fought me so hard over them seemed compelling evidence that she was to be trusted.

'Thank you,' I said.

She rubbed her hands together. 'Well, now.'

I cleared my throat. 'A few weeks ago, I met a woman in a country church. It was the chancest of chance encounters: we were both taking shelter from the rain. But we got into conversation, and she told me something about herself. She was abandoned at birth by her parents, it seems, and grew up without even knowing who they were. The happiest moments, she

133

said, in what was obviously a fairly wretched childhood – the happiest moments, in fact, of her entire life – were when she was at your school.'

'Ah.' She nodded, and let out a long sigh. 'And would this young woman happen to have been called Mary Stone?'

'Mary Wilson. But –'

'Wilson, yes, of course. I'm still thinking of her maiden name. As you get older, it becomes more and more difficult to adjust, I'm afraid.'

'Well,' I said, shaking my head in wonder. 'Did she write to you, then? About our meeting?'

'No. But it wasn't difficult to guess her identity, from what you said. It was a small school. We never had more than a few girls. And Mary is really the only one who would fit your description.' Her eyes drifted towards the window. When she looked at me again, they were bright with tears. 'This may sound unduly harsh, Mr. Roper, but when a man says he wishes to help a young woman whom he scarcely knows, there is usually a reason for it. Beyond, I mean, the natural impulse to do good. And more often than not, in my experience, I'm sorry to say, it's the most obvious one. Sometimes he may not even be aware of it himself. But the result, in that case, can be even worse – because by the time he and . . . the object of his philanthropy discover his true motives, it is too late.'

I had expected this, of course, and was ready for it.

'What I have in mind doesn't concern *my* relations with Mary Wilson, Miss Robinson, but her own family's. It seems to me that *they* are the root cause of her unhappiness, and that only they have the power to alleviate it. So my aim is to find them, if I can, and learn why they treated her as they did, and try to bring about a reconciliation. There is no reason why Mrs. Wilson should even know I am involved – in fact, it would clearly be better if she didn't, and the family could claim the credit for initiating the *rapprochement* themselves.' I hesitated, and then – without pausing to consider the full implications – added: 'If it would make you more comfortable, I could sign a legal undertaking never to tell her anything about my part in the matter at all.'

She studied me closely for a few seconds, then smiled and said:

'I don't think we need to bring the lawyers into it, Mr. Roper. They do perfectly well without our creating more work for them. You have convinced me that you are acting honourably, and that is enough. Let's just shake hands on it, shall we?'

Her fingers were cold and tremulous; but when she finally found her grip, it was unexpectedly strong.

'I do have to say, though,' she murmured, as I sat down again, 'that I'm curious to know what kind of a man can simply give up his own life on a whim, and take to being a knight-errant.'

'I'm not sure I should call it a whim. But the truth is my life has rather given *me* up, and I'm at something of a loose end at the moment.'

She waited, giving me an opportunity to say more. When it became clear that I was not going to, she coloured slightly and dropped her gaze.

'Well,' she said. 'I should just be grateful, I suppose, that poor Mary has found a true friend at last. If you succeed in nothing else, it is a great thing, at least, for her to know that there is someone she can confide in.'

'Is that the best I can hope for, do you think?'

She nodded sadly. 'Frankly, I do.' She reached out towards the tree standing next to her and – taking one of the long drooping leaves in her hand – began to stroke it absently, as you might a favourite pet. 'I don't dispute your diagnosis of her – I was going to say *problem*, but perhaps *affliction* would be a better word. But after thirty years, I think it's very unlikely that anything can be done to put it right.'

'Why? Are her parents dead?'

'They may be, for all I know. But even if they're not, you'd have very little chance of ever finding them.'

'Because they're foreigners, you mean?' I asked, suddenly remembering Mary Wilson's idea that she might be a Balkan princess, and imagining myself hammering at the gate of a half-ruined castle in the Carpathians.

'I've no idea who they were, I'm afraid.'

'Who placed her in the school, then?'

'Her guardian, Mr. Cooper. I did try, on several occasions, to discover something from him about the family. But he was the discreetest man I've ever met, I think – which is one reason, no doubt, why he was charged with her care.'

'What did he say when you asked him?'

'He was always very pleasant.' She smiled. '*At the risk of sounding like a novel by Mrs. Braddon –*' her voice slipping surprisingly into a fair imitation of a worldly lawyer's – '*I am afraid I am not at liberty to say. The reputation of a very great family is at stake, Miss Robinson. Perhaps it would not be stretching things too far to say even the national interest.*'

'Heavens!'

'Of course, this set my imagination racing, as it couldn't fail to. My first thought – well, I'm sure you can guess what *that* was.'

'Yes.'

'But then I reflected that – even if her father had been no more than a distant cousin, and her mother a serving-girl – she would have been provided for differently. Not simply cast away in a house in Paris, and then sent to a school such as ours.'

'I don't quite follow that. I should have thought –'

She shook her head. 'There would have been *some* acknowledgement of her position – if only to lessen the scandal if the truth ever *did* come out. And by bringing her up in a city where her presence was certain to be remarked upon, and entrusting her to strangers who – wittingly or unwittingly – could all too easily betray her secret, they were making it infinitely more likely that it *would* come out.'

'But what if the strangers simply didn't *know* her secret?'

'There was bound to be at least one link in the chain who did, wasn't there? And why take that chance, when you already have hundreds of royal servants whose loyalty you can count on absolutely, and scores of places you can hide a child without attracting – ?'

She stopped abruptly as the maid appeared with the tea. Miss Robinson watched fondly as the girl manoeuvred a table in front of her, and then painstakingly laid everything out where it was in easy reach.

'Will that be all, Miss Marion?' she asked, when she had finished.

'Yes, thank you, Fanny,' said Miss Robinson, beaming up at her. 'You're very good to me.'

'Thank you, miss.' She gave me a quick sidelong glance and smiled. 'Hope it's to your liking.'

'The kindest girl in the world,' said Miss Robinson, as the door closed behind her. She lifted the pot with both hands, and started trickling tea into the cups. 'When I hear what an awful time of it other people have with their servants, it makes me realize just how lucky I am.'

'It may not be simply a matter of luck. Kindness tends to breed kindness, don't you think?'

She flushed. 'I'm glad to hear you say so, Mr. Roper,' she murmured, nudging a cup in my direction. 'That is my view, and I have always tried to live by it. But sometimes one has to admit that kindness is not enough.' She hesitated. Then looking oddly at me, like a bird examining a worm, she said: 'If it were, you would not be here now.'

'Oh, you can hardly –' I began.

'Not that I mean to say that Mary is unkind, exactly,' she went on hurriedly. 'She has great natural affection. But it is invariably driven from its course. What starts as love always manages to curdle, somehow, into fear and suspicion. It's as if . . . she is so convinced she will be rebuffed, she has to make the thing a certainty by her behaviour.'

'*There, I told you so: they hate me.*'

She nodded. 'We did our best, my sisters and I, to make her *less* fearful. It was impossible, of course, to undo the wrong that had been done to her – but we hoped we might soften its effect, at least, by giving her some of the experience of home and family that she had never known. And we tried to instil in her – as we did in all our girls – the belief that in bearing her own cross cheerfully, she was following in the footsteps of our Lord.' She shook her head sadly. 'But it was not enough, I'm afraid.'

'I think you are being very hard on yourself, Miss Robinson. No one could have done more for her, I am sure, than you and your sisters did.'

'I don't say we were entirely unsuccessful. When I remember the Mary Stone who came to us at the age of nine, it seems something of a miracle that she turned out as well as she did. She certainly isn't lacking in accomplishments. And nobody could doubt that she is a young woman with a strong feeling of religious duty. But that . . . that joyfulness that comes from knowing you are the beloved child of God, and that He delights in your existence – that, sadly, is a gift that has always eluded her.'

'But that is a matter of grace, surely? Or of belief? In any event, it's not something a school can be expected to teach.'

'A school can be expected to teach the truth, Mr. Roper. And for a Christian, that *is* the truth, is it not? In most children, the *feeling* is already there, and they merely need to be guided to a grateful understanding of it. In a few, there is just a faint inkling – a tiny frail shoot, that requires constant care if it is ever to grow into a healthy plant. In Mary, there was nothing. We planted the seed – we tended it every day – but . . .' She shook her head again. 'I often thought that not the least of her parents' cruelties to her was their choice of name. Mary *Stone*. As if it were not enough to cast her out, but they must curse her with barrenness, too.'

'Life seems to have connived with them,' I said.

'What, by banishing her to dusty Tenerife, you mean?'

That wasn't what I'd meant, of course. But either she didn't know about the still-born child, or else she assumed that I didn't, so I merely nodded.

'Even Tenerife produces the fig-cactus,' she went on, pointing to a fleshy pea-green plant in the angle of the bay-window. 'Mary sent that to me, as a present, while she was there. Not beautiful, you see, but fruitfulness of a kind.'

'Well, we must show up life's shabbiness, then, mustn't we, by refusing to accept its judgement on her, and treating her better ourselves? You've done your part. Now it's my turn to carry on the fight.'

'And I wish I could help you. But really, I don't see how . . .'

'Well, the first thing thing to try, I suppose, would be a direct appeal to Mr. Cooper. How might I set about finding him?'

She shook her head. 'He wasn't a young man, even then, so it's quite likely he's dead. And, even if he isn't, I very much doubt whether he would be any more forthcoming with you than he was with me.'

I shrugged. 'There's nothing to be lost by trying. At the very least, if he *is* still alive, he might unwittingly let slip something useful. Would you still happen to have his address, by any chance?'

She shook her head. 'I *never* had it, I'm afraid.'

'How did you communicate with him, then?'

'Through his bank. I *do* recollect that: Cox and Co. in the Strand. They sent a cheque every term for the fees, and if we required anything more we were to write to him there. It would be easier, he said, because he was abroad a good deal. India, I believe. I thought very little of it, because a lot of our girls' parents made the same arrangement.'

'And you've *no* idea where he lived, when he was in this country?'

'None whatever. I'm sorry.'

For a moment I was at a loss. Then I said:

'Well, there must be somebody in Paris who knows something about her, mustn't there? You can't simply set an infant up in her own establishment without offering some explanation of how she happens to be there.'

'Perhaps. But, if so, I don't know who he is. Or *she* is, more likely. Mary did mention a nurse called Adèle, but there must be ten thousand Adèles in Paris – and who's to say the woman didn't marry, and –' She stopped suddenly. 'Wait a minute.' She shut her eyes, and clamped her brow with one hand. 'Periwinkle. Periwinkle.'

'I beg your pardon?'

'The feebleness of age. One's mind becomes a sieve. The French for periwinkle?'

'*Pervenche.*'

'That's it!' – opening her eyes again, and holding up a quivery finger in triumph – '*pervenche*! That's where she was brought up: the Rue Pervenche. It always struck me as such a quaintly rural name for a street in the middle of one of the largest cities in the world. I don't know how easy it would be to find the exact house. But if you could, well . . . then . . .'

Her voice faltered, as if, having gamely kept up a conversation with me for half an hour, she had finally worn herself out in the struggle to remember *pervenche*.

'You've been very patient with me, Miss Robinson,' I said, getting up. 'But I'm afraid I've exhausted you.'

'Oh, no.' She raised a hand, and I thought she was going to try to detain me; but the effort to be polite was too much for her, and she dropped it again.

'I'm only sorry I couldn't do more,' she said, ringing for Fanny to show me out.

I shook my head. 'You've done a great deal. Including' – forcing myself to smile – 'giving me a perfect excuse to go to Paris.'

We had said our goodbyes, and I was half-way to the door, when she called after me:

'I wish I could give you some helmet flower to wear in your buttonhole. That is the flower for chivalry, you know.' She twisted herself round, and pointed at a plant on the mantelshelf. 'But at least I can offer you heliotrope, for faithfulness. Please take a sprig before you leave, and my prayers with it.'

X

Though I was three-quarters convinced that my enquiries in Paris would lead to nothing, I still found the business of getting there exciting. Since my marriage, my wife's aversion to boats had kept us pretty much penned up in England; so travelling to the continent – like roaming the countryside with Jessop – was something I associated with youthful adventure. Seeing the weald of Kent sweep by – the orchards already snowy with the first apple-blossom – and joining the luggage-laden exodus at Folkestone, and tramping up the swaying gang-plank, made me feel like a schoolboy given an unexpected holiday. I stood at the rail, relishing the smack of the breeze on my cheeks, and the squawk of the gulls, until the chalk cliffs had dwindled to a brush-stroke on the horizon. And then I inverted the telescope, as it were, and turned to watch the French coast growing from a moth-eaten, dun-coloured ribbon into a living landscape of dunes and beaches and villages. It was odd to reflect that the last time I had seen them the old queen had been on the throne, and I had never even heard of anyone called Violet Ashburn. The thought of the wrong turnings I had taken since, and the dead-ends and tragedies they had led to, inevitably pricked me with sadness. But as we came alongside the long wooden pier at Boulogne, and I caught sight of the purple-trousered workmen swarming over the quays, and beyond them, blurred by its own smoke, the train waiting to carry us to Paris, I had the thrilling sense that my younger self was not dead, but had merely lain dormant all these years, and was now starting to wake again.

I shared my compartment with a friendly American, who lent me his Baedeker guide. I spent most of the journey scouring it for some clue to the whereabouts of the Rue Pervenche, but could find no mention of the name, either on the map, or in the text itself. As I returned the book to him, he said:

'Didn't see what you were looking for?'

'No, I'm afraid not. But thank you anyway.'

He laughed. 'I ought to ask for my money back. They said it had everything.'

'It's probably just a tiny *sans issue*.'

He nodded, in a vague abstracted way that made me think he hadn't understood me, and turned to look out of the window. We were in the outskirts of the city now. Dusk had fallen, and dark little streets were slipping by like fish glimpsed from a ship.

'There's been a tremendous amount of construction going on, you know,' said my companion. 'Hundreds of neighbourhoods demolished. And a whole lot of new roads made.'

As if to prove the point, there was a sudden burst of light, and we found ourselves rattling past a broad modern boulevard, brilliant with gas-lamps and lit shop-fronts, that seemed to have been cut with ruthless geometric precision through the tightly packed clusters of older buildings.

'Maybe your place was knocked down to make way for that,' said the American, nodding towards it.

'Oh, I hope not!' I said, smiling. But the thought that he was probably right haunted me as we drew into the Gare du Nord, and I fought my way through the crowds in search of a cab. I considered trying to set my mind at rest by asking the driver if he knew of Rue Pervenche, but – worrying that he might misunderstand me, and take me there directly – I finally decided against it. Giving him the address of the Casque d'Or instead, I settled back in my seat and pulled the curtain across the window – feeling curiously like a fugitive or a spy, as if the possibility that the house I was looking for no longer existed had somehow robbed me of legitimacy. Though I knew it was ludicrous, I could not help imagining being stopped by the police, and struggling to explain in my unwieldy French what I was doing there.

Tiredness is making you fanciful, I told myself. *You'll see things more clearly in the morning. Settle the matter then.* But when I got to the hotel – a fairy-tale confection of marble and velvet and gilt – my resolve began to weaken. My room was so stuffy that walking into it felt like being wrapped in warm flannel. The radiator gurgled dyspeptically, and light and laughter and the sound of traffic spilled in through the window, making it almost an extension of the street. It would be hard enough to sleep there at the best of times. In a state of mental turmoil, it would be next to impossible.

I decided to try, nonetheless. I had a sandwich and a bottle of mineral water brought up for my supper, then closed the shutters, and went to bed. But it was hopeless. After twenty minutes, I was more wide awake than ever, and so tense that it felt as if my neck had turned to cement.

I got dressed again, and went down to the lobby. The man at the desk told me the name Rue Pervenche meant nothing to him. But as I turned away, he motioned me to wait, and – taking a creased map from his drawer – opened it on the counter. Painfully slowly, he began to pore over it, moving his stubby finger in tiny half-inch increments, and all the time muttering *rue Pervenche, rue Pervenche* under his breath. Finally, I could stand it no longer, and asked:

'Well?'

He grimaced and cleared his throat. And then, rat-tatting the paper triumphantly, he drew himself up and said:

'*Voilà!*'

I craned forward to see what he was pointing at: a small crescent-shaped street, close to the place des Vosges.

'Excellent,' I said. 'But are you quite sure this is up to date?'

He shook the map out like a laundress hanging up a sheet, and nodded at the cover: *Nouveau Plan de Paris. 1910.*

'Thank you,' I said. I slid a franc on to the desk, but he held up his hand, in a gesture that said: *I don't expect to be paid. I was just doing my job.*

'Please,' I said. 'It's worth far more to me than that to know what you've told me.'

And leaving the money where it was, I went upstairs again.

My room had a different aspect when I returned to it. What had been intrusive now seemed romantic. I re-opened the window, and stood looking down at the jostling crowd in the street. Somewhere in the distance a band was playing a quickstep, and every now and again a couple would dance to it for a few seconds, before resuming their stroll. The cool air smelt of drains and garlic and grilling meat and women's scent. The dark walls of the building opposite were broken here and there by regular slashes of yellow light leaking through the louvres of closed shutters. The effect was almost coquettish, like a well-calculated display of ankle: you could see just so much, and must imagine the rest.

There was a flutter in my temple, and I began to stroke the skin over it companionably.

'Yes, old fellow,' I said. 'And tomorrow we'll see where *she* grew up.'

I went out early the next morning, bought my own map at a *tabac*, then returned to the hotel with it and studied it over breakfast. There was no direct way to Rue Pervenche, but – even allowing for all the zigs and zags and doubling-backs – I estimated it would take me less than an hour to walk there. Going on foot would not only give me much-needed exercise, I thought: it would also help me to draw my very fractured knowledge of the city – really no more than a series of fuzzy impressions, if truth be told, gained during two short visits almost half a life-time ago – into a coherent picture.

I sauntered eastwards, enjoying the spring sunshine, and the exhilarating sense that Paris itself was encouraging my progress, by artfully presenting me with one glorious vista after another, like an unfolding series of lantern slides, that made the prosaic business of putting one foot in front of the other a kind of enchanted journey. There was misery to be seen, of course, and poverty, and ugliness; but the overwhelming sense was of a place that – as far as any human community can – had freed itself of shadow, leaving only light and colour.

It was hard, in such an atmosphere, to feel anything but uplifted; and I was soon optimistically sketching out a strategy in my head. From the plan, it was obvious that Rue Pervenche was a short street, which meant that – even if the houses were small and cramped – there were unlikely to be more than fifty or so on each side. I could try half of them in the morning, and the rest in the afternoon. If there was anyone there who had known Mary Stone, I should – with reasonable luck – have found her (it seemed almost certain it would be a woman) by night-fall.

It was only when I turned into the Rue Pervenche itself that I realized how woefully my ignorance had betrayed me. Apart from a huddle of old tenements at one end, there were no houses at all. In the middle, where the street bent like a crooked elbow, stood a boarded-up shop, with posters pasted over the shutters. Otherwise, I could see nothing but apartment buildings. I counted: they were all six storeys high. That must, at a stroke, increase at least threefold the number of doors I should have to knock on – and that was assuming I should be allowed in in the first place, which seemed far from certain.

But wait, I thought. *Surely Mary Wilson said she lived in a house?* I leaned against a wall and closed my eyes, trying to imagine myself on the windswept road between Heanor and Langley Mill again. Fragments of conversation started to come back to me: *Nurse . . . Governess . . . Sur le pont d'Avignon.* And then I had it: *An entire household . . .*

Household. Not *house*. *Ménage*, not *maison*. And for most Parisians, except perhaps the very poorest and the very richest, *ménage* would suggest an apartment.

I was already in front of the first building. I pushed open the massive glazed entrance-door, and found myself in a cool, dimly lit hall floored with black-and-white tiles. To the left was a heavy marble staircase, and next to it the ornately barred cage of a lift. Opposite them was a small booth with a half-open stable-door, beyond which I could see a mahogany cabinet divided into pigeon-holes, and an empty chair.

I started quietly towards the stairs. As I reached the bottom step, a woman's face suddenly appeared in the booth, like a puppet at a seaside Punch-and-Judy show.

'*Bonjour, monsieur.*'

'*Bonjour, madame.*'

She shaded her eyes and squinted at me. When she was sure she didn't recognize me, she said:

'*Excusez-moi, mais où est-ce que vous allez, Monsieur?*'

I explained as best I could. She nodded sympathetically; but when I had finished she shook her head and said she was sorry, but I could not go up. It was nothing personal, she was sure I was an honest gentleman, but the rules were quite clear: no unauthorized strangers. Otherwise the place would be full of hawkers and other undesirables.

I tried two more buildings, with no better success. Then I stood outside, wondering what to do next. I could simply walk up and down the Rue Pervenche, of course, accosting the residents as they came out; but it would be impossible to be systematic about it, and the chances of discovering anything remotely useful before I started to find myself being shunned as a nuisance were negligible.

A policeman appeared at the far end of the street, and began walking towards me. Not wanting to arouse his suspicion by seeming to be loitering, I set off again, strolling past him with a nonchalant *bonjour*. As I turned into the boulevard at the bottom, I heard the mournful swoop of a violin, and the next second almost collided with a small crowd of people gathered outside a café on the corner. Peering over the head of the woman in front of me, I saw a dark-skinned girl of nine or ten dancing barefoot to a gypsy fiddler.

It was an oddly engrossing spectacle, touching and squalid at the same time. Want had made her prematurely old: she moved well enough, but it was the motion of a mechanical toy, rather than a spontaneous expression of innocent high spirits. As she hopped and twirled, her face fixed in a joyless smile, she hoisted her dirty dress above her knees, revealing her naked legs. They were as spindly as a scarecrow's, and covered with a fine powdering of dust, which turned them from chestnut brown to a sickly corpse-grey – so giving the startling impression, when you first saw her, that while the top part of her was still a living child, the bottom half was already dead. It seemed such an image of a life withering before it had truly begun that I was suddenly stabbed by the memory of poor Elspeth. I quickly threw a couple of coins into the upturned hat lying at the musician's feet, and then hurried away, before anyone could see my tears.

I crossed to a small park on the other side of the road, and sat on a bench near the entrance. Try as I might to think clearly, and work out what I should do next, I could not put the dancing girl from my head. I found myself wondering if the young Mary Stone had witnessed something similar when *she* lived here, and – looking into the child's face – seen a mirror of her own blighted existence. Not blighted by material need, of course, like the gypsy's; nor by ill-health, like Elspeth's – but by something all the more disfiguring, perhaps, for being invisible.

I shut my eyes, listening to the faint strain of the violin, and imagining all three of them – Mary, and Elspeth, and the gypsy girl – moving to it in a sad *ring o' roses*. After a few moments, the whirligig music metamorphosed, almost without a break, into something calmer and more stately. I knew at once that I had heard the tune before, and that it had some significance, but I could not immediately put a name to it. Then some of the children in the crowd started to sing along with it:

Sur le pont d'Avignon, on y danse, on y danse.

I got up, and retraced my steps to the Rue Pervenche. The first *concierge* I had spoken to had been the friendliest, so – assuming she was the one most likely to help me now – I decided to start with her. She was still in her little booth, and smiled when she saw me walk through the door.

'What, have you remembered who you came to see?' she said.

I laughed. 'A music teacher.'

'A *music* teacher!'

'The little English girl I mentioned had a music teacher. There can't be many round here. Most of the children, I take it, go to the same one?'

She jutted her lower lip and frowned. Then she nodded. 'Mme. Loubet.'

'How old is she?'

She shrugged. 'Sixty-five. Seventy.'

'Has she been here long?'

'As long as I can remember.'

My pulse fluttered. 'Where does she live? Do you know?'

'The Place Colombe. Above the dress-shop.'

'How far is that?'

She made a finger-post with her hand. 'About two hundred metres. In that direction.'

It wasn't difficult to find. There was only one dress-shop in the Place Colombe, and on the entrance next to it was a list of names. Second from the top was *Mme. L. Loubet*.

I opened the door, and found myself in a narrow hall, lit only by a grey funnel of light from the upper storeys. It was bare of furniture except for a chair with an untidy ball of knitting on the seat, as if whoever normally sat there had been suddenly called away, leaving her work behind her.

I went quickly upstairs, making as little noise as I could on the stone steps. There were two flats to each floor. Mme. Loubet's was on the second, marked by an engraved brass plate with *Professeur de musique* under the name.

I rang the bell, and almost immediately heard rapidly approaching footsteps inside. I expected a maid, or possibly even Mme. Loubet herself; but in the event the door was opened by a plump, harassed-looking man of about forty. He was respectably dressed, but had taken off his jacket and tie, and his shirt was stained with sweat. His arm was crossed over his chest as if to bar my way, and he was fidgeting nervously with the latch, clearly impatient to be rid of me, and return to whatever he had been doing.

'Yes?'

'May I speak to Mme. Loubet, please?'

'The elder Mme. Loubet? Or the younger?'

'I didn't know there was more than one. The elder, I imagine.'

He cleared his throat. 'She's dead. I am her son. I'm here to remove her things.'

It would have been hard enough to know how to answer in English. In French, it was impossible. I made a pitiful attempt, mumbling *je suis désolé* and *c'est une tragédie*, then ran out of words altogether, and was reduced to merely shaking my head.

'Did she owe you money?' he said.

'No, no, I just wanted to ask her some questions.'

He seemed to relent slightly. 'What sort of questions?'

'I was hoping she might be able to give me the address of one of her former students.'

He hesitated a moment, then stood back, pulling the door wide. 'Well, you can look, if you like, I suppose. Lucky for you you came today. All her books are still here. Tomorrow they'll be on the fire.'

'Thank you.'

He turned, and led me into a cluttered *salon* overlooking the street. The shutters were half-closed, leaving only a narrow rectangle of daylight, too feeble to fill the entire room. In the middle of the floor stood a round table crowded with boxes and old newspapers and piles of bills – the top one, I noticed, stamped *dernier avertissement*, which presumably explained his assumption that I was a creditor. In the furthest corner, draped in a dust-sheet, was an elephantine grand piano. Next to it, and taking up the rest of the end wall, was a pretty mahogany bureau, with a glass-fronted cabinet above it.

'Here,' said M. Loubet, unlocking the doors and spreading them open. 'Help yourself.'

The shelves were lined with thick, red-covered exercise books. I took one down at random, and saw *1897* written on the front. I pulled out the two before it: *1896* and *1895*. They must be in order. I counted back, and found *1886*.

I opened it. The first page was headed *Célestine Boudin, 12 rue du Renouard*. The space below had been divided, with ruled pen-strokes, into differently sized sections, like an *ad hoc* diary. At the top of each one was a date, and then – underneath – the titles of the pieces played, with comments scribbled next to them in illegibly crabbed writing.

I turned over. Celestine Boudin went on for two more pages. Then came *Amélie Corot, Marianne Franck, Delphine de Grandcourt.*

Clearly a methodical woman, Mme. Loubet. I turned to the end of the book, and started to flick backwards through it. *Caroline Villefranche, Estelle Vitry, Dominique Thiers . . .*

And then, all of a sudden, there it was: *Mary Stone, Apt. 4, 18 rue Pervenche.*

I read it again, to make sure I had not deluded myself. No, there was no question about it. There was even a crossed-out *Marie* before the *Mary*, as if the English spelling had initially taken Mme. Loubet by surprise.

I shut my eyes and muttered a prayer of thanks. Then I closed the book quietly, and turned round. The man was energetically balling newspaper in his big hands, then stuffing it into a box of china ornaments to protect them on their journey.

'Abracadabra,' I said.

He did not even look up. 'What, found what you wanted already?'

'Yes.' I hesitated a moment, then added: 'Would you mind if I took this with me?'

He glanced at the book and shook his head. 'Just means a slightly smaller fire, that's all.'

'Thank you,' I said. I started to the door, then stopped and said: 'And – my condolences.'

He nodded, and went on with his work.

18, Rue Pervenche was not one of the buildings I had been to that morning, mercifully, so at least I was spared the embarrassment of having to explain myself again to someone who had given me short shrift before. But there was no guarantee that, when I did get there, I could expect a better reception than I had had everywhere else. I knew the address of Mary Stone's apartment, but I had no idea who lived in it now. The *concierge* might not believe my story. Or she might believe it, and still feel it was her duty to protect the current tenants from being disturbed by a stranger.

There was a café a few doors down from the dress-shop. I took a table outside, and ordered a large coffee and an omelette. By the time it had arrived, I had what I thought was a workable plan.

I settled my bill, then pulled on my right glove and went in search of a *librairie*. I soon found one: a dim badger's den of a place at the corner of the square. The *patron* was starting to close for lunch, but waited patiently while I selected a small notebook.

'Would you write something in it for me?' I asked him, after I had paid.

He looked at me quizzically. I held up my gloved hand.

'Ah,' he said. 'An accident?'

I nodded. He took the notebook, and opened it at the first page.

'What would you like me to write?'

'*Il me faut m'excuser, mais je ne parle pas français.*'

He smiled. 'That's not true.'

'You're very kind. But it's for someone else,' I said, hoping it was too dark for him to see my blushes.

He nodded again, and slowly wrote it out. 'And after that?'

'*Rendezvous à 2 heures.* And then the address: *Appartement 4, 18, rue Pervenche.*'

'Is that all?'

'That's all. Thank you.'

Outside, I removed my glove, then tore the sheet from the notebook and folded it into my pocket. I was too nervous to sit still, so I filled in the rest of the time by walking back and forth, more or less aimlessly, between one little street and the next. Finally, just before two o'clock, I turned into Rue Pervenche again, and made my way to number 18.

It was so like its neighbours – even down to the harlequin floor, and the ponderous wedding-cake moulding of the ceiling – that I could only conclude they must all have been built at the same time to the identical design. The *concierge* was in her booth, and watched scowling as I clattered towards her across the hall.

'*Bonjour, monsieur.*'

I removed my hat, then took out the torn-off page, and – jettisoning my French accent altogether – haltingly read:

'*Il me faut m'excuser, mais je ne parle pas français.*'

Her face relaxed into a smile.

'*Anglais?*'

I nodded. She laughed, and waggled a finger at the paper. I gave it to her. It was possible, of course, that she knew the tenant of Apartment 4 well enough to be able to recognize his – or her – hand-writing, but I doubted it. It must be obvious, at least, that *I* hadn't written it: the script had that distinctive mixture of the careful and the spendthrift – a row of tiny miserly letters suddenly broken by a huge plunging flourish – that French children must learn at school, and no Englishman could ever hope to imitate.

She scanned it, mouthing the words as she read.

'*Ah, numéro quatre! Mme. Gaston!*' she said.

I nodded. '*Oui.* Mme. Gaston.'

'*Deuxième étage,*' she said, holding up two fingers.

'*Merci.*'

I started for the stairs – relieved, but troubled, too, by that vague sense of dissatisfaction you feel when you have deceived a child with a too-easy trick. As I was approaching the first landing she called after me:

'*Mais je crois que Mme. Gaston est sortie!*'

I could not show I understood, so I merely smiled and shrugged at her, and continued up to the second floor. If Madame Gaston *was* out, I thought, I was doomed. My only hope was that the *concierge* had made a mistake.

Number 4 was at the front of the building, overlooking the street. I rang the bell and waited. There was no response. I rang again. Still nothing. I began to knock, thumping the wood repeatedly with my fist. After a few seconds I heard a click behind me, and a voice saying:

'*Monsieur?*'

I turned round. There was another flat, immediately opposite, and a plump woman in a maid's cap was peering out of the half-open door.

'Excuse me, sir,' she said, 'but my mistress asks if you would please stop making that noise? She has a headache.'

154

'Oh, I'm sorry.'

She smiled and nodded, grateful that I wasn't going to be unpleasant about it. As she started to close the door again I took a couple of steps towards her and said:

'You wouldn't happen to know who lived in number four before Mme. Gaston, would you?'

'M. Perruquier.'

'And before him?'

She shook her head.

'In the eighties there was a little English girl there called Mary Stone. I'm trying to find the people who looked after her.'

Her eyes widened, and darted towards the interior of the flat. There was no doubt about it: she had heard the name before. I rested my hand on the jamb, so that if she tried to shut me out she would squash my thumb.

'You don't know how I could discover where they are now, do you?'

'No.' But she seemed flustered and uncertain, and cast another hurried look into the hall.

'Is there anyone else I could ask?'

Her mouth opened, then shut again. From behind her, a woman's voice called:

'Who is it, Felicité?'

She half-turned her head, but kept her eyes fixed on me. 'A gentleman, madame.'

'What does he want?'

'He ... he ...'

'Did I hear him mention Mary Stone?'

She hesitated. 'Yes.'

'Why?'

'I ... I don't know, madame.'

'It's a little complicated,' I said. 'But I can –'

'Ask him to come in!'

The maid raised her eyebrows and pursed her lips – reminding

155

me, suddenly, of our poor house-maid when I was a child, who had made exactly the same expression when my drunk father ordered her to bring another bottle of wine. Then, accepting the inevitable with a sigh, she ushered me inside, and shut the door.

'Your name, sir?'

'Corley Roper.'

I followed her down the hall into a drawing-room so murky that at first I could see nothing but the thin slivers of light falling through a venetian blind.

'M. Roper, madame.'

Something stirred under the window. I half-closed my eyes, and was just able to make out the figure of a woman on a *chaise longue* struggling to sit up.

'*Roper?*' she said, her voice croaky with pain. 'You are English?'

'Yes.'

'Let us speak English, then.'

'It's no trouble to speak French, if you prefer.'

'I don't,' she said in English, with scarcely a trace of an accent. 'But forgive me if I neglect the formalities. I can't stand. I can't shake hands.'

'I could come back later, when you're feeling better.'

'No, no, it will *make* me better to talk to you. A visit from the past is always welcome. Sit down, please.'

I felt my way to a chair.

'Mary Stone,' she said. 'Do you know her?'

'Yes.'

'She is alive, then?'

'Yes. Or she was, anyway, two weeks ago.'

'Good. Good. I –' She started to sway, and for the next few seconds was entirely occupied with trying to keep herself upright, thrusting her fists into the upholstered seat and bracing her arms like a pair of callipers. To avoid embarrassing her, I looked away, and began to take stock of where I was. It was a large, high-ceilinged room, which the architect must have conceived as the setting for a scene of Victorian – or Second Empire – domestic harmony, with Papa seated by the hearth, and Mama kneeling at his side, and three children playing happily on the rug in front of them. Reduced – as it appeared to be – to an invalid's sick-room, it felt sadly empty. The mantelshelf was bare of ornaments; and, aside from the *chaise longue* and a couple of chairs, there was no furniture except a table and a slender tallboy, so much of the floor was a desert waste. Only the walls seemed populated: I counted fifteen picture frames – though it was too dark to see what they contained; and over the fireplace hung an enormous rococo looking-glass, a muddy puddle of light in the surrounding gloom.

'Did she send you to look for me?' said the woman suddenly.

I turned back to her. She was propped against a pyramid of cushions, rubbing her neck with her fingertips.

'I beg your pardon?'

'I am Françoise Revel. I thought perhaps that's why you'd come? To find me?'

'Well, no, not exactly. She didn't send me at all, in fact. She doesn't even know I'm here.'

'Ah. She mentioned me, though?'

'I . . . The truth is, she told me very little about her time in Paris. It's taken me all morning just to discover where she lived. I've no idea whom she knew, or –'

'She knew me. I was her friend,' she said – as if friendship were a legally recognized relationship, like marriage, and you could no more have two friends than you could two spouses. 'I saw her almost every week. Sometimes I went there. More often, she came here.'

I narrowed my eyes again, trying to guess her age.

'Yes, I know,' she said. 'You think I am too old for that.'

'No –'

She batted my protest away with an impatient wave.

'It's true. I was almost a young woman, and she was only a child. But still we loved each other.'

'You didn't live on your own, as she did?'

'No, of course not! My parents were not monsters. They thought it odd that I wanted to play with the strange little *anglaise*. But they did not try to stop me.'

'Did Mary have no other . . . I mean, was there no one else . . .?'

'No one capable of understanding her as I did. I am an artist, you see. And that gives one a certain sensibility. A certain natural affinity with the world of a sensitive child like Mary. Perhaps the true artist never entirely grows up.'

She paused, gathering up the reins of the conversation and preparing to take it firmly in the direction of her own life. Hurriedly I said:

'But what about the people looking after her?'

'Oh, they were all quite unsuitable. The governess was a frightful woman. A grim-faced purveyor of facts, without a spark of imagination. And Mme. Bournisien, the housekeeper, was no better. She might have been caring for a parrot, for all the interest she showed in Mary. There was a vile old nurse, to begin with – what was her name – ?'

'Adèle?'

'Adèle Lamarthe, yes, that was it. *She* at least was loyal, I suppose. But more like a sly old dog than a human being. You know, grey whiskers, and the foulest breath you've ever smelt. And no conversation beyond the state of the weather, and the price of things in the market. And she left, of course, when the governess came.'

'What happened to her? Do you know?'

'No. But she must certainly be dead by now. She was at least sixty-five, even then.'

'And Mme. Bournisien?'

'Oh, yes, I know what happened to *her*. She came back, no more than a year ago – expressly to tell me, I think, how well she has done. *I'm with a family in Cabourg now, madame. Very respectable people. Good Catholics. A large house near the sea, with six children and a staff of eight. Certainly a more responsible position than looking after one little bastard, wouldn't you agree?'*

'Is that really what she said?'

She nodded again. 'And the other children in the building shunned Mary for being, you know, different from them, and *not quite respectable.* So that just left me. She used to like coming here for all kinds of reasons. One was that it gave her an opportunity to practise her English.'

'You do speak it extraordinarily well, I –'

'Ah, well, I was brought up more or less bilingual. My mother was from Kent, you see, so –'

'She *considered* herself English, then, did she? Mary, I mean?'

She hesitated a second, then nodded again. 'She knew she had an English name. And that one day, when she was old enough, she would be going to school in England. That's why she wanted to speak the language perfectly: she was frightened, if she didn't, the other girls would laugh at her accent. But she really had no idea *what* she was. People would put all kinds of silly notions in her head.'

'That she was the daughter of a Balkan grand duchess?'

'Yes, that kind of thing. They weren't serious ideas, needless to say: just romantic fairy-tales, really. But sometimes she'd take one of them quite literally, and for a week or two wouldn't talk of anything else . . .'

There was a sudden commotion in the street: shouts, and the blare of a horn. She immediately grimaced and clamped her hands over ears. After a few seconds she gingerly removed them, and – when she was sure it was quiet again – folded them in her lap.

'It's killing me,' she said.

'What? The noise?'

She gave a quick flick of the head. 'Anyway,' she said, with the air of someone forcing herself back into a pleasanter train of thought, 'I used to have an old dolls' house, you know, and Mary would always make me fit it up to match the latest story. Turning it into a Bohemian castle wasn't easy, I can tell you. Though not as hard as Versailles.' She tried to laugh, but the effort made her wince. 'That . . .' she said, catching her breath again, 'that's what I had to do when my father suggested she was the daughter of the comte de Chambord, and would go to live at court when the monarchy was restored. It was a joke, of course. But Mary insisted I should make one of the dolls Marie Antoinette, even though she'd been dead for almost a hundred years. And paint a backdrop showing the park and the *petit hameau*. I was always painting things for her. She adored my pictures.'

'I'm sure she did.' I was anxious to ask about Mary's servants, but didn't want to seem to be changing the subject too precipitately. I left what I thought was a decent pause, and was about to go on when she said:

'Would you like to see some of them?'

'Hm?'

'The pictures? Most of them were done after she left, of course. But I can show you her particular favourite.'

'Well, yes, that would be very interesting.'

'Open the blind, then, would you?'

I got up, and started towards the window.

'Not completely,' she called after me. 'Just the slats.'

I pulled on the string until the strips were horizontal. Muted daylight filled the room.

'Thank you,' she said, staring at me over her shoulder, as if she were as curious to see me clearly as I was to see her. She was a striking-looking woman, dark-haired, with a pale, square-jawed face. She wore a high-collared silk dress the colour of oyster-shell, setting off the startling flint grey of her eyes. As she studied me she ran one finger absently around the neck.

'Not too bright for you?' I said.

'No. I think I'm feeling a little better, thank you.'

I started back towards my seat – not pausing to examine any of the pictures closely, but conscious of a general impression of clouds and river-banks and little girls in smocks. As I passed the *chaise longue* she put out a hand and touched my wrist.

'There,' she said, pointing. 'That was the one.'

It was hanging next to the fireplace, half hidden by shadow from the chimney breast. I saw speckles of blue on a dark background, but it wasn't until I went and stood directly in front of it that I was able to make out what they were: wild flowers carpeting a beech wood.

'Yes,' I said. 'It's lovely.'

'*The Bluebell Wood*. My first oil. I did it on a visit to my grandparents in England.'

It was skilfully painted, and you could see why a child would like it: the atmosphere of mysterious calm was so alluring that you longed to feel the mossy ground under your feet, and the glance of the sun on your cheek as you moved from shade to light. But to an adult eye, it was almost too sweet – the tree-trunks soft and indistinct, the bluebells like flecks of coloured sugar on a cake. You could smell their faint hyacinth scent, all right – but not the musty humus of the earth, and the sour whiff of rabbit droppings.

'I asked Mary once why she loved it so much,' said Françoise Revel. She had got up, and was standing next to me now. 'She said it was like looking out of a window. One day, she thought, she would come in and find it open. And then she would be able to climb through it, and disappear into the wood.'

'I can understand that.'

Her headache seemed to have evaporated entirely. 'And here's another one,' she said, grabbing my arm excitedly and turning me round, so that we were facing a large gilt-framed canvas on the opposite wall. 'Some people like this even better.'

She jostled me towards it. It showed a small fair-haired girl in a blue dress watching gold-fish in a weedy pond, while a woman holding a parasol – presumably the child's mother – looked on smiling. It was defter than *The Bluebell Wood* – and the effect was sicklier, too. Stare at those pinks and golds and creams and blues for more than a few seconds, and you felt as if you had eaten a surfeit of *bonbons*.

'M. Durand-Ruel said it reminded him of Renoir.'

'Yes, there's a strong resemblance.'

'You have taste, Mr. Roper. You appreciate beauty.' She was moving me on again, this time towards the tallboy. 'But beauty is out of fashion now, of course. People don't want it. Or rather they are told they *shouldn't* want it. They should want this instead.'

She pulled open one of the drawers, and carefully eased out a sheet of paper. It was covered in a web of of sanguine pencil strokes that at first sight looked like the random scrawling of a demented child. Only when she had laid it out on the table did I realize that it was a portrait – though a portrait utterly unlike any other I had ever seen, with the ears and eyes and nose and mouth jumbled together in a single plane, as if the head had been flattened like a cardboard box, allowing you to see all the sides simultaneously. What made it odder still was that – despite the brutal rearrangement of the features – I instantly recognized the sitter as Françoise Revel herself.

'Did *you* do this?' I said.

'You think I am mad? Or a savage?'

'No, but –'

'No, the culprit is M. *X*. You do not know him yet, but you will. In a year or two he will be rich and famous, you may be certain of it. The critics and the dealers will see to that.' She lifted nine or ten more sheets from the drawer, and neatly spread them out. 'And I shall be rich too. That is my one consolation. They won't take my work, but they'll buy my poor mutilated face.'

162

Only a couple of the images were as distorted as the first one she had shown me. The rest seemed to date from an earlier phase of the artist's development – or from earlier *phases*, rather, because they were not of a piece, but ranged from an almost naturalistic bust to a nude in which the features were still in their true position, but the cheeks had been pared into sharp triangles, and the limbs and breasts had lost the particularity of flesh, and metamorphosed into an abstract pattern of geometric forms.

'Here,' she said, moving so near that I could feel the warm pressure of her shoulder against my arm. 'This is how I will be remembered. Do you think that is just?'

She turned and gazed directly up at my face with a slight frown. I couldn't tell exactly what she was looking for – whether desire, or approval, or admiration – but I was certain she would not find it there. I had nothing but counterfeit currency to offer, and anything I was weak enough to give her would only leave her feeling hungrier in the end.

'Well, thank you,' I said, backing away. 'I'm really glad to have seen those. And what you told me about Mary Stone was very helpful.'

I hurried to the door, half-expecting to hear her running after me. But when I turned, she was still standing where I had left her, head bowed, clamping her temples with her thumb and fingers.

'By the way,' I said, 'you wouldn't happen to have Mme. Bournisien's address, would you?'

She looked up, with the baffled expression of a dog that finds itself banished from the warmth of the house and tied up outside. She said nothing, but as we gazed at one another her eyes started to flood with tears.

If I hesitated, I knew I should relent.

'Well, thank you again, then,' I said. 'Goodbye.'

When I reached the hall, I found the maid hovering by the door.

'Please go in,' I said. 'Your mistress isn't well.'

The girl shook her head sadly. 'No, I know.'

Then I let myself out, and made my escape.

This encounter left me feeling oddly shaken, so – although it was still broad daylight when I emerged once more into Rue Pervenche, and I knew I should have more than enough time, if I wanted, to walk back to the hotel before dinner – I decided to distract myself by taking the new Métropolitain instead. I paid my fifty centimes for a first-class ticket at the Bastille station, then briefly reverted to excited schoolboy-hood as the train appeared by some invisible force. Less than ten minutes later I found myself at Lancry, being swept up to the surface on a great well-spring of humanity that finally deposited me on the street directly opposite the Rue Casque d'Or.

I crossed towards it, pausing in the middle of the road to avoid a cab. Rather than hurrying past, however, the driver slowed suddenly, as if to let me go in front of him. I raised a hand in thanks, and went on – half-running, so as not to delay him any more than was necessary. But when I reached the other side, I was conscious that I had still not heard the horse starting off again.

Curious, I looked back. The cab had not moved, and there was a blurred face peering out of the window at me. I narrowed my eyes, trying to see it more clearly; but it promptly receded into the darkness, and the curtain fell back across the glass. The next moment, the driver cracked his whip, and the horse jolted into action.

A coincidence, I told myself: someone who thought he knew you, and then realized he didn't.

But still, as I entered the hotel, I could not shake off a faint feeling of unease.

XI

I had no idea how to get to Cabourg, but the next morning the obliging man at the desk showed me where it was on a map, and then – magicking an *Indicateur Chaix des chemins de fer* from his drawer – looked up the times of trains from the Gare St. Lazare for me. I discreetly gave him another franc when I paid, and by eleven o'clock was installed in a first-class carriage, watching the grimy western suburbs of Paris drift by.

As *banlieue* gave way to country, and the oppressive noise of the train began to dissipate itself across the flat fields, I took out my notebook and started to write down everything I could remember of my conversation with Françoise Revel. I had been working only a couple of minutes when I felt that odd, tingling pressure on the skin that tells you you are being watched.

I looked up. As I did so, the man sitting opposite ducked abruptly behind his newspaper. I continued writing. Almost immediately the same thing happened again. I was quicker this time, and just managed to catch two dark eyes under heavy black eyebrows and a pale flash of forehead before they disappeared behind *Le Figaro*.

It was impossible to know how close the resemblance was without seeing the rest of him, of course, but from that one brief glimpse he might have been Mary Wilson's brother.

And I suddenly found myself thinking, for the first time that morning, of the incident of the cab outside Lancry station. Perhaps I had been wrong to dismiss it so lightly. If – as was quite conceivable – her parents had somehow got wind of my search, was it not more than likely that they would try to stop me? After all, they had clearly gone to considerable lengths already to conceal their identity, and must have imagined they had been entirely successful. To hear that someone was now trying to uncover it again would be unsettling, at the very least. And might be something considerably worse, if Mr. Cooper had been right, and the reputation of a great family had been at stake. Or, even more alarmingly, the national interest.

How do great families protect their reputations? How does a country defend its national interest?

I told myself that I had broken no law, and that – if I could not trust the French authorities – there was bound to be a British consul at Cabourg who would give me protection. But what if the British government itself were behind the conspiracy? Or, worse still, the British and the French were in it together?

It was not warm, but by the time we drew into Lisieux, I was drenched with sweat.

And then, just as we were about to pull out again, the man opposite me suddenly looked out of the window, and – realizing where we were – leapt up, and hurried from the train without so much as another glance at me.

At a stroke, the convoluted labyrinth into which I had been winding myself for the past hour or more unravelled.

It took me a few minutes to re-adjust myself to the reality of a world in which no one was pursuing me, or wanted me dead – or even, in all probability, knew what I was doing, or would be the least bit interested if he did. When I finally had, I felt as limp as a glove-puppet that has lost its animating hand. I promptly fell asleep, and dozed the rest of the way.

Since the start of the summer season was still two or three months away, I imagined it would be easy enough to find a room for the night at Cabourg, but I was wrong. The first three hotels I tried were all full, and I was finally forced to take the last available bed in a small *auberge* half a mile or so from the front, overlooking the market. The *patronne* – a bulging, grey-haired woman in an ill-fitting black widow's dress that made her look like a lumpy cushion – insisted I should pay her in advance. As I was doing so, I asked why the town was so packed with people.

'Because it's Saturday, monsieur.' Her breath was like a blast from a garlic-fuelled oven. 'And on Saturdays, the Parisians come.'

'Even at this time of year?'

'At every time of year.' She jutted her lip, and gave a disdainful shrug that said: *They're mad, but what can we do? And at least they bring us money.*

I left my bags in my room, and walked down a street of half-built houses towards the sea, thinking that a saunter along the promenade would blow the stink of the woman from my nostrils and the clamminess of the journey from my skin. The water was grey and sullen-looking, dulled by a covering of high cloud and licked by a cold north-easterly that broke the surface into long foamy wrinkles and sent them racing to the shore. The sand was almost deserted, but here and there a few brave souls pitted themselves against the weather, the women laughing as they clutched their hats and tried to control their wayward skirts, the men huddled inside their coats, their pale faces slapped red by the wind.

I pulled up my collar, and ventured on to the beach myself. After fifty paces or so, I turned and looked back towards the town. It was dominated by the Grand Hôtel, an imposing mock-château with a towering mansard roof and a gracious façade that seemed to promise you – for a night, or a week, or as long as you could afford – the chance to live as an *ancien régime* aristocrat. It was flanked on one side by the casino, and on the other by a row of apartment buildings.

Beyond them, strung out at regular intervals along the coast, a procession of huge turreted houses, as massive and forbidding as mediaeval fortifications, loured forbiddingly at the English Channel. From Françoise Revel's description, there was a fair chance that one of them might belong to Mme. Bournisien's

167

good Catholic family. Perhaps, indeed, the woman herself was even now looking down at me from an upstairs window . . .

The thought of it gave me a flurry of excitement. But it was frustrating, too: she was almost certainly somewhere within the range of my vision, but I had no idea how to identify the exact spot. I felt like a blindfold child at a party, vainly trying to pin the tail on the donkey.

Cabourg was reassuringly small, at least: I guessed it would take me no more than a couple of days to visit every house in the place, asking if Mme. Bournisien lived there. But that, I knew, was not the way to find her. She was clearly someone who valued the proprieties, and if I wanted her help, I must show I respected them, too. If I flustered or embarrassed her, she would probably simply shut the door in my face.

I made my way back past the Grand Hôtel towards the town. Immediately behind the casino was a small garden, with six or seven little roads radiating from it like the ribs of an open fan. After hesitating a moment, I took the central one, a kind of narrow high street lined with shops. That, I thought, would be the most obvious place to start: the good Catholic family must eat.

I tried a baker first, then a butcher, then a *pâtissier*. None of them had heard of Mme. Bournisien. Then, near the end of the street, I spotted a couple of well-dressed women coming out of a large grocer's. As I approached it, I saw written in the window, in prominent gold letters: *livraisons*.

I went inside, and asked the young man at the counter whether he knew someone called Mme. Bournisien.

He frowned, then shook his head. 'No, monsieur, I don't think so.'

'She's the housekeeper in a large house here. I thought perhaps you might deliver to them?'

'It's possible.' He took down his order-book. 'What is the name of the family?'

'I don't know, I'm afraid.'

'Then I'm sorry, I can't help you.'

I thanked him, and turned to leave. As I reached the door, I heard footsteps behind me, and felt a hand on my elbow.

'Monsieur?'

I looked round, and found a small man squinting up at me. He was wearing a darned woollen jacket and a red kerchief discoloured with grease and sweat. He had taken off his cap and wound it into a rough tube, which he ran up and down his thigh like a rolling-pin.

'You are looking for . . .?'

'Mme. Bournisien.'

'Ah, ah.' He screwed up his eyes and squinted past me, rubbing his cheek and the side of his neck with his free hand.

'Why?' I said. 'Do you know where I can find her?'

He made an odd noise, like the mewling of a small animal. He squeezed his mouth into a fish-pout, then let it go again and began gnawing his upper lip. He seemed incapable of stillness: his facial muscles were in constant motion, and when they could not produce enough twitches and contortions on their own, his hands joined in the scrummage, prodding and tugging and pinching his features into a kind of living gargoyle.

'This requires some consideration,' he said finally, stroking the side of his strawberry nose with his thumb.

'You think you can help me?'

He shrugged his eyebrows. 'Well, it's an interesting problem. But' – pointing at his temple – 'in principle, I don't believe it should be beyond the power of a couple of fellows like us to resolve it satisfactorily. All it requires is time. And the application of reason. In a congenial atmosphere.'

He held out his fingers and wiggled them suggestively.

'May I buy you a drink?' I said.

He smiled, as if I had successfully passed some esoteric initiation, by demonstrating a sublime intellectual subtlety that matched his own.

Without another word, he crossed the road, and led me into a side-street. Half-way down was a small *bar tabac*. He lingered for a moment, then plunged down the handle and opened the door.

I followed him inside, and was instantly hit by a pungent smell of coffee and aniseed and French tobacco. Four or five men, reduced almost to silhouettes by the smoke, were sitting at tables, talking or reading newspapers. My companion smiled and murmured *bonjour*. The response was decidedly chilly: no more than a couple of barely perceptible nods.

We found a place in the corner, and sat down. A thick-necked, square-shouldered fellow came out from behind the bar and wiped the table with a tea-cloth. His mouth was half hidden by a heavy moustache that stirred like a curtain when he spoke.

'*Monsieur?*' He said it to me – but his eyes, I noticed, were on the other man. It was hard to read their expression: not surprise, exactly, but a kind of grudging wonderment.

'A coffee, please,' I said. My companion ran his tongue over his lips, then – trembling slightly, and blinking his teary eyes – ordered an *eau-de-vie*.

'So,' he said, as the *patron* left. 'What do you know about this Mme. Bournisien?'

'She's a housekeeper. Her employers have a large house here, near the sea. With a staff of eight, and six children. Or they *had*, at least, a year or so ago.'

He nodded. 'We must use deduction,' he said. He closed his eyes and started counting on his fingers, muttering under his breath. 'Problem,' he said at length, opening his eyes again and laughing. 'Come on, children. Take out your pencils and exercise books. There are thirty large houses near the sea, but twenty-one of them have fewer than eight servants. We are left, therefore, with nine. House A has eight servants, but we do not know the number of children. House B, by contrast –'

He stopped as the *patron* reappeared with our drinks. He drained his at a gulp, then held the glass up with a shaking hand.

The *patron* gave me a quizzical look. I nodded.

'Very well,' he said, with a shrug. 'I'll bring the bottle.' He thought I was allowing myself to be made a fool of, it was clear – and, indeed, I thought so myself. But for the cost of a couple of glasses of brandy I might learn *something* – and I could not immediately think of any other course of action more likely to be productive.

'House B, by contrast, has nine servants, although one of them may have been taken on in the last twelve months. *Ergo*, at the time in question, it is possible that it fitted your description. Why are you not writing this down? We cannot hope to solve the problem if we do not have the facts in front of us.'

Feeling more stupid with every moment, I slipped my fountain pen and notebook from my coat.

'That's better. House A, you recall –'

'Yes, I remember. Eight servants. Unknown number of children.'

'Good. Good.'

We continued in this vein as he drank a second and then a third brandy, all the while adding more and more extravagant details: House D was home to a pair of parrots; House E was reputedly haunted by the ghost of a man with one eye; House F boasted the most insatiable dog in Christendom, so notorious for his exploits that a group of local ladies, outraged at seeing their spaniels and whippets produce litter after litter of mongrels, had petitioned the mayor to order it to be castrated.

We had still only reached House G when I heard the door of the bar open, and someone walking in from the street. He took three or four steps, then abruptly stopped, as if something had caught his attention. In the same moment, the whole room suddenly fell silent. The back of my neck prickled: I could not help imagining that the *something* must be the sight of the man in the red kerchief fleecing yet another unsuspecting victim, and that – seeing the newcomer watching it – the rest of the clientèle had decided to enjoy the spectacle, too.

'In House G,' said my companion, 'we have the most curious plant that was ever seen in France.'

He paused, and reached for the brandy bottle. The sight of his tremulous fingers closing on it yet again finally made me snap. I snatched it away from him and plugged the open neck with my thumb.

'Do you or do you not know Mme. Bournisien?' I said.

He jerked back, with a *you-don't-have-to-talk-to-me-like-that* look on his face.

'We are proceeding,' he said, with a wheedling smile, 'one step at a time, towards –'

'Of course you know her, don't you, Renaud?' said a voice behind me. Startled, I twisted round, and saw a looming black figure that seemed to be half man and half woman. Then I blinked, and realized that what I had taken to be a dress was a *soutane*.

'Ah, father,' said the man in the kerchief, half getting up and bobbing his head. 'We were just eliminating certain other possibilities.'

The priest smiled, pursing his lips into a sceptical *moue*. He was no more than thirty, impressively tall, with a florid complexion and the crude, unformed features of a young bird. With surprising lightness he moved behind my companion's chair and laid his fingertips on the man's shoulders.

'What possibilities?' The backs of his large hands, I noticed, were covered with a thick mat of curly black hairs.

'This gentleman wanted to know where she lived. And I could not quite remember.'

'Ah.' He nodded, breathing out softly through his nose. He was still smiling, but his eyes had the blank defeated look you see in a mother worn down by an incorrigible child. 'And do you remember now?'

'Yes, father. *Chez* Dubucq.'

'Chez Dubucq, monsieur,' repeated the priest, looking at me. 'On the Promenade des Français.'

'Thank you.'

'Only don't tell her you had it from me.' He seized a chair from a neighbouring table, spun it round on one leg and sat down next to me. 'I am a disgrace to the Church, you see,' he said, with a laugh. 'I consort with tax collectors and drunkards.'

I had no desire to add to the little man's humiliation by watching him squirm, so I quickly paid for our drinks, and hurried out into the street. When I glanced back through the window, he had his hand over his mouth, and was pressing the thumb and forefinger so deep into his eyes that he seemed in danger of gouging them out altogether.

It did not take me long to find where the Dubucqs lived: the first person I asked directed me to an enormous house overlooking the beach, no more than a few hundred yards from the casino. Like its neighbours, it was a mad jumble of canopies and balconies and jutting windows, with – as if even a square inch of uncluttered space were an affront to the architect – snake-skin patterns of red and white brick festooning the few patches of bare wall.

Feeling like the lost child in a fairy-tale approaching the ogre's castle, I climbed the steps and rang the bell. Almost immediately, a house-maid opened the door.

'Good evening, monsieur.'

'Good evening. Is Mme. Bournisien in?'

Her eyelid flickered, as if she had a tic. 'I'll go and see, sir. What is your name?'

'Corley Roper.'

She tried to repeat it, but couldn't.

'I'll just say an English gentleman,' she said, laughing at her own ineptness. 'Please come in.'

She ushered me into a cavernous hall lined with hunting

trophies, then vanished through a baize-covered door at the back. I found myself standing under a pair of antlers as big as the branches of a small tree, and staring uncomfortably into the maledictory glass eyes of a stuffed boar's head. After a couple of minutes I heard the sigh of the baize door again, and turned to find a woman striding towards me. She was perhaps fifty-five, but still trim and erect, and moved with an almost girlish nimbleness. She wore a neat black dress, with a bunch of keys and a watch hanging from the belt. Her thick silver hair was wound behind her head in a tight whorl.

'Monsieur?'

'Mme. Bournisien?'

She nodded. She seemed neither friendly nor unfriendly, but only coolly enquiring, as if the fixed rhythm of her daily routine had developed an unexpected irregularity, and she was curious as to the cause.

'Please forgive my intruding on you,' I said.

She gave a twitch of the head. 'How can I help you?'

I introduced myself. We shook hands. I said:

'I should like to ask you some questions. About a former charge of yours, Mary Stone.'

She breathed in deeply, half-closing her eyes. Then she nodded and said:

'Ah, Mary, yes. What has happened to her? Is she dead?'

'No, no. But she is troubled.'

She nodded again, unsurprised – giving me the odd sense that, alone of all the people I had met, she immediately understood the reason for my quest without my having to explain it to her.

'I'm sorry to hear that,' she said quietly. 'But that is the price we pay, isn't it? When we do as her mother did.'

My pulse quickened. 'Why, do you know who her mother is?'

She half-shut her eyes again, and shook her head. 'No. I knew only the sin. Not the sinner.'

'Who actually employed you to look after her, then?'

'A man . . . A man . . . I forget the name . . .'

'Cooper?'

She nodded. 'Cooper, yes, that was it.'

'Did you ever meet him?'

'No. But it was he who paid us.' She glanced at her watch. 'Look, Mr. Roper, I would be happy to tell you what little I know. But now, I'm afraid, I have to supervise the family's dinner.'

'Oh, of course, I'm sorry –'

'But I have tomorrow afternoon off. If you would care to meet me at three o'clock, in front of the Grand Hôtel . . .?'

'Thank you,' I said. 'I would, very much.'

XII

I went down the steps feeling half a stone lighter than I had going up them – which was strange, considering that I had learned nothing of any significance, and had only the slenderest reason to hope that my interview the next day would yield anything more valuable. But at least I had found Mme. Bournisien, and she had turned out to be neither Françoise Revel's heartless functionary, nor the scolding Pharisee the priest had led me to expect. Or perhaps she was both those things, but had chosen to show a different face to me. That she had grasped the reason for my quest, at any rate, and was broadly sympathetic to it, I was almost certain – and I found that curiously reassuring.

To lift my spirits still further, the weather was starting to improve. The wind had dropped, and the gauze of high cloud had retreated to the horizon, turning the sky a brilliant powder blue and allowing the low evening sun to flood the sea with light. The incoming tide had swallowed up two-thirds of the beach, and what remained was now thronged with people. Knowing there was nothing more I could usefully do that day, I picked my way between them and started walking eastward along the ribbon of wet sand at the edge of the water, with no particular aim except to enjoy the smell of salt and seaweed and the half desolate, half thrilling sensation of being poised between the world of familiar things on one side and the inhuman vastness of the sea on the other.

I was almost past the Grand Hôtel when I was suddenly struck, yet again, with the feeling that someone was watching me. I stopped, and looked around. The crowd seemed denser than ever: immediately next to me, a group of fashionably dressed women sauntered by, twirling their umbrellas, and followed by a chattering train of small girls in frocks and boys in sailor-suits, while further afield three or four hardy young men in striped bathing costumes were daring each other to be first into the water. None of them showed the least interest in me.

Stop being so fanciful, I told myself. *Remember the man on the train this morning.* But as I was turning back, I was dazzled by a needle of light so brilliant that it hurt my eyes. I looked in the direction it had come from, and saw a woman on a balcony on the third floor of the Grand Hôtel peering at me – or so it seemed – through a pair of field-glasses. She must have realized that I had noticed her, because the next second she lowered the binoculars, and hurried inside.

I counted: four windows from the end. I started towards the hotel, then almost at once stopped again. It was scarcely conceivable that the staff there would help me to identify the room, or tell me who was staying in it – and even if they did, it was almost certain the name would mean nothing to me. In the very process of asking, moreover, I should only be exposing myself to greater danger.

As I went on, all the questions that I thought I had set to rest at Lisieux station suddenly erupted again, sending wilder and wilder ideas galloping through my head. What if the man that morning *had* been following me, and had got off the train to wire the time of my arrival to his accomplice in Cabourg? Or perhaps Mme. Bournisien was in league with my pursuers, and had arranged our *rendezvous* the next day in accordance with their instructions? She *had* specified the Grand Hôtel, after all . . .

'Mr. Roper?'

I spun round, to find a young woman half-running to catch me up. The exertion had made her flushed and breathless, but she still had energy enough to give me a tentative smile.

I knew I had seen her before, but, in that first instant, I could not for the life of me have said where. I was conscious, though, that the sight of her provoked a paradoxical mix of emotions: pleasure, and astonishment, and exasperation, and something very close to despair.

'Don't you remember me?' she asked.

No Englishwoman ever spoke quite like that. No Frenchwoman, either . . .

I had it.

'Miss Dangerfield!'

Her face relaxed. 'That's right.'

'Was that you on the balcony just now? With the field-glasses?' She nodded.

'What are you . . . why are you . . .?'

'I just . . . No, I won't pretend. I followed you here.'

I tried to speak, but my tongue seemed paralysed, and I was reduced to mutely shaking my head.

'I know,' she said. 'It was the strangest thing in the world to do. I'm as surprised by it as you are.' She held out her hand and marched a couple of fingers. 'Shall we walk?'

'All right.'

'I saw you in Paris,' she said, as we started along the beach. 'Or at least, I was pretty sure it was you. Last night.'

'Ah, the cab!'

She nodded again. 'I was on my way to meet someone, and couldn't stop. But I went to the Casque d'Or this morning, and asked for Mr. Corley Roper. And the man at the desk said Mr. Roper had just left. Which was annoying – but at least it meant I was right, and it *had* actually been you that I'd seen. So I asked him if he knew where you'd gone, and he told me Cabourg. And I thought, well, it's the week-end, and I could just as well spend it at the seaside as in Paris. Do you mind if I take your arm?'

'I beg your pardon?'

'All the ladies are holding the gentlemen's arms.'

'Ah.' I took her arm, and drew it through mine. 'But I don't think it's obligatory.'

'No. But still, I don't like people to guess I'm a foreigner.'

'They can't really help it, can they? It must be pretty obvious the moment you open your mouth.'

'*Before* then, I mean,' she said, dropping her voice. 'Most of *them*' – jerking her head at the crowd milling past us – 'will never hear a word I say. And I'd prefer them, when they look at me, to think I know how to behave. The French have a wonderful gift for making you feel . . . making you feel . . .'

'*Gauche*?'

'Yes.' She hesitated a moment, then laughed and went on: 'Yes, that's it, isn't it? We even have to use a French word for it.'

I laughed too – then stopped abruptly when it occurred to me just how utterly absurd this was: to be walking along arm in arm and exchanging pleasantries with a woman I had met only once before, and whom, until five minutes ago, I had assumed to be hundreds – if not thousands – of miles away.

'At least at the Grand they speak English,' she said. 'So I don't have to watch them smirking as I mangle their language.'

'How did you get a room there?' I asked. 'When I tried, they told me they were full.'

'I telegraphed them before I left Paris.'

'Very prudent of you,' I said. 'I imagined I should find the place deserted, and the desperate hoteliers competing to get my custom.'

'And so they should be, if they only knew who you were.'

I smiled and shook my head. 'You greatly over-estimate my reputation, I'm afraid.'

'Is it – ? Dare I – ?' she began. She looked up at me to see if I could complete the question for myself. When it became clear that I couldn't, she went on:

'I was wondering if perhaps you had come here to write?'

'Ah.' I smiled. 'No, no, I haven't, I'm afraid.'

'That's a pity.'

I felt a surge of anger, which dissipated the instant I glanced down and saw her expression. The skin around her eyes was stretched tight and she was biting her lower lip, like a hurt child trying to stop herself crying.

'I'm sorry to disappoint you,' I said.

She shook her head.

'I did try to explain –'

She nodded. 'I know. And I've no right to keep on . . . to keep on . . .' She broke off, as if she suddenly found herself teetering on the edge of a precipice.

'Badgering me?'

She grimaced. 'That is what I was going to say, yes.'

'Better than frog-marching me, I suppose.'

She laughed. 'Yes, I guess so.'

We walked on in silence. I could not help being struck by the change in her since our last conversation. Obviously, she had not entirely lost her self-assurance – if she had, she would not have been here now – but it was clear that over the past few weeks it had taken something of a battering. Before, she had had the hard rosebud perfection of someone whose will has never been seriously thwarted, and who takes it for granted that she will inevitably get her way; now the petals seemed to have half-opened, and been nibbled by slugs and nipped by their first frost. Her behaviour was no longer all of a piece: confidence kept being capsized by diffidence, and diffidence slipping into melancholy.

'It would have been a consolation, that's all,' she said at length.

'What?'

'To know that you were working on a story.'

'Well, that's very flattering. But . . .' I hesitated, then plucked up my courage and went on: 'Why do you need consoling?'

'Oh, I don't, really.' But the sigh with which she said it belied her. 'I'm just being selfish, I suppose. Probably all it is, really, is that another adventure with Alcuin Hare and Mr. Largo Frog and the Coneys sounds awfully appealing to me right now. I could shut the door, and close the curtains, and curl right up, and just *devour* it, the way I did when I was a little girl.'

'Is your . . . is the tour not going well, then?'

'Hm? Oh, no, no, it's going fine.'

'Miss Dangerfield, the English doubtless appear to you a most obtuse race. You probably have no idea what we are talking about, and assume that we, for our part, are incapable of understanding even the simplest thing you say to us. But the one area in which we cannot be deceived is brave-facery. It is an English vice, and we are experts at detecting it. And that *oh, no, it's going fine* was as unmistakable a piece of brave-facery as I have heard in years.'

This was the longest speech I had ever made to her, and it took her quite by surprise. She gave the kind of embarrassed giggle you hear when you walk in on a woman unexpectedly, and discover her half-undressed.

'Very well, then,' she said. 'The truth is, it's a whole lot more lonely than I thought it would be. I write home, of course, every day. And my family write me. But that's not the same as having somebody to talk to. A *friend* to confide in. And I have no friends here at all.'

'Well, *that*, at least, I understand,' I said.

'You have no friends here, either?'

'Not a solitary soul.'

'Oh. Then why – ?'

'Listen, Miss Dangerfield, as one foreigner to another, would you care to have dinner with me?'

'Well, yes, thank you. That would be . . . that would be . . . oh, just –'

'Not the Grand, I think, don't you? Too *grand*. We'll find somewhere rather cosier.'

We fought our way back to the promenade, and then – as if by some previous agreement, though neither of us had suggested it – looked back to watch the death-throes of the sun as it plunged into the sea and broke up, strewing the surface with fiery wreckage. For ten minutes or more we stood there, still arm in arm, saying nothing. Only when the last pulsing sliver of red had finally sunk below the horizon did we turn again, and continue into the town.

It didn't take long for us to stumble on what we were looking for: a small, snug, softly lit restaurant in one of the streets leading inland from the casino. It was still early, and the only other customer was a lone man with a fierce moustache who sat half lost in shadow next to the fireplace.

A waiter bustled to the door to greet us, and – with a kind of grave but teasing courtliness that made me think he must have taken us for a honeymooning couple – led us to a table by the window. It might just have been a coincidence, but I couldn't help observing that, as we settled ourselves, and I offered her my packet of Players, Alice Dangerfield slipped her left hand under the table before taking the cigarette with her right – as if she had noticed the fellow's manner, too, and wanted to preserve the illusion that we were married by concealing her naked ring-finger.

'*Monsieur dame*, can I bring you something to drink?'

'Perhaps just some wine with our meal?'

'Yes,' said Miss Dangerfield. 'That would be nice.'

He nodded. 'I will bring the menus.'

Before he left, he leaned forward to light our cigarettes, dropping the matchbox on the table to coax the flame into life with his cupped hands. As he did so, Miss Dangerfield's face was thrown suddenly into sharp relief. I could not imagine how I had failed to *see* her before – the startling brilliance of her amber-flecked eyes, and the way her cheek glowed as if there were fire trapped under the skin, like a burning phoenix inside its egg. Had my dismay, the first time we had met, at discovering that she was not Mary Wilson, and my irritation and embarrassment at what she asked me to do, simply blinded me to her? Or had I merely assumed that I should never experience again the mill-race of feelings that was all at once tumbling through me as I watched her across the table?

I took a deep breath, and prepared to try to navigate my way out of danger.

'So,' I said, in what I hoped was a tone of polite interest, 'what were you doing in Paris?'

'Oh, I had come to see Gertrude Stein.' The *Stein* was on a rising note, suggesting that I ought to recognize it.

I shook my head. 'I'm sorry, I dare say I should know who she is, but I don't.'

She laughed. 'Well, I can only say I wish I didn't, either.'

I unfolded my napkin as carelessly as I could, and wafted it debonairly on to my knees.

'It wasn't a success, then?'

She shook her head.

'*She's* not French, though, is she, with a name like that? American, I take it? Or – ?'

She nodded. 'But one of those Americans who don't like America very much. She was always trying to make me feel like an ignorant little country girl. You know, talking about writers and painters I'd never heard of. Or pretending to be surprised that I didn't know what *Cubism* was.'

The waiter reappeared with the menus, and hovered nearby as we scanned them. When we had ordered, I said:

'And what exactly *is* Cubism?'

She laughed again. 'Oh, that makes me feel so much better!' She cast around, like a magician at a children's party looking for a watch or a trinket he can make vanish into thin air. 'Ah,' she said, picking up the waiter's matchbox and rattling it. 'Do you think I could have this?'

'Why?' I said, nodding at her burning cigarette.

'It's the box itself I need.'

I shrugged. 'Well, we can always offer to pay for it, I suppose.'

She slipped out the tray of matches and set it down. Then she split open the cardboard cover, unfolded it, and laid it flat on the table. 'There,' she said. 'Do that to a human head, and you've got Cubism.'

'Ah, yes,' I said. 'I was shown something of the kind in Paris.' And then, seeing a tiny spasm of disappointment in her face: 'Though I haven't a clue what the point of it was. Can you enlighten me?'

'Miss Stein did try to explain to me. And I . . . well, I think I can understand it, in a way. The object is to show several different aspects of something at the same time. So when you look at it, you're not just seeing what you *expect* to see. You're taken by surprise, and forced to examine the thing afresh, perhaps even from quite contradictory points of view. And that makes you really *think* about it.'

It took me a few seconds to assimilate this idea. And when I had, finally, the first thing that came into my mind, for some reason, was Mme. Bournisien, and how poorly the priest's and Françoise Revel's snap-shots of her character had prepared me for the reality.

'Yes,' I said. 'I can see that makes a certain sense, though I should never have thought of it myself, if you hadn't told me.'

She nodded. 'And *I* wouldn't have thought of it, if Miss Stein hadn't told *me*. It's the future, she says. Not just of painting, but of everything – poetry, novels –'

She broke off as the waiter arrived with our wine. While he was opening it I showed him the flattened carcass of his matchbox.

'We must apologize,' I said. 'But it was sacrificed on the altar of art.'

He waved his hand and made a contemptuous *phhh*, as if it were too trivial to mention.

'Thank you,' I said – and the next instant found myself, without quite knowing why, slipping the thing into my pocket.

'So are we to expect a Cubist Mr. Largo Frog one day?' she asked.

'Possibly. But the only way to do it would be to have him run over by a motor-car.'

She flinched. 'Oh, please! Don't!' She was quiet for a moment, fingering the stem of her glass. Then she seemed to shake off her melancholy, and looked up with a smile.

'Anyway,' she said, toasting me. 'Thank you. Your very very good –'

I raised my glass in return. 'And yours.'

'This really is such a treat for me,' she said.

I almost said *for me, too*, but managed to stop myself. Instead I murmured:

'Well, I'm delighted. But still I'm sorry to hear you've been having such a rotten time of it.'

'Oh, I wouldn't say *rotten*, exactly. Just . . . Just not quite what I expected, I suppose.'

'How was Mr. H. G. Wells?'

She flushed and her eyes widened. 'Why do you ask about *him* all of a sudden?'

'Oh, for no particular reason.'

'Did he say something?'

I laughed. 'No. Or not to me, at any rate. I've never met the man. His was more or less the only name on your list I knew, if you want the truth.'

'Oh.' She slackened, like a sail that's lost the wind.

'Why? What did he do?'

'He . . .' She drew in her breath, and started fiddling with her glass again. 'He didn't seem much interested in literature, to my surprise. Instead he gave me what amounted to a lecture on eugenics, and the need for the Anglo-American stock of my country to renew itself before it's too late.' She paused a moment, glanced over her shoulder, as if she imagined the place might be thronged with eavesdroppers, then went on in a half-whisper: 'American gentlemen, I know, are meant to be freer than the English kind, but no American I ever met would have dared to touch me where he did.'

'Really?'

She nodded, and tapped her haunch with one finger.

'Good God!'

'It was a purely scientific investigation, you understand. To discover whether or not I have good child-bearing hips.'

I had to bite my thumb to keep myself from bursting out laughing.

'Apparently I do, you'll be glad to hear. And I think he'd have been only too happy to prove it there and then, if I'd let him.'

I could contain myself no longer. 'Oh, do forgive me,' I said. 'It's just so . . . so . . . oh . . .'

'I know. It's totally outrageous, isn't it?' She was laughing too, now, but more with embarrassment than mirth. 'I'm sorry, I really don't know why I just told you that. I haven't mentioned it to a single other living soul.'

'No,' I said. 'I'm sure you haven't. But don't worry: I've heard worse things.'

She shook her head in disbelief – though whether at what I had said, or at her own audacity, I couldn't tell – then stopped abruptly as the waiter materialized with our soup. She waited until he had gone again, before gratefully seizing the opportunity to change the subject.

'And what about you?' she said. 'You still haven't told me what you're doing here?'

I smiled, trying to make light of it. 'No, I haven't, have I?'

She gave me a moment to elaborate. When I didn't, she said softly:

'Is it something very shaming, then? More shaming than being touched on the you-know-what by H. G. Wells?'

I laughed. 'I hope not. Just a small matter of private business, that's all.'

'Ah.'

'Anyway, what about the other authors you went to see? They didn't all behave as disgracefully as he did, I hope?'

186

'No.' She took a sip of wine, watching me all the while, with an odd, contradictory expression that seemed both to reproach me for having evaded her question, and to implore me to trust her as she had trusted me.

'That's good,' I said. But it had no more effect than a pebble kicked into the abyss. She did not even dignify it with a nod, but simply went on looking at me.

I tried to swallow, but the saliva had dried in my mouth. She seemed, simultaneously, unsettlingly close, and enormously far away. I suddenly had the strange sense that for days, perhaps weeks, without even being conscious of it, I had been living in utter darkness. Mme. Bournisien had opened a tiny chink, allowing in just enough light for me to glimpse the barn-like extent of the place in which I had unknowingly imprisoned myself. And now Miss Dangerfield stood outside, offering to share my confinement with me if I would only unbar the door and let her in.

'Why will you not tell me?' she said suddenly, putting her head to one side and smiling at me.

'What?'

'You know what.' She darted out a hand and touched mine. 'Does it concern a woman?'

'Well, yes. Though not in the way I think you mean.'

'In what way, then? I'm quite broad-minded, you know – and very discreet. I promise it'll go no further.'

I longed to do it – to feel the immense release of unburdening myself to another human being. But suppose the weight of it was too much for her? What if, having heard me out, she concluded I was mad, and recoiled in disgust – leaving me more acutely alone than I had been before? Even more alarming still, in some ways, though less dispiriting: what if she accepted it? I had given Miss Robinson and Jessop edited versions of my story, and Enticknap rather more – but none of them had heard the entire thing. What would it be like to wake up in the morning, and go to the window, and know that somewhere out there in the world I had a confidante? And not just any confidante, but a dizzyingly attractive young American woman, for whom my feelings seemed suddenly to have become dangerously complicated?

'I don't know,' I said. 'It's a strange tale.'

'I love tales. Especially yours.'

I smiled. 'You may feel differently about this one.'

May rather than *might*: that was a slip. The wine and the warmth must be melting my resistance.

'I'm sure I shan't,' she said.

'There's a complete absence of talking frogs and hares and enchanted woods, I'm afraid.'

She gave a quick shake of the head: *it doesn't matter*.

'Though there is . . . something.'

'Mm?'

'And it's that something, frankly, that makes me so hesitant.'

'Oh, you *have* to tell me now!' she cried. And then, catching the imperiousness in her own voice, her new self hastily intervened. 'No,' she said, 'I didn't mean that, I'm sorry, of course you don't have to. But I'd be so honoured if you would.'

I was undone.

'Well, all right,' I said. 'But only if you promise me one thing. If you find yourself getting weary, or thinking *this man is a lunatic, and I don't want to listen to any more of his ravings*, you are to tell me at once, and I'll stop.'

'All right. I promise.'

So I told her. To begin with, fearing I might be tiring or repelling her, I was careful to pace myself, pausing every five minutes or so to ask her about her food, or make some hushed comment about the waiter. But these interruptions always seemed to frustrate her, and she would invariably draw me back again by nodding impatiently and muttering *go on, go on* – with the result that I soon lost the queasy feeling that I was taking out a basketful of soiled linen and exposing it to the gaze of a complete stranger, and found myself becoming more and more expansive. Only when I got to my second meeting with Mary Wilson did I slow down again for a moment, like an engine-driver approaching a particularly tricky stretch of track. But – though she put a hand to her mouth and gasped with astonishment – even the fantastic idea of the still-born child having found its way inside my head did not make Miss Dangerfield instinctively shrink from me, or dissolve into embarrassed sniggers. Instead, the next second she impulsively reached out and touched me again, and – her eyes full of tears – murmured:

'Oh, my goodness!'

After that, I held back nothing – not even my suspicions about Dolgelly, or my wife's request for a separation, or Dr. Enticknap's needling questions about the state of my marriage, and his unsettling theory as to the cause of my disturbance. I did not finish, finally, until we had eaten the last of our *tarte tatin*, and the waiter had cleared away the plates and brought coffee. My throat was so sore from the talking that the first gulp I took made me wince.

Neither of us spoke for a few seconds. Then I said:

'Well?'

She shook her head, as if she were still trying to take in everything I had said, and didn't know what she made of it yet.

'You deserve a medal,' I said. 'Please forgive me. I have never talked so much in my entire life.'

'No, no, not at all. I'm grateful to you. Truly.'

'What, for boring you silly?'

She smiled. 'I wasn't bored. Not for a moment. It was fascinating.'

She said it pleasantly enough, but there was an unmistakable change in her manner. I couldn't have defined it – she didn't seem angry, exactly, or repelled, or disapproving – but the effect was as palpable as the sudden disappearance of the sun behind a cloud.

'You don't think I'm insane, at least?' I said.

'Insane people drool and slaver, don't they? And I don't see you drooling and slavering.'

I hesitated a second. Then, ashamed of my own nakedness, I said:

'What *do* you think, then?'

'I think you're an exceptionally kind man.'

'Just rather misguided.'

'I didn't say that.'

'No. But it's obviously what you mean.'

She reddened, and drew in her breath sharply.

'I'm sorry, but you've no right to put words into my mouth like that.'

'No,' I said. '*I'm* sorry. You made it pretty clear, when we met before, how you thought I *ought* to be spending my time, so it was quite unreasonable of me to expect you to understand why I decided to devote myself to this instead. I should have stood firm, and not told you about it. All I've done by giving in, I'm afraid, is spoil what ought to have been a lovely evening, and place you in an impossible position.'

'I don't know how I gave you that impression,' she said quietly, shaking her head in wonderment at my obtuseness. 'It simply isn't true. But . . .' She crumpled her napkin and dropped it on to the table. 'Excuse me, I have to go wash my hands.'

I felt humiliatingly close to crying. When she had left, in an effort to preserve the appearance of normality, I summoned the waiter as nonchalantly as I could, and asked for the bill.

But the sudden cooling of our relations had evidently not gone unnoticed. While I was paying, the man who had been sitting in the corner when we arrived got up and sauntered towards the door. As he passed my table, he leaned over and murmured:

'Your wife is very beautiful, monsieur. But be careful. If you make her unhappy, she will look for consolation elsewhere. And she will have no difficulty finding it.'

*

When Miss Dangerfield returned, she did not sit down, but hovered by her chair, saying she was tired and would like to go back to the Grand Hôtel.

'All right,' I said, signalling for our coats. 'I'll walk with you.'

She did not refuse, but neither did she take my arm again. On the way, I tried several times to coax her into conversation, but it was useless as struggling to re-light a fire with wet tinder. Every time I asked a question or made an observation she would reply with one or two words, before lapsing back into silence.

And then, when we reached the hotel entrance, she surprised me again. As I held out my hand, preparing to say goodbye, she snatched it suddenly, drew herself towards me, and – to my utter amazement – kissed me on the mouth.

'Thank you,' she said. 'And I *am* your friend, whatever you may think. Don't forget I said so.'

I plodded back to the *auberge*, feeling as knocked-off-balance and removed from myself as if I'd had a blow to the head. My room was simultaneously frowsty and cold, and permeated – like the rest of the place – with a heavy stench of garlic and drains so potent that it lay on my tongue like a coating of oil. I opened the window, hoping to let in some fresh air, but all I got was the same ubiquitous smell, laced with a faint tang of sea-salt, and the sour rotten-cabbage odour of the market.

I half-undressed, then lay down and folded the counterpane over myself. There was, I knew, no immediate prospect of sleep; so, rather than closing my eyes, I twined my fingers under my head, and stared up at the cracks and patches on the ceiling, which – in the dim glow of the street-lamps – looked as remote and mysterious as the surface of the moon.

I was paralysed by confusion, like a man with a broken arm and a broken leg who can't decide which one hurts the more and should be treated first. I felt disappointed by my behaviour, and puzzled by Alice Dangerfield's; but it would have been just as true to put it the other way round, and say that I was disappointed in her and puzzled by myself. I should not have told her about Mary Wilson, that much was plain. But why had I felt such an overwhelming *urge* to tell her – and why, when I succumbed, had she reacted as she had?

It took me only a few seconds to find the answer to the first question. It had been a kind of test: I had wanted her to like me, not just as the idealized author of a series of books she had enjoyed as a child, but as I was, in all my weakness and complexity. That, of course, was why I had been so dashed by her cool response. But what else had I expected? That she would be moved to tears by my chivalrous spirit, and – before she could stop herself – blushingly declare her love for me?

No, I hadn't expected it. But, if I was absolutely honest, I had to admit that it wasn't far from what I had hoped.

How could I have been so foolish? Perhaps Enticknap had been right, and I was simply so starved of female affection that I was bound to fall for any woman who showed the least interest in me. That was why I had become obsessed with Mary Wilson, and imagined I had been possessed by her child. That was why, like an infatuated undergraduate, I had indulged the pitiful fantasy that Miss Dangerfield could fall in love with me.

Then I remembered her kiss and her parting words to me. Didn't they suggest that perhaps she *might* love me, after all?

To which, with withering contempt, the opposition would reply: it might be true that I had been a fool about Mary Wilson – but the answer wasn't simply to become a fool about Alice Dangerfield instead. No, if the whole sorry episode had taught me anything, it was this: I should detach myself from both of them – retreat with as much dignity as I could still muster – and live out my days in wintry solitude.

For I don't know how long these two contesting moods battled for supremacy. At some point – it must have been after two, because I remember hearing a distant clock striking the hour – it finally hit me that I was exhausting myself for nothing. The civil war would rage all night, if I let it, without either side winning a decisive victory. If I was to get any sleep at all, I must arrange a temporary truce, and try to choose between the opposing sides in the morning, when I was feeling fresher.

I did not hear the clock strike three.

When I came to again, it was still dark. For a moment, I wasn't sure what had roused me. And then I heard it: an infant crying. Not the angry animal howls of a baby, but the hiccoughing sobs of a child old enough to know that it's distressed. It was so much like the noise Elspeth had made when she had been woken by a nightmare that I almost called out: *Don't be frightened, darling.*

I put my head against the wall. No, the only sound from the neighbouring room was a slow whistling snore. I went to the window. Nothing but the sigh of the waves, and the faint clip of some early riser's horse at the other end of the town.

I stuffed my fingers in my ears. The noise grew louder.

I sat down on the bed.

'Please,' I said. 'Hush.'

The sobs became more agitated.

'What is it?' I said.

You . . . you . . . you . . .

'I what?'

You're going to leave us.

'Why do you say that?'

I heard. I heard. I heard.

I took a deep breath. As I exhaled again, I was suffused with a tremendous sense of calm. A storm had blown me from my mooring, and sent me pitching and plunging into a turbulent sea that threatened to capsize me. Now, suddenly, miraculously, I seemed to be at anchor again.

'It's all right, old fellow,' I said. 'All just sound and fury, signi-fying nothing. I won't leave you, I promise.'

Gradually, the sobs diminished, until at last they were no more than the soft regular murmur of untroubled sleep.

The next morning, I wrote to Miss Dangerfield, apologizing for being a morose dinner companion the night before, and wishing her luck with the rest of her tour. I made no mention of another meeting, nor did I give her the address of the *auberge* – so, even if she took it into her head to suggest one herself, she would not know where to find me.

I left the note at her hotel, then bought a *ficelle* and a Camembert and a bottle of Perrier water, and walked eastwards out of the town, along a narrow spur running between the beach on one side and a natural harbour dotted with fishing-boats on the other. After half a mile or so it became wilder and rougher: a lost kingdom of tussocky dunes, where the wind had scalloped the sand into deep smooth hollows. I found one sheltered from the breeze, and – lulled by the sea and a choir of jeering gulls – settled down to make up some of the sleep I had lost the night before.

It was almost two by the time I woke again. I ate my picnic, then sauntered back for my three o'clock *rendezvous*. I arrived early, and stopped short of the hotel, to avoid any unnecessary risk of Miss Dangerfield spotting me again. But then I noticed that Mme. Bournisien was already there, standing at the edge of the terrace, looking first left and then right, in hope of seeing me coming.

She recognized me while I was still fifty feet away. Her face cleared, and she smiled and fluttered her fingers.

'Good afternoon, monsieur.'

'Good afternoon.'

We shook hands. She was wearing a tall, old-fashioned black hat, and a black coat that flapped and billowed around her ankles. From her left wrist dangled a bulging reticule, which flew up like a kite every time a gust of wind caught it.

'Thank you for coming,' I said.

'It's nothing, monsieur.'

'Where can we go? Would you like coffee? Or –'

'I should prefer to be outside, if you don't mind. I love the sea, but my duties, of course, tend to keep me indoors. So every time I can, I like to come to the beach.'

I steered her towards a bench in front of the casino. As we sat down, she said:

'Poor little Mary. I don't think of her as often as I should, I'm sorry to say – though I do still try to remember her in my prayers occasionally. You know: at Christmas and Easter. And on her birthday. But yesterday, after your visit, I found it impossible to get her out of my head. It was very sad. A lot of sad memories. After dinner, I went to my room and sat down and tried to write them all down for you.'

'That was very good of you. Thank you.'

She shook her head. 'It wasn't so hard. But none of them, I'm afraid, is going to be much help to you. I can recall nothing about her family at all. I wonder, now, that I wasn't more curious. But I was young, and being kept in ignorance of my charge's background seemed a small price for such an opportunity. Looking back, I can see that I perhaps paid it too willingly.'

'Who actually engaged you?'

'An agency. I had been head house-maid for a Swiss family in Paris. When they returned to Geneva, I might have gone with them. But I am French, and my parents still lived at Bar-le-Duc, so I decided to seek another position. My former employer was kind enough to give me excellent references. So – although I imagine Mr. Cooper was probably looking for someone older and more experienced – they finally recommended me for the place.'

'And what about the rest of the staff? Were they appointed in the same way?'

'The woman who came in to help with the cleaning, yes. I interviewed her myself. The governess, Mme. Groves, was found through an agency in London, I believe. But she didn't arrive until Mary was five, of course, so she knew even less than I did.'

'And the nurse?'

'Ah, Mme. *Lamarthe.*' She pressed her lips into a thin smile – whether of rueful affection or contempt, it was impossible to tell. 'She was a character, that one. A real old Norman peasant. Could barely write her own name. But as cunning as Talleyrand. The only time I ever saw her truly happy was after she'd been to the market. *Do you know how much he wanted for these, madame? Fifteen centîmes. I told him they weren't worth half that. In the end, he let me have them for eight – and gave me this turnip into the bargain.*'

I laughed.

'Where they found *her*, I don't know. She was from Avranches originally. And I assume that's where Mary was born, because Madame Lamarthe said she'd taken her in when she was just a day old.'

'So *she* must have known the mother, at least?'

She shook her head. 'Not necessarily. The midwife could have taken the child to her. Or the doctor.'

'And she never said anything to suggest who the parents were? Or why they might have chosen her to look after their daughter?'

'No. I did ask her, once or twice. But she'd only sigh, and say, *oh, just two of God's creatures, I suppose, madame, like the rest of us. And speaking for myself, I hope I know my duty better than to go asking questions, and prying into other people's business.*'

'Do you think that means she *did* know something, then?'

She splayed her fingers and looked at them. She was not wearing a wedding-ring, I noticed. *Madame* must be a courtesy title, in recognition of her position.

'Possibly,' she said finally. 'But if she did, it will have gone to her grave with her. I'm sorry, you must reproach me for not having pressed her more.'

'No, not at all –'

She held up a hand to stop me. 'I doubt if she would have told

196

me even if I had. But I have found something that might help you.' She hoisted the reticule into her lap and prised it open. 'I used to have to take Mary to the English church in Paris every week. And she would always carry this with her.'

She pulled out a prayer-book and handed it to me. It was not particularly old, but had faded boards and a worn spine, as if it had seen a lot of use.

'She left it behind when she went to England,' said Mme. Bournisien. 'And since neither she nor Mr. Cooper sent for it, I decided to keep it to show my uncle. He was a priest near Rouen, so I thought he would be interested.'

'But he wasn't?'

She smiled, and shook her head. 'He said he could read English, but I don't think he could.'

I opened the book. On the fly-leaf was written:

A birthday present to Henry Malden Studd
  From his affec^te
    Mamma

Underneath, a childish hand had added something in pencil. It had since been rubbed out; but – when you tilted the page to catch the light – you could still clearly see the impression it had left:

Henry Malden Studd
  Hallaton Hall
    Leicestershire

'How did Mary come by this, do you know?' I said, looking up.

'She had always had it. I had the impression it had been given to her by her parents. Or by Mr. Cooper.'

I nodded. 'Thank you,' I said, fumbling for my fountain pen. 'Let me just make a note of the name, if I may –'

'Please,' she said. 'Take the book. And give it to Mary, when you see her again, with my apologies for having kept it so long.'

XIII

Henry Malden Studd. Hallaton Hall. Leicestershire. It was little
enough, for all the trouble it had taken me to get it. But, unlike
the succession of maddeningly vague clues that had eventually
brought me to Mme. Bournisien, it was at least admirably specific: there must *be* a Hallaton Hall in Leicestershire; and even if
Henry Malden Studd no longer lived there, there was a strong
possibility that whoever had the place now would be able to tell
me what had become of him. And, childish though it may seem,
as I strolled back to the *auberge*, clutching the prayer-book, I
could not help remembering my walk from the church to the
Railway Inn with *She* in my hand, and drawing a kind of superstitious courage from the symmetry of the thing. Perhaps, I
thought, books were lucky for me, and, having been taken to
Mary Wilson by H. Rider Haggard, I should find that Thomas
Cranmer led me to her parents.

I could have done the journey from Cabourg to Leicestershire
in three days; but that would have meant arriving rumpled and
travel-weary, with a trunk full of dirty clothes. So I decided to
stop in London for a couple of nights, to allow enough time to
get my washing done and my suit cleaned, to have my hair cut,
and to replenish my stock of collars and ties. The outcome of my
visit to Hallaton Hall was, I knew, largely in the lap of the gods;
but I could at least marginally improve my chances of success by
ensuring that I turned up looking the part.

What I should find there, of course, I had not the slightest
idea. As I sat in the train, first in France, and then in Kent, and
then steaming steadily north into the grey flat Midlands, I told
myself half a dozen stories about Henry Malden Studd: he was

Mary Wilson's father; he was her grandfather; he was the clergy-man who had baptised her, who – horrified at her parents' callousness towards her – had wanted her to have his own prayer-book. None of them seemed entirely plausible – and yet I couldn't help feeling it was equally unlikely that the man had no link with Mary Wilson at all. A prayer-book, after all, is a private, personal thing; if you give a child someone else's, rather than buying one new, surely it can only be because the previous owner has some special significance for her, or her for him?

After the seaside giddiness of Cabourg and the beauty of Paris, it was depressing to find myself being drawn inexorably further and further into the sooty heart of England. But when I reached Market Harborough, and changed to the Melton Mowbray branch for the last ten miles of my journey, my spirits started to rise again. The line ran through an elysian landscape of lush pastures and dark huddled woods pricked with spring green, which seemed to grow lovelier with every mile. Finally, as we were drawing into Hallaton itself, I stuck my head out of the window and saw, through the gouts of smoke, one of the pretti-est villages I have ever set eyes on: a glorious, tight-knit jumble of thatch and whitewash and brick and stone, spread – like a kind of roughly made cap – over a low hill at the edge of a grassy valley.

A porter opened the door and helped me with my luggage. As we were walking along the platform, I asked him:

'Do you know where I might be able to get a bed for the night?'

'What, here in Hallaton, you mean, sir?'

I nodded. He pursed his lips.

'Well, there's the Royal Oak. That's where gentlemen usually put up, if they're not stopping at the Manor or the Hall. But if it was me, I'd go to the Bewicke Arms. More old-fashioned than you're used to, I dare say. But you'll eat well there. And there's nowhere'll make you welcomer.'

'All right, then,' I said. 'Thank you. I'll try the Bewicke Arms. How far is it?'

'Far end of the village, sir. But that's no great matter, in a place the size of this. Theo there' – nodding at an old fellow waiting in the station yard with a pony cart – 'will have you there in no more'n ten minutes.'

He was right. The Bewicke Arms was barely bigger than a cottage, and squeezed like an afterthought into an odd corner at the edge of a patch of green at the bottom of the high street; but the landlady – a large woman of fifty or so, who emerged from the kitchen wearing an apron powdered with flour – greeted me with such a show of relaxed friendliness that you'd have thought she'd been expecting me. She led me to a tiny room just large enough for a bed and a washstand, gave me a little handbell to ring if I needed anything, and – with a sweet smile, and a bob of the head – asked me what time I would like my dinner, and whether I'd prefer steak pie or rabbit stew.

After she'd gone, I opened the little casement, and peered out under a heavy brow of thatch at the view across the valley. It was idyllic: a sloping meadow, fringed by trees and burnished to a brilliant green-gold by the afternoon sun. For a long time I stood there, listening to the song of a thrush in a nearby garden, trying to fit this arcadian scene into the same reality as Mary Wilson's blighted life, and failing.

Then I put on a clean collar, brushed my hair, pocketed the prayer-book, and went out to look for Hallaton Hall.

Some instinct of caution made me wary of asking my landlady for directions. If she knew where I was going, she might naturally enquire the reason – and then I should have either to lie, or to explain that I was looking for Henry Malden Studd. And if – as seemed a fair bet, given the way I had come by it – the name was associated with a scandal of some kind, then even to mention it might rouse her suspicions, and send the whole village into a defensive spasm. News, after all, would travel through such a tiny place at telegraph speed; and I might turn up at the Hall only to find the people there forewarned, and determined not to help me. And its very smallness meant it could not be too difficult for me to find the house on my own.

On the green in front of the inn was a curious old conical stone structure, which might have been the stump of a mediaeval cross. Around the base ran a low seat, where two boys sat playing marbles. I casually asked one of them if he could tell me how to get to the Hall.

'Up there,' he said, pointing towards the high street. He shut his eyes, and waved his hand from side to side like a fish-tail, trying to remember his left from his right. 'Then you just jog over a bit,' he said, looking at me again, 'and it's straight in front of you.'

I thanked him, and slipped them threepence apiece. Five minutes later I found myself peering through the gates at a square, stately stone-built house set well back behind a long wall that seemed to run almost the entire breadth of the village. I had been prepared for a certain grandeur, of course; but nothing quite on this scale. It wasn't the size of the Hall itself that took me aback: rather the extent of its grounds and outbuildings, and the way the main front was turned at right angles to the road, as if it had deliberately averted its gaze from *hoi polloi* to enjoy the spectacle of its own woods and gardens.

It suddenly occurred to me that, without even thinking about it, I had been visualizing my visit to Hallaton Hall as a kind of repeat of my expedition to Miss Shaw's house, but with a different book. That, I could see now, as I ventured on to the drive, had been a mistake. Miss Shaw's house, for all its seclusion, had looked out upon the world, and admitted the possibility you might have some business with it. This place, by contrast, seemed to repel you by the monumental mass of its indifference – which increased, like a sort of inverse gravity, the nearer you got to it, making each step harder than the last. The door would be opened, in all probability, not by a friendly housekeeper or maid, who might be appealed to as a fellow human being, but by an inscrutable footman trained to keep undesirables at bay. I could sense his withering stare already, and see the twitch in the corner of his mouth, as my carefully rehearsed phrases bounced off him like arrows loosed against a dreadnought . . .

It was no good: I needed to think of another strategy. I turned, and started back towards the gate. At any moment, I thought, there might be a bellowed *Hey, you!* behind me, followed by the sound of pursuing footsteps; but all I could hear, beyond the scrunch of my own feet on the gravel, was a leisurely tattoo of hoofbeats from the road outside, and two men calling to each other in the stable-yard. I had just reached the entrance, and was on the point of making good my escape, when a horse suddenly appeared in front of me, blocking my path into the street. I tried to dodge round it; but the rider, a girl of no more than eighteen or nineteen, stopped the beast abruptly, and sat staring curiously down at me.

'Good evening,' I said.

She nodded. She didn't speak, but her insolent blue eyes demanded to know who I was, and what I was doing there.

'Excuse me,' I said. I made another attempt to get past. She responded by urging the horse a couple of paces forward to stop me.

I started to blush. There was nothing for it: I was going to have to account for myself. And reluctant though I was to tell her the truth, I knew that if I tried to make up a more convincing story on the spot I should almost certainly end by being caught out.

'I was looking for Mr. Studd,' I said.

'*Studd?*'

I nodded.

'There hasn't been a Studd here since before I was born. Longer ago than that.'

'Well, I'm sorry, but this is the only address I have.' I took the prayer-book from my pocket, and opened it to show the inscription, pointing to where *Hallaton Hall* had been written and then rubbed out. She frowned at it, with the sulky look of a stupid child who suspects you're playing a trick on her, but can't quite understand how it's being done.

I remembered that the surest way to disarm suspicion is to ask for help.

'Do you know where I might find him?' I said. 'Or, at least, where I might find someone who could tell me what happened to him?'

She continued gazing at the book for a second or two, then glanced over her shoulder and called:

'Carter!'

I looked back along the road. Fifty yards or so behind her sat a groom on a bay gelding. As I watched, he nudged the horse into motion and began trotting towards us.

He was a burly, bull-necked fellow who looked like a prize-fighter, and there was only one reason I could think of why she should have summoned him. I instinctively rose on the balls of my feet, preparing to run. Then I realized that it would not simply make me look ridiculous, but would also be entirely pointless, since the only way open to me was back into the grounds, where I should be trapped.

'Yes, miss?' he said as he came up to us – all the while studying me with a sardonic grin, as if he were measuring me up as a potential opponent and finding me less than impressive. His forearms, I noticed, were so thick that they threatened to split the sleeves of his jacket.

'Pick,' said the girl.

'Beg pardon, miss?'

'Old Pick – what's his name – ?'

'John, would that be?'

She nodded impatiently. 'John, John, yes. Where does he live?'

'Pudding Lane, miss.'

'There,' she said, looking down at me. 'If you want to talk about Studds, go to Pudding Lane and ask for John Pick.' And without waiting for a reply, she tapped the horse into life with her crop and rode on.

The groom smiled as he passed me – and then, looking back, called:

'Pudding Lane's off the high street, sir. You can't miss it. And Pick's is three down on the right.'

I raised my cap in thanks, but he had already turned away, and didn't see it. I watched them both into the stable-yard, before setting off for the high street.

My first idea was that I should simply establish where Pudding Lane was, and then return to the pub to gather my thoughts before going in search of John Pick. But when I got there, and found a grassy track, bordered on one side by neat gardens and on the other by an orchard teeming with squawking hens, it looked so enticing that I couldn't resist seeing where it led. And as I reached the third gate, I saw – not more than six feet away, stooped behind a low hedge – a stocky man of sixty or so tending a line of bean-poles in front of his cottage. I tried to edge past without his noticing me, but he sensed my presence, and looked up smiling.

'Lovely evening.'

Impossible, now, to extricate myself. 'Yes,' I said. 'It is. Are you Mr. Pick, by any chance?'

He grabbed the handle of his fork and pulled himself up, then stood squinting into the setting sun behind me, trying to see if he recognized me. He was broadly built, with close-cropped silver hair that ran seamlessly into a well-trimmed beard, giving the queer impression that his whole head was covered with a continuous grey pelt. The effect was to make him look startlingly like a badger.

'Yes, that's right,' he said, after a couple of seconds.

'My name's Corley Roper.' I held out my hand. He glanced down at it in surprise, then – after brushing the earth from his palm – reached out and took it. He said nothing, but from his perplexed expression I think he must have thought I had come to try to sell him something.

'A young lady at the Hall said you might be able to help me,' I said.

'What, Miss Bankhart, you mean?'

I smiled. 'I don't know. I only met her by chance. But when I mentioned that I was trying to find out something about Mr. Studd, she suggested I should come and see you.'

He did not reply at once, but leaned heavily on his fork, his jaw working as if he were chewing a plug of tobacco.

'Which Mr. Studd?' he said at last.

'Henry Malden.'

He sucked his cheeks in surprise. 'Ah, poor Master Henry. What's happened to him, then?'

I shook my head. 'I know nothing about him at all, I'm afraid. All I have is this.'

I opened the prayer-book and held it out to him. He took it and scanned the inscription, moving his lips as he read.

'And how come you *do* have it, if you don't mind my asking?' he said, as he handed it back again.

'Well, that's something of a story.' I glanced past him. 'Perhaps . . .?'

He turned to see what I was looking at, then got my meaning, and nodded.

'Very well, sir,' he said, opening the gate. 'Please come in.'

'Thank you.'

He led me up an uneven path towards his plain little red-brick cottage. Under the window, wedged against the wall, was a weather-stained wooden bench.

'We'll do well enough here, don't you think, sir?' he said, prodding it with his foot.

'Yes, of course.'

We sat side by side, looking out at the hills rising above the orchard. I could hear children playing in the neighbouring garden, and see a woman taking down laundry from a line.

'Don't trouble yourself about them, sir,' he said. 'They won't pay us any heed.'

I tapped the prayer-book on my knee. 'Thirty years ago,' I said, as softly as I could, 'someone gave this to a little girl living in France. She was far too young to remember who it was. But there must have been a reason for it.'

He nodded. 'Well, her parents would know, wouldn't they?'

I looked across at the woman. He was right: she was showing no interest in us at all. Dropping my voice to a whisper, I said:

'She doesn't know who her parents were. But . . .'

'Oh, I see!' He was stage-whispering himself now. 'And you imagined Master Henry might have been the – ?'

'Yes. Is that possible, do you think?'

'No, sir. Well, I shouldn't say *no*, because you never really know another human creature, do you, and what you might find in him, if you looked deep enough? But if you was to ask me, which member of that family was least likeliest to go and make a child he didn't want the world to know about, I'd say Master Henry.'

'And which would be the *most* likely, do you think?'

He started, as if he had only realized too late that I was almost certain to ask him that question, and regretted laying himself open to it.

'I was only a stable-boy, sir,' he mumbled, his cheeks reddening beneath the grey furze of his beard. 'And then a groom. It was just *Good morning, sir*; *good morning, miss*; *good morning, Pick.* They were pleasant enough to me, most of the time. And Mr. Studd, that's the father, he was a fine gentleman, who knew a good horse when he saw it. But that's about as much as I can tell you about them. And it wouldn't really be my place to say more in any case, would it, even if I could?'

That didn't stop you offering an opinion on Henry, I thought. But to say so would only make him retreat further; so instead I simply asked:

'Why did you call him *poor* Master Henry?'

He grinned with relief. 'I'd say they was both of them poor, truth be told. Him and Master Edward, I mean. But Master Henry was the worser.' He spread his fingers on his knee and looked down at them, shaking his head. 'Not poor the way *we* were, of course. Poor like a couple of young saplings that find the other trees have growed up around them, so they can't get enough light.'

'Master Edward . . .?'

He scowled at me, wrestling with the impossible challenge of imagining what the world must look like to someone who had never even heard of the Studds.

'Master Edward was Master Henry's elder brother,' he said finally. 'Mr. Studd, see, had four children by his first wife: Master Edward and Master Henry, and then the . . . the two young ladies. But –'

'Listen,' I said, drawing out my pen and notebook. 'Do you mind if I write this down?'

He shook his head. 'It's not a secret. Leastways, not so far as I know.'

I started sketching a rough family tree. 'So: the brothers are Edward and Henry. What about the sisters?'

He hesitated a second, before clearing his throat and saying gruffly:

'Miss Henrietta and Miss Emily, sir. But their mother died, that's the tragedy of it, when they was all just mites. And Mr. Studd re-married. And he and the second Mrs. Studd, they come back to England, and had five boys of their own. And –'

'Wait, wait – came back from where?'

He raised his eyebrows, as if he were surprised that I needed to ask. 'Why, from India, sir. They went first to Wiltshire, I think it was. And then, after a few year, they come here, and took the Hall.'

'And when was that, do you remember?'

'Oh, that would have been . . .' He screwed up his eyes and stared into the distance, whistling silently. 'About 1862, I reckon. Or sixty-three. I was just a lad at the time. But when my dad – he was groom to Lady Hinrich, who had the house before them – when he saw how many hunters Mr. Studd meant to keep, and how many staff he was going to need to mind them, he suggested me for a stable-boy. And that's how I got my start.' He shook his head again. 'Crazy for the horses he was, Mr. Studd.'

'And Henry and Edward were what, overshadowed by their half-brothers, were they?'

He nodded. 'Well, not to begin with, maybe, on account Master Kynaston and Master George and Master Charles weren't much more'n babes when they come here. But by the time they was old enough to run around, it was soon pretty clear who ruled the roost. You'd have thought Master Kynaston was the Prince of Wales, the way he'd stride about, ordering everything to his liking, and Mrs. Studd looking on like this.' He pressed his hands together, and somehow managed to pull his bearded face into a grotesque parody of a doting madonna's smile. 'Always got his way, did Master Kynaston. *And*'d make sure Master George and Master Charles got theirs, too, when it didn't interfere with his.' He shook his head, and laughed almost noiselessly. 'Funny, when you think what become of them. Just goes to show, you never can tell with folks, can you?'

'Why, what *did* become of them?'

He lifted his arms, and wielded an imaginary cricket bat.

'Oh, what, the Studd brothers?' I said. 'Who played for England?'

He nodded, pleased to discover that – alien though I undoubtedly was – even the universe I came from was not entirely Studdless. 'And then went on to be missionaries, so I heard.'

'Really? I didn't know that.'

He nodded again. 'Leastways, Master Charles did. Went off to China or some such, I believe. Hard to imagine, that, when you think of how he used to torment poor Master Henry.'

I shifted position on the bench – taking the opportunity, as I did so, to turn my head for a moment and glance in at the window. The sunlight was too bright for me to be able to make out much; but through a ghostly image of the garden I glimpsed a cluttered table with an open beer-bottle on it, and – hanging at a skewed angle on the wall beyond, where in a religious household you would expect to see *The Light of the World* – a dull print of a rural scene.

'Perhaps', I said, 'the habit of supposing you are always right and the other poor chap is always wrong is exactly what you need to be a missionary.'

I had not misjudged him. He chuckled and said:

'I never thought of that, sir. But maybe you're right. Master Henry might just as well have been a savage, the way they treated him sometimes – and that's the truth.' He paused for a moment, startled by his own frankness; then – fearing I might think him disloyal – turned towards me and said: 'Not that I'm saying they were wrong, mind. They were only favouring their own, after all, and that's natural enough, isn't it? It was just hard to watch sometimes. Put me in mind of a lot of healthy young piglets jostling a couple of runts to keep them from the teat.'

'And what about the girls? Did they get jostled too?'

He hesitated, then shook his head. 'Not so much, sir, no.'

'What, they were stronger-willed, were they?'

He let out a soft *phew*. 'That's a tidy way of putting it. I can think of another word. Any road, they were Mr. Studd's darlings – and if the mistress or one of the boys crossed them, they'd have him to answer to for it.'

'And what became of *them*? Do you know?'

The skin tightened around his eyes, and for a moment he

seemed at a loss what to say. Then he mumbled:

'Miss Henrietta married the doctor. Dr. Crane.'

'And do they still live here?'

'No, sir,' he muttered, barely moving his lips. 'They moved away a good while ago now.'

'That's a shame. Do you know where they went?'

He shook his head.

'How about Miss Emily? Did *she* marry?'

He breathed in sharply, then tried to cover it by coughing.

'I couldn't say, sir. All I *do* know is, she hadn't by the time she left here.'

'And when was that?'

He squirmed, almost imperceptibly. 'You'll have to give me a minute, sir. I'll need to work it out.' He leaned forward, dropping his hands between his knees, and stared out at the horizon again. His eyes, I noticed, had gone suddenly dull and milky, as if a cloud were passing across the sun, and they had picked up its reflection.

'Seventy-one, sir,' he said finally, levering himself up.

'That's when she went?'

'When they *all* went. Save Miss Henrietta, of course. *She* stayed, on account she was Mrs. Crane by then.'

1871. A good nine or ten years before Mary Wilson was born. Whatever her connection was to Henry Malden Studd, it looked as if I wasn't going to find it in Hallaton.

'And what about Master Henry?' I said. 'Do you know what happened to *him* after they left?'

'Him and Master Edward was sent off to India again, to run the plantation. That's what I understood, any rate.' He saw the question in my eyes and added quietly, as if he were committing an indiscretion: 'Indigo. That's what all the horses and the houses and the money is, if you come down to it. Indigo. Made by a lot of poor barefoot heathens.'

'And you don't know if they ever came back?'

'No, sir. That were pretty well the last I heard of them.'

I nodded. 'And the rest of the family – ?'

'They went back to Wiltshire. A big place, seemingly, bigger'n the Hall, they say. I might have gone with them, only I was courting by then, and my girl was in service at the Manor, and didn't want to leave.'

'Do you remember what it was called? The house in Wiltshire?'

He chewed his lip for a moment, then shook his head. 'Tell you what I do have, though, sir,' he said, getting up. 'And that's the letter Mr. Studd were good enough to send, when Amy and me was married. It weren't from Wiltshire, it were from their London house. And of course, it's a good few years ago now. But there'll be someone living there, won't there – and if it isn't Master Kynaston, then whoever it is might still be able to tell you where you can find him.'

He went inside, and reappeared a moment later carrying a black-bound scrap-book, which he had wedged open with one finger.

'Here you are, sir,' he began. 'Number two –' And then, losing confidence in his ability to read it, he bent down and showed me the page:

Gummed to the middle was a letter written on expensive blue paper. The ink had already started to yellow, but the engraved address at the top was as clear as ever:

2, Hyde Park Gardens.

I wrote it down, then – slipping my notebook back in my pocket – got up and thanked him.

'It's been a pleasure, sir,' he mumbled. 'I'm only sorry I couldn't tell you more.'

I went back to my cupboard of a room at the Bewicke Arms, and opened the casement to let in some fresh air. The sun had almost gone now, and the breeze had a hard edge to it. I shut my eyes, and stood for a minute or two thinking of nothing, luxuriating in the coolness on my cheeks and the smell of the dewy grass and the melancholy bleating of the sheep on the far side of the valley. Then I roused myself, lit the lamp, and lay down on the bed to consider what I had learnt.

Not a great deal, on the face of it – certainly nothing that seemed to take me any closer to explaining why Mary Wilson had had Henry Malden Studd's prayer-book. But in some odd corner of my mind I was conscious, nonetheless, of that tantalizing sense you get when – after casting your line in vain for hours on end – you feel the first tentative tug of a bite.

In an effort to locate it, I went through everything John Pick had told me – projecting our conversation like a kind of spectral cinematograph film on the rough ceiling, in hope of catching the crucial gesture or expression. After no more than five minutes or so, I thought I had the answer. And, what's more, I could see a relatively simple way of putting the matter to the test.

I washed and went down to the dining-room. When the land-lady had brought my pie, and was turning to leave, I said, as casually as I could:

'By the way, didn't there use to be a Dr. Crane in Hallaton?'

She stopped, pirouetting back towards me so abruptly that she almost lost her footing. 'Yes, sir, that's right.'

'I thought so. He was a friend of my uncle's. Must be getting on a bit now, I suppose. He's not still here, I take it?'

'Oh, no, sir. He's been gone a good long time, Dr. Crane has.'

'How long?'

'Oh, thirty year, it must be, now.'

The hairs on the back of my neck stirred.

'Really?'

She nodded.

'Well, you do surprise me, I must say. Surely he didn't *retire* then, did he? He wouldn't have been old enough?'

'Oh, no. Just about your age now, I should say.'

I laughed. 'Well, there you are: I've certainly no intention of retiring. So why did he go, do you know?'

She shook her head.

'I mean, it's quite unusual for a doctor in a good practice simply to up and leave like that, isn't it?'

She flushed, and the muscles in her jaw hardened. 'I'm sure I couldn't say, sir.'

I had pushed her too hard, clearly. For the rest of the meal I left the subject alone – confining my conversation, whenever she appeared, to anodyne comments about the weather and the beauty of the countryside. Only when I had finished, and was half-way to the door, did I suddenly turn back and say with a laugh:

'You're not going to tell me he did something terrible, are you? Killed a patient with an overdose of chloroform, or cut off an arm instead of a leg?'

She did not even pretend not to know what I was talking about. Her neck stiffened as she bent over my table, and – without looking at me – muttered:

'It was nothing like that, sir. He was a good doctor, as doctors go. No one had a bad word for him till Miss Studd come back. That was what did it.'

'Miss Studd?' I said. 'But surely she was Mrs. Crane by that point?'

'I'm not talking about that Miss Studd,' she said – and vanished into the kitchen with a jangling stack of dirty plates.

I went back up to my room, re-lit the lamp, then opened my notebook, and – on a fresh page – wrote:

Emily Studd.

XIV

I took an early train from Hallaton the next morning, and by tea-time was back in London. At first I tried to persuade myself that I could justify putting up at the Great Western at Paddington, on the grounds that it was no more than a few minutes' walk from Hyde Park Gardens; but in the end I settled for a small private hotel off the Edgware Road instead. And not just for reasons of economy – pressing enough though these were starting to become, as the costs of my travels steadily mounted. I was, I felt fairly sure, finally closing in on my quarry; and while I knew rationally that Emily Studd – assuming she were still alive – could not conceivably have the first inkling that I was looking for her, I nonetheless felt the hunter's natural urge to keep to the shadows, and avoid advertising my presence more than was necessary. To have kept her secret successfully concealed for thirty years, she must have developed a wild animal's nose for danger; and if, when I appeared, she had even the faintest intimation of why I was there, she would simply refuse to see me.

Not, of course, that I really knew what her secret was. It was a fair guess that she was Mary Wilson's mother – though even that was far from certain; but who the father might be, and why they had gone to such enormous lengths to keep their daughter from knowing her true identity, I still had not the least idea. One possibility that occurred to me was that perhaps Miss Studd had originally hoped to avoid the issue altogether, and that that was why she had gone back to Hallaton: her brother-in-law, after all, was a doctor, and she could reasonably have expected that he might be able to help her induce a miscarriage. When he failed or refused to do so (I reasoned), it soon became impossible to

214

disguise Miss Studd's condition – and the consequent scandal drove the family to leave the village in disgrace. But – while it fitted the few facts I had – I had to admit that this was pure conjecture; and that even if it were true, it still brought me no nearer to answering the most fundamental question.

I unpacked, changed my shirt, and set off for Hyde Park Gardens immediately. I had revolved a number of different plans in my mind, but in the end decided that my best hope was again to use the prayer-book as my *entrée*. It might seem eccentric, to say the least, that a perfect stranger should go to the trouble of trying to find Henry Malden in order to return his property to him – but the story had the advantage of simplicity, if nothing else; and his name on the fly-leaf should be enough to convince them that it was true, and to dispel any suspicion that Emily might be my real target. And if it turned out – as John Pick had suggested – that he was still in India, then it would be natural enough for me to ask for his sister's address, so as to be able to give the book to her instead.

But when I reached Hyde Park Gardens itself my nerve failed. The fronts of the houses were shut away behind a private garden overlooking the park, so that all you could see were the backs: towering cliffs of brick and stucco, approached by blind little entrance doors that seemed to have been added on as an afterthought – as if it were only as the most grudging concession to necessity that the architect had been persuaded to allow any communication with the outside world at all. The whole place, in fact, might have been expressly designed to keep the lives of its inhabitants hidden from view. And staring up at the blank walls, I suddenly knew, almost beyond doubt, that if Henry Malden had given his prayer-book to the young Mary, then at least some of the other members of the family must have been aware of it, and would immediately guess that I had got the thing from her. I might artfully slip in some reference to having found it in a second-hand bookshop, of course, but I doubted if they would believe me:

the natural assumption, after all, when you buy something second-hand, is that the previous owner has no further use for it, and
it was hard to think of a plausible reason why anyone but a lunatic
would deliberately set out to re-unite him with it.

I paused in front of number 2, debating what I should do.
While I was standing there, I noticed a slight movement out of
the corner of my eye; and, looking towards it, saw a shadow
moving across the ceiling of one of the rooms on the second
floor. Fearing that someone might come to the window and spot
me, I bent down and performed a dumb-show of removing a
stone from my shoe. Then I retraced my steps into Clarendon
Place, stopping only when I had gone far enough to be sure I
could no longer be seen from the house.

What I needed, it finally struck me, was another John Pick: an
elderly servant, who knew the family well, but was not sufficiently privy to its secrets to understand the full significance of
what I was asking. And the easiest way to find him – or her –
would be to watch, and wait for a suitable candidate to emerge
from number 2.

Behind the houses ran a large mews. I crossed the road, and
stationed myself immediately opposite the entrance. Then, to
avoid looking like a detective policeman, I took the prayer-book
from my pocket, and – as soon as I heard anyone approaching in
the street – opened it, and began earnestly studying whatever
page had presented itself to me.

Though it brought me some curious looks, this device worked
well enough for half an hour or so. But then one man, instead of
glancing nervously at me and hurrying by, stopped in front of
me and ducked down to see what I was reading. When he stood
up again, he cleared his throat and said:

'Hullo! What's the matter?'

He was about fifty, wearing a light suit too big for his lean
frame, and with a bony, sun-darkened face sheathed in a dense
black beard. It seemed oddly familiar, somehow, but I could not

for the life of me say why.

'Nothing,' I said.

'I've an eye for people who're lost. And you have the look of one to me.'

'Oh, no, really, I'm perfectly all right, thank you.'

He smiled, and tapped the book.

I shook my head. 'Ah, that. No, I was just reminding myself, that's all. Good thing to do every once in a while. Such marvellous language.'

'Marvellous *language*?'

He leaned towards me, searching my face. His dark eyes seemed to fix themselves to mine, making it impossible for me to look away, and giving the unpleasant sense that something was burrowing inside my brain.

'Well,' I said. 'The spirit of the thing, as well, of course. The Psalms . . .'

'Are you a Christian?'

'I . . . well . . .'

He took the book from me, riffled through until he found the Creed, then held the page up in front of me.

'Can you say that?'

'Of course. I know it by heart.'

'I mean, can you say it and *mean* it?'

My neck flushed with anger. 'I'm sorry,' I said. 'I don't see that's any of your concern.'

'Ain't it, though?'

'No.' I held my hand out. 'May I have that back now, please?'

He continued staring at me for a few moments, then smiled and started to close the book. But then, at the last second – doubtless hoping to learn my name – he glanced quickly at the fly-leaf, and stopped dead.

'Where did you get this?' he said, looking up.

I felt a sudden rush of annoyance. Without pausing to think, I snapped:

'Look, I've no idea who you are, but we're not living under the Inquisition. And you really have no business interrogating me like –'

He smiled. 'Studd.'

'I beg your pardon?'

'That's who I am. C. T. Studd. And whoever *you* are, it ain't my half-brother Henry.'

A desert wind seemed to blow across me, searing my cheeks and drying my mouth.

'Ah,' I said.

He looked towards the mews, then squinted at his wrist-watch.

'I think', he said, 'that you and I should take a walk together.'

He pinched my sleeve, and started leading me towards the park. I felt like a spy, deep in enemy territory, who – having imagined his disguise to be impenetrable – suddenly finds himself humiliatingly exposed. But I knew it would be as pointless to try to flee a world-class cricketer as it would have been to run from the groom at Hallaton Hall; so I went along meekly, and concentrated all my resources on trying to work out what I should tell him. By the time we had tacked our way across the Bayswater Road and entered the park gates, I had more or less made up my mind: I would not lie, because there was too great a danger of being found out, but neither would I volunteer anything that I felt might compromise either me or Mary Wilson.

'So,' he said, striking south in the direction of the Serpentine. 'Here's my story: I was on my way to my mother's house when I found a fellow I've never clapped eyes on before loitering near the mews, reading my brother's prayer-book. What's yours?'

'I was standing looking at a prayer-book when a fellow *I've* never clapped eyes on took it from my hand and began interrogating me about my religious beliefs.'

He laughed. 'Ah, and what, you think that makes us pretty well square, do you?'

'Pretty well.'

'Well, I suppose if you put the matter before the readers of the *Daily Mail*, three-quarters of them would probably agree with you. But they'd be wrong. It's my business to win souls, you see. If it's *your* business to loiter a stone's throw from my mother's house with her step-son's prayer-book, I'd be very glad to know why.'

I rehearsed several different replies in my head. Finally I said:

'You might say I'm trying to do much the same thing.'

'What?'

'Save a soul. Or two souls. Or even three.'

'*Whose* souls?'

'Ah, well, that's not so easy to explain.'

He didn't press me to elaborate, but walked on in silence, staring abstractedly at the trees fringing the lake. After a few seconds, he nodded suddenly, and said:

'All right. Can you at least tell me how you happened to have the prayer-book?'

He sounded less suspicious now, for some reason, and more genuinely curious. I took a calculated risk and said:

'It was given to me in France.'

'Was it, indeed? By whom?'

'A woman.'

'A *French* woman?'

I nodded. He waited a moment for me to go on. When I didn't, he waved his hand impatiently and said:

'Oh, don't worry, the name would mean nothing to me in any case. And why did *she* have it, do you know?'

'It had been given to . . . to someone she looked after, many years ago.'

He gave me a sharp sidelong glance, raising his eyebrows. 'A child?'

'Yes.'

He nodded again, exhaling slowly through his teeth. 'Well, I think I've an idea who these souls of yours may be. But I still haven't a clue who *you* are. Or what your connection with them is.'

I hesitated only a moment. 'My name's Corley Roper.'

He took my hand, then leaned back and scrutinized me, his eyes wide with surprise.

'The Mr. Largo Frog kind of Corley Roper?'

'Yes.'

He started to laugh. 'Well, that answers the first question, at least.'

'I . . . Well, the truth is, Mr. Studd, I met a woman. Purely by chance. And was so . . . moved by her predicament that I decided to try to help her.'

'When you say a woman, you are talking about the . . . the child, I take it?'

'Yes. Only she's not a child any more.'

'No, no, of course not. She'd be, what, thirty now?'

'About that.'

'And what has become of her?'

Since he had guessed so much already, I could see no reason not to tell him.

'She's married. Not very happily, I think. To a curate in Derbyshire.'

'Ah. And your reasoning is, what, that if she could be reconciled with her mother, she might be *less* unhappy?'

'More or less.'

'I see.' He hesitated, then added: 'And the mother too, perhaps?'

'Perhaps. But of course, I don't know her. What sort of a person she is.'

'A stiff-necked sort of a person. But we can none of us be happy if we don't acknowledge our sins, and ask God to forgive them.'

For perhaps half a minute he didn't speak again, but seemed to be pursuing some train of thought of his own, leaving me to reflect on what he had said. *Thirty, would she be now? A stiff-necked sort of a person.* It was as if, entirely unexpectedly, he had been giving me a kind of a shadow-play performance of Mary Wilson's story, in which the characters were faceless, and yet it was taken for granted that we both knew who they were. And the miracle was that, thanks to the hints and scraps I had picked up on the way, I *did* know – enough, at any rate, to follow the broad gist of what he was telling me. It was frustrating, of course, that I could not understand more; but I feared that if I revealed the extent of my ignorance by asking him to be more explicit, he might clam up altogether.

'Do you know what I thought?' he said, turning to me suddenly, with a laugh. 'I thought you must be a blackmailer, and I should have to box your ears, and call the police. But you didn't seem quite the type . . . And then when I heard your name . . . You do quite well enough out of yarn-spinning, I imagine, not to have to resort to *that* sort of a crime.'

'You make it sound as if the yarn-spinning's just *another* sort of crime.'

He laughed again, more loudly. 'Do I? Well, I have to say, there was a time, when our girls were small, that I might have thought so. You could put them to bed and tell them a story about the young Jesus, but there'd be no chance of getting them to go to sleep until they'd had a visit from Alcuin Hare and Mr. Largo Frog. I began to despair, thinking we'd spawned four little heathens. But they soon all decided for Christ, thank God, so that was all right.' He paused in front of a park-bench, and, patting the back, said:

'I say, would you mind waiting here for a moment?'

I sat down. He walked fifty yards on to the grass, then dropped to his knees and began to pray. I looked away, towards a cavalcade of riders on Rotten Row; but there was something so fascinatingly alien about a man who was prepared to make such a public spectacle of his private convictions that, embarrassed though I was, I could not keep my eyes from drifting back to him.

After five minutes or so he got up again, and returned to the bench, walking with a cricketer's lope, as if he were carrying an invisible bat.

'You say you met her purely by chance,' he said, as he settled himself beside me. 'And you probably think *we* met by chance, too. But a Christian looks at things differently. Where you see chance, *he* sees the hand of the Lord at work. Or the hand of the Devil.' He turned towards me and smiled. 'Normally it isn't hard to tell which it is. But just occasionally you get a poser like this one. And then there's nothing for it but to ask the Lord Himself.'

I couldn't think of a response that wouldn't sound sarcastic or defensive, so I merely nodded. When he saw I wasn't going to challenge him, he went on:

'I had to find out why He sent you to *me*, you see – rather than to my mother, say, or one of my brothers. And I know the answer now. None of them would have helped you. Too much family pride for that. Too much anger. *She had her chance*, they'd say, *and she rejected it; and she must go her own way to hell.* Whereas I don't care a fig for family pride, if it stands in the way of *anyone* being kept from hell. God knows my sister would never let *me* bring her to the rescue shop. So He's picked you for the job instead.'

My mouth was dry. I said: 'Well, naturally, I . . . I hope to be of some service to them . . . But I doubt if I'm quite equal to that, I'm afraid.'

'Of course you doubt it. We all doubt it. We just have to open ourselves to the Lord, and ask Him to fill us with His Holy Spirit. Only put your trust in Him, *truly*, and He won't fail you, I promise.'

I was at a loss. To accept his assistance on those terms seemed shabby, if not downright dishonest; and yet to refuse it would not simply be churlish, but would rob me of my best – and probably my only – chance of doing what I had set out to do. Before I could resolve the issue one way or the other, he unclipped a fountain pen from his pocket and said:

'Have you got some paper?'

I handed him my notebook. As he started to write he murmured:

'I shouldn't tell her how you got this, at least to begin with. If she knows it came from me, it'll only make her close her heart to you, and to God. Here.'

He screwed the cap on to his pen again, and held the notebook out to me, together with the prayer-book. But – as if, despite his protestations, he still could not suppress the queasy sense that he was betraying a family secret, and wanted to spare himself the sight of my actually reading it – he did not let go of them until he had shaken my hand, and was turning to leave.

'God bless you,' he said. And, without so much as another glance, started hurriedly back towards his mother's house.

In deference to his feelings, I did not look at what he had written at once, but sat down on the bench again, and waited a few moments before finally letting my eyes drift towards the page – so casually that anyone watching me would have assumed he had given me nothing more contentious than the address of his tailor.

It was as well I did. What he had written was:

Mrs. Samuel Cooper, 109, Gipsy Hill, Lambeth.

It was so utterly *not* what I had expected that I had to re-read it a few times to get it clear in my head. My first thought then was that somehow Studd and I must have misunderstood each other, and been talking about different people. *Cooper*, after all, was the name of Mary's guardian, not her parents. And it was inconceivable, surely, that my journey from Hampshire to Paris to Hallaton to Hyde Park Gardens should end at such a dowdily mundane destination as 109, Gipsy Hill, Lambeth?

But then I reflected that it was Mary's old housekeeper in

Cabourg who had given me the prayer-book – and that when I had mentioned its connection to a small girl abandoned by her mother thirty years ago, Studd had not only seemed entirely unsurprised, but had even provided some of the details himself. What were the chances of the same book being associated with two almost identical cases – and of the name *Cooper* featuring in both of them? Almost non-existent. Far more likely was that we *had* both been talking about Mary, but that my knowledge – derived almost entirely from Mary herself – was so limited and partial that it had given me a fatally distorted picture of her story.

I quickly looked up, and saw what I thought was Studd vanishing among the crowds that were surging into the park to enjoy the evening sunshine. I could still run after him, and make a full confession of how little I actually knew. But to do that would be tantamount to admitting that I had been acting under false pretences – which could only shake his confidence in me, and make him repent of having helped me at all.

I looked down again at the prize I had gone to such lengths to get. It suddenly appeared as flimsy and valueless as a counterfeit bank-note. It told me where I could find Mary Wilson's mother – but as to how I might contrive a meeting with her, or persuade her to acknowledge her long-lost daughter, it gave me not the slightest hint. And what, anyway, if I succeeded? Was it really conceivable that an anguish as profound as Mary Wilson's could just be magicked away by a kindly word or two from Mrs. Samuel Cooper of 109, Gipsy Hill, Lambeth?

Watching the paper fluttering in the breeze, I was all at once overwhelmed by the most tremendous tiredness. It bore down on me, scattering my thoughts before I could begin to assemble them into any kind of logical sequence. There was no point in even trying to think about what I should do next until I had slept.

I trudged back to the hotel, told the owner I should not be requiring dinner, and went straight to bed.

*

At some point during the night I woke up suddenly. Or so, at least, it seemed: I can't be certain that I wasn't still unconscious, and merely *dreamed* I had woken. At all events, when I came to – or imagined I did – I was no longer lying down, but found that in my sleep I had somehow managed to get out of bed, switch on the lamp, and settle myself on the stool next to the dressing-table. Since I had never sleep-walked before, this should have surprised me; but it didn't. So utterly unaware of myself was I, indeed, that if, at that moment, you had asked me to recall a single incident from my life, or even to tell you my name, I doubt if I would have been able to do it. All that interested me was the clutter of objects I had taken from my pocket the night before and spread out in front of the looking-glass: notebook, wallet, pen, change, prayer-book . . .

Prayer-book. I couldn't have said that was what it was called, but I knew it was the thing I wanted. I reached for it, and set it on my knee. As I started to thumb through it, I was startled by the sight of my own hands. Their shape and colour looked familiar enough; but there was something clumsy and tentative about the way they moved, as if some usurper were trying to take control of them, and had not yet succeeded in fully mastering the complex machinery of nerve and muscle.

We were at the Psalms now. I was racing through the pages, flitting from one paragraph to the next but assimilating nothing. Again, I had the vertiginous feeling that my eyes had been commandeered by someone else, who was using them to look for something quite specific. But what it was, and why he wanted to find it, I had not the least idea.

And then all at once we stopped, and I found myself reading: *Cast me not away from thy presence.*

Consciousness seemed to be returning to me now, like feeling to a numbed limb. And suddenly I was awake enough to realize what was happening.

'Is that you, old fellow?' I said.

In my temple, I heard – or sensed – a sort of involuntary gasp, as if he were astonished to have been so easily found out.

'Don't worry,' I said. 'Don't be frightened.' And then, when there was no response: 'I'd been wondering what had become of you. I thought perhaps you'd left.'

There was a soughing noise, like the wind whining through an empty attic.

Where would I have gone?

The voice was different: a child's, still, but no longer babyish.

'I don't know,' I said.

There's nowhere I can go.

'Oh, I'm sure that isn't true,' I said brightly. But the truth was I *wasn't* sure. I had always assumed that when I had brought Mary Wilson and her mother together again, the unquiet ghost in my head would be satisfied, and leave me again. But, now I came to reflect upon it, I had had no *reason* to believe that. And I had given no thought at all to what would happen to it if I failed.

You are going to throw me out.

'No, no, old fellow . . .'

Yes. I know it. You're getting ready to abandon us . . .

'Not at all. As a matter of fact, I'm getting ready to go and see your grandmother –'

There was a sudden thumping on the wall, and a muffled voice from the next room called:

'Keep it down, will you! Some of us are trying to sleep!'

I thought I heard a faint intake of breath just above my ear. And then – as if it feared being taken for a trouble-maker, and expelled without further ado – the child was silent again.

'Don't fret,' I whispered, as I crawled back into bed. 'We'll work something out, I promise.'

I awoke, in the morning, with the consciousness that there was some momentous decision I had to make. As soon as I tried to focus my mind on it, however, I felt giddy with panic. So I gave up, and walked to my lawyer's in Gray's Inn Square to collect my letters instead.

The clerk, a thin, fidgety man with a prematurely lined face and a fine dusting of scurf on his collar, put on a great charade of searching for my post, scanning shelves, and peering into piles of documents that looked as if they had been there since the eighteenth century – all the while making exasperated little *tck-tck*s with his tongue that suggested his time was precious, and he really shouldn't have to waste it doing something so menial. At last he tugged open the bottom drawer of his desk, and, after rooting around for a few seconds, drew out a modest bundle held together with a rubber band.

'There you are,' he muttered, jabbing it towards me.

'Thank you.' I slipped it into my pocket, then retreated to a bench in the Inn gardens, where I knew I should be able to read undisturbed.

I had ten letters in all, which seemed a meagre crop for the time I had been away. The first was from Jessop, asking whether I had got home safely from Langley Mill, and was recovered from my illness. Most of the others were predictably dull: a bill from Dr. Enticknap; another nagging note from my publisher; and a letter from some poor fellow trying to establish himself as a wine merchant who would be *honoured to receive my order* for almost anything that comes in a bottle. One, though, I saw – there was no mistaking the hand-writing this time – was from Miss Dangerfield.

I set it aside until I had finished ploughing through the others, and returned them to their envelopes. Then, with a tiny tremor of excitement, I slit it open. Inside were two closely written sheets. I unfolded them and read:

My dear –
   I have been debating for days how I should begin this letter.
'My dear Mr. Roper' sounds so coldly formal; 'My dear Corley'

dreadfully familiar. I even consulted an etiquette book – only to find, of course, that it was all about calling cards and how to address a baronet, and had no useful advice to offer a young woman in my situation at all. This morning it finally dawned on me that I might knock the question back and forth for a year without finding an answer, and that if I meant to write at all, I must do so without one. So, as you see, I have left a blank, which you may fill in as you please.

I wanted first to thank you again for a delightful evening in Cabourg: it was very good of you to take pity on me, and gather me up as you did. And second, I feel I owe you an apology for my conduct that night. You did me the honour of confiding in me; and the manner in which I responded must have appeared cold and unsympathetic. My true feelings, I promise you, were neither of those things. But I did not express them as I should; and for that I ask your forgiveness.

I am back in London now, and will be staying at Fleming's Hotel until April 25, when I at last sail for America. It seems barely credible that in less than a month I shall be in Albany again, surrounded by people who have never seen the Eiffel Tower or Piccadilly Circus, or met you. I have no idea where _you_ are, or how – if at all – this letter will find its way to you. But if it happened to reach you in time, and you felt inclined to let me know how you are, and how your quest is progressing, I should be very happy.

Very sincerely yours,
Alice Dangerfield

I re-read it twice. And then – as gingerly as I could, so that even the strange presence in my head should not be alerted to what I was doing – I folded it up again, and slipped it into the inside pocket of my coat.

Its almost imperceptible pressure against my chest, as I made my way back to the hotel, was curiously reassuring, for some reason. It seemed to work on me like a talisman, soothing my doubts, and allowing me to start thinking lucidly again. By the time I reached Sussex Gardens, I felt sufficiently calm and clear-headed to confront the huge unresolved question that I had left in abeyance since the previous evening: how was I going to approach Emily Cooper?

XV

There was a small writing-table in my room. I sat down at it, and took a thick sheaf of paper from the drawer. Then I started to make a list of everything I knew – or could confidently guess – about my quarry.

It turned out that I had more than I had expected – enough, in all, to cover nearly three sides: her maiden name; her family circumstances; her childhood in Hallaton; and the fact that her return there as an adult was somehow connected with the disgrace of the local doctor. Thanks to John Pick and C. T. Studd – whose accounts were strikingly similar – I had some idea of her character. I had seen the enormous trouble and expense she had gone to to keep Mary in ignorance of her identity. I knew her current name and address, and had strong grounds for believing – however improbable it might seem – that the man she had married was also Mary's guardian.

These were only isolated fragments, of course; but – just as a few random highlights can sometimes be enough to give you the whole shape of a wild animal crouching in the shadows – they could be assembled into a more or less coherent pattern, from which it should be possible to fill in some of the gaps, and get a sense of what kind of a plan of attack was most likely to be effective.

It was obvious, to begin with, that I was dealing with an obstinate, strong-willed woman, who had ruthlessly set out to create a life in which she would be insulated, as far as possible, from the consequences of whatever it was she had done more than thirty years before. And it was equally clear – otherwise, what was I doing here? – that she had very largely succeeded. To take the conventional route, therefore, by writing and asking for a meeting, would be as useless as trying to seize a besieged castle by knocking on the portcullis: if my letter told her everything, and ended with a passionate plea for her to acknowledge Mary, she would simply ignore it, as she had presumably ignored appeals to her better nature in the past; if, on the other hand, I hinted darkly that I knew something about her life that I wished to discuss with her, she would naturally assume I was threatening her, and become even more defensive. I should face exactly the same problem if I managed to cultivate an acquaintance with one of her friends, and contrive an introduction to her at some social event. As long as she was on familiar ground, and could easily retreat behind the barriers she had erected to protect herself, I was doomed. My only hope was to wait for her to emerge for a moment into the open, as it were, and then take her completely by surprise.

But how? That was where my limited stock of knowledge finally failed me.

On an impulse, I pulled on my coat and set off for Victoria, where I was just in time to catch the 4.10 for all stations to Stoat's Nest.

I had never been to Gipsy Hill before; but I imagined it – despite the romance of its name – as one of those soulless Victorian suburbs where the buildings are so uniform that they look as if they have been taken out of a giant toy-box, and spread across the landscape with no thought of what had been there before. And I was not far wrong, as it turned out: after an uncomfortable half-hour journey wedged between two heavily sweating gentlemen reading newspapers, I emerged to find myself in a long sloping street lined with squat, frumpy houses and parades of identical flat-fronted shops that stretched almost unbroken to the horizon. Even on a pleasant spring evening, with birds singing and hazy sunshine mottling the endless progression of unadorned brick with faint patterns of light and shadow, it made a depressing sight. *We're plain, practical people here*, it seemed to say, *who understand the way of the world, and you shan't fool us into parting with a penny for what you're pleased to call beauty.*

A quick glance at the buildings either side of the station told me that number 109 must be down the hill. It took me only a couple of minutes to find it: an utterly unremarkable red-brick villa, set well back from the street, with the name *Oaklands* engraved on the gate. There was a pleasant garden, with a couple of little bridges, each covered by a rustic pergola, leading across the herbaceous border separating the gravel sweep from the front lawn; and the house itself – tall, and square, with steps up to the door, and a generous bay under a steep gable jutting out to one side of it – looked comfortable enough. But it seemed too large for its plot, like a fat schoolboy jammed into a row of equally ungainly fellows; and, fanciful though the idea was, I could not help imagining that – for all its effort to appear imposing – it was somehow aware of how pitifully it compared with Hallaton Hall and Hyde Park Gardens, and the knowledge had made it sour.

I looked around for some vantage-point from which I could observe the place unnoticed. Facing it, on the other side of the road, was a long, narrow strip of greenery fringed with trees. Thinking I might find a bench there, where I should be able to sit and pretend to read without drawing attention to myself, I crossed towards it – only to discover that it was not a modern public park, as I had supposed, but a strange little remnant of farmland, hemmed in by a wire fence, and with a five-bar gate at the top, that had somehow been left behind in the rush to transform Gipsy Hill from countryside into suburb.

I found a wicket-gate, and went in. As I did so, a mass of crows rose cawing from the branches of a fallen oak lying at the far end. Apart from a solitary cat hunting among the thistles, there were no animals to be seen, but the rough tussocky ground was dotted with fresh cow-pats. I picked my way among them, relishing the spring of the long grass under my feet, and took up position behind a young lime tree directly opposite number 109. The trunk was too narrow to conceal me completely, but the canopy of overhanging branches meant I should be visible only from the ground-floor windows. And if somebody appeared in one of them, I would simply bend down, like a walker who has paused for a moment to re-tie his boot, and then move on again.

For almost two hours I stood there, as the air cooled, and the shadows grew longer and fainter, and finally melted away altogether in the deepening dusk. In all that time, though there was an almost constant traffic to and from the neighbouring houses, no one either came to Oaklands or left it. Then, just as the clock from a nearby church struck half-past six, lights appeared – first in the basement, and then in the hall. A couple of minutes later, an elderly man walked stiffly into view from the direction of the station and slowed in front of number 109. As he turned in at the gate, I caught, in the glow from a street-lamp, a fleeting glimpse of a pale, tired face, with heavy bags under the eyes, and a straggly grey moustache. It was hard to believe this was Emily's husband: he looked closer to the age I should have expected her father to have been. But – after struggling painfully up the steps to the front door – he went inside without ringing, taking off his hat and glancing down at the letters on the hall table with the unmistakable air of the master of the house returning home.

I was still trying to square this frail old figure with the picture I had formed of Mr. Cooper – a man whose ability to manage every detail of Mary's upbringing and preserve the secret of her parentage had imbued him, in my imagination, with almost superhuman powers – when I heard a sudden commotion at the top end of the field. I spun round, and saw a herd of cows being chivvied through the five-bar gate by two men and a dog. Not wanting to have to explain my presence there, I edged quickly along the line of trees, and managed to slip out through the wicket before I was spotted.

It was already clear, from the little I had seen, that Emily Cooper's life would not easily open itself to me; and that if I were to find an opportunity to accost her, I must be prepared to keep the house under surveillance for several days. The question was: how could I do it without arousing her suspicion?

I wrestled with this conundrum all the way back to my hotel. By the time I got there, I thought I had the answer.

After breakfast the following morning, I walked to Cornelissen and Son in Great Queen Street, and bought myself a sketch-book, a box of charcoal and a folding stool. Then I made my way back to Victoria, and by mid-day was walking down Gipsy Hill again. The cattle raised their heads and watched with sullen curiosity as I entered the field, opened the stool beneath the lime, sat down, and – squinting at them, in what I hoped was a convincing impersonation of an artist sizing up his subject – began to draw their collective portrait. It took me several attempts; but after an hour or so, I had finally succeeded in producing something that seemed just about competent enough to justify the pretence that I was an enthusiastic amateur enjoying a day's sketching in a picturesque spot.

I had just finished, and was starting to try my hand at a general view of the field and the cluster of buildings beyond, when out of the corner of my eye I noticed a flicker of movement in front of number 109. I glanced towards it as discreetly as I could, and saw two women climbing the steps to the front door. One of them was leading a small black spaniel, which, in its eagerness to get inside, barged against her legs, almost knocking her off balance. She grabbed the handle to steady herself, then started to turn towards the street, as if she imagined someone might have witnessed her near-accident and be laughing at her. I dropped my gaze; but not quickly enough to avoid seeing a strong, jowly profile, with a prominent nose and heavy black eyebrows. I dared not look again; but I turned to a new page, and, my heart thumping, dashed off a quick sketch of it. When I at last had the thing to my satisfaction, I was pretty certain I was looking at an image of Mary Wilson's mother.

It was a fair bet that they had come home for lunch, and that I could count on their remaining there for at least an hour or two while I went in search of something to eat myself. But I was too excited to relish the thought of a steak-and-kidney pudding in a smoky pub; and by the time my appetite returned, it was too late. So all afternoon I stayed doggedly at my post, waiting for something else to happen.

It never did. There was a constant hammering and shouting from the builders working on a rash of new houses further down the hill, and every half-minute or so a wagon or a motor-lorry would trundle past, laden with bricks or timber; but number 109 seemed to have lapsed back into a state of suspended animation. At about four o'clock, I noticed a thin stream of sulphurous smoke starting to drift from the chimney. Otherwise, there was no sign of life at all.

By the time the dairy-men arrived to round up the cows for their evening milking, it was pretty obvious that Emily Cooper meant to be at home for the rest of the day. Rather than continuing to wear myself out to no purpose, I decided, I should conserve my energy for the morning – when, if today's experience was anything to go by, I should have a better chance of seeing her.

And so it turned out. At nine the next day, I was back in the field. At a quarter past, the door to Oaklands opened, and Mrs. Cooper appeared, leading the little spaniel on a leash, and accompanied, this time, by two younger women. I started to pack up my things, but remained sitting down until they had reached the street and set off up Gipsy Hill. Then I quickly folded up my stool, and – after giving them a hundred-yard start – slipped out of the wicket-gate and began to follow them.

They passed the station, then crossed the road and halted at the entrance to a side-street. They seemed to be debating which way they should go, because one of the younger women was pointing towards a cross-roads further up the hill, while Emily Cooper stood repeatedly shaking her head. After fifteen seconds or so the younger woman capitulated with a nod, and they disappeared from view. I hurried after them, and reached the corner just in time to see Emily Cooper, magnanimous in victory, drawing her two companions to her and walking arm in arm with them down the middle of the road, with the dog scampering eagerly ahead, like a small tug pulling three ships under sail. As they swayed along together, so nearly in step that they looked as if they were dancing to the same inaudible music, it was impossible to mistake the easy air of familiarity and affection between them. For one instant, I had the odd sensation that I and Mary Wilson and her still-born son were all looking at them through the same pair of eyes, and I had to bite my lip to keep from yelping with anger and despair.

Apart from a delivery boy on a bicycle and a couple of women scrubbing doorsteps, we were the only people in the street; and – knowing how conspicuous I must appear, with my stool and artist's sketch-book – I hung back, in case one of the Coopers glanced behind them. For ten minutes or more I trailed them through a web of modest little terraces, losing them at one corner, and then catching sight of them again at the next. Finally, they emerged into a bustling, shop-lined road running at right angles to Gipsy Hill. A second or two later they stopped, as a respectable-looking man in a dark suit intercepted them, raising his hat.

I was, of course, too far away to hear what they said; but I noticed that Mrs. Cooper retreated a step or two, making a great show of managing the dog, and leaving the burden of carrying on a conversation to the two younger women. The fellow – I should have taken him for a prosperous tradesman, or perhaps the manager of a bank – at first seemed slightly taken aback by her reserve; but he soon adjusted to the situation, and stood turning from one daughter to the other, with the pursed-up little smile of an older man plying a younger woman with gallantries. After a minute or so he lifted his hat again and hurried off, and they continued on their way.

As soon as I turned into the main road I guessed where they were going. There on the horizon, looming up incongruously between the drab rows of shops like a pagoda, was one of the Crystal Palace water-towers. I followed them into the park, and along the upper terrace running in front of the Palace itself. Even though I had been here as a boy and knew what to expect, I was still shocked by the sheer scale of the place. I stopped, and for a few seconds stood staring up in childish awe at the massive central bay, with its huge ziggurat steps crowned by a gargantuan arch. For all its impressive size, it seemed somehow to have grown tired and frail since my last visit, like a giant green-house left untended in a corner of the garden, giving you the unpleasant sense that at the first puff of breeze the whole thing might come tumbling down on top of you.

I shook myself free of its spell and looked about for the Coopers again, but they had already disappeared in the sea of hats eddying in front of the building. I quickly made my way to the far end, keeping close to the wall, where the crowd was thinnest, but I could not spot them in the crush. I looped round and went back along the other side of the terrace, scanning the faces coming towards me, but there was still no sign of them.

I began to wonder if they had somehow realized I was following them, and deliberately given me the slip. But then, as I was approaching the main entrance again, I heard an excited yapping coming from the park below; and, looking down, saw the little dog tearing wildly across the grass, watched by the two younger women, who were perched together on the edge of an ornamental pond, smiling at its antics. But I could not immediately see their mother; so I squeezed my way into the line of people ranged along the balustrade, and began searching the garden for her.

As I did so, the spaniel spun round and bolted back towards the pond, running so furiously that it seemed bound to overshoot and end up in the water. But at the very last moment it spreadeagled to a halt, and streaked off in another direction. The two young women got to their feet, weeping with laughter, and stood gazing up at the terrace, like a couple of comedians acknowledging the applause of the crowd. Their likeness to Mary Wilson, now I could see them clearly, was striking: they both had the same pale delicate skin and dark hair and strong eyebrows. But it was the relationship of two healthy young flowers to a withered bud: where she frowned suspiciously at the world, they beamed confidently at it, certain of its admiration.

For a moment I had the unnerving impression they must somehow have sensed my interest in them, because they seemed to be looking directly at me. Then I heard a low, knowing laugh to my left. Turning towards it, I saw Emily Cooper leaning on the balustrade, gazing down at her daughters with an expression – complicit and tender and ruthlessly oblivious to everything else around her – that reminded me of a buzzard or a kite surveying its young.

She was so near that I could have reached out and touched her. I edged a couple of inches closer. She must have noticed the movement out of the corner of her eye, but did not allow it to divert her attention for even a fraction of a second. She fluttered her fingers at the younger women. They waved back, turned and started sauntering after the dog, whistling and calling to it, and then – when, instead of coming to them, it merely twitched its ears quizzically and rushed off again – doubling over with laughter at its naughtiness. The sound of their voices grew fainter, until – after a couple of minutes – they were out of earshot altogether.

Emily Cooper was still watching them, bent over the parapet

with her elbows splayed and her face bracketed in her hands, as if she were fixed to the stone. It would be the easiest thing in the world for me to lean down and whisper something to her. She could, of course, move away, but only at the risk of making a spectacle of herself – which everything I had seen of her so far suggested she would be reluctant to do. And if she tried to recall her daughters, and take refuge behind them again, they wouldn't be able to hear her.

I had visualized talking to her somewhere less exposed, and with fewer unknown quantities to contend with: in a tea-room, say; or a railway compartment. But there was no guarantee – however long I followed her – that fate would throw me together with her in such a setting. There was no guarantee, in fact, that it would throw me together with her *anywhere*. This might be the only opportunity I should ever get.

I eased myself on to the balustrade beside her. I was close enough now to feel the heat of her body against my hand and cheek. I ran a few phrases through my head, before deciding that only one could be sure of really harpooning her.

I turned towards her, silently mouthing *Mary Stone, Mary Stone*.

I could not have said what it was that stopped me. Nothing she said or did, certainly: even now, she gave not the slightest sign that she was aware of my presence. Perhaps that very indifference, in circumstances where most people could not have helped responding, either by returning my gaze or retreating from it, persuaded me that I should not be able to penetrate the invisible no man's land she had created around herself.

For a second or two I stood there, studying the obstinate set of her heavy mouth and snuffing the warm bedroom smell of rosewater on her skin. Then, as quietly as I could, I gathered up my things, and set off for the railway station.

XVI

The next morning I was up early, intending to take the 8.20 from Victoria and be back opposite the house again by nine. But I was aware, as I went down to breakfast, that I felt none of the excitement about it that I had the day before. My legs were leaden; I had virtually no appetite; and when I peered out through the dining-room window, the world outside had that cold, flattened-out greyness it seems to take on when you have some thankless duty to perform.

My porridge tasted of soap. I pushed it away after a couple of mouthfuls, then fell at the first hurdle with the scrambled eggs, which stuck like rubber to my palate, making me retch. Perhaps, I thought, I had caught a chill standing in the field, and was sickening for something. If so, the sensible thing would not be to drive myself back to Gipsy Hill, but to take a day off. I was pretty certain I knew Emily Cooper's routine now; and there would be nothing to be lost if I delayed going after her again for twenty-four or forty-eight hours. In fact, there would be everything to be gained, because it was essential that, when I did finally speak to her, I was absolutely at my best.

I went up to my room, and – though I had had no conscious thought of doing it when I left the table – immediately began fumbling in my jacket for Miss Dangerfield's letter. She was leaving, it said, on the 25th. Today was the 24th.

Some nannyish voice told me that if I was well enough to see Miss Dangerfield, I was well enough to go to Gipsy Hill. But it was too late now to catch the 8.20; and the next train would almost certainly not get me there until after Emily Cooper had left her house. And, besides, had I not already persuaded myself that Emily Cooper would be there tomorrow – whereas Alice Dangerfield, I knew, would be gone?

I put on my coat; and – taking care to avoid Hyde Park Gardens – made my way across the park and down Piccadilly. I had not given much thought to where Miss Dangerfield would choose to stay in London; but when I turned into Half-Moon Street and saw Fleming's Hotel, it seemed reassuringly in keeping with her character: an unpretentious, quietly elegant place, formed out of two Georgian terraced houses.

The hall smelt pleasantly of starch and furniture polish and spring flowers. I asked the soberly dressed man at the desk if Miss Dangerfield was in.

'Miss Dangerfield?'

'Yes.'

He glanced down, looking for something among the pile of papers in front of him. 'Would you be Mr. . . . Mr. – ?'

'Roper.'

He nodded, although his face had a slightly pained expression, as though that were not quite what he had expected to hear. 'I think you'll find her in there, sir.'

She was sitting in a window at the far end of the lounge, reading a book. On the table in front of her was a large vase of daffodils that gave her bowed head a faint yellow halo. She was so engrossed in what she was doing that it was only when I had gone the entire length of the room and stopped in front of her that she finally looked up. Her eyes widened. She dropped the book, and her hand sprang like a jack-in-the-box to her throat.

'Good morning,' I said.

'Good . . . Oh . . . My gracious . . .'

'You're waiting for someone else, I know –'

'Yes.' She seemed confused. She swallowed, flushed, then searched the wall for the clock. Watching her, I could not suppress a spasm of jealousy – made all the worse by the knowledge that I had no business feeling it.

'So I won't detain you,' I said. 'I simply wanted to say goodbye.'

She hesitated a moment, then got up and took my out-stretched hand. 'I *would* have been waiting for *you*, if I'd known,' she said, with a directness that made the back of my neck prickle.

'Yes, I know, it was dreadfully rude of me to turn up unan-nounced like this. But I've not been back in town long, and –'

'It doesn't matter. It's just rather a shame, that's all.'

I nodded. 'I'm sorry. Anyway . . .' I started to withdraw, then stopped and said: 'Would you be free later on, by any chance? For lunch, say?'

'No, I'm afraid I have appointments all day.'

'Then for dinner, perhaps?'

She shook her head, colouring more deeply. 'I'm sorry.'

'Well, in that case –'

'But the gentleman I'm expecting', she said hurriedly, glancing at the clock again, 'won't be here until half-past eleven, which gives us almost an hour. So why don't you sit down – if you'd like to – and – ?'

'Are you sure you can spare the time? It looks as if you're rather busy.'

'Oh, I was just trying to finish his book before he gets here, that's all.'

'Well, I should probably leave you to it, then, shouldn't I?'

She wavered for a second, then said:

'No, no, that's all right.'

'You're sure?'

She nodded. I sat down opposite her. She studied me for a moment with an odd expression I had never seen before: eyelids half-lowered, head slightly to one side, as if she feared her gaze might give away too much, and she was all ready to avert it.

'So,' I said. 'How are you?'

'Oh . . . quite well, thank you.'

'Authors all doing as they're told?'

She gave a laugh that sounded more like a cough. 'With one exception.'

'Oh, Lord, you're not going to tell me, I hope, that Mr. G. K. Chesterton made an improper suggestion to you?'

She smiled – but awkwardly, compressing her lips and twisting them, so they looked like a squirl of unrolled pastry. And, indeed, even to my ear, the avuncular playfulness of my tone rang false. It might be appropriate to a conversation between an author and a young journalist who admired his work; but that, as she had acknowledged in her letter, no longer adequately described our relationship – though what it had become instead, and what the rules were for it, I could not have said.

'And how about you?' she said. 'Did you find out who they were?'

'I beg your pardon?'

'The parents of that poor woman? Mary Wilson?'

'Oh, yes. Well, no, not her *parents*. But I think I've traced her mother.'

'Really?'

I nodded. 'The day after we . . . we last met, I had a stroke of luck. I was given a prayer-book with a name in it. And that name took me to a village in Leicestershire. And from there back to London, and to a grand house in Hyde Park Gardens.'

'Gracious! How very *Lady Audley's Secret*. Am I allowed to know what it is? The name, I mean?'

'No one you'll have heard of, I'm sure.'

'Still . . .'

I had the powerful sense that I should be betraying someone if I told her. But when I tried to work out *who*, exactly, I couldn't: neither Mary nor her mother even knew what I was doing, and the only person who did, C. T. Studd, had not told me anything in absolute confidence.

'Studd,' I said.

'A *Miss* Studd?'

'Once upon a time. Now Mrs. Cooper.'

'But you've no idea who the father was?'

'Not really.'

'So what makes you think she's the mother?'

I told her everything I had been able to piece together from my visit to Hallaton and my conversation with Studd. When I had finished, she nodded and said:

'And is she still alive?'

'Yes.'

'Do you know where she lives?'

'Better than that. I've seen the house.'

'*Really?*'

'I've seen *her*. Twenty-four hours ago I was standing closer to her than I am to you now.'

'Oh, my.' She pressed her hands together, in a gesture that reminded me so vividly of Elspeth readying herself for the dénouement of an Alcuin Hare adventure that my heart skitted. 'And what did she say?'

'Nothing.'

'She refused to speak to you?'

'I didn't give her the chance. I walked away.'

'Why?'

'Well, it was a tricky situation. We were in Crystal Palace park – which, if you've been there, you'll know isn't really the ideal spot for an intimate *tête-à-tête*.'

'No, I can imagine. But –'

'I'm like a big-game hunter, you see. I've got just one shot; and if I miss with that, my prey will be off, and I'll never see her again. So I've got to make sure the conditions are right before I finally pull the trigger.'

Plausible – but I knew even as I said it that I was putting a rational gloss on an entirely *irrational* act. The uncomfortable fact was that I *had* intended to speak to Emily Cooper, and then balked at the last second – and there was nothing to say that, when it came to it, I would not do so again.

Miss Dangerfield did not reply at once, but frowned intently at me, as if she knew I had been lying, and was trying to burrow out the truth. Finally she said:

'But how can you be sure the conditions will *ever* be right?'

'I must just bide my time until they are.'

She gave a slight shake of the head.

'You don't think that's reasonable, in the circumstances?'

She sighed. 'Oh, I don't know. Maybe. I just . . .' She hesitated a moment, then snapped her mouth shut, guillotining the end of the sentence.

'No, go on, please.'

She shook her head again. After a moment she folded her hands across her stomach and hunched forward, clutching herself.

'Are you cold?' I said.

She glanced towards the window. 'A little.'

'Shall we have coffee, to warm you up?'

She nodded. I summoned the waiter hovering inside the door. As he was leaving, I said:

'You just what?'

'I'm not sure I ought to say . . . I . . . You did get my letter, did-n't you?'

'Of course.'

'So what's the answer?'

It took me a second to remember. 'Oh, Corley or Mr. Roper, you mean?'

'Yes.'

'Oh, Corley, please.'

'Thank you. But your just saying it doesn't make it right. What would be *proper* . . . In the . . . you know . . .?'

For a moment, the invisible curtain separating her conscious-ness from mine seemed to dissolve, and we saw the same memory in each other's eyes. I felt myself starting to blush, and looked away.

'I'm blowed if I know, to be honest,' I said.

She gave a rueful grimace. 'Only if I knew a Mr. Joshua So-and-so in America, and it was proper for me to call him Joshua, I could say things to him I couldn't while he was still Mr. So-and-so.'

'Well, I should certainly prefer it if you felt able to say those things to me.'

She nodded again. 'Then what you just told me – about Mrs. Cooper – makes me very uneasy.'

'Really? I don't see why it should.'

'Because I think you're deceiving yourself. You've been looking for this woman for weeks. Against all the odds, you've succeeded in finding her. But then, when a perfect opportunity presents itself to speak to her, you lose your nerve, and decide it isn't quite perfect enough, and you'd better leave it for another time. And I can imagine you doing the same thing over and over again for the rest of your life, if you're not careful – steeling yourself to say something, and then at the last minute finding some excuse not to.'

I wanted to protest, but the heat in my face betrayed me.

'You're frightened to bring things to a head,' she went on. 'Because if she spurns your good offices and refuses to be reconciled to her daughter – and the chances are, after all this time, that she will – then there's nothing more you can do. That will be the end of the matter.' She paused for a moment, then leaned towards me and said quietly: 'And I suspect what you're really afraid of is waking up the next morning and remembering what has happened. And all of a sudden thinking: *I have nothing to live for.*'

I tried to say *Oh, I don't think it's quite as bad as that*, but a pain like cramp had closed my throat. What saved me was the arrival of the waiter with our coffee. As he was setting out the cups, I forced myself to look again into the mirror Miss Dangerfield had unexpectedly held up to me – and came to the startling conclusion that she understood my feelings better than I did.

'And the idea of that saddens me,' she said, when the fellow had left again. 'Because I had hoped that perhaps by now . . . You would have seen . . . You would have realized . . . That there *are* other things.'

I recovered my voice enough to say: 'You're very perspicacious.'

She smiled quickly. 'Not really. I've been thinking a lot about you, that's all.' She hesitated, as if she were about to elaborate – then appeared to think better of it, and picked up the book from her lap. 'This has helped, in an odd way,' she said, tapping the spine against her palm, like a lecturer emphasizing some important point.

'What is it?' I said, craning to see the title.

'It's called *The Serpent and the Dove*.'

I shook my head. 'No, sorry, never heard of it, I'm afraid.'

'You wouldn't have done. It's a first novel, and the fellow who wrote it's completely unknown. Except to my editor, that is, who read a story and a couple of poems he did, and thought it was the voice of the future, or some such.'

'And you agree with him, I take it?'

She raised her eyebrows, then opened the book and began riffling through it. 'Well, I don't know that I care for it, particularly, but it's . . . interesting. I certainly never read anything quite like it before. It's about a man and a woman – just ordinary people, a clerk and a pupil teacher – who are . . . deluded, I guess you could say, into denying their own destinies. One by the fear of being ostracised. And the other by grief for . . . for someone he loved very much.'

She glanced up at me, to make sure that I hadn't missed the significance of what she had said. I nodded. She went on with her search. After a couple of seconds she stopped and said:

'Ah, here we are.' She folded the page open, and began to read:

247

'"If we accept what our conscious minds *tell* us is good, then we are no better than poor pale second-hand images of human beings. We have to have the courage to grasp what we intuitively desire, and know intuitively that life demands of us – to seize it, and grapple with it until our broken fingers bleed, and our blood mingles with it, and with the earth. Only then shall we be *truly* good – for only then shall we truly express the great elemental force that called us into existence and pounds through our veins."'

She half-closed the book and raised her head again. Something went through me that started as a laugh and ended as a sob. I choked it back, and pulled my face into a smile.

'Well,' I said, spreading my hands in front of me. 'I'm afraid I don't measure up awfully well, do I? Fingers all perfectly hale and hearty, and not a drop of blood to be seen. The great elemental force can't be terribly pleased with me, can he – or she – or it?'

She didn't laugh, but continued to look at me unflinchingly. 'Can you honestly say you don't feel a pang of recognition when you hear that?'

'Well, I . . . No . . .'

'I know *I* do. I've tried to grasp things, all right – and then shrunk back, because I was frightened of what people would think of me. Particularly since I came over here.'

My mouth was dry. I reached for my cup, but my hand was trembling so much that I ended up slopping coffee into the saucer.

'I realize that's not quite your predicament, of course,' she said gently, leaning forward to blot the spillage up. 'You're not worried about anyone else's opinion of you, only your opinion of yourself. You feel responsible for your daughter's death. So you have to punish yourself for it, by renouncing your vocation.' She paused, refolding her napkin to find a dry spot. 'And', she muttered, barely audibly, as she set to work again, 'any prospect of happiness you might have.'

248

'Well, I don't know about that,' I said, struggling to keep myself afloat. 'Everyone makes far too much of happiness, in my view. It's all the fault of your Mr. Jefferson, I'm afraid, telling people they had a right to pursue it. Do that, and it'll run away from you. Leave it be, and if you're lucky it just might hop up and take you by surprise.'

She raised her head again. 'But isn't that what *you're* doing? Pursuing it, I mean? For Mary Wilson? Surely the only reason you've been looking for her mother is in hope of making her happy – or *happier*, at any rate?'

'I . . . Well . . . Yes . . . But it's different, isn't it, when you're doing it for someone else?'

She shook her head. So quietly I could barely hear her, she said: 'You want to make Mary Wilson happy only because you know she can't make you happy in return. She's already married. And even if she weren't, from your description of her, she isn't capable of loving you. She isn't capable of loving anyone, poor woman. So there's absolutely no danger that she might try to rescue you from the tower in which you've imprisoned yourself. The most you can hope for is a kind of cold, monkish satisfaction if you succeed.'

I shook my head, biting my lip to try to stop the tears flooding my eyes.

'But, as I said,' she went on, 'it's almost certain that you *won't* succeed. And you'll take that as proof of your own guiltiness, and a pretext to give yourself an even harsher sentence. That's what *really* frightens me.'

I lowered my head, to hide my face. Seeing the effect she had had on me, she said nothing more; but after a few seconds I felt her lay her hand on mine.

'Please,' I muttered, shrinking back into myself, and clenching my fists. 'This really won't do.'

'No one's looking at us.'

'But your chap's going to be arriving in a minute, isn't he?

Can't have him finding us like this.' I took out my handkerchief and dabbed my eyes. 'Can't have him finding *me* here at all, if you come to that.' I squinted up at the clock, but my vision was too blurred for me to be able to read it.

'We still have a quarter of an hour,' she said.

'But you've got to finish the book, haven't you?'

She smiled. 'All right. Ten minutes, then.'

'Are you sure that'll give you enough time?'

'I just have to find out whether *he* drinks himself to death, and *she* marries her horrid *fiancé*. And, to be honest, I'm much more interested in what's going to happen to you.'

'Well,' I said, after a second's pause. 'When I've spoken to Mrs. Cooper, and told her where she can find her daughter, I suppose I shall return home.'

'What, back to the wife who doesn't care for you, you mean? And the garden hut to which she's banished you, so that she can consort with her spiritualist friends in your house?'

'I don't really have much choice in the matter, Miss –'

She smiled. '*Miss?*'

I nodded. 'I'm sorry. Alice. No one else will take me in. And I can't go on being a vagrant for ever. For one thing, there's the sordid business of making a living to consider.'

'And how do you propose to do that?'

I shrugged. 'I've no idea, I'm afraid. Over the past few weeks I really haven't given it much thought. But I'd better *get* an idea pretty sharpish, or in no time at all we'll find the duns hammering at our door.'

She didn't reply at once; but I could tell from the abstracted way she pursed and relaxed her lips that she was wrestling with some complex question in her own head. Then, as if she had finally settled it to her satisfaction, she nodded and said:

'*I* have an idea.'

I managed a smile. 'I've a suspicion I know what it is.'

She shook her head. 'No, I'm not talking about another book

– though of course . . . one day . . . I hope . . . No, this is something quite practical. Will you promise me you'll at least consider it?'

'I don't know what it is, yet.'

'But if I tell you, will you promise?'

I bowed my head.

'A lecture tour.'

'*What?*'

'A lecture tour of the States. I know I could arrange it for you: you have so many admirers in America who'd be just thrilled to hear you speak. And it would be the perfect solution, wouldn't it – you could go on being a vagrant, and get handsomely paid for it at the same time? Two birds with one stone.'

'I . . . I don't think I could.'

'Why?'

'I should feel a fraud.'

'I don't see why.'

'It would be a kind of false pretences. People would expect to hear the man I used to be. Not' – tugging on my lapels – 'this.'

She held up a hand to silence me. 'Well, don't make a decision now. You promised you'd think it over.'

I nodded.

'And', she went on, more quietly, 'I'm sure you would find someone to take you in there, if . . . if that's what you wanted.'

She tried to hold my gaze but couldn't, and turned away, pressing her fingers to her cheeks in an effort to extinguish the fire that had suddenly suffused them.

'Well, that's a very kind offer,' I said.

Still holding her face in her hands she turned towards me and shot me a furious glance.

'I know, I know,' I mumbled. 'But this isn't the place for a grand scene. Let me have your address, and I'll write to you.'

'Really?'

'Of course really. I give you my word.'

251

She stared at me for a second more, then tore a page from her notebook. While she was writing I called the waiter and paid him. Then I got up and pulled on my coat.

'There you are,' she said, handing me the sheet.

'Thank you. No, please, don't get up.' I held out my hand. She looked at it incredulously for a moment, as if she had given me a jewel and I was offering her a bus ticket in return. Then, with a sigh, she took it and gave it a perfunctory shake.

I turned and hurried to the door. I could imagine her hurt gaze following me all the way across the room, but I dared not look back for fear that, if I did, I should break down and howl.

XVII

As I made my way back to Sussex Gardens, I was afflicted by an unpleasant sensation I had not felt since my first experiences of drunkenness as a young man. The city seemed to be revolving slowly, like a sluggish roundabout, so that with every step I was forced to compensate for some faint centrifugal pressure; and several times I had to stop and cling on to a railing to stop myself from falling. I knew I needed to take stock of everything that had happened in the past hour, and begin to try to adjust myself to the strangely altered vision of the world it had created; but it is impossible to think clearly when you feel at any moment you may be violently sick.

By the time I reached the park I was so unsteady that I decided to stop for a while. I spread my coat out among the trees bordering the Serpentine, then lay down, wrapped it round me like a blanket and shut my eyes.

When I finally came to again, it was the middle of the afternoon. I sat up. The vertigo, thank God, had vanished. And – as if, even while I was sleeping, some part of my mind had been continuing to order my thoughts – I knew exactly what I should do.

It was quite straightforward: Miss Dangerfield was right: I had been a coward, and I must redeem myself. At the next opportunity I had – however unpromising it might seem – I must speak to Mrs. Cooper. Until I had done that, there was no point in even thinking of anything else.

That evening, I treated myself to dinner at a small French restaurant in Covent Garden, savouring each sip and mouthful as if – instead of merely being a kind of bridge to carry me through to the next day – the meal were itself the whole object of my existence. Then I returned to my hotel, and slept better than I had for weeks.

I woke early, and was at Victoria in time to take the 7.15 to Gipsy Hill. As I emerged from the station, I noticed a strong cattle-yard smell, and, looking down the road, saw the cows being driven back to the field after their morning milking. I dawdled along in their wake, and loitered on a corner while they were herded through the entrance and the five-bar gate closed behind them. Then I slipped in through the wicket, and set myself up in my usual place under the lime tree.

Thinking that Emily Cooper and her daughters might come out at any moment, and that I should be ready to follow them when they did, I only half unpacked, and sat with the sketch-book open on my knee, squinting at the horizon as if I had not yet quite decided what to take as my subject. But by ten o'clock there had been no sign of them; and – on the off-chance that someone might have noticed me, and begun to wonder at my strange behaviour – I pulled out the box of charcoal, and started to draw.

All morning I stayed there, covering sheet after sheet with per-functory pictures of trees and cows that – as my boredom and frustration grew – came more and more to resemble the scrib-blings of a two-year-old. When the church clock struck one, and the Coopers had still not shown themselves, I knew that the logical thing would be to give up for the day and go back to town. But I was not in a logical state of mind; and though I tried hard to persuade myself that their failure to appear was just an unlucky aberration, I could not entirely suppress a superstitious fear that Fate might have punished me for squandering my opportunity to speak to Emily Cooper by ensuring that I did not get another one. Perhaps, in the forty-eight hours since I had seen her, she had moved house. Or gone abroad. Or, worse still: been taken ill suddenly, and died in the night.

These thoughts would not be reasoned away; and as the afternoon went on, they fed on my mounting hunger and despair to become ever more insistent, until eventually they were powerful enough to squeeze everything else from my mind. If I left now, I knew, they would merely pursue me, baying in triumph: the sole thing that would silence them was categorical proof that they were groundless.

And finally, a little after four o'clock, just as I was beginning to lose hope altogether, the proof miraculously materialized. A cab appeared from the direction of the station and stopped in front of the house. Two women got out, laden with bags and hat-boxes; and as the elder one turned to pay the driver, I caught a glimpse of that unmistakable bird-of-prey profile.

Instantly, the bugbears that had been battening on me all day were routed. I felt a surge of relief – but tinctured with incredulity that I had allowed myself to be tormented by such gothic-novel imaginings, rather than guessing the obvious, mundane truth: that she had simply broken with her normal routine to go shopping with her daughter. At all events, I had learned my lesson: there was nothing sinister about her absence, and no reason to suppose that – if I came back tomorrow – I should not find her taking her walk to Crystal Palace park as usual.

I lingered for a few minutes, so as not to give the impression that my departure was in any way connected with their arrival, and then started to pack up. While I was walking to the gate, however, I heard the slamming of a door; and, looking towards it, saw one of the young women coming down the steps with the little dog. As she reached the road, I stopped and waited for her to pass, to avoid the risk of meeting her in the street; but instead of turning right up the hill, she crossed over and entered the field by the wicket.

She obviously had not noticed me before, because when she caught sight of me she stiffened with surprise and dropped the end of the leash. She bent down to retrieve it, but too late: after boggling at me for a split second, the dog twitched into life and started tearing towards me, yapping furiously, his ears flying like unsheeted sails. She chased after him, clapping her hands and calling *Stop it! Stop it! Grrr, come here, you bad boy!*; but he was impervious to her, and hurled himself upon me, scrabbling wildly with his paws and jolting the sketch-book free of my grasp. To my embarrassment, it fell open at the last drawing I had done: an incompetent jumble of squiggles and smudges that would have shamed a schoolboy.

'Oh!' she gasped, coming up to me. 'I'm so dreadfully sorry!' She caught the leash, tugged the dog away from me, then crouched down to pick up the sketch-book.

'Don't worry,' I said. 'No harm done.'

'Still . . .' She shook her head, then stood up and handed me the pad. 'You're an artist, I see.'

'Not a very good one. As you can tell.'

She smiled. 'I'm not much of a judge, I'm afraid. Pictures are a bit of a mystery to me. Well, modern ones, anyway. I don't really understand them.'

'Then take my word for it. This is atrocious.'

She laughed. 'And as for you, you reprobate,' she said, wagging her finger at the dog, 'you're an absolute disgrace. I've a good mind never to take you out again.'

'Oh,' I said. 'That seems rather a harsh sentence.'

She laughed again. Close up, the family resemblance was quite unnerving: if I relaxed the focus of my eyes for a moment, I could half convince myself that I was looking at Mary Wilson. But not Mary Wilson as I had seen her in the church porch and at Langley Mill: Mary Wilson as I still clung to the hope I might see her yet, relieved of the invisible yoke on her shoulders.

'It wouldn't be *that* harsh,' the young woman said. 'He's my mother's dog, really, and she usually brings him over here her-self. Only she's been up to town today and she's tired, so she asked me to do it instead.' She bent over, took the dog by the ears, and gave him a play-scolding shake. 'That's why you won't obey me, isn't it, you horrid animal? You don't think I'm your mistress.' She cocked her head, and gave me a conspiratorial glance. 'I actually don't think he's much more obedient to her, if truth be told,' she said, in an amused undertone. 'Only she doesn't notice, because it's always dark.'

Something suddenly seemed to start crawling through the hairs on my forearms. 'What,' I said, 'you mean she walks him here in the middle of the night?'

She shook her head. 'Not the middle of the night. But late. Just before bed-time, usually, when there's nobody else about. I find it a bit eerie then, and lonely. But she likes it. Says it reminds her of when she was a girl, and lived in the country. The *proper* country, I mean.'

I nodded. And then – fearing that if I showed too much interest she might think it strange, and mention me to her mother – raised my hat, and said: 'Well, good afternoon.'

'Good afternoon.'

I started towards the gate. Instantly, the dog began barking behind me. A moment later, I heard the girl shout exasperatedly:

'Oh, *Largo*, come *here!*'

I stopped and turned round. She was jerking at the leash, to keep the writhing dog from trying to follow me.

'I beg your pardon?' I said.

'Sorry.' She gestured helplessly at the spaniel. 'I was –'

'*What* did you call him?'

'Oh, oh, *Largo*.'

'Largo?'

She started to giggle. 'I know, it does sound rather funny, doesn't it? We named him after a character in a book my mother used to read us when we were small and we all loved. Mr. Largo Frog. And he's pretty much as silly and vain as the original. If we'd called him something sensible like *Banister* or *Toppy*, he'd probably have been better behaved. Wouldn't you, boy?'

Mercifully, the dog started squirming and yelping again, and she was too taken up with trying to control him to see my reaction. By the time she looked up again I had regained power over my face, and was even able to manage a smile.

'Ah, well,' I said. 'Good afternoon again. And good afternoon to *you*, Largo, too.'

Then, before she could say anything more, I turned back, and continued on my way to the station.

I awoke the next morning in an almost narcotic state of calm. For a while I lay there, listening to the world getting up around me, my body so light and relaxed that when I closed my eyes again I felt as if I were levitating. The dawn chorus of *what if*s and *hold on*s and *but suppose*s that had greeted me every day for the last few months was quiet. There was nothing to debate any more: I had made up my mind. I would return to the field in Gipsy Hill that night, and if Emily Cooper was there I would speak to her.

I had a leisurely bath, then carefully reviewed my wardrobe, trying to decide what to put on. I finally settled for my homeliest suit and a well-loved old shirt that was starting to fray around the cuffs. She would be unable to see it, in all probability; but – just as a crown will enable an actor to transform himself into Henry V – I thought the mere feel of it against my skin would help me to be the man I wanted to present to her: a quiet, modest, unassuming fellow, whose experience of life had knocked the fresh-starch sheen from him, leaving him sadder but full of a gentle understanding of human weakness.

It was only when I took out my nail-scissors and sat down in front of the glass to trim my moustache that my mood changed. The man gazing back at me looked sad, all right; but so shockingly alone and out of place that he appeared to belong to a different reality altogether.

All at once the silence around me seemed not restful, but frightening. I was suddenly acutely aware that – now that the clamour of voices in my own brain had stopped – I could hear no voices at all.

To whom could I turn for help, or encouragement, or approval – or even just a wave and a breezy *good luck*? My only true confidante, Miss Dangerfield, had gone; and though I did not doubt that she, more than anyone else in the world, was genuinely concerned for me, I could not help remembering the look of pained constraint on her face when she talked about Mary Wilson, and feeling it as a mute rebuke to what I was doing. Jessop? My only means of reaching him quickly would be by wire – and, in any case, for all the sympathy he had shown when I embarked on my quest, I could not expect him to follow me through the labyrinth into which it had led me since. I briefly thought of telephoning Miss Robinson; but there was something so repugnant about the idea of trying to draw vital strength from a frail old woman twice my age that I abandoned it again – even before I had got round to considering the practical problem of how to get her number.

I could not think of anyone else. Finally, I retreated to the bed again, shut my eyes, and murmured: 'Well, at least *you're* still there, anyway, aren't you, old fellow?'

I could have imagined it, but I thought I felt a tiny tightening in my temple, like the contraction of a small animal rolling itself into a protective ball.

'Don't you *want* to meet your grandmother?'

There was no response. I waited for perhaps fifteen minutes, alert to every flicker of light or sound. Nothing but the distant music of the city, and the slow procession of brilliantly coloured shapes drifting in front of my eyelids like globules of oil on water.

I gave up, feeling troubled and oddly aggrieved. I had an early lunch, then spent the afternoon wandering in the park, losing myself in the crowds, drawing from the warmth of their bodies the spurious sense that I had rejoined the human race.

Just before bed-time, the girl had said. But I had no idea when bed-time at Oaklands was; so, to be absolutely certain, I took the 8.25 train, and was back in Gipsy Hill by nine. I thought if I went to my usual place under the lime I might be seen in the light from the street-lamp; so instead I waited by the entrance at the top of the field, leaning on the five-bar gate and exchanging curious stares with the cattle congregated just below it.

It was as well I hadn't left it any later. I had not been there ten minutes when I heard the sound of a door in the distance, followed by the thin clip of a woman's footsteps. Shortly afterwards, a figure emerged into the street, leading the dog. For a moment I could not be certain it was her; but then – as if she sensed, somehow, that she was under surveillance – she began peering around her, craning her neck into the darkness, and I caught a glimpse of the hawk-beak nose and heavy mouth.

I held my breath. After a few seconds, apparently satisfied, she nodded, and crossed the road. I hid behind a tree until I heard the clang of the wicket, then quickly walked down and followed her in, taking care to cushion the gate with my fingers as I closed it, so as not to alert her to my presence.

She was already almost at the bottom of the meadow. I started after her, moving as quickly as I could without making too much noise – although even if she heard me now, she would not be able to escape, because she could not get back to the gate without passing me. When she reached the fallen oak, she sat down on the trunk, and – thinking, presumably, that she was now far enough away from the cattle for the dog not to be tempted to chase after them – bent forward to release him from his leash. He tore around for a few seconds, then caught my scent and started running towards me. I squatted down to greet him. Whimpering with excitement, he levered himself up on my knees and began licking my face.

'Largo,' I heard her calling. '*Largo!* Come here!'

He took no notice of her. She got up, and bustled over to us, folding the leash-strap in two and then snapping it against itself so that it made a sound like a whip-crack.

'Where on earth did you spring from?' she said, in a tone that suggested that her failure to control her dog was my fault for being there rather than hers for not having trained him properly.

I pointed towards the gate. 'But don't worry,' I said. 'Largo and I are old friends.'

As if to bear me out, he slithered back on to the ground and rolled over on his back. I started to rub his stomach.

'Really?' she said. Looming above me, her face was just a featureless black aberration in the faint silver of the night sky; but I could feel the intensity of her gaze as she squinted at me through the gloom, trying to tell if she knew me.

'I met him yesterday,' I said. 'With your daughter.'

'Ah, so you're the artist, are you?'

I went on petting the dog for a few seconds, deliberately taking my time. Then I gave him a valedictory pat and got up.

'I'm not an artist,' I said. 'My name is Corley Roper.'

She hesitated a moment. 'Corley Roper the author, do you mean?'

'Yes.'

Now that I was standing up, and she no longer appeared silhouetted against the sky, I could see the puzzlement in her eyes. She was reluctant to believe me, clearly – but couldn't imagine why I should be lying.

'That's very strange, if you are,' she said finally.

'Because of the dog, you mean?'

'Ah, Muriel told you, did she?'

I nodded. 'Very gratifying.'

'Well, you've no idea how much those books meant – mean

– to all of us . . .' she said – the words trailing off as the thought that I might not actually *be* Corley Roper, after all, reasserted itself.

'Thank you,' I said. I took a few steps towards the fallen oak. 'I'm going to sit down, if you don't mind.'

She shook her head. 'It isn't mine.'

'Still, you were here first, weren't you?'

She gestured at the tree with a graceless flick of the hand. I sat down. I was, I knew, taking a chance; but I was pretty certain that – however unsure she still felt about me – she was too curious now simply to walk away.

I sighed, and looked up at the stars. At the edge of my vision I could just make out the glint of her eyes as she stood watching me, like the gleam of coal in a scuttle. She seemed to be wrestling with the urge to say something, and I hoped she might be going to clear the way for me by asking what I was thinking about. But she held her tongue, and in the end I said:

'Shall I tell you a story?'

She did not reply. But, hearing my voice, Largo slunk up to me, and I began stroking him again. As he inched nearer, nuzzling my leg with his wet nose, I discreetly hooked a finger through his collar. She would not leave while I still had her dog.

'I don't know if you take *The Times*?' I said.

Still she said nothing. I went on:

'Only if you do, you might have seen the announcement. A few months ago. My daughter Elspeth. Scarlet fever.'

I glanced towards her. She shook her head.

'No? Well, at all events, when it was over I took myself off to the Sussex downs and lived like a savage in the woods for a while. I still don't quite know why I did it. To be wet and cold and hungry, to feel bark grazing your skin and stones sticking through your boots . . . Those seemed the only terms, at that moment, on which it was possible to go on living.'

I looked at her again. This time she nodded.

'Well,' I continued, 'one miserable evening, when I hadn't slept in a bed or had a proper meal for a couple of days, I had a . . . an experience that made me think I'd better go in search of food and somewhere to stay. So, as darkness fell, I slipped and stumbled down through the trees, looking for an inn, or even simply a farmhouse, where I might spend the night. And eventually, just as I was beginning to give up hope, I saw, in the distance, the faint yellow glow of an oil-lamp.'

I sensed her starting to edge towards me. I looked up at her, and smiled. She hesitated, then settled herself on the trunk, no more than a couple of yards from me, to listen.

'It turned out to be the light from a small game-keeper's cottage, standing all by itself in a clearing,' I said. 'I knocked on the door. A young man appeared, who said he was just leaving and would be happy to show me the quickest way to the nearest village. He led me through a queer old overgrown gateway into a beautiful rolling park, where the grass shone silver in the moonlight. Half-way across it he said: "I must leave you here. But if you continue straight you'll come to a drive that will lead you out on to the road."'

I turned towards her. She was sitting hunched forward, her hands pressed together, her mouth half-open.

'Well?' she said. 'What happened?'

'I followed his directions, and they brought me into the village, exactly as he had said. But just as I got there, it started to rain – not just a shower, but a biblical deluge – and I decided to take shelter in the church porch. It was completely dark by this point, but I could see just far enough inside to make out the end of a stone bench where I could sit and wait out the storm.

'As I groped my way in, I felt something brush against my hand. I picked it up, and found it was a rose – a cut rose, in February! It smelt wonderful – but when I held it to my nose, one of the thorns jabbed my finger, and I let out a cry of pain.'

Her anticipation was palpable. I could feel it prickling my

cheek like a rash. I paused, playing out the line for a moment, then started to reel it in again:

'Naturally, I had assumed I was quite alone. So you can imagine my astonishment when the next moment, out of the darkness, no further away from me than you are now, I heard a woman's voice speaking to me.'

'Oh!' she gasped, shrinking back and putting a hand over her mouth. 'Was it a ghost?'

'No,' I said. 'It was a real woman. She'd come in to take refuge from the rain, as I had.'

Her shoulders slumped – half with relief, and half with disappointment. 'Ah.'

'But there was a mystery about her, nonetheless.'

'Really?'

I nodded. 'The flower was hers, it seemed. I held it towards her, and a hand appeared from the darkness to take it. I could hear her sob as she sniffed it, so I asked her if she had brought it to put on her parents' grave?

'"No," she said. "I've no idea where my parents are buried – or even if they are alive or dead."'

I leaned forward, consolidating my grip on Largo's collar. But it was an unnecessary precaution: she clearly still had no inkling where I was leading her.

'So who was the rose for?' she asked impatiently.

'For her son. He was still-born, so he couldn't have a proper funeral. But she had saved a lock of his hair, and wanted to bury it in the churchyard.'

'Oh, the poor woman.'

'Yes,' I said. 'Only there were too many people there, so she hadn't been able to. So in the end I said I'd bury it for her.'

I suddenly remembered the smell of the damp earth, and its pliancy beneath my fingers as I pressed it down on the box. I shut my eyes, trying desperately again to summon up the child, to make him incarnate for long enough to be a witness to the

264

dénouement of the journey we had embarked on together that evening.

'And did you?' she asked.

It was no good: he was still obstinately coiled away in his hiding-place. I opened my eyes again. 'Yes. But that wasn't the end of it. Afterwards I found myself . . . haunted, you could say –'

'By him, you mean?'

'By both of them. By the situation.'

She nodded. 'Well, of course . . . For a mother . . . The loss of a child is the most dreadful thing that can happen.' She shivered, and clasped her hands about her knees.

'Yes,' I said. 'For a father, too. But for this woman it wasn't just an isolated horror. It was symptomatic of her entire existence.' I hesitated, considering how much more I could say without making it obvious whom I was talking about. The answer, I decided, was very little: the enchantment would start to fade soon, and then it could only be a matter of time before she deduced why I was here. So, lame though I knew it sounded, I added simply:

'Or that's how she felt it, anyway.'

She nodded. Then, glancing down, and busying herself with straightening her coat, she said quietly:

'I think I can understand that more easily than you might imagine, Mr. Roper.'

Had she guessed already? I couldn't be sure. But I forced myself not to show my anxiety by looking at her.

'Well, I'm sorry to hear it,' I said. 'But – forgive me if this seems impertinent – you at least have other children to console you. This woman has nothing. I'd defy anyone to see such unhappiness and not feel moved to try to alleviate it, if they could.'

I heard the rustle of her clothes as she re-settled herself on the tree. 'And can you?'

'*I* can't. But I think I know how it could be done. With someone else's help.'

'Well, that's very noble of you, Mr. Roper,' she said, getting up abruptly. 'And I wish you luck. I must be going in now. Come on, Largo!'

He tried to follow her, but I pressed him down and closed my hands around his neck.

'Mrs. Cooper,' I said. 'Please don't imagine I am judging you. I know only too well, believe me, how easy it is to make mistakes. My own life is a catalogue of them. My only reason in coming here is to appeal to you, as one flawed human being to another, to –'

She darted towards me suddenly, snapping the leash again. For a second I thought she was going to hit me with it; but instead she bent down, brushing my face with her hat, and began fumbling the clasp back on to the dog's collar.

'Do you not think, in all honesty,' I whispered, trying to turn our brief awkward proximity into a kind of intimacy, 'that it would be a relief to you?'

She was quiet for a moment. Perhaps, I thought, against all the odds, I had winged her with my last shot. But then, squaring her shoulders like a boxer, she said softly:

'Please let Largo go, Mr. Roper.'

I let him go. She got up and started towards the wicket at a regal pace that challenged me to try to overtake her. After she had gone thirty yards or so she wheeled round and called:

'What you want me to do is quite impossible.'

Then she turned again, and continued to the gate without looking back.

XVIII

Alice Dangerfield had warned me I should fail. I had known it myself, rationally. And yet, however hard you try to imagine how the world will appear to you when the last thread of hope has gone and the thing you fear established itself as irrevocable fact, it is impossible. I had prepared myself for deep despair or guilty relief, but in the event I felt neither – only the flat, fatalistic sense you get as a child when, at the end of the summer, reality finally breaks in, and you're waiting for the train that will take you back to school. There was the same sense of desolation; the same unaccustomed hardness in the air, making it sound as if the boots clacking along the platform had all been soled in concrete; the same sense that all the light and shadow in the world had been averaged out to a dull warship grey.

My first thought, naturally enough, was that I ought to go to see Mary Wilson again; but after a few minutes' reflection I realized that I was under no obligation to tell her what I had learned. She might, of course, be gratified that someone cared enough for her to take so much trouble on her behalf; but discovering the depth of her mother's indifference to her could only leave her feeling more unwanted and abandoned than ever.

What I should do instead, I finally decided – not with much enthusiasm – was go home, and take a few days to recover from my fruitless quest before starting to consider my future. To reassure my wife that I had no intention of laying claim to the house, or of intruding permanently on her life again, I sent her a telegram, warning her of my arrival, but saying I should not be staying long, and asking her to tell Chieveley to make up the bunk in the cabin. She must have received it, because the gardener's boy was waiting for me at the station with the trap. But when we got home, Chieveley greeted me at the door with the news that she wasn't there, but had gone to stay with her brother.

'Really?' I asked. 'When did she leave?'

'This afternoon, sir. Luke dropped her when he came to meet you.'

'Ah. That's a bit of a . . . Did she arrange this a long time ago, do you know?'

'I'm afraid I couldn't say, sir.'

'Well, when did she tell you about it?'

'Just this morning, sir.'

I expected to find a note in the cabin, saying when she would be back; but there was nothing from her at all. Apart from the freshly-made bed, in fact, the place appeared exactly as I had left it, so that when I went inside, I had the eerie sense that I was entering a photograph from some earlier stage of my own life.

I was past feeling hurt by Violet's behaviour, but I was troubled by it. My intention had been to concede her demand for a permanent separation – asking, in return, only that she should allow me a grace period of a week or two in which to make the necessary arrangements. But her sudden flight suggested that the idea of my being there at all had become intolerable to her, and that the best I could hope for would be a return to the prickly armed truce under which we had lived before I had embarked on my adventure. Even that, in fact, seemed optimistic now.

I was too tired to do anything that night, but the next morning I finally settled down at my desk and forced myself to take stock of my situation. It was, I soon concluded, quite lamentable – and, what was worse, almost entirely of my own making. I was like a man who deliberately turns his back on the sun to walk headlong into driving rain. I had squandered time and money I could not afford in a doomed attempt to save a poor lost woman who had not asked for my help, and to accommodate myself to a wife who only wanted to be rid of me. In doing so, I had neglected my true gift – and my one practical hope of earning a living again – and systematically ignored the advice of my real friends, and those who wished me well.

It suddenly struck me that perhaps Alice Dangerfield had been right: my inability to write had been nothing more than a kind of temporary paralysis, brought on by grief – and it was my failure to *understand* that it was only temporary that had sent me blundering off so blindly in the wrong direction. And, if that were the case, perhaps it was not too late to go back, and pick up the path I had foolishly abandoned then.

I opened the drawer in my desk, and started to gather up the story I had been working on when Elspeth had died – but one glimpse of the words *Little Mouse* was enough to make me drop it back again. It was asking too much of my own fortitude to start there. Better to try to reintroduce myself to the business of being an author more gently, by embarking on something new.

I picked up my pen, took a fresh notebook from the cabinet, turned to the first page, and settled back in my chair to stare at it. For a long time nothing happened, and I began to wonder if, after all, the old magic had really deserted me. But then I felt a familiar shiver tightening my skin, and saw an image, like the faint impression left by a traced drawing, form itself on the whiteness: a caravan.

There: I still didn't know who the hero was, or why he was doing it, or whom he would meet along the way; but of one thing I was already certain: he would go on a journey in a caravan.

I started to scribble some notes about the adventures he would have: sharing a picnic with a family of new-found friends in a meadow; meeting a strange old woman (or was she a bird?) who lived in a hut in the woods woven from the tendrils of creepers; finding a map buried under a tree, and following the route it showed, down winding lanes scented with wild garlic and over a queer crooked bridge, until he reached . . . What? I couldn't say, yet. But that didn't trouble me: scattered and incomplete though they were, these few ideas had the authentic, fecund feel – how exhilarating to experience it again! – of seeds that would grow while my attention was elsewhere, so that when I went back to them again I should find they had worked themselves into a story of their own accord.

But the moment I turned to the hero himself, for some reason, my inspiration left me. When you find the right character, you know it at once, as if it had been there in the shadows all along, and all you have done is to reveal it by shining your torch into the corner where it has been hiding. But none of the possibilities that suggested themselves now – a mole? A vole? A squirrel? – had that sense of inevitability about it. I tried to make them more interesting by giving them idiosyncrasies: the mole stuttered; the vole had a sweet tooth, and kept a bee for a pet. But it was useless: simply pinning trinkets on a line of tailor's dummies in the hope of bringing one of them to life.

Perhaps the mistake was to think he must be an animal. Why could he not be a child instead? But as soon as I began to consider what he might be called, and who his parents were, and where they lived, and how he came to be in possession of a caravan, I found myself in the same difficulty. He just hung there, inert and featureless, like a sail refusing to take the wind.

I was still vainly struggling to animate him when I became aware of a fluttering in my temple. It was not particularly violent or insistent: in fact, there was something almost joyful about it, like the delighted splashing of an infant in its bath. But it was disturbing to know it was still there. For some days, it had seemed to be dwindling away; and since my abortive interview with Emily Cooper I had assumed it had finally evaporated, together with the fantasy that I could help its mother.

Come on, old fellow, time to go, I said. Instantly it was still, and – imagining it had grown so weak that one gentle injunction had been enough to remove it – I went back to work. But no sooner had my thoughts settled themselves in the caravan again than it returned – hovering at the edge of my consciousness like a buzzing fly that you can never quite swat or shoo out of the window. I struggled on; but after half an hour or so it had become so distracting that I admitted defeat, and took myself off for a walk on the hill behind the house.

I had gone no more than a quarter of a mile when I realized that the whirring had stopped, and my head was clear again.

I had a late lunch of bread and cheese in a little riverside pub, enjoying the smoky frowst of the bar, and the noise of real people discussing real things: horses; the king's health; the state of the weather. Watching their flushed, earnest faces, it was hard to believe that any of them had ever fretted over an invented character, or imagined that a ghost had taken up residence in his brain, or considered for a moment that there might be anything beyond the immediate reach of his own senses. And, as can sometimes happen, the effect of the warmth and the beer was to blur the boundaries between us and make me somehow a temporary member of their number; so that by the time I left I had convinced myself that the spirit of the dead child was an utter absurdity, and that only a fool would allow himself to be held to ransom by it for even a second.

This John Bull-ishness started to fade on the way home, as the influence of the alcohol wore off; but there was still enough of it left when I got to the cabin to make me open the notebook again, and settle myself determinedly back in my chair to work. I had not been there five minutes, however, when I was distracted by a movement out of the corner of my eye.

A man was walking towards me across the lawn. For a second or two he was too far away for me to be able to tell who it was; but as he emerged from the shadow of the cedar I recognized my brother-in-law, Hubert Ashburn. He peered in at the window as he passed, and – seeing I had noticed him – pulled his face into a comical grimace. A moment later, he lifted the latch, opened the door a couple of inches, and called through the crack:

'Knock! Knock!'

Then, without waiting for a response, he came inside and said:

'Hullo, old man. Thought I'd find you here.'

I stood up, but was too taken aback to say anything.

'Sorry just to barge in like this,' he said. 'But I'm afraid we need to have a bit of a chat.'

'About what?'

'Oh, you know . . .' He started edging towards my chair. 'Mind if I sit down?'

I stood my ground. 'Let's go up to the house, if it's that important. We'd be more comfortable there.'

'Hm.' He grimaced again. 'We probably would. But you know how it is. The very walls have ears. And eyes.'

'What, is Violet here?'

He shook his head.

'Then – ?'

'That's what we have to talk about.' He nodded towards the chair. 'Please, Corley.'

I hesitated, then sat down in it again myself. He looked round, discomfited, before finally perching awkwardly on the edge of the bunk.

'You've been away, I gather,' he said.

'Yes.'

'Anywhere nice?'

'A few days in France. Some time in London.'

'Ah.' He ratcheted his face into a smile. But it did not reach as far as his eyes, which continued to watch me apprehensively. 'I think Violet was under the impression you'd gone for good. Bit of a surprise for her when all of a sudden you just popped up again, what!'

'I did tell her I wasn't intending to stay long.'

'Did you? Ah. Didn't realize that.' He took in a deep breath, then let it out again as a ragged sigh. 'Look, Corley, this is damned ticklish. I don't know when I've ever had to do anything I hated more. But there it is. She's asked me to ask you to ... Well, not to put too fine a point upon it, to vacate the premises again.'

'Why couldn't she ask me herself?' I said.

'Um ... Well, the fact is, old man, she won't come back while you're still here.'

'What, not even to the house now, you mean?'

He shook his head. Something burned my throat like bile, making it impossible for me to speak.

'I know, I know,' he said softly. 'And, of course, it makes *me* feel an absolute worm. Because I'm sure you must think it's all my fault, for advising you to let her have her way the last time. I can only say I honestly believed that, if you did, the whole thing would blow over in a few weeks. But there: I've never understood women, and I never shall.'

'Well,' I said, 'you can tell her I shall be out in a month. If she can't bear to be here with me, she'll just have to stay with you till then.'

He did not reply at once, but stared at the cabin wall, as if it might suggest some other solution that we could all agree on. Then he shook his head again, and laughed.

'She's obviously never forgiven me,' he said. 'For the time when I was seven that I shut her in a trunk and said I'd have her shipped to Timbuktu. This must be her way of punishing me for it.' He cleared his throat, and gave me an apologetic grin. 'She wants you to leave now, I'm afraid.'

'What, permanently, you mean?'

He nodded. 'I'm not to return home until I can tell her you've gone.'

'Well, I'm sorry, but that's just not –'

He held up a hand to stop me. 'I know, I know,' he said again, wearily. 'It's utterly unreasonable. But the woman's hysterical.

She won't eat. We couldn't even persuade her to go to bed last night. She said there'd be no point, because just knowing you're here would make it impossible for her to sleep.'

'Why? What on earth does she think I'm going to do?'

He lifted his eyebrows and shook his head.

'Nature knows her job, Corley. And just as well she does, I suppose, else we should all still just be bobbing around in the aboriginal soup, shouldn't we? But she's not very particular about how she goes about it. That's what I learned in Africa. Chap I met there once, a settler, told me – as matter-of-factly as if he'd been admitting a fondness for bridge – that he'd used to hunt bushmen for sport. I gave the fellow the eye, and said – a trifle stiffly, you can imagine – *well, that doesn't sound very good sport to me.* And he said: *Why? You hunt the fox, don't you?* And I said: *Yes. Well,* he said, *your bushman'll give you a better run for your money than a fox. He's a wily little brute, and will lead you the devil of a dance if he puts his mind to it.*'

I stared at him, so flabbergasted I could not even find the words to ask him why he was subjecting me to this story. But he must have seen the question in my face, because he ducked his head and lifted a finger, urging me to be patient.

'Well,' he went on, 'I said to the chap – Beauvais his name was, came from an old Huguenot family – *But don't you think there's a bit of a difference between a bushman and a fox? Besides, I mean, the difficulty of killing them?* And he laughed, and said: *Oh, bosh! That's all sentimental humbug! Just look around you. Do you think Nature cares a straw for the feelings of the zebra mare as a lioness disembowels her young? Or the lion when the Zulu spears it? Or the Zulu when a bullet rips through his shield and tears his throat out? Of course she doesn't. She only cares that the fast get faster and the strong get stronger, and devil take the hindmost. So when we're clearing bushmen to make way for farms where blacks can grow tea and oranges and grapes for us, we're just doing her work for her.*'

'Well,' I said, not daring to raise my voice above a stage-whisper in case it betrayed me, 'he sounds like an admirable fellow. And a fine advertisement for civilization. Evidently, no one seeking proof of its practical benefits and moral superiority could do better than apply to him.'

Hubert smiled, and attempted a laugh. 'It's hard to accept, I know,' he said. 'For a chap who's spent the best years of his life spinning yarns about talking animals who live in cosy holes and conduct themselves like maiden aunts. But the truth is, he's right, isn't he? It's just that most of the time we don't get our noses rubbed in it, because we're at the top of the tree. Only now Violet *has* had her nose rubbed in it. Because all of a sudden, for the first time in her life, she's the zebra, not the lioness. And the long and the short of it is, it's driven her mad. Ably assisted, I'm afraid, by that scoundrel Dolgelly.'

'Ah, Dolgelly. *He's* behind this, is he?'

'He put the notion in her head.'

I settled back in my chair, bolstering myself for the next blow.

Hubert swallowed uncomfortably. 'I'm sorry, old man. There ... I mean, this is bound to sound awful, however I put it ... He's persuaded my poor foolish sister that he's made contact with Elspeth on ... on the other side. But that little E. won't come back and appear to her while you're here. And that if you stay, there's a danger she'll never come back at all.'

I felt as if I were – at the same time – turning to ice and melting away to nothing. I was stunned, not only by the cruelty of the idea, but by the brilliance of its conception: having succeeded in estranging me from my wife and turning me out of my house, the devious little charlatan would seal his victory by posthumously taking my daughter from me as well. Not only, on its own terms, did it make perfect logical sense, but it was also completely unanswerable: the more I tugged at the hook, by arguing that it was simply a callous lie, the deeper it would embed itself in Violet's flesh.

And yet, even if it *were* no better than a lie, I could not help seeing – with a shocking, inescapable clarity – that there was a kind of poetic truth to it, too. I *had* closed myself to Elspeth after her death, because to keep myself open to her would have been unbearable. I had abandoned the one place in which we might have continued to meet: the world that I had created for her and shared with her. I had turned my back on my own grief, to occupy myself obsessively – madly – with Mary Wilson's instead. The dead child that had found a refuge in my head was not mine, but hers.

'Well, old man?' said Hubert, his eyes boggling anxiously as he studied my face for a reaction.

I looked away.

'It's hard, I know. Damned hard,' he went on. 'I'm sure you feel you've already been a good deal more accommodating than she had any right to expect. And, brother or no brother, I'd agree with you. Absolutely. Any sane man would.' He hunched forward, clasped his hands over his knees, and began to massage them nervously. 'So if the question should arise . . . Well, it's bound to, isn't it?'

'Of what? A divorce?'

He gulped and nodded. 'You'd need to talk to a lawyer, of course. But I don't imagine . . . Given the circumstances . . .'

He stopped and shook his head. To my astonishment I saw his eyes were bright with tears.

'It's the most damnable thing,' he went on, after a few seconds. 'First poor little E., and now this.' He levered himself up suddenly and held out his hand. 'But we can still be pals, can't we?'

'Yes, of course.'

He could not speak, but, pressing his lips together, nodded his thanks.

'Give me three days,' I said, 'and I'll be gone.'

That night, I walked through the house, deciding what things I should take. I had expected it to be a maudlin experience; but all

I felt, in the event, was a kind of wonderment that my life had ever been large enough to fill the place. Even a single room appeared too much, now, for what I had become. I could not find the tiniest trinket or keepsake that seemed to have the least connection with me any more. I was on the point of leaving again when I remembered something of Elspeth's: the battered rag toy with uneven ears and a pearl-buttoned waistcoat that had evolved, over the course of a dozen bed-time stories, into the character of Alcuin Hare. I retrieved it from the nursery, and then fled back to the cabin, hobbled by the unnerving sense that I had undergone some Alice-in-Wonderland transformation, and that if I did not stop the process by removing myself to a world that fitted my new doll's-house scale, I should shrivel away altogether.

In the morning, I telegraphed Jessop: *May I, once again? A week, at most, I promise*; and was reassured, three hours later, to receive the answer: *As long as you like. C.J.* But still, as I bustled about over the next couple of days, packing and writing letters, I could not escape the feeling that I was failing to cast off the ropes attaching me to my old self quickly enough, and that my existence, as a result, was continuing relentlessly to shrink. I found myself incapable of giving orders for meals, or deciding what clothes I should wear.

One morning, as I was flipping through the paper over breakfast, my eye was caught by a book review: *The Serpent and the Dove*, by Mr. Davey Riddick. I knew perfectly well I should feel something: surprise; curiosity; perhaps even a stab of envy. But it seemed like intelligence from Brobdingnag, that had no significance for a Lilliputian like myself, and I turned the page without so much as glancing at the thing.

And when Chieveley appeared the next day to announce that the king had died at Buckingham Palace, I struggled to make anything of the news at all.

'*Who* did you say?'

'The king, sir.'

I was conscious of the concern in his eyes, but could not think how to allay it.

'Ah, poor old chap, eh?' I said.

'Yes, sir.'

'And poor old queen, too.'

As if to compensate for the numbness of my waking life, at night I was visited by a series of harrowingly intense dreams. In one, I was standing with Violet under the shade of a tree, looking out at a sun-yellowed savannah wavery with heat. Some way off, next to a dried-up pool, a lioness was devouring a zebra foal. As the little creature writhed and flailed piteously, Violet started to pummel me, shrieking *Save her! Save her!* I ran forward, shouting and waving a stick; and the lioness backed away, snarling. Throwing myself down, I scooped the zebra up in my arms, thanking God that I could still feel her pulse. But then she turned her black-striped face towards me, and I saw that the tongue was hanging half torn from the mouth, and the throat had been torn out, leaving only a jagged crater in her neck. She gazed wonderingly at me for a moment, as if she were trying to understand how I could have let this happen to her; and then her eyes filmed over, and I knew she was dead.

I woke feeling half-suffocated. For a moment I lay there, steadying my breathing, telling myself: *it was only a dream, it was only a dream.* And then, to my horror, I was aware of a familiar sound in my head, as sickeningly intrusive as a too-intimate touch from someone you scarcely know: the childish sobbing I had heard in the middle of the night in Cabourg.

And I knew instantly that he had dreamed the same dream I had, and finally understood that, when life has made her decision, however cruel it may seem, there is no appeal against it.

Ahunh-ahunh-ahunh.

'Listen –' I began.

What is going to happen to me?

278

'I've no idea. But you can't stay here.'

Ahunh-ahunh-ahunh.

'Look, I'm at my wits' end. I –'

Where can I go? You must find a place for me.

'How can I?'

Ahunh-ahunh-ahunh.

I could not stand it any more. It was no longer in my power to try to console him. I clenched my jaw, and muttered:

'I'm sorry, I've done what I can, but the game's up. Now be quiet, so I can sleep.'

And immediately he was. For half an hour or so I lay there, listening to the echo of my own words in the silence, and wondering if I had been too harsh. And then, at last, I drifted off again, and dreamed I was on a tiny boat, and about to set sail for America.

On the fourth day, as good as my word, I was ready to leave. The operatic show of emotion required to bid a permanent farewell to the Chieveleys was far beyond me by that point; so I merely told them I did not know when I should be returning, and would write as soon as my plans were clearer. Then I got into the trap, and – without looking back – set off for the station.

By seven that evening, I was sitting in Jessop's study, drinking whisky from a scuffed old tumbler, while he crouched by the grate, trying to coax a recalcitrant fire into life.

'So,' he murmured, 'you're quite over it, are you?'

'What?'

'Whatever it was that led to your precipitate departure from Derbyshire?'

'Oh, yes, yes, thanks.'

'That's good.' He began weighing an ash-log in each hand, trying to decide which would burn better. 'And so now, what, you're just having a bit of a holiday to recuperate, is that it?'

'Not exactly. Violet and I, we're . . . Well, we've separated.'

'Oh, I'm sorry to hear that.' He chose the slenderer log and craned forward to put it on the fire, taking as much care to place it in exactly the right position as if he were playing spillikins. 'Mary. Mary *Wilson*, was that her name? Been in touch with her at all, have you?'

'Not since then.'

'Ah.'

He went on tinkering with the fire. But I felt no desire to unburden myself, this time; so I ignored his unspoken invitation to elaborate, and merely said:

'I'm hoping to take rooms somewhere by the sea. I was thinking of Lyme, perhaps.'

I knew he must have noticed my evasiveness, and interpreted it as a tacit admission that my marital difficulties were something to do with Mary Wilson. But I hadn't the energy to disabuse him; and he was too tactful to press me. Instead, he sat back on his heels and said:

'Well, in that case Mrs. Batty in Thrift Street's your woman. It's a queer old house, where you half expect to find a brandy-smuggler hiding from the Excisemen under the stairs. But quite comfortable, I believe, and pretty reasonable.'

Then he bent forward, and – thrusting his hand so far into the flames I thought he must burn his fingers – set about finessing the arrangement of the logs.

The next morning I took his advice, and went to see Mrs. Batty. Her house was not quite as romantic as Jessop had suggested; but it was quiet and clean, and when I told her what I wanted, she showed me up to a pleasant room on the first floor, with a big bay window overlooking the harbour, and a small bedroom behind. Its good-hearted simplicity seemed perfectly adapted to my reduced state: after days of flight, I could imagine finally taking my ground here. In the mornings, I should go to the library, and divert myself with some modest project or other; in the afternoons I should walk along the beach, picking my way through the fossilized remains of all those countless creatures that had lived and died to make the fast faster and the strong stronger, consoled by the sound of the sea; in the evenings, I should sit at home, reading; or find a cosy fishermen's inn where I could drink by the fire, feeling the winter gradually thawing from my cheeks.

I quickly agreed terms, and told Mrs. Batty I would return that evening with my luggage. Then I hurried back to Jessop's house to tell him the news.

He was in the barn, touching up the paintwork on the shafts of the caravan. As I came in, he picked up a package lying on the step and held it out to me.

'Post,' he said.

'For me?'

He nodded. I took it. It had been redirected, first from my publishers to Oxfordshire, and then from Oxfordshire to Dorset. The original name and address had been written in a tight, strong hand-writing I did not recognize.

I opened the envelope, and found a sheaf of twenty or more pages, torn from an exercise book, and held together with a loop of black ribbon. I drew it out, and started to read.

XIX

109, Gipsy Hill, Lambeth

May 15, 1910

Dear Mr. Roper,

You will be surprised, I am sure, to receive this from me. I am surprised myself, to be writing it. I do not owe you – or anyone else – an explanation for my past actions, still less an apology; and it was quite inexcusable of you to ferret me out in that underhand way and try to hold me to account for them. Nonetheless, I have to admit that our encounter in French's Meadow last week left me feeling strangely uneasy. I find myself constantly wondering how you found me, and what impression the search has given you of my character. A poor one, probably, since I have many enemies and few friends, and it must have been the enemies who led you to me. I know only too well the kinds of words they use to describe me: stiff-necked; obstinate; heartless; wicked; cruel.

I am quite indifferent to the opinion of the world in general, but the thought that you should believe those things of me is hard to bear. Reading your stories to my girls when they were young made me a girl again, too, admitting me, for the first time, to a world that is the birthright of more fortunate children. To know you think ill of me would poison it for me, cheating me – as I have been cheated of so much in my life – of the most truly innocent delight I have ever known. And that is something I am not prepared to allow to happen, if it is in my power to prevent it.

So I have decided to do what I have never done before, and

shall never do again: lay out a brief account of my early years,
and the horror that overtook me when I was a young woman.
Because I have no idea how much or how little you may know
already, I shall tell you everything. When I have finished, you
will see, I am certain, that – far from being the monster you
imagine – I was the unwitting victim of a catastrophe that
most women would not have survived.

I was born in 1852, at Tirhoot, in India, where my father had
an indigo plantation. Three years later, life delivered the first of
the many blows it had in store for me, by robbing me of my
mother. I remember the suffocating silence, and everything in
the house turning black, and my three-year-old self crying
'Mama! Mama!' and being told she had gone to heaven, and
saying 'then I want to go to heaven, too, to be with her.'

Soon afterwards, we returned to England, and the following
year my father re-married. My step-mother was a hard, sour
unsmiling woman with big bulging eyes that seemed to find
fault with everything. From the very beginning she showed
nothing but coldness and indifference to me and my sister and
our two brothers. I thought she was a witch, who had put a
spell on our mother, and – as soon as my father's back was
turned – would try to magic us all into animals. Once I found a
toad on the doorstep, and thought it was my brother Edward,
who had gone out riding for the day.

We moved from one house to another, living a year here and
a few months there, until, when I was ten, my father took
Hallaton Hall in Leicestershire. The place meant little to him, I
think, beyond good hunting and ample stabling for his horses;
but I fell in love with it at once. It stood at the edge of an
enchanting village, full of quaint old cottages and queer little
alleys, and paths that led you through sloping meadows up into
the woods. Though I had no inkling of it at the time, I later
came to think that the cruellest trick Fate played on me was to
make me give my girlish heart to Hallaton.

What deepened my attachment to the countryside was the ever-increasing dominance of my step-mother and her brood within the house itself. I already had three little half-brothers by the time we settled in Hallaton; and shortly afterwards she produced a fourth. Her own children were not only the centre of her world; as they became bigger, she was more and more successful in making them the centre of my father's, too. And, of course, they soon came to realize the superiority of their position; and, being boys, and enjoying nothing more than torturing creatures weaker than themselves, took every opportunity they could to make our lives a misery.

My brothers, Edward and Henry Malden, accepted the endless injustices against them, and their banishment to the shadows of family life, meekly enough, as if they knew they could not win, and had decided to give up even before the race was run. But I and my elder sister Henrietta (God, how it pains me now to write that name again) were made of sterner stuff. Henrietta used every feminine wile she could to retain our father's affection, and her power over him, making much of him, and calling him her darlingest papa, when he let her have her way; and sulking when he crossed her; and running to him for protection when our half-brothers tormented her.

I took another course: to make the hills and the trees and the fields my friends, and to look for solace in their company. I would ride for miles along the narrow, overgrown lanes; or climb into the woods and run until I was exhausted – not returning until late in the evening, looking like a gypsy, with mud on my boots and thorns in my cloak and burs sticking to my dress, to find my father half mad with worry, and getting ready to send out a party of grooms and stable-boys armed with lanterns to look for me.

There is an old custom in Hallaton, called the annual hare-pie scrambling and bottle-kicking contest, which takes place every Easter Monday. It is a frantic rough-and-tumble, more

284

like a drunken brawl than a game, in which all the men join together to fight the men of a neighbouring village for possession of a cask of ale. My father considered it an unsuitable spectacle for girls; and for the first few years we were there he kept Henrietta and me indoors while it was going on, though the boys were allowed to watch from the safety of the grounds – after which, of course, they would invariably drive us to distraction by refusing to report what they had seen, saying it was too horrible to tell us. So one Easter, when I was fourteen or fifteen, I made up my mind to find out what happened for myself, and slipped out of the house and into the village without anyone noticing. I found a vantage-point in a little side-street, where I thought I should be protected from the mêlée; but after half an hour or so, as if it had been caught by a sudden squall, the crowd abruptly changed direction and started rushing towards me.

I had only two alternatives: to be knocked to the ground and trampled underfoot, or to be swept up and carried along. I chose to be carried along. It was terrifying, but thrilling, too, like finding oneself, all at once, on an enormous horse – only a horse that would pay not the slightest heed to reins or crop or spurs, but simply went its own wild way, rearing and plunging, willy-nilly. I shut my eyes for a moment, feeling the energy surging through the press of bodies around me, and imagining that when I looked again I should discover I had been borne away to another place entirely, where I could be free. In the event, needless to say, it turned out I had been taken nowhere more exotic than Hallaton high street. But in that instant, I vowed that one day I should find a means to get away.

The same idea, I think, must have occurred to Henrietta; and soon afterwards, the opportunity for _her_ to escape presented itself. In 1867, a young doctor called Albert Crane came to live in the village. In so small a place, it was almost inevitable that we should see a good deal of him, and he quickly

285

became a regular visitor at the Hall. He was always particularly animated with my sister; and after a few months, he began to make love to her. It might appear strange, given the difference in their positions, that my father did not whip him for his impudence, thereby averting the disaster that would all but destroy the Studd family. But Dr. Crane had a kind of lazy insolence – as unconscious as a lion's as it pads round its cage at the zoo – that somehow conveyed that it was _he_ who was bestowing the favour by deigning to take an interest in _us_. And my father, having spent almost his entire life in India, had little understanding of the niceties of English social distinction. My step-mother might have enlightened him; but the truth was that it suited her well enough if Henrietta made a poor match, because that meant her own children would shine all the more brilliantly by comparison. I think she would have had us all packed off to the workhouse, if she could.

I cannot bring myself to give you a physical description of Dr. Crane. Imagine a sleek animal, that happened to speak, and walk upright, and wear clothes, and smoke cigars, and you have enough. Even his hair had a pelt-like sheen, so that when he bent down to pet a favourite gun-dog you could not tell where dog ended and man began. He was a fine horseman, and gained quite a reputation for his exploits on the hunting-field. 'Damn me', my father would say admiringly, 'if Crane ain't the pluckiest man alive. Or the luckiest. He took a hedge as though the furies were after him, and by rights should have fallen and broken his neck; but he kept his seat, deuce knows how, and was across the field before the rest of us were over the gate.'

If I could go back in time and change only one thing, I should make sure that hedge knew its business better.

Henrietta was little more than a girl, and – it is obvious now, though I was too young myself to see it then – a foolish girl, at that. The only grown man she had ever known intimately was our father; and to find another, who gave her his attention freely, without her having to compete for it, and who was self-evidently accomplished enough to command the grudging respect even of our half-brothers, was hugely flattering to her. When he asked her to be his wife, she accepted him at once; and, though she was not yet of age, she soon persuaded my father to give his consent. She and Dr. Crane were married in 1868, in Hallaton church; and began their life together in a handsome old house near the centre of the village called the Grange.

I shall not tire myself needlessly with a detailed account of the next few years, but merely give you the one fact pertinent to my story: in 1871, wanting a larger place, with provision for a race-course and a racing stable, my father decided to leave Hallaton Hall and take Tedworth House, in Wiltshire, instead. It was a blow for me to leave my sister – whose jealous and spiteful nature I was yet too innocent to suspect, and to whom I still felt closer than anyone in the world, except our father – and to lose my brothers, who were sent back to India to manage the plantation. But there was one consolation: my elder half-brothers were now away at school; and when they came home for the holidays they were – if not kinder to me – at least more civil, in a distant, off-hand way. So I bore the move as best I could, and bided my time, imagining that among the young men who came to stay at the house, or whom I might meet at dances and dinner parties and at homes when we went to London, I should at last find one carrying a glass slipper who would deliver me from my misery.

It was an innocent enough dream, I think you will agree. Certainly countless thousands of other young women have shared it, without provoking Fate to punish them for it – and some have even had the good fortune to see it come true. But not I. Just as a real prospect of happiness was finally starting to open up before me, life abruptly closed it off again.

To do so, it resorted to the most snivelling trick of them all: a

pair of pious American busybodies called Moody and Sankey.
Perhaps you have heard of them: they were much talked about
in the 1870s and 1880s, when they came to England to 'convert'
us – as if we were a nation of heathens, and their own country
were not Christian at all only because <u>ours</u> had been first. They
held public meetings in theatres, where they sold religion as if it
were a patent medicine – exhorting their listeners to test its
efficacy there and then, by kneeling down and praying, after
which some of the more credulous got up noisily declaring
themselves to be 'saved'. One of the noisiest, unfortunately, was
a friend of my father's called Vincent, who – determined that
he should be 'converted', too – insisted on taking him to one of
the meetings. My father sat at the front, just under Moody's
nose, and was mesmerized by the man. A few weeks later, he
followed Vincent's example, and became 'a Christian'.

Our lives changed almost overnight. My father withdrew
from the Turf, and – after giving a race-horse to each of the
older boys as a hunter – sold his racing stable. He filled the hall
at Tedworth with chairs and benches, and invited preachers
down from London to hold meetings there. There were no more
dinner parties, no more dances. The only young men who
entered my world now were pale, earnest fellows with
prominent Adam's apples, armed with bibles rather than glass
slippers, and interested – if they were interested in me at all –
exclusively in the state of my soul.

And the contagion soon spread. Within a year, my three
eldest half-brothers, now all at Eton, had 'converted' too. Our
house in town became more like a chapel than a home, full of
hymn-singing, and bible-reading, and jocular, back-slapping
good-fellowship. At night, I would lie in bed, dreading the
tramp of my father's footsteps on the stairs, because when he
reached the landing he would invariably hammer loudly on my
door, and call: 'Are you saved yet?'

I endured this purgatory, for my father's sake, for as long as

he was alive; but when he died in 1877 I could stand it no more.
The last connection with my own family had gone, and I was
entirely at the mercy of my step-mother and her children, who
no longer made the least effort to conceal their contempt for
me, and took every opportunity to vaunt their supposed
superiority – which seemed, now, to their eyes, to have been
confirmed by God Himself, Who had chosen to save them, and
not me. I had no suitor to marry me, and – after years of social
isolation – no possibility of meeting one. In desperation, I
decided to flee to the one place where I thought I could still be
sure of finding a welcome: my sister's house in Hallaton.

It was a bitter return. When I had left the village, five years
before, it had been in the confident expectation that I should
soon have a husband of my own – and not a country doctor,
either, but a man closer to my station in life, who, if he lived in
Hallaton at all, would inevitably have taken the Hall as my
father had done, so allowing me (I cannot deny that I dreamed
of this sometimes) to make a triumphant reappearance as
mistress of my girlhood home. Instead, I found myself little
better than a pensioner at the Grange, where it was agreed I
should contribute £250 a year towards the household expenses.
I did not begrudge the money – my father had left both
Henrietta and me comfortably provided for; what I resented
was how even this, the one relationship to which I should
naturally have been able to look for uncalculating love and
consolation, was reduced to a squalid commercial transaction.
And I could not help noticing the way the villagers glanced at
me as I went about the place, and guessing what was passing
through their minds: why had the woman who had left the Hall
as Miss Studd now, still as Miss Studd, come back to the
Grange?

This is proving harder than I had imagined. I wrote what you
have just read in a great rush, in twenty-four hours; but the

effort and anguish of doing it, and the dread of relating what comes next, made me ill, and for two days I could barely move from my bed. I got better by telling myself I should not have to go on, if I did not want to. But I knew it was a lie, even as I said it; and so here I am, back at my desk, determined to finish, whatever the cost.

My sister had five children by now, the youngest no more than a few months old. There was a nurse, of course; but Henrietta was one of those mothers for whom the baby in its cot is the centre of the world, and she could not bear to be away from it for more than a few minutes before creeping back to gaze on its face in wonder. Her infatuation was so overpowering that for days at a time she seemed barely to notice either me or her husband – and when she did, it was usually to express irritation at some trifling thing that one of us had done, or failed to do.

It was inevitable, in these circumstances, that Albert and I should find ourselves thrown together more than would have usually been the case. And – where before he had shown only polite indifference to me, and I had considered him, if anything, faintly repellent – the effect of our common exclusion from my sister's affections was to start to forge a fragile bond between us – just as, when we were children, our common exclusion from our step-mother's affections had forged a bond between Henrietta and me. Sometimes, when she had been particularly impatient with him, he would try to lessen his humiliation by making light of it, rolling his eyes and smiling at me, in a way that invited me to share his exasperation at her unreasonableness – and, more out of awkwardness than anything else, I would find myself smiling back.

After dinner, Albert and I began playing cards together in the drawing-room, or – on fine evenings – walking out in the garden, to admire the view of the hills rising up behind it. I never felt any impropriety in what we were doing, although I did occasionally wonder whether the sight of us sauntering arm in arm back to the house could cause Henrietta some unease. But so much the better if it did, I thought, because then she might be less inclined to take her husband's and her sister's love for her for granted, and try a little harder to deserve it.

But it soon became clear that that was a vain hope – at least so far as her husband was concerned. One morning, I came out of my room on to the landing, to catch the end of a conversation between my brother-in-law and my sister in the hall below. He was speaking too softly for me to make out what he was saying; but I think he must have been proposing that she should go out riding with him, because she angrily replied:

'I've far too much to do here. Why don't you ask Emily to go? She likes to be out of doors – and _she_ has no household to manage, and no children to attend to.'

I did not want to embarrass them by letting them know I had overheard this outburst; so I crept back in to my bedroom and closed the door. When I finally came downstairs, five minutes later, I found Albert standing in the dining-room, smoking a cigar.

'Ah, Emily,' he muttered carelessly, his eyes on the window. 'I was just wondering whether you'd care to come riding with me today?'

And so began our long expeditions together, roaming the countryside I remembered so vividly. I felt no compunction about them on Henrietta's account: not only had she herself encouraged Albert to take me with him in the first place, but – after the third or fourth time – her attitude towards me started to grow noticeably warmer. When she saw me, now, I was rewarded with a smile, and even kisses and caresses. One evening, after we had got back, and my brother-in-law had gone into his study to consult his books about a case that was troubling him, she drew me aside and, blushing, said:

'You have no idea how grateful I am to you, darling, for

taking Albert off my hands like this. One never imagines . . . before one's married . . . just how _insistent_ men's needs are. One may feel as dull and wrung-out as an old dish-cloth, it makes not the slightest difference to them. Sometimes I quite dread going to bed at night. But when he has been out with you, I know I am quite safe, because he is too tired to . . . to make demands on me.'

But even though our jaunts together had Henrietta's blessing, I could not help wondering what other people would suppose when they observed the doctor venturing out, time after time, with his sister-in-law at his side rather than his wife. One morning, as we were turning into the high street, I tentatively suggested that in future it might perhaps be better if we left the house separately, and met again later, a little outside the village. He immediately stopped his horse, and – in full view of a group of urchins playing on the green – said:

'What, are you ashamed to be seen with me, then?'

'No,' I stammered, stung, 'of course not. I'm only thinking of your reputation, and Henrietta's.'

'Well, then,' he said, 'don't. I don't concern myself with other people's affairs, except when I'm paid to; and they've no business concerning themselves with mine.'

As we grew bolder, I began sometimes to accompany him even on his professional visits, going as far as the gate with him, and then waiting outside with the horses. When he came out again, he would invariably divert me by describing the patients he had seen – always in the most contemptuous terms, as if they were animals rather than people, and he a vet rather than a doctor. 'What an evil-smelling old dog,' he would say. Or: 'I don't like to leave that fat sow alone with her litter. I'm afraid when I go back again I shall find she's eaten the lot of them.' There was something wearying about his relentless unpleasantness; and yet I have to admit I found the comical turns of phrase he used amusing. And it was exhilarating, too, *for a young woman who had always lived at the margins of other people's lives to find herself admitted to his confidence, which seemed to make us conspirators in a secret compact against the folly of the world.*

On the Monday after my second Easter at the Grange, Albert was called to an isolated farm, where the tenant's wife had gone prematurely into labour and was bleeding heavily. He asked me to go with him; and I stood in the yard, refusing the farmer's distracted offers of hospitality, and listening to the strange, trapped-hare shrieks of his wife from the house. When Albert came out, his hands were covered in blood. He washed them at the pump; but the cuffs of his shirt were still speckled with red.

'What happened?' I asked, as we started to ride off.

'She'll live,' he said, with an abrupt nod.

'And the child?' I said.

'He'll live, too,' he said; and then lapsed into a moody silence, as if having succeeded in saving two human lives had not made him glad, but melancholy.

It was the day of the annual hare-pie scrambling and bottle-kicking contest, and as we neared Hallaton we could hear the roar of voices rising towards us. We stopped at the edge of a wood overlooking the village, dismounted, and stood watching the great mass of bodies swarming through the streets below. After a minute or so, I suddenly became aware that Albert was no longer beside me. I looked round, and saw him about fifty yards away among the trees, standing with his back to me, his hands held in front of him and his legs splayed. It was perfectly obvious what he was doing, and I did not want him to know I had been a witness to it; but before I could look away again, he turned, and I saw, quite clearly, what he should never have allowed me to see. I let out a cry, and felt myself starting to colour furiously. But he appeared totally unconcerned, and went on buttoning up his trousers as easily as if he had been slipping a cigar into his case. I was so shocked, I could not even find the words to reproach him; but as he came towards me, I started to back away, wondering whether or not I should accept the apology I assumed he must be about to offer me. In the event, however, all he did was shrug, and say:

'Well, what did you expect to see there?' And then he nodded down at the heaving crowd of men jostling its way up Hare Pie Bank, and said: 'There's not a one of them would look any different. Under our clothes we're all the same. All just beastly animals.'

I was careful to keep a little distance from him on the way back, and we did not exchange another word until we had reached the Grange. But that evening, half-way through dinner, I was suddenly aware that he was looking at me in a strange way. When I turned towards him, he did not drop his gaze, but continued to stare at me, with an air of quizzical reflection, as if he were appraising a horse he was thinking of buying. And in that instant I again heard his drawling voice saying 'under our clothes we're all the same', and knew, somehow, with absolute certainty, the thought that was going through his head. The idea of it made me feel so faint and sick that I had to get up and leave the table.

For some weeks afterwards, whenever he invited me to accompany him again, I found some pretext to refuse. He never pressed me; but there was a kind of sulky irritability in his manner as he shrugged and said, 'Very well, then, you must please yourself, I suppose,' that suggested I was being petty, and inflicting a punishment on him that was quite disproportionate to his offence. Soon, I began to catch myself wondering if perhaps he was right. After all, I had very little experience of the world; and – for all I knew – what had happened might be a common enough accident when a man and woman went riding in the country together. And, aside from that one unspoken insult at dinner, he had never acted in an improper way towards me since.

But still I continued to resist, until, one morning, Henrietta came into my room before breakfast, sat down on the bed, and asked me outright why I had stopped going out with him. I could not, of course, tell her the truth, and fumbled an excuse.

'Well,' she said, 'you'd be doing me a great kindness if you started again. He has become more demanding than ever lately, and I begin to fear I shall go mad. You may think it a shocking thing to say, but I can't help feeling perhaps the Moslems are wiser than we are. Where there are two or three wives in a house, at least one of them can be sure of an uninterrupted night's sleep. And if things go on as they are, that's something *I* shall never have again.' And she started to cry, and asked me to hold her; and for ten minutes we clung to one another as we had as little girls.

That afternoon, when Albert suggested I should go with him to see a patient in an outlying hamlet, I said: 'Yes.'

After that, I started accompanying him regularly again; and for a while things were exactly as they had been before. But then, one day, as we were riding through the woods above the village, we heard a shot, and a moment later came upon a wounded rabbit lying by the side of the track. It was twitching and screaming piteously, and I asked Albert to stop and put it out of its pain. He dismounted, and I watched as he knelt down and ran his fingers over its flailing body, murmuring, 'There, there, easy now.' And then, without warning, I heard the snap of its neck; and the next moment saw him stand up again, holding the wretched creature by the ears.

'There,' he muttered, through clenched teeth, tying it to his saddle, 'that will make a fine present for my wife, won't it?'

We rode on, but the mood had changed: he was silent and morose, and I unnerved by the demonstration he had given me of his effortless power over life and death. After another mile or so, as I was following him along a dark, rutted path hemmed in by trees, he stopped again, and waited for me to draw *alongside. The instant I did so, he reached out his hand and seized my wrist.*

'Emily,' he said, in a queer, half-strangled voice.

'What is it?'

'I have been so unhappy.' He was not looking at me, but straight ahead, his head slightly bowed, so that he appeared to be staring between his horse's ears.

'I am sorry to hear that,' I said. And then, thinking that perhaps he was going to reproach me for having neglected him so long, I added: 'I hope I am not to blame in some way?'

'No. Yes. Well, no. But you are the one person in the world who could make me happy again.'

I said nothing. My heart was starting to beat faster, and my mouth was dry.

'You know how, don't you?' he said, turning towards me at last. And as soon as I saw his eyes I did know, as surely as I had understood what he was thinking that evening at dinner.

You will think I should have cried: 'How dare you!' and lashed him with my crop; but the sense of my own powerlessness before him still seemed to bear down on my shoulders.

'Please,' I said, trying to break away from him, 'let me go.'

But he only tightened his grip, and said: 'Surely, it's a natural enough thing, isn't it?'

'No!'

'Of course it is,' he said firmly, punching the dead rabbit. 'Look at this poor little brute. How'd you think he came into the world?'

'But we're not even . . . I mean –'

'Ah, what, you're thinking of Henrietta, are you? Well, I can promise you: she won't mind. Far from it: she'll be eternally grateful to you.' He leaned closer, so I could smell the cigar smoke on his breath. 'In fact,' he said, with an apologetic little smile, like a chastened schoolboy, 'truth be told, this is actually

*her idea. Naturally, I'd thought of it myself. But I don't think
I'd ever have dared suggest it, if she hadn't given me the signal.'*

'I don't believe you.'

*'What, you mean she hasn't said anything to you? About my
<u>needs</u>? And how she wishes there were someone else to satisfy
them?'*

*I shook my head; but my eyes must have betrayed me,
because he nodded and said:*

'There, well, then.'

*'But even if she did say it,' I said, rallying, 'that does not
mean it would not be wrong. And unnatural.'*

*He raised his eyebrow, in a kind of weary amusement, as if I
had been a child talking of fairies.*

*'Nonsense,' he said. 'It's quite usual, I assure you. Half the
families where there's an unmarried girl living with her sister
have an arrangement of the sort. Not here, of course, I mean –
but in society.'*

*'I . . . I'm sure you must be wrong. What if the girl wants to
get married herself?'*

*He shrugged. 'Then she does. There's no difficulty there.
Plenty of chaps prefer a woman who knows what she's about.'*

'Well, I never heard of such a thing.'

*'Well, you wouldn't have done, would you? Not living with
those milk-and-water half-brothers of yours. What would <u>they</u>
know about the beau monde, when they get their notion of the
world from a two-thousand-year-old book of Jewish gibberish?'
He hesitated a second, then smiled as a thought struck him.
'Shall I tell you what I'd do, if I had my way? I should
confiscate their damned bibles and not return them until they'd
all read Mr. Darwin, word for word. My, wouldn't you hear
some pretty squeals and shrieks then? Mama! Some beathly
chap'th got my Book of Leviticus. Make him give it back!'*

*It was such a ridiculous picture that I couldn't help laughing,
despite myself. He took advantage of the moment to lean*

forward and kiss me. But then, instead of forcing himself on me
as I feared he might, he drew away again.

'Well,' he said, 'I shan't press you for an answer now. Think
about it.'

And without looking back at me, he rode on.

What should I do? I was at a loss. Both my parents were dead.
My brothers were in India. My sister, who ought to have been
the first, was the last person I might confide in. I had not a
single friend in Hallaton – and, even if I had, I could not have
unburdened myself to her without risking the utter destruction
of my own family.

The next morning, I stayed in bed, complaining that I felt
unwell. But I knew that could only be a temporary expedient,
particularly in a doctor's house; and, sure enough, after forty-
eight hours, Henrietta insisted, despite my protests, on sending
Albert up to see me. He behaved entirely professionally, made
no mention of what had passed between us, and ended by
diagnosing over-excitement of the nerves, and prescribing
laudanum and a week's complete rest. Both he and my sister
showed me the greatest solicitude; and, as I lay there, listening
to the murmur of their voices outside my room as they
discussed my condition, united in their concern for me as they
might have been for one of their own children, I began to
wonder, just as I had before, whether perhaps I had not been
brought up to have an excessively narrow view of the world?
Might it not be simple prejudice and superstition to assume
that love must always be rigidly confined to two poles, and
could never open itself to embrace a third?

And then, the instant I caught myself entertaining the idea, I
would feel a sudden rush of panic, and an overwhelming urge
to flee. But flee where? Was not Hallaton already my last resort?

At length, as the week drew to a close, Henrietta came to see me one evening by herself – taking the unusual precaution of locking the door behind her.

'How are you, my pet?' she asked, as she sat down next to me.

'Much the same, I think,' I said.

'Oh, I'm sorry to hear that. We all miss you so very much. Especially Albert, I have to say.' She took my hand in hers, and began to stroke it. 'Is there some . . . awkwardness between you and him?'

I could barely speak; but I just managed to blurt out: 'Why do you ask that?'

'Oh, only that you seem rather constrained with him sometimes. And when you're constrained with him, he's . . . He's very <u>un</u>constrained with me.'

I summoned up all my courage, and said: 'Would you rather I <u>weren't</u> constrained with him, then?'

'Much rather.'

There was a long silence, which I broke, finally, by saying: 'I think perhaps it would be better if I went away.'

She put her hands on my shoulders, and, leaning close, murmured in my ear:

'If you left now, darling, I truly believe it would kill me.'

After she had gone, I began to pray to our mother for guidance; but as I tried to put my predicament into words, I was so overcome by shame for Henrietta and for myself that I had to stop.

That night, I woke to find a figure standing by my bed. It was too dark for me to see the face; but the strong odour of wine and tobacco told me who it was. He was wearing a dressing-gown; but the next moment slipped it off, allowing me to see the dim glow of his skin in the moonlight. He started towards me, then stopped again when he saw that I was awake.

'She's been to see you, hasn't she?' he whispered.

I did not reply. And suddenly he was kissing me. I tried to push him away, but he was too strong for me. When he lifted his mouth from mine for a moment I started to cry out; but he clamped his hand over my lips, and said:

'Sssh! Rouse the servants, and we're all ruined.'

I knew it was true. And, feeling the full depth of my own impotence and loneliness, I submitted.

I do not remember how many more times I yielded myself to him after that. But I do know that, even then, I somehow contrived to persuade myself that what took place when he came to me was not what normally occurs between a man and a wife, but a sort of lesser adjunct to it, which could not have the same consequences. So it was a double devastation when, in October 1879, I realized that the regular monthly visitation that every young woman learns to expect had missed its time.

Day after day I waited for it, taking every opportunity to go up to my room to see if the first signs had appeared, praying fervently that God would take pity on me, and promising that – if He would only spare me this once – I should never sin again. But He did not take pity on me; and at the end of a week, unable to bear it any longer, I went to Albert, and confessed my anxiety to him. He examined me, then told me to get dressed again, and stood looking out of the window.

'Well?' I said.

'Too soon to tell,' he said. But his face had turned the colour of fish-skin.

That evening, we played cards not in the drawing-room, but in his study, where he plied me with wine. It seemed much stronger than usual; so that when the time came for bed I could barely get up by myself, let alone climb the stairs. He insisted that I should take a bath, which was so hot that I almost fainted, and had to be lifted out again by two of the maids. In the morning, he asked me if I had noticed anything unusual in the water; and when I answered 'No' seemed dreadfully disappointed.

I soon deduced what he had been trying to provoke, and allowed myself to be subjected several more times to the same treatment, but always without success. Finally, I said to him:

'It won't be long before my condition starts to become obvious, will it? What are we going to do?'

'Well, what do *you* suggest?' he snapped, as if it were entirely my own concern, and I were imposing on him unjustly by asking him to share the burden with me.

I felt mad with anger; but by an effort of will I managed to contain it, and said: 'Perhaps you could say I was ill again, gravely ill, this time, and would see no one but you and Henrietta. And then, when the child came, you could deliver it –'

'Henrietta!' he said. 'You haven't mentioned this to her, have you?'

'No, of course, not.'

'Well, for God's sake, don't!'

'I won't, if there is a way to avoid it. But surely, if she encouraged our – whatever you may call it – she could not be entirely surprised at the result?'

'You might think so,' he said. 'But women are not rational creatures.' He reached for a cigar, and his hand was shaking as he lit it. 'You must leave this to me. I shall think of something, I promise you.'

I had little enough reason to believe his promises by this point; but I could see the fear in his face, and trusted that to succeed where appealing to his honour had plainly failed. And it did. Within two days he came to me with a scheme: we would go to Normandy, where he had grown up until the age of ten, and take a house in Avranches. There he would engage servants, who would care for me until the baby was born. Afterwards, he would make provision for the child in France, and I might come back to England without a stain on my character.

I did not care for the idea, even then; but with certain and utter disgrace the only alternative, I reluctantly agreed to it. In November 1879, Albert and I left the Grange separately and travelled to London. We spent two nights as man and wife at the International Hotel while he made the necessary arrangements, and then took the boat train to Folkestone.

I cannot begin to convey to you the horror of the next seven months, as, little by little, I was robbed of everything – love; dignity; self-respect;and even the most rudimentary amenities of civilized existence – that separates our lives from the brutes'. The house in Avranches turned out to be a delusion; there were houses to be had, sure enough, but no landlord (or so, at least, Albert said) willing to risk scandalizing the English colony settled there – all colonels, and spinsters, and younger sons of baronets, as sensible of rank and respectability as if they had been in Cheltenham – by letting one of them to two people in such obviously embarrassed circumstances. Instead, Albert asked his old nurse, Adèle Lamarthe, to take me in. She was married now, and living on a tiny farm a few miles outside the town, where there was barely enough space for her own family, let alone a guest. While Albert was still with me, they put me in their own bed, and made much of me; but as soon as he left to return to England I was relegated to a makeshift room next to the cattle-shed, full of the stink of ordure, and the sound of beasts lowing and fidgeting beyond the flimsy partition; and, as winter turned to spring, and spring to summer, an ever-increasing population of flies. My schoolgirl French was quite unequal to communicating my needs to a pair of uneducated peasants, or of penetrating the thick Norman accent in which they replied. Everything was all unspeakably sordid; and the more my existence descended to the level of their own cows, the more my gaolers treated me like one of them, bringing me food two or three times a day, and taking away my filth, but otherwise leaving me entirely alone in my misery.

Albert had promised faithfully to write to me at least twice a week; but at the end of a month or so the stream of letters from him dwindled to a trickle, and eventually dried up altogether. Not long afterwards, I received a furious broadside from my sister, to whom he must have treacherously given my address. In the course of five venomous pages, she called me a string of names I would blush to repeat, even now, and accused me of betraying her, and cold-heartedly ruining her family. I wrote back, reminding her of everything she had said to me, and protesting that all I had done – against my own inclinations – had been to please her. I had a four-line reply, which I can still remember, word for word: 'You _cannot_ have imagined that I meant such dreadful things, or that any wife who was not either mad or depraved could have viewed them with anything but utter abhorrence. I never wish to see or hear from you again.'

I cannot deny that sometimes, in the middle of the night, as I heard the senseless noises of the animals next door, and felt the child growing remorselessly within me, bending and twisting my body to its blind will, I considered doing what so many poor women in that predicament have done before. It would not have been difficult; half a day's walk would have taken me to the coast, and then it would simply have been a matter of weighing myself down with stones, struggling a few yards out into the sea, and letting the waves take me. But always, in the morning, the determination to fight on came flooding back to me. Whatever others might have done, _I_ was not going to allow myself to be destroyed. Some day soon, the horror would be behind me; and then – though I still had no idea where I should go, or what I should do – I would recover every fragment I could from the wreck of my old life, and exert myself tirelessly to make a new one.

One hot afternoon in June, when I was already so swollen that it was agony to move, Mme. Lamarthe told me I had a

303

visitor. She led me in to the squalid little room that served as both kitchen and parlour, where, to my astonishment, I found my brother Henry standing in front of the fireplace. He seemed dreadfully ill at ease, and winced when he saw the all-too-evident change in me. But then he recovered himself, and said:

'I can't stay long. And we've a good deal to talk about.'

'How on earth did you find me?' I said.

'Henrietta,' he muttered, not looking me in the eye.

'Dear God!' I began. 'I hope you didn't believe what _she_ told you –'

'Don't trouble to explain,' he said, raising a hand to stop me. 'The whole story's come out. Crane's a scoundrel, and there's an end of it.'

'Come out?' I cried. 'How?'

'In court. She's divorced him.'

'What! Was I named?'

He nodded. 'Of course.'

I toppled on to a chair, and was only stopped from slumping to the floor by Mme. Lamarthe, who, if she could not grasp the sense of what we were saying, clearly understood the tone.

'At any rate, that's all finished now,' said Henry. 'All that's left is to try to mend matters as well as we're able to.'

I merely shook my head in despair. He reached out, and – gingerly, as if it were a duty he had to steel himself to perform – touched my shoulder.

'Since the divorce case,' he went on, 'Crane has refused to accept any responsibility either for you or for the baby. The Studds have conspired to ruin him, he says, and the Studds can pay the price for it. So I've come back to see what I can do.'

And he quickly sketched out the plan that he and Edward had devised between them to rescue me, and – as far as was still possible – save the honour of the family. When the child was born, it would be sent back to England, where a home would be found for it in some remote part of the country, either

304

with a distant relative of my mother's, or with a respectable farmer and his wife, who would be glad of a little extra money, and – in due course – another pair of hands. I, meanwhile, would return with Henry to London, where he would take lodgings for me, and then, when the moment was right, introduce me to a friend of his from India, a widower called Mr. Cooper, who had shown a lively and sympathetic interest in my case. Cooper was not a young man, nor a particularly wealthy one: after years in the Uncovenanted Civil Service, he had worked his way up to the rank Deputy Opium Agent, and was not expected to climb any higher. But he was kindness itself; and – while of course my brothers could not presume to speak for him – they thought it very probable, if we liked one another, that he would be prepared to marry me, and take me back to India with him. If he were, and I refused, then they would be forced to wash their hands of me altogether.

I asked for twenty-four hours to consider his proposal. The next day, when he returned, I told him I would accept it, provided he would make one change: instead of coming back to England with us, the child must remain here in France.

'Why?' he said. 'What difference does it make – especially when you are going to be in India?'

'We don't know that I shall be in India,' I said. 'We don't know that Mr. Cooper will ask me to marry him. And I cannot bear the thought that it might come looking for me. Or that I could happen upon it by chance in the street.'

'But if we leave it here, it will grow up _French_,' he protested.

'It may grow up a Chinaman, for all I care,' I said. 'Or not grow up at all.'

'That's not fair,' he said. 'The poor little thing will still be a member of the family, however disreputable, and it deserves some recognition of the fact. It's not _its_ fault, after all, that you –'

'It's not _my_ fault, either!' I screamed.

He continued to argue; but when he realized how adamant I was, he began to relent, and eventually we reached a compromise: the child would stay with Mme. Lamarthe until it was three or four, and then an establishment would be provided for it in Paris, where it might receive an education more appropriate to its parents' position in society. And, as a token, to preserve some thread of a connection to the family, he insisted on giving Adèle Lamarthe his prayer-book, instructing her to keep it until the infant was old enough to have it himself.

A few weeks later, I finally went into labour. The pain was indescribable – and, to a man, I am sure, unimaginable; but it was tempered by great, gushing waves of relief that I should finally be rid of the monster that had invaded and all but destroyed me. When the doctor, whose French, mercifully, I could understand, told me it was a girl and asked if I wanted to see her, I rammed my fingers into my eyes. To see that, the bawling, stinking incarnation of heartlessness, of deceit and bad faith, would, I knew, have killed me.

My subsequent life, as you will have deduced, has more or less followed the path laid out for it by my brothers: Mr. Cooper did take pity on me, and I did go to India with him; and since his retirement we have lived modestly and quietly in Gipsy Hill. It is a testimony to his goodness that, soon after we were married, at his own suggestion, he became the child's guardian; and when we returned to England, he prevailed on me to allow her to be moved from Paris to a school on the South Coast, on condition that he never revealed my identity or our address to the old spinsters who owned the place, so that she should not be able to find me. But I have never deviated from the belief that to see her or speak to her would be a sentence of death to me. That is why I told you, in French's Meadow, that what you wanted me to do was impossible.

I am not her mother, for a mother gives life freely, and she took it from me by force. But I will, nonetheless, end by offering her one piece of advice, if you care to pass it on to her: that she should stop snivelling at the injustices she has suffered, and make the best of what she has, as I have. I was robbed of almost everything; but that did not stop my being a dutiful wife, and a respectable member of society, and bearing four children of my own, and giving them the love I never knew as a child myself.

Yours sincerely,
Emily Cooper

XX

On a hot afternoon at the end of May, I arrived back in Derbyshire. For nearly a week – sitting at breakfast in the window of my room in Mrs. Batty's house, or walking along the undercliff, desultorily looking for fossils – I had been debating whether or not I should come, and on more than one occasion I had almost persuaded myself that I shouldn't. I had already decided, after all, not to tell Mary Wilson that her mother still refused to see her, and the letter – for all the additional information it gave – did not alter that essential fact. Indeed, it re-iterated it so brutally that it could only leave her feeling more utterly rejected than ever.

And yet, and yet . . . It was *her* history; and to keep it from her – try as I might to put a different gloss on it – seemed like a kind of theft. She had the right at least to know that it existed, and to choose for herself whether or not she should read it. I tried composing a covering letter, explaining how I had come by it and warning her of what it contained; but after half an hour or so I gave up, realizing that I did not have her address – and that, in any case, however carefully I attempted to soften the blow, it would be a horrible shock for her to receive the thing in the post. The only humane course, I saw, would be to take it to her in person.

Though the idea of it filled me with dread, once I had finally taken the decision I felt curiously liberated. On the way there, I kept drifting off to sleep, and finding myself in the world of my half-formed caravan story – as if, in facing up to doing my duty, I had somehow licensed my imagination to begin working again. So powerful was this dream-reality that, even when I was awake, a ghostly image of woods and animals and streams seemed to remain at the edge of my consciousness, tempting me to return to it and make it concrete. By the time we reached Derby, there was a kind of tremulous, electric lightness in my limbs that I had despaired of ever feeling again. I did not want to examine it too closely, for fear it would simply evaporate. But I promised myself that – whatever the upshot of my meeting with Mary Wilson – when I got back to Lyme Regis I would take out my notes, and see whether, after all, something might be done with them.

As we drew in to Langley Mill, I saw a little local train standing at the next platform, and heard the guard shouting that it was for Heanor and all stations to Butterly. To spare myself labouring up the hill on foot and arriving in a sweat, on an impulse I scrambled on board, and spent most of the six-minute journey with my head out of the window, enjoying the cool bluster of smoky air against my face. When I ducked inside again to gather up my things, the pleasant-looking woman sitting opposite gave me a droll smile, and dabbed her cheek with her finger.

'You might want to know', she said, 'that you've got a big smudge of soot here.'

'Thank you.' I rubbed it with my handkerchief. 'Is that better?'

Her smile deepened, half-closing her eyes. 'Much better.'

'Glad to hear it. It'd be no good calling on a Sunday School teacher looking like a minstrel, would it?'

She laughed. 'Which Sunday School teacher is that?'

'Mrs. Wilson.'

'The new curate's wife?'

I nodded.

'Why, then looking like a minstrel would be just the thing. Her husband's mad keen on amateur theatricals. Never happier than when he's wearing some silly costume, or decked out in a false beard and a wig.'

She laughed again. Her expression was so friendly and free of guile that I decided to press my advantage.

'Well, that's good,' I said, patting my breast pocket, and then pulling my face into a dumb-show of dismay.

'Have you lost something?'

'The address.' I frowned into the empty pocket and shook my head. 'I could have sworn I had it here. But it seems to have slipped out somehow.'

'Oh, that's easy,' she said, getting up, and retrieving her hat from the rack. 'They're just round the corner from where I live. Come on, I'll show you.'

I was worried that on the way she might try to prise from me how I knew Mary Wilson, or what my business with her was; but she merely chattered happily about nothing very much at all until we reached the entrance to a street of nondescript little semi-detached villas.

'There,' she said. 'That's their house. Number three.'

There was a strong chance, I knew, that the curate would be at home; and for a few minutes I lingered on the corner, hoping that if I waited long enough Mary Wilson would eventually emerge on her own, saving me from the need to explain my presence there to her husband. But when I heard the church clock striking three I suddenly decided I had spent too much time lurking outside other people's houses. I should go to the door, and ask for Mrs. Wilson. If Mr. Wilson was there, then so be it. I would simply tell him the truth: that I had something of importance to discuss with his wife.

I walked up the short path and rang the bell. It was answered by a flustered, red-faced girl who held the door open with her foot while she hastily finished taking off her apron.

'Is your mistress in?' I asked.

She glanced down the hall behind her. 'I'll just go and see, sir. What name shall I say?'

'Corley Roper.'

While she was gone, I stood fidgeting in the stuffy hall, half expecting the curate to appear at any second, and rehearsing what I should say to him if he did. But then I heard a woman's footsteps approaching, and a moment later a door opened at the back of the house, and Mary Wilson hurried into the hall. I feared that she might be angry with me for calling on her at home, and so – as she would almost certainly see it, if she were in a suspicious mood – compromising her reputation. But as soon as she caught sight of me she stopped, and gave a little shiver of excitement.

'I hope you will forgive my intruding like this,' I said.

She dismissed my apology with a shake of the head, then suddenly darted towards me. For one giddy instant I thought she might be going to embrace me; but instead she rushed past, opened the front door, and peered up and down the street.

'Where is it?' she said.

'What?'

'The caravan.'

'Oh, I took the train this time.'

'Ah.' Her shoulders drooped, and she gazed sadly across the rooftops on the other side of the road. But then she recovered herself, and – turning towards me – said:

'I knew you'd come back, anyway.'

'Did you? How?'

She shrugged. 'Because I've discovered your secret. And I know now I was right. You really *were* an angel sent to help me.'

Somehow, she must have caught wind of what I had been doing. But who could have betrayed me to her? Any one of a number of people, now I came to think about it: Miss Robinson; C. T. Studd; even old Mr. Cooper, if his wife had confided in him.

'Not a very effective angel, unfortunately,' I said.

She shook her head, smiling, then reached out impulsively and touched my lapel. The awful thought struck me that perhaps Miss Robinson had been right, and the poor woman had been dazzled by my quixotic efforts on her behalf into imagining I was in love with her, and she with me.

'Please,' I said, taking a step back. 'You mustn't turn me into something I'm not. I won't deny I meant well, in my clumsy way. But the truth is that the whole thing's been a ghastly failure, I'm afraid.'

'No, it hasn't. I can vouch for that.' There was a brightness in her eyes I had not seen before, and her heart-shaped face was tinged with colour. 'Look, why don't we go outside? That's where I've been. It's lovely.'

'I really don't want to disturb you. Or your husband. But –'

'Oh, don't worry about him,' she said, starting back along the hall. 'He isn't here. He's gone to see a parishioner.'

I followed her into a little dining-room still fuggy with the smell of lunch, and out through french windows into the garden. Two chairs and a table were arranged at the edge of the narrow lawn, in the dappled shade of a cherry tree.

'Please,' she said. 'Sit down.'

I settled myself opposite her. Between us lay the remains of her siesta: an empty coffee-cup and an open book, the pages pinioned by a huge shell. I leaned down and took Emily Cooper's letter from my bag. I meant merely to slip it surreptitiously on to my knee, so it would be to hand when the moment seemed right to produce it; but I was not deft enough, and – like a child spotting her present on Christmas Eve – Mary Wilson saw it, and cried out:

'What's that?'

'Oh, just something I thought you might be interested in.'

'A story?'

'Well, in a manner of speaking, I suppose.'

She smiled. 'In a *manner of speaking*? Surely, either it is or it isn't?'

I hesitated, not sure how to reply. Finally, I muttered: 'Very well, then, it is. But not in the usual sense. Let's say it's *your* story.'

She flushed. 'You mean you wrote it for me?'

I was completely nonplussed now. I opened my mouth, then shut it again. She laughed.

'You can't imagine how I found out, can you?' she said. 'Well, I have to say, it was an accident, really. Over the Easter holidays, my brother-in-law, Jimmy, came to see us. He's just started working at a prep school in Surrey, and one evening at dinner he told us an anecdote about one of the boys in his form, who'd been reading under his desk when he should have been paying attention to the Norman Conquest. Jimmy confiscated the book, but then didn't have the heart to keep it – because, as he said, *it turned out it was one of my favourites, too, when I was a kid, and I knew how much the poor little fellow would miss it.* And Chris – my husband – said: *Why, what was it?* And Jimmy said: The Mists of Time. And Chris said, *What, by Corley Roper?* And Jimmy nodded, and said: *That's right. My, what I wouldn't give to be able to write a yarn like that one day!* He's an author himself, you see. Or means to be – he's only twenty-two. But he's had a few poems and stories published already.'

I felt the heat climbing my neck, and a pool starting to form in the small of my back.

'So I knew then who you must be,' she said. 'Though of course I didn't tell *them* I'd actually met you, and you'd brought me back my copy of *She*. But the next day I went to the library, and borrowed *The Mists of Time* for myself, and simply – I cannot tell you – *adored* it. So when I returned it, I took *this* out.' She picked up the book on the table, and folded it so that I could read the title on the spine: *The Little Mouse*. 'And, if such a thing were possible, I'm loving *it* even *more*! And because . . . well, because I know you, it's almost as if I can hear you telling it to me . . . I mean, to me personally . . . as I read. And that's wonderful, because no one's *ever* told me stories before in my entire life.'

'Well, that's very gratifying, of course,' I said at last. 'I'm naturally delighted you've found some enjoyment in my books. But I wish I could have succeeded in doing more.'

She frowned. 'But what? What more *could* you have done?'

I shrugged. 'I should have liked to have tried to heal the

wound in some way. Rather than simply applying a temporary balm to it.'

She shook her head, puzzled. 'What wound?'

I cleared my throat. 'Your wound.'

'*My* wound?'

'The . . . the suffering inflicted on you by your parents.'

'Oh.' She rolled her eyes, as if the subject exasperated her, and she was already impatient to change it. '*No one* can do anything about that now, can they? It's all over and done with.'

'Well, yes. But I thought . . . if it were somehow possible . . . to track down your mother, and ask her –'

'What, Emily Cooper!' she cried.

I must have made some noise, because she stopped and looked oddly at me for a moment.

'That was her name,' she said. 'Emily Cooper. *Née* Studd.'

'But . . . but you told me,' I said, 'I'm sure you did . . . when we first met . . . that you had no idea who your parents were –'

'I told you I had no idea where they were buried. Or even whether they were alive or dead. Not that I didn't know who they were.'

'But what about all the stories you used to tell yourself? About how your mother was a Balkan grand duchess? Or you'd been stolen by gypsies as a baby?'

'That was when I was a child. Just before my wedding, my guardian told me the *true* story.' She glanced quickly at the house, and then into the neighbouring garden, as if she had suddenly remembered where we were, and was frightened of being observed or overheard. 'He said he was not my father, but that he had married my mother after I was born, and they had four children of their own, who would like to meet me. And I said: *what about my mother? Would she like to meet me, too?* And he said no. That she . . . that she wanted nothing to do with me. Ever.' There was a tremor in her lip that seemed to chop the words in the wrong places, dicing them into a barely comprehensible mush.

She hesitated a moment, to bring it under control, before going on, in a half-whisper: 'And if Emily Cooper were to come through that french window now, and throw herself at my feet, and beg my forgiveness, I would get up and walk away.'

'Well,' I said, as gently as I could, 'that's absolutely natural, of course. But – you never know – perhaps *she* had her sufferings, too. And if you could begin to understand them, and why she behaved as she did, it might make you feel –'

She clamped her hands to her ears. 'Please! Don't speak about it! Don't speak about her!'

'I'm only thinking of you,' I said. 'If you realized how unhappy *she* had been –'

'No!'

'But don't you – ?'

She began pushing her head violently from side to side. 'People will see!' she moaned. 'People will hear! They'll say things about me!'

'Who will?'

She drew a circle in the air, encompassing the whole world. Then she put her face in her hands and began to sob – not tearfully, but with a dreadful dry screeching that shook her entire body.

'I'm sorry,' I said. 'I really didn't –'

She started to wail, blocking out my words. I was at a loss what I should do. I shut my eyes. What I was hoping for, I am still not sure: guidance or inspiration, perhaps, though from what or from whom I have no idea. What I found was that I was immediately back, once again, in the world of the caravan story. But there was a difference, this time: drifting through it, like visitors to a theatre waiting for the play to begin, was a crowd of people from *other* worlds: Elspeth, and the Little Mouse, and Mme. Bournisien, and Alice Dangerfield, and Emily Cooper – and, flitting between them all, barely more than a stirring of the air, the ghostly child that had found refuge in my head. That was strange

315

enough: odder still was that, instead of jostling or fighting one another, as I would have thought such a disparate hotchpotch of characters must inevitably do, they seemed to acknowledge each other quietly and politely – united, or so it appeared, by a common expectation of resolution and pleasure.

I opened my eyes again. Mary Wilson had stopped crying, and was peering at me from behind her hands. I heard myself saying:

'Shall I tell you a story?'

'*My* story?'

'No,' I said, leaning down, and slipping the letter back into my bag. 'A new story, that I've never told anyone before. About Alcuin Hare and Mr. Largo Frog.'

She did not reply, but through the lattice of her fingers I could see her nodding her head. 'Very well, then,' I said. I gazed up at the sky. For a moment all I saw was an expanse of blue. Then, in sure, quick pencil-strokes, a picture started to form.

'Well,' I went on, 'one evening, when he was at home, finishing his supper, Alcuin Hare heard a strange noise outside the house. Even afterwards, when he was telling me about it, he couldn't find the right word to describe it. "It wasn't a *sighing*, exactly," he said. "But then nor yet a *groaning* or a *roaring*, either. A mixture of all three of them, if you can imagine such a thing." So he decided he had better go and see what it was – though, being a thoughtful, careful sort of an animal, not before putting his knife and fork neatly on his plate, and wiping his mouth with his table napkin.

'"Oh, my ears!" he cried, when he got to the window. For there, on the other side of the grassy meadow, the trees in the wood were rustling and roaring and throwing up their branches, as if someone had just told them the most tremendous news, and they were all in a great taking about it. "There's a storm brewing, and no mistake," he thought. "Pity the poor creatures that can't get home in time before it comes. But at least *I* shall be cosy enough, thank goodness." And he went into

316

his study, and took down his long churchwarden pipe, and put another log on the fire, and then sat contentedly with his slippers on the fender, listening to the song of the wind in the chimney, and the tattoo of rain on the roof, and saying to himself: "You know, Hare, old chap, I think you really must be the luckiest animal alive!"

'The next morning, when he was still in his dressing-gown, there was a knock on the door. And when he went to open it, who do you think he found standing on the step?'

'Mr. Largo Frog?' said Mary Wilson.

'That's right, Mr. Largo Frog, boggle-eyed, and dreadfully out of breath. "Ah, Hare, Hare," he gasped. "I'm so glad you're in."

'"Why?" said Alcuin Hare. "Whatever is the matter?"

'"Well, this morning, after all that *lovely* rain, I thought the pond would be just *perfect* for a swim; so without even stopping for breakfast I put on my togs and hurried off. But I hadn't gone quarter of a mile when I *found* something."

'"Found what?"

'"That's just it. I haven't a clue."

'"Well, where was it?"

'"In the woods. Please, Hare, won't you come and have a look at it, like a good fellow, and tell me what I should do?"

'So Alcuin Hare got dressed, and followed his friend back across the wet meadow. Mr. Largo Frog, of course, was incapable of remaining serious for very long, and every few yards or so he would completely forget the purpose of their expedition, and stop to splash in a flooded lark's nest, or to shake the water from a particularly thick blade of grass, laughing and crying out, "Oh, this is delicious, delicious!" as the drops showered down on his upturned head. Years ago, Alcuin Hare might have argued with him, but he knew better now, and merely continued on his way. He had never gone very far before he heard Mr. Largo Frog's voice calling frantically after him:

'"I say, slow down, won't you, Hare, and wait for a chap!"

'Proceeding in this three-legged-race kind of a way, they at length came to the wind-racked wood, where Mr. Largo Frog paused at the base of a tall beech tree ringed by bluebells.

'"There," he said.

'"Where?" asked Alcuin Hare.

'"There," said Mr. Largo Frog, prodding a pile of fallen leaves and broken twigs with his webbed foot.

'Alcuin Hare saw a flash of pink and yellow stirring amongst the browns and greens. He squatted down to take a closer look at it. A tiny, shivering thing with a gaping orange-lined beak stared helplessly back at him.

'"What is it?" asked Mr. Largo Frog.

'"It's a bird."

'"A bird! Birds *fly*, don't they?"

'"They do when they're grown up. This one's a baby. Its nest must have been blown down in the storm."

'"Well, what are we going to do with it?"

'"I don't know. We'll have to ask Theophilus Owl."

'Owl was not best pleased at being disturbed so early, complaining that he didn't know what things were coming to, when a respectable creature like himself couldn't get a good day's sleep any more. But as soon as they had explained why they had come, he opened his eyes, and puffed out his feathers, and said he would fly down and take a look for himself.

'"Well," Alcuin Hare asked him. "What do you think?"

'"The parents won't be able to look after it now," said Theophilus Owl. "There's only one thing for it. You'll have to take it to the country beyond the bridge, or else it will die."

'"The country beyond the bridge!" scoffed Mr. Largo Frog. "There's no such place! It's just a fairy-tale!"

'"There *is* such a place," said Owl. "I saw it myself, once, when I was young, though I've never been there. It's where all the lost creatures in the world are found again."

'"And how do we get there?" asked Alcuin Hare.

"'You just have to follow your heart.'"

"'Oh, but honestly!' said Mr. Largo Frog. "It's all very well for fellows like you to go *gallivanting* off like that, I dare say. But some of us, you know, are busy animals. We have *responsibilities*. We can't simply –'"

"'I'll go on my own, then, if you like,' said Alcuin Hare."

"'Oh, no, Hare, of course, I didn't mean that!' spluttered Mr. Largo Frog. "If you're going, naturally I will, too. Who knows what trouble a silly ass like you might get into if I weren't there to keep an eye on you? And, besides, after all, it was me who *discovered* the thing, wasn't it?'"

"'Very well,' said Alcuin Hare. "Then we'll ask Badger if we can borrow his caravan, shall we?'"

I glanced across at Mary Wilson. She was still watching me, but her hands were now folded in her lap. The hard lines of her face had softened into a smile, and her eyes were half closed – not with tiredness, but with blissful relaxation. As I sat looking at her, wondering if I should go on, I felt a familiar agitation in my temple, and for a moment almost panicked. Then, slowly, I realized there was something different about it: rather than blindly thrashing about, it seemed to be moving purposively, straining to prepare itself for some great effort.

'One day, if you like,' I said, 'I'll write down for you the whole story of their journey together – of the adventures they had, and the people they met, and how Mr. Largo Frog used to catch flies for the little nestling, and ended by fancying himself the best nurse-maid in the world.'

Her smiled deepened, and she settled luxuriously against the back of her chair.

'But not now,' I said. 'Because you're starting to doze off, and before you do I want to tell you about the moment when they finally came over the top of a hill, and saw below them a wide river, and beyond it the most beautiful country they had ever laid eyes on.

"'Oh, my!" gasped Mr. Largo Frog. "Is that the place, do you suppose, Hare?"

"'Yes," said Alcuin Hare, wonderingly.

"'How can you tell?"

"'Because it couldn't be anything else."

I paused. Mary Wilson nodded dreamily.

"'*He* knows," said Alcuin Hare.

"'Who does?"

"'The little nestling."

"'Knows what?"

"'That he's almost home. Listen."

'A sound was coming from the caravan. It was a sound they had never heard before: a wild, joyful cheeping.

"'And how do we get to it?"

"'Look," said Alcuin Hare. "There's the bridge."

'At first, it was no more than a vague shadow on the water; but as they descended towards it, it began to take shape, and they saw it reaching out towards the other side, as slender and perfect as a rainbow.

"'It looks awfully *thin*, doesn't it?" said Mr. Largo Frog doubtfully. "Do you think it'll bear the weight?"

"'It's borne more before," said Alcuin Hare. "And it'll bear more again."

I heard a long, soft whistling sound. Mary Wilson was asleep.

Go on. Go on, said a voice in my temple.

'All right,' I murmured.

And I shut my own eyes, so that I could see what happened next. First there was some comic business with Mr. Largo Frog getting tangled in the reins; then Alcuin Hare brought the nestling from its box and, holding it before him, so that it should be the first to reach the other side, slowly led the horse on to the bridge. I watched them until they had grown so faint that it was impossible to tell what was caravan and what was bridge and what was mist.

And, in that moment, I felt a strange shuddering, such as a branch must feel when a bird that has been perched on it takes flight, and knew – with a shock of grief and relief that remains with me even as I write this, looking out of my window, more than three thousand miles away – that the still-born child had finally left my head.

Albany, New York

1913

ACKNOWLEDGEMENTS

I must begin by gratefully acknowledging the support of Arts Council England, for their generous assistance during the writing of *Consolation*.

Thanks to the many friends who have contributed encouragement, inspiration or practical help, among them: Nicholas Alfrey; Martine Annandale; June Burrough; Sally Darius and Derek Robinson; Louise Greenberg; Tony Hipgrave and Sue Barlow; Muriel Mitcheson Brown; Roland and Kaye Oliver; Dominic Power; Richard Skinner; and Steve Xerri.

I'm indebted for their professional advice to Professor Peter Atkins, of Durham University; Heather Joynson; Carol Kirby, of Hallaton Museum; the staff of the Lambeth Archive; M. Jean-Luc Leservoisier, Conservateur de la bibliothèque municipale d'Avranches; the Archivist of the National Army Museum; Jane Russell Hurford; and Karen Sampson of the Lloyds/TSB Group Archives.

Sue Hourizi did a magnificent job of genealogical detective work uncovering Mary Wilson's story. Her efforts finally led me to a long-lost cousin, Jenny Pugh, who provided a treasure-trove of invaluable material. My warmest thanks to both of them.

Special thanks, as ever, to my exceptional agent, Derek Johns, and all his colleagues at AP Watt; and to everyone at Faber – Kate Burton, Lee Brackstone, Neal Price, Kate Ward, and the rest of the team – for their help and kindness. I am particularly grateful to Angus Cargill, who edited the finished manuscript with his usual intelligence and sensitivity.

And thanks, finally, as always, to my family: to my mother, for her unstinting moral and practical support; to Tom and Kit, for offering such a heartening antidote to the shadowy world into which the writing led me; and to Paula, for her unwavering love and understanding.